NIGHTSHADE

BY ANDREA CREMER

Nightshade

Coming soon

Wolfsbane

NIGHTSHADE

ANDREA CREMER

www.atombooks.net

ATOM

First published in the United States in 2010 by Penguin
First published in Great Britain in 2010 by Atom

A CIP catalogue record for this book
is available from the British Library.

ISBN 978-1-907410-27-7

Printed and bound in Great Britain by
Clays Ltd, St Ives plc

Papers used by Atom are natural, renewable and
recyclable products sourced from well-managed forests and certified
in accordance with the rules of the Forest Stewardship Council.

Mixed Sources
Product group from well-managed
forests and other controlled sources
www.fsc.org Cert no. SGS-COC-004081
© 1996 Forest Stewardship Council
FSC

Atom
An imprint of
Little, Brown Book Group
100 Victoria Embankment
London EC4Y 0DY
An Hachette UK Company
www.hachette.co.uk

www.atombooks.net

For Garth, the first to read this book
and the first to love it

As for witches, I think not that their witchcraft is any real power.

Thomas Hobbes, *Leviathan*

ONE

I'D ALWAYS WELCOMED WAR, BUT IN BATTLE

my passion rose unbidden.

The bear's roar filled my ears. Its hot breath assaulted my nostrils, fueling my bloodlust. Behind me I could hear the boy's ragged gasp. The desperate sound made my nails dig into the earth. I snarled at the larger predator again, daring it to try to get past me.

What the hell am I doing?

I risked a glance at the boy and my pulse raced. His right hand pressed against the gashes in his thigh. Blood surged between his fingers, darkening his jeans until they looked streaked by black paint. Slashes in his shirt barely covered the red lacerations that marred his chest. A growl rose in my throat.

I crouched low, muscles tensed, ready to strike. The grizzly rose onto its hind legs. I held my ground.

Calla!

Bryn's cry sounded in my mind. A lithe brown wolf darted from the forest and tore into the bear's unguarded flank. The grizzly turned, landing on all fours. Spit flew from its mouth as it searched for the unseen attacker. But Bryn, lightning fast, dodged the bear's lunge. With each swipe of the grizzly's trunk-thick arms, she avoided its reach, always moving a split second faster than the bear. She seized her advantage, inflicting another taunting bite. When the bear's back was turned, I leapt forward and ripped a chunk from its heel. The bear swung around to face me, its eyes rolling, filled with pain.

Bryn and I slunk along the ground, circling the huge animal. The bear's blood made my mouth hot. My body tensed. We continued our ever-tightening dance. The bear's eyes tracked us. I could smell its doubt, its rising fear. I let out a short, harsh bark and flashed my fangs. The grizzly snorted as it turned away and lumbered into the forest.

I raised my muzzle and howled in triumph. A moan brought me back to earth. The hiker stared at us, eyes wide. Curiosity pulled me toward him. I'd betrayed my masters, broken their laws. All for him.

Why?

My head dropped low and I tested the air. The hiker's blood streamed over his skin and onto the ground, the sharp, coppery odor creating an intoxicating fog in my conscience. I fought the temptation to taste it.

Calla? Bryn's alarm pulled my gaze from the fallen hiker.

Get out of here. I bared my teeth at the smaller wolf. She dropped low and bellied along the ground toward me. Then she raised her muzzle and licked the underside of my jaw.

What are you going to do? her blue eyes asked me.

She looked terrified. I wondered if she thought I'd kill the boy for my own pleasure. Guilt and shame trickled through my veins.

Bryn, you can't be here. Go. Now.

She whined but slunk away, slipping beneath the cover of pine trees.

I stalked toward the hiker. My ears flicked back and forth. He struggled for breath, pain and terror filling his face. Deep gashes remained where the grizzly's claws had torn at his thigh and chest. Blood still flowed from the wounds. I knew it wouldn't stop. I growled, frustrated by the fragility of his human body.

He was a boy who looked about my age: seventeen, maybe

4

eighteen. Brown hair with a slight shimmer of gold fell in a mess around his face. Sweat had caked strands of it to his forehead and cheeks. He was lean, strong—someone who could find his way around a mountain, as he clearly had. This part of the territory was only accessible through a steep, unwelcoming trail.

The scent of fear covered him, taunting my predatory instincts, but beneath it lay something else—the smell of spring, of nascent leaves and thawing earth. A scent full of hope. Possibility. Subtle and tempting.

I took another step toward him. I knew what I wanted to do, but it would mean a second, much-greater violation of the Keepers' Laws. He tried to move back but gasped in pain and collapsed onto his elbows. My eyes moved over his face. His chiseled jaw and high cheekbones twisted in agony. Even writhing he was beautiful, muscles clenching and unclenching, revealing his strength, his body's fight against its impending collapse, rendering his torture sublime. Desire to help him consumed me.

I can't watch him die.

I shifted forms before I realized I'd made the decision. The boy's eyes widened when the white wolf who'd been eyeing him was no longer an animal, but a girl with the wolf's golden eyes and platinum blond hair. I walked to his side and dropped to my knees. His entire body shook. I began to reach for him but hesitated, surprised to feel my own limbs trembling. I'd never been so afraid.

A rasping breath pulled me out of my thoughts.

"Who are you?" The boy stared at me. His eyes were the color of winter moss, a delicate shade that hovered between green and gray. I was caught there for a moment. Lost in the questions that pushed through his pain and into his gaze.

I raised the soft flesh of my inner forearm to my mouth. Willing my canines to sharpen, I bit down hard and waited until my own blood touched my tongue. Then I extended my arm toward him.

"Drink. It's the only thing that can save you." My voice was low but firm.

The trembling in his limbs grew more pronounced. He shook his head.

"You have to," I growled, showing him canines still razor sharp from opening the wound in my arm. I hoped the memory of my wolf form would terrorize him into submission. But the look on his face wasn't one of horror. The boy's eyes were full of wonder. I blinked at him and fought to remain still. Blood ran along my arm, falling in crimson drops onto the leaf-lined soil.

His eyes snapped shut as he grimaced from a surge of renewed pain. I pressed my bleeding forearm against his parted lips. His touch was electric, searing my skin, racing through my blood. I bit back a gasp, full of wonder and fear at the alien sensations that rolled through my limbs.

He flinched, but my other arm whipped around his back, holding him still while my blood flowed into his mouth. Grasping him, pulling him close only made my blood run hotter.

I could tell he wanted to resist, but he had no strength left. A smile pulled at the corners of my mouth. Even if my own body was reacting unpredictably, I knew I could control his. I shivered when his hands came up to grasp my arm, pressing into my skin. The hiker's breath came easily now. Slow, steady.

An ache deep within me made my fingers tremble. I wanted to run them over his skin. To skim the healing wounds and learn the contours of his muscles.

I bit my lip, fighting temptation. *Come on, Cal, you know better. This isn't like you.*

I pulled my arm from his grasp. A whimper of disappointment emerged from the boy's throat. I didn't know how to grapple with my own sense of loss now that I wasn't touching him. *Find your strength, use the wolf. That's who you are.*

With a warning growl I shook my head, ripping a length of fabric from the hiker's torn shirt to bind up my own wound. His moss-colored eyes followed my every movement.

I scrambled to my feet and was startled when he mimicked the action, faltering only slightly. I frowned and took two steps back. He watched my retreat, then looked down at his ripped clothing. His fingers gingerly picked at the shreds of his shirt. When his eyes lifted to meet mine, I was hit with an unexpected swell of dizziness. His lips parted. I couldn't stop looking at them. Full, curving with interest, lacking the terror I'd expected. Too many questions flickered in his gaze.

I have to get out of here. "You'll be fine. Get off the mountain. Don't come near this place again," I said, turning away.

A shock sparked through my body when the boy gripped my shoulder. He looked surprised but not at all afraid. That wasn't good. Heat flared along my skin where his fingers held me fast. I waited a moment too long, watching him, memorizing his features before I snarled and shrugged off his hand.

"Wait—" he said, and took another step toward me.

What if I could wait, putting my life on hold in this moment? What if I stole a little more time and caught a taste of what had been so long forbidden? Would it be so wrong? I would never see this stranger again. What harm could come from lingering here, from holding still and learning whether he would try to touch me the way I wanted to him to?

His scent told me my thoughts weren't far off the mark, his skin snapping with adrenaline and the musk that belied desire. I'd let this encounter last much too long, stepped well beyond the line of safe conduct. With regret nipping at me, I balled my fist. My eyes moved up and down his body, assessing, remembering the feeling of his lips on my skin. He smiled hesitantly.

Enough.

I caught him across the jaw with a single blow. He dropped to the ground and didn't move again. I bent down and gathered the boy in my arms, slinging his backpack over my shoulder. The scent of green meadows and dew-kissed tree limbs flowed around me, flooding me with that strange ache that coiled low in my body, a physical reminder of my brush with treachery. Twilight shadows stretched farther up the mountain, but I'd have him at the base by dusk.

A lone, battered pickup was parked near the rippling waterway that marked the boundary of the sacred site. Black signs with bright orange lettering were posted along the creek bank:

NO TRESPASSING. PRIVATE PROPERTY.

The Ford Ranger was unlocked. I flung open the door, almost pulling it from the rust-bitten vehicle. I draped the boy's limp form across the driver's seat. His head slumped forward and I caught the stark outline of a tattoo on the back of his neck. A dark, bizarrely inked cross.

A trespasser and trend hound. Thank God I found something not to like about him.

I hurled his pack onto the passenger seat and slammed the door. The truck's steel frame groaned. Still trembling with frustration, I shifted into wolf form and darted back into the forest. His scent clung to me, blurring my sense of purpose. I sniffed the air and cringed, a new scent bringing my treachery into stark relief.

I know you're here. A snarl traveled with my thought.

Are you okay? Bryn's plaintive question only made fear bite harder into my trembling muscles. In the next moment she ran beside me.

I told you to leave. I bared my teeth but couldn't deny my sudden relief at her presence.

I could never abandon you. Bryn kept pace easily. *And you know I'll never betray you.*

I picked up speed, darting through the deepening shadows of the forest. I abandoned my attempt to outrun fear, shifted forms, and stumbled forward until I found the solid pressure of a tree trunk. The scratch of the bark on my skin failed to repel the gnat-like nerves that swarmed in my head.

"Why did you save him?" she asked. "Humans mean nothing to us."

I kept my arms around the tree but turned my cheek to the side so I could look at Bryn. No longer in her wolf form, the short, wiry girl's hands rested on her hips. Her eyes narrowed as she waited for an answer.

I blinked, but I couldn't halt the burning sensation. A pair of tears, hot and unwanted, slid down my cheeks.

Bryn's eyes widened. I never cried. Not when anyone could witness it.

I turned my face away, but I could sense her watching me silently, without judgment. I had no answers for Bryn. Or for myself.

TWO

WHEN I OPENED THE FRONT DOOR TO MY

house, my body went rigid. I could smell the visitors. Aged parchment, fine wine: Lumine Nightshade's scent exuded an aristocratic elegance. But her guards filled the house with an unbearable odor, boiling pitch and burnt hair.

"Calla?" Lumine's voice dripped with honey.

I cringed, trying to gather my wits before I walked into the kitchen with my mouth glued shut. I didn't want to taste the creatures as well as smell them.

Lumine sat at the table across from her pack's current alpha, my father. She remained impossibly still, posture perfect, chocolate tresses caught in a chignon at the back of her neck. She wore her typical immaculate ebony suit and crisp high-collared white shirt. Two wraiths flanked her, looming shadow-like just over her slim shoulders.

I sucked in my cheeks so I could bite the insides. It was the only thing that kept me from baring my teeth at the bodyguards.

"Have a seat, my dear." Lumine gestured to a chair.

I pulled the chair close to my father, crouching rather than sitting in it. I couldn't relax with the wraiths nearby.

Does she already know about the violation? Is she here to order my execution?

"Little more than a month of waiting left, lovely girl," she murmured. "Are you looking forward to your union?"

I let out the breath I didn't know I'd been holding.

"Sure," I said.

Lumine brought the tips of her fingers together in front of her face.

"Is that the only word you have to offer about your auspicious future?"

My father barked a laugh. "Calla's not the romantic her mother is, Mistress."

His tone remained confident, but his gaze fell on me. I ran my tongue along my canines, which were sharpening in my mouth.

"I see," she said, eyes moving up and down my body.

I crossed my arms over my chest.

"Stephen, you might teach her better manners. I expect my alpha females to embody finesse. Naomi has always had the utmost grace in the role."

She continued to watch me, so I couldn't bare my teeth at her the way I wanted to.

Finesse, my ass. I'm a warrior, not your child bride.

"I thought you might be pleased with the match, dear girl," she said. "You're a beautiful alpha. And there hasn't been a Bane male the likes of Renier before. Even Emile admits that. The union bodes well for all of us. You should be grateful to have such a mate."

My jaw clenched, but I met her eyes without blinking.

"I respect Ren. He's a friend. We'll be fine together."

A friend . . . sort of. Ren watches me like I'm a cookie jar he wouldn't mind being caught with his hand in. And he's not the one who'd pay for that theft. Though I'd been stuck with lock and key from day one of our betrothal, I hadn't thought playing policeman over our relationship would be that hard. But Ren didn't like to play by the rules. He was just tempting enough to make me wonder whether giving him a taste might be worth the risk.

"Fine?" Lumine repeated. "But do you desire the boy? Emile would be furious at the idea you might scoff at his heir." She drummed her fingers on the table.

I stared at the floor, cursing the flames that raced over my cheeks. *How the hell does desire matter when I'm not allowed to do anything about it?* In that moment I hated her.

My father cleared his throat. "My lady, the union has been set since the children's birth. The Nightshade and Bane packs remain committed to it. As are my daughter and Emile's son."

"Like I said, we'll be fine," I whispered. The hint of a growl escaped with my words.

Tinkling laughter brought my eyes back to the Keeper. As she watched me squirm, Lumine's smile was patronizing. I glared at her, no longer able to hold in my outrage.

"Indeed." Her gaze moved to my father. "The ceremony must not be interrupted or delayed. Under any circumstances."

She rose and extended her hand. My father briefly pressed his lips to her pale fingers. She turned to me. I reluctantly took her vellum-like skin in my own hand, trying not to think about how much I wanted to bite her.

"All worthy females have finesse, my dear." She touched my cheek, letting her nails scrape hard enough to make me flinch.

My stomach lurched.

Her stiletto heels struck a sharp staccato on the tile as she left the kitchen. The wraiths trailed behind her, their silence more disturbing than the unnerving rhythm of her steps. I drew my knees up to my chest and rested my cheek against them. I didn't breathe again until I heard the front door close.

"You're awfully tense," my father said. "Did something happen on patrol?"

I shook my head. "You know I hate wraiths."

"We all hate wraiths."

I shrugged. "Why was she here anyway?"

"To discuss the union."

"You're kidding." I frowned. "Just me and Ren?"

My father passed a weary hand over his eyes. "Calla, it would be helpful if you wouldn't treat the union like a hoop to jump through. Far more is at stake than 'just you and Ren.' The formation of a new pack hasn't occurred for decades. The Keepers are on edge."

"Sorry," I said, not meaning it.

"Don't be sorry. Be serious."

I sat up straight.

"Emile was here earlier today." He grimaced.

"What?!" I gasped. "Why?"

I couldn't imagine a civil conversation between Emile Laroche and his rival alpha.

My father's voice was cold. "The same reason as Lumine."

I buried my face in my hands, my cheeks once again on fire.

"Calla?"

"Sorry, Dad," I said, swallowing my embarrassment. "It's just that Ren and I get along fine. We're friends, sort of. We've known the union was coming for a long time. I can't see any problems with it. And if Ren does, that would be news to me. But this whole process would be much easier if everyone would just lay off. The pressure isn't helping."

He nodded. "Welcome to your life as an alpha. The pressure never helps. It also never goes away."

"Great." I sighed and rose from my chair. "I have homework."

"Night, then," he said quietly.

"Night."

"And Calla?"

"Yeah?" I paused at the bottom of the staircase.

"Go easy on your mother."

I frowned and continued up the stairs. When I reached my bedroom door, I shrieked. Clothes were strewn everywhere. Covering my bed, on the floor, hanging from the nightstand and lamp.

"This will never do!" My mother pointed an accusing finger at me.

"Mom!"

One of my favorite vintage T-shirts, from a Pixies tour in the eighties, hung from her clenched fists.

"Do you own anything beautiful?" She shook the offending T-shirt at me.

"Define *beautiful*," I returned.

I swallowed a groan, searching for any clothes I particularly wanted to protect, and sat on top of my Republicans for Voldemort hoodie.

"Lace? Silk? Cashmere?" Naomi asked. "Anything that isn't denim or cotton?"

She twisted the Pixies shirt in her hands and I cringed.

"Do you know that *Emile* was here today?" Her eyes moved over the bed, assessing the pile of clothes.

"Dad said that," I replied quietly, but inside I was screaming.

I stroked my fingers along the rope of hair that hung over my shoulder, lifted the end, and caught it between my teeth.

My mother pursed her lips and dropped the T-shirt so she could extract my fingers from the twisted hair. Then she sighed, took a seat on the bed just behind me, and pulled the elastic from the end of the braid.

"And this hair." She combed out the waves with her fingers. "Why you bind it up all the time is beyond me."

"There's too much," I said. "It gets in the way."

I could hear the chime of my mother's chandelier earrings when she shook her head. "My lovely flower. You can't hide your assets anymore. You're a woman now."

With a disgusted grunt I rolled across the bed, out of her reach.

"I'm no flower." I pushed the curtain of hair back behind my shoulders. Free of the braid, it felt cumbersome and heavy.

"But you are, *Calla*." She smiled. "My beautiful lily."

"It's just a name, Mom." I began to gather up my clothes. "Not who I am."

"It is who you are." I started at the warning note in her voice. "Stop doing that. It's not necessary."

My hands froze on the T-shirt I'd grabbed. She waited until I placed the half-folded shirt back on the coverlet. I started to say something, but my mother held up a silencing hand.

"The new pack forms next month. You'll be the alpha female."

"I know that." I fought off the urge to throw dirty socks at her. "I've known that since I was five."

"And now it's time for you to start acting like it," she said. "Lumine is worried."

"Yeah, I know. Finesse. She wants finesse." I wanted to gag.

"And Emile is concerned about what Renier wants," she said.

"What *Ren* wants?" I said, wincing at the shrillness of my voice.

My mother lifted one of my bras from the bed. It was plain white cotton—the only kind I owned.

"We need to think about preparations. Do you wear *any* decent lingerie?"

The burning in my cheeks began again. I wondered if excessive blushing could cause permanent discoloration.

"I don't want to talk about this."

She ignored me, muttering under her breath as she sorted my things into piles, which, since she'd ordered me to stop folding, I could only presume were "acceptable" and "to be discarded."

"He's an alpha male and the most popular boy at your school. At least by all accounts I'm privy to." Her tone became wistful. "I'm sure he's accustomed to certain attentions from girls. When your time arrives, you must be ready to please him."

I swallowed sour bile before I could speak again.

"Mom, I'm an alpha too, remember?" I said. "Ren needs me to be a pack leader. *Wants* me to be a warrior, not the captain of the cheerleading squad."

"Renier needs you to act like a mate. Just because you're a warrior doesn't mean you can't be enticing." The sharpness of her tone cut me.

"Cal's right, Mom." My brother's voice piped in. "Ren doesn't want a cheerleader. He's already dated them all for the last four years. He's probably bored as hell. At least big sis will keep him on his toes."

I turned to see Ansel leaning against the door frame. His eyes swept over the room.

"Whoa, Hurricane Naomi strikes, leaving no survivors."

"Ansel," my mother snapped, hands on her hips. "Please give your sister and me some privacy."

"Sorry, Mom." Ansel continued to grin. "But Barrett and Sasha are downstairs waiting for you to go with them on night patrol."

Her eyelids fluttered in surprise. "Is it that late already?"

Ansel shrugged. When she turned away, he winked at me. I covered my mouth to hide my smile.

She sighed. "Calla, I'm serious about this. I put some new clothes in your closet and I expect you to start wearing them."

I opened my mouth to object, but she cut me off.

"New clothes starting tomorrow or I'll get rid of all your T-shirts and ripped jeans. End of discussion."

She rose and swept from the room, her skirt swirling around her calves as she moved. When I heard her steps on the staircase, I groaned and flipped over on the bed. The mound of T-shirts offered a convenient place to bury my head. I was tempted to shift into wolf form and rip the bed apart. But that would get me grounded for sure. Plus I liked my bed, and at the moment it was one of the few things that my mother wasn't threatening to toss out.

The mattress creaked. I propped myself up on my elbows and looked at Ansel. He perched on the corner of the bed.

"Another heartwarming mother-daughter bonding session?"

"You know it." I rolled onto my back.

"Are you okay?" he asked.

"Yeah." I put my hands on my temples, attempting to massage the new throbbing pain away.

"So—" Ansel began. I turned to look at him. My brother's teasing smile had vanished.

"So what?"

"About Ren . . ." His voice thickened.

"Spit it out, An."

"Do you like him? I mean for real?" he blurted.

I collapsed back onto the bed. My arms covered my eyes, blotting out the light.

"Not you too."

He crawled toward me.

"It's just," he said. "If you don't want to be with him, you shouldn't be."

Beneath my arms my eyes snapped open. For a moment I couldn't breathe.

"We could run away. I'd stay with you," Ansel finished in a voice almost too low to hear.

I sat bolt upright.

"Ansel," I whispered. "Don't ever say anything like that. You don't know what . . . Just drop it, okay?"

He fiddled with the coverlet. "I want you to be happy. You seemed so mad at Mom."

"I am mad at Mom, but that's Mom, not Ren." I wound my fingers through the long waves that spilled over my shoulders and thought about shaving my head.

"So you're okay with it? With being Ren's mate?"

"Yeah. I'm okay with it." I reached out, ruffling his sand brown hair. "Besides, you'll be in the new pack. So will Bryn, Mason, and Fey. With you guys at my back, we'll keep Ren in line."

"No doubt." He grinned.

"And don't breathe a word about running away to anyone. An, that's way out of line. When did you become such a free thinker anyway?" My eyes narrowed.

He bared sharpened canines at me. "I'm *your* brother, right?"

"So your traitorous nature is my fault?" I smacked him on the chest.

"Everything I need to know I learned from Cal."

He stood up and began jumping on the bed. I bounced close to the edge and then rolled off, landing easily on the balls of my feet. I grabbed the edge of the coverlet and gave it a sharp jerk. Ansel fell laughing onto his back and bounced once on the mattress before he lay still.

"I'm serious, Ansel. Not a word."

"Don't worry, sis. I'm not stupid. I would never betray the Keepers," he said. "Unless you asked me to . . . alpha."

I tried to smile. "Thanks."

THREE

WHEN I ENTERED THE KITCHEN FOR BREAKFAST,

my family fell silent. I made a beeline for the coffee. My mother rushed over, grasped my hands, and turned me to face her.

"Oh, honey, you are a vision," she said, kissing me on both cheeks.

"It's a skirt, Mom." I wrenched free. "Get over it."

I grabbed a mug from the cupboard and poured coffee. At the last second I managed to push my long hair out of the way before blond tendrils dunked in the black liquid.

Ansel tossed me a Luna bar and tried to hide the smirk on his face.

Traitor, I mouthed as I sat down. Two bites into my breakfast, I realized my father was gaping at me.

"What?" I asked around a mouthful of soy protein.

He coughed, blinking several times. Then his eyes darted from my mom to me. "Sorry, Calla. I guess I didn't expect you to take your mother's suggestions to heart."

She glared at him. My father shifted in his seat and unfolded the *Denver Post.*

"You're quite fetching."

"Fetching?" My voice jumped up a couple octaves. The coffee mug shook in my hand.

Ansel choked on his Pop-Tart and grabbed for a glass of orange juice.

My father lifted the newspaper to hide his face while my mother patted my hand. I allowed myself one glare at her before losing myself in the haze of caffeine.

We spent the rest of breakfast in awkward silence. Dad read and tried to avoid any eye contact with me or my mother. Mom kept throwing encouraging glances in my direction, which I deflected with cold stares. Ansel ignored us, happily munching on his Pop-Tart. I threw back the last dregs of coffee.

"Come on, An."

Ansel bounced from his chair, grabbing a jacket on his way to the garage.

"Good luck, Cal," my father called as I followed my little brother toward the door.

I didn't respond. Most days I looked forward to school. Today I dreaded it.

"Stephen." I heard Mom's voice rise as I walked out the door and slammed it shut behind me.

"Can I drive?" Ansel's eyes were hopeful.

"No," I said, heading for the driver's seat of our Jeep.

Ansel gripped the dashboard as I squealed out of the driveway. The scent of burnt rubber filled the cab. After I cut off the third car, he glared at me, struggling to buckle his seat belt.

"Just 'cause wearing panty hose gives you a death wish doesn't mean I have one too."

"I am not wearing panty hose," I said through clenched teeth, swerving around yet another car.

Ansel's eyebrows shot up. "You're not? Isn't that, like, unseemly or something?"

He grinned at me, but the dagger glare I threw at him made him cower against his seat. By the time we reached the Mountain School's parking lot, his face was ghost white.

"I think I'll get Mason to drive me home," he said, slamming the door behind him.

When I noticed how white my knuckles had become as a result of my grip on the steering wheel, I took a deep breath.

They're just clothes, Cal. It's not like Mom made you go get a boob job.

I shuddered, hoping no such ideas ever entered Naomi's mind.

Bryn intercepted me halfway across the parking lot. Her eyes widened as she looked me up and down.

"What happened?"

"Finesse," I grumbled, and kept walking toward our school.

"Huh?" Her tight bronze ringlets bounced around her head as she trotted beside me.

"Apparently being an alpha female involves more than fighting off Searchers," I said. "At least according to Lumine and my mother."

"So Naomi's trying to give you a makeover again?" she asked. "What's different this time?"

"This time she's serious." I adjusted the waistband of my skirt, wishing I were in jeans. "And so is Lumine."

"Well, I guess you'd better get with the program." Bryn shrugged as we passed the chalet-like residences from which bleary-eyed human students stumbled.

"Thanks for the vote of confidence." I couldn't figure out how the skirt was supposed to lie, so I gave up trying to straighten it.

We walked in silence through the entrance and down the hall to the long row of senior lockers. The smell of the school that greeted me each day had changed. The sharp metallic of the lockers, acrid floor polish countering the freshness of the ceilings' cedar beams were familiar, but the fear that usually seeped from the skin of the humans was missing.

Instead they smelled curious, surprised, a strange reaction from the boarders, whose lives were carefully segregated from the local Keepers and Guardians. The only activities we shared were our classes. Having their eyes on me as we moved through the crowd of students jostling through the narrow space proved more than a little unsettling.

"Is everyone staring?" I tried not to sound nervous.

"Yep. Pretty much all staring."

"Oh God," I moaned, tightening my grip on my bag.

"At least you look hot." Her cheerful response made my stomach flip.

"Please don't say stuff like that to me. Ever." *Why did my mother do this to me?* I felt like a sideshow freak at a carnival.

"Sorry," Bryn said, toying with the multi-hued metallic bangles that jangled along her arm.

I switched out my homework for the books I needed in first and second period. The din of the hallway dropped to a buzz of curious whispers, and Bryn abruptly straightened from her casual pose.

I knew what that meant. He was nearby. I slung my bag over my shoulder, slammed my locker door, and hated that my heart sped up as I looked for Renier Laroche.

The crowd of students parted for the Bane alpha and his pack. Ren, flanked by Sabine, Neville, Cosette, and Dax, seemed to float down the hallway. He moved as though he owned the school. His eyes darted from side to side—ever a wolf, always predatory.

I'll bet he's never had to suffer a makeover.

When Ren found me, a half-cocked smile played along his mouth. I stood perfectly still, matching his challenging gaze. Bryn stepped closer. I could feel her breath on my shoulder.

Activity in the hall stilled. Eyes fixed on our meeting, whispers traveling from mouth to ear.

A movement to my right caught my eye. Mason, Ansel, and Fey

emerged from the throng of students and took flanking positions around Bryn. I stood a little taller.

Not the only alpha now, are you?

Ren's eyes narrowed as they focused on the Nightshade wolves behind me. An abrupt laugh escaped his throat.

"You going to call off your soldiers, Lily?"

I glanced at the Banes, who stood like sentinels around their alpha.

"As if you're flying solo?" I leaned back against my locker.

His laugh became a low chuckle, not unlike a growl. He looked at Sabine.

"Get out of here. I need to speak to Calla. Alone."

The inky-haired girl to his right stiffened, but she turned and walked back in the direction of the commons. The other three wolves fell in behind her, though Dax cast a glance back at his alpha before they melted into the crowd.

Ren raised an eyebrow. I nodded.

"Bryn, I'll see you in class."

I heard the rustle of her curls as she bobbed her head. Out of the corner of my eye I caught Mason and Fey leaning in and whispering to her as they moved off. I waited, but Ren's eyes remained focused over my shoulder. I turned to see Ansel still standing behind me.

"You too. Now."

My little brother ducked his head and dashed after the other Nightshades.

Ren laughed. "Protective of you, eh?"

"Whatever." I tightened my arms over my chest. "What's with the show, Ren? You've got half the student body watching us."

He shrugged. "They always watch us. They're afraid of us. It's the way it should be."

My lips thinned, but I didn't respond.

"That's a new look," he said, letting his eyes move slowly over me.

Damn you, Mother.

I gave a reluctant nod and looked down. Ren's finger caught the underside of my chin and tilted my face upward. When I raised my eyes, he was wearing his most appealing smile. I jerked away from his fingers. A soft, low growl rumbled in his chest.

"Easy, girl."

"The look doesn't matter." I pressed closer to the locker. "Stop toying with me. You know who I am."

"Of course," he murmured. "That's why I like you."

My teeth clenched as I struggled against the warm, bubbling tension that the alpha boy provoked from the tips of my toes to the crown of my head.

"I'm immune to your charms," I lied. "Cut the act, Bane. What do you want?"

He laughed. "Come on, Cal. I thought we were friends."

"We are *friends*." I let the phrase hang between us. "Until October thirty-first. Then it changes. Those are the rules. You're the one acting like a buck in rut today. Just tell me what's on your mind."

I held my breath, wondering if I'd gone too far. But no angry retort came, and for a split second his expression was tender.

"The Keepers are coming down hard on us," he said. "I, for one, am tired of being scrutinized twenty-four seven. I wondered if you were interested in doing something about that."

I waited for the joke. None came.

"H-How?" I finally managed to stammer.

He took a hesitant step closer.

"What's the stick up their ass?" he murmured, leaning toward me. Breathing became a challenge.

I am in control. I am in control.

"The union. The new pack," I said. He was close enough that I could see the flecks of silver inside his dark eyes.

Ren nodded. His smile became a grin.

"And who has control over its success or failure?"

My heart hammered against my rib cage. "We do."

"Exactly." He straightened, and I could breathe again. "I thought we might do something about that."

"Like what?" I watched his neck and shoulders tighten and almost shivered. *He's nervous. What has the power to make Ren nervous?*

"Like spend more time together. Get the pack's loyalty transferred to us instead of the elders," he said. "Maybe convince our friends to stop hating each other. Could make the Keepers relax, lay off a bit."

I pulled my lip between my teeth as I considered his words. "You want to start moving toward the union now?"

He nodded. "Ease in. It will make the adjustment easier for everyone instead of going cold turkey in October. I thought we could hang out."

"Hang out? *Together?*" I bit my lip hard so I wouldn't laugh.

"Couldn't hurt," he said quietly.

The laugh died in my belly when I realized how serious he was. *Unless they rip each other's throats out.*

"It's risky," I said.

"Are you saying you can't control your Nightshades?"

"No. Of course not." I glared at him. "If I say so, they'll toe the line."

"Then it shouldn't be a problem. Should it?"

I sighed. "The Keepers have been on you too?"

Ren pulled his gaze from mine. "Efron expressed some concerns about my . . . habits. Worried that you'd be unhappy or concerned about fidelity." He chewed on the last word like a piece of gristle.

I doubled over laughing. For a minute he looked chagrined.

"Serves you right, Romeo." I aimed my fingers at his chest, miming a cocked pistol. "If you weren't Emile's son, your pelt would already be nailed over a fireplace belonging to the father of some brokenhearted girl."

Ren flashed a wicked smile. "You're not wrong." He put his hand against the locker just above my shoulder. "Efron has visited our house once a week for the last month." His grin didn't fade, but his eyes looked troubled.

Fear curled my fingers around his shirt, pulling him closer. "Every week?" I whispered.

He nodded, passing a hand through his espresso dark hair. "Don't be surprised if he's packing a shotgun at the union."

I smiled, but my breath caught in my throat as he leaned down. His lips brushed against my ear. I pulled away. The Keepers took this purity thing seriously, even if he didn't.

"I think they're worried the next generation might not fall into line. But I'd never leave you at the altar, Lily."

I punched him in the stomach and instantly regretted it. Ren's abdomen was rock hard. I shook my aching hand as I drew it back.

He braceleted my wrist in a fierce grip. His smile didn't fade.

"Nice hook."

"Thanks for noticing." I tried to pull my arm away, but his lock on my wrist remained firm.

"So what do you think?"

"About hanging out?" I couldn't meet his eyes. He was much too close. I could feel the heat of his body, and it was making my own temperature rise.

"Yes." His face was inches from my own. He smelled like leather and sandalwood.

"It might work," I said, certain I'd melt into the locker at any second. "I'll think about it."

"Good." He pulled back and dropped my wrist. "See ya, Lily."

He danced out of reach. I could hear him laughing as he disappeared into the crowd of students.

FOUR

I BOLTED FOR MY DESK AS THE FIRST BELL

rang. From the desk behind mine Bryn clucked her tongue. "Spill."

"It was interesting," I said, sliding into my seat.

Mr. Graham cleared his throat. "Ladies, gentlemen. A moment of your precious time."

I gasped as Bryn's hand shot out, fingernails digging into my forearm. "Bryn, what?"

Her eyes were locked on the front of the classroom. The roar of student chatter faded.

"Much obliged." Mr. Graham's raspy tone wafted through the room. "We have a new student matriculating at the Mountain School today."

I began to turn in my chair and winced, certain that I'd lost some skin to Bryn's claw-like grip. Then I froze, catching the scent of a spring breeze full of sunlight. *No, it can't be.* But it was.

Standing in an uneasy pose next to Mr. Graham's desk was the hiker I'd saved not twenty-four hours earlier.

"This is Seamus Doran," our teacher continued, beaming at the boy, who looked distinctly uncomfortable.

"It's Shay. I go by Shay," he said quietly.

"Welcome then, Shay." Mr. Graham's eyes cast about the room.

My heart dropped when I saw his gaze fix on the empty seat to my right. "There's a seat for you next to Miss Tor."

Bryn kicked the back of my chair insistently.

"Knock it off," I snapped, half turning toward her. "What am I supposed to do?"

"Something." Her voice was low but alarmed.

I was trapped between being thrilled and horrified to see him again. Even if I couldn't sort out my muddle of feelings, I still knew that when he recognized me, it would be disastrous. I pulled my hair forward in an attempt to veil my face.

Where is my hoodie when I need it?

Shay walked slowly to his desk. When he reached his designated seat, I met his pale green eyes for a moment before looking away, but there was no doubt. He knew it was me. I was afraid, as I should have been, but the fear was tinged with satisfaction. In the mere seconds our eyes had locked, I'd seen his astonishment. I'd been a dream to him, and now I was real. His backpack slipped from his hands. A couple of pens rolled along the floor between our desks. I swallowed a groan and visored my face with my hand; it felt like flames were licking my belly. Bryn kicked my desk again so forcefully that it scooted forward an inch.

I panicked and bolted to the front of the classroom. Mr. Graham took several steps backward as I rushed toward him.

I whispered, "Cramps," and, "Bloating." Mr. Graham blushed and scribbled out a hall pass. I ran down the hall to the girls' bathroom. Fortunately it was empty. I sank to the floor, shaking. The bathroom door creaked open.

"Cal," Bryn whispered as she knelt beside me.

I tempted fate and now it's hunting me down. I should have let the bear kill him. But the thought of anything hurting the new boy snatched my breath away. "He cannot be here."

"I know." Bryn scuttled closer and wrapped her arms around me.

"But he must be somebody. I mean, in the human world. Why else would he transfer in as a senior? That never happens."

"Oh God, Bryn." I raised my face from behind my fingers. "What if the Keepers know?"

She shook her head. "No. They don't. When something goes wrong, our mistress deals with it. Instantly. You're safe."

"You're right." I got up and went to the sink. "They don't know." I caught her glance in the mirror. "But who could he be?"

"Just the kid of some banking czar or a hotshot senator, like all the rest of the humans that go to school here," she said. "He's nothing to us."

I'm such a fool. My legs were still rubbery. *I can't believe I saved him.*

"Put this on; you're pasty." Bryn pulled blush from her bag, handing it to me. "No one knows about what happened but us and this boy. And he probably barely believes it himself. I mean, what outsider would? Just pretend it never happened."

"Okay." I swallowed my own horror at the realization that I actually wanted to see him. I felt his mouth against my arm and shivered. *The stress of the union has finally gotten to me. I'm losing it.*

I decided to skip the rest of first period, but I knew hiding from Shay Doran wasn't a realistic option. Considering that fewer than thirty students constituted the senior class, I was bound to see him in another course later in the day.

French?

No.

AP Biology?

No.

Organic Chemistry?

Yes.

Ms. Foris directed the should-be-dead hiker to join a pair of human students. As if he sensed my watchfulness, Shay turned and caught my stare. I quickly looked away, wishing I could keep my eyes on him. Instead I turned to Ren, who was arranging our lab materials. I tried to focus on the lab, but I could sense the stranger's inquisitive glances from across the room. I bit my lip to stop my smile. *He wants to watch me too.*

Ren handed me a beaker. "So have you thought about it?"

"Thought about what?" I set the beaker down and reached for another bottle.

"Hanging out," he said, resting his hand on my lower back. "Or are you still doubting your ability to control your pack?"

The rush of heat was as sudden as if I'd been branded by his handprint. I didn't look at him. "I've got a bottle full of hydrochloric acid in my hand, Ren. Don't piss me off. You know you're not playing by the rules."

He laughed but snatched his hand back. When I'd finished measuring the volatile liquid, I set the bottle down.

"I've had other things on my mind," I muttered, wishing I didn't want him to reach for me again.

"That's too bad." His teeth flashed partly in friendship, the other part in warning.

"And why is that?" I leaned against the table.

"Because I was going to offer a rare invitation." He began to make notes in his workbook.

"An invitation to what?" I peered over his shoulder. As ever, his notations were perfect, but I enjoyed pretending I doubted his studiousness. I fought off the desire to snatch the pen and start a game of keep-away.

He wore a wry smile. "I don't think I could extend any courtesy if you have doubts about our ability to interact peaceably."

I didn't take the bait. "I'm interested, Ren. What are you offering?"

His eyes flashed, streaks of silver against black.

"Efron's having a VIP party at one of his clubs in Vail this Friday.

Some new bigwig's in town, and our master is wining and dining him as usual. We were going to hit it. You could come. Bring your pack."

I started at his words. "Seriously?"

"Would I toy with you?" He cocked his head at me, eyes wide in affected innocence.

"Yes," I said, and he laughed. This time he reached for my hand. I didn't flinch when his fingers trailed over mine.

"The offer stands. Take it or leave it," he said, turning back to his workbook. He pulled his hand away, leaving my heart to its own ferocious pumping.

"Which club?"

"Eden."

I clenched my teeth together so my jaw wouldn't drop.

"Okay. We'll be there. Thanks." I kept my tone nonchalant though anticipation made my limbs quiver.

He didn't hide his smile. "All your names will be on the list."

I chewed on my lip.

"What?" Ren frowned.

"I'm not sure about Ansel."

Ren shrugged. He gripped the sides of the table and bent forward, arching his back in a languid stretch. "If his name is on the list, he'll get in."

I put my hands behind my back, threading my fingers so I wouldn't reach out to feel the flexing of his muscles.

"He's fifteen." I averted my eyes from the fluid lines of his body.

"Cosette's fifteen and she'll be there." He moved closer to me. "Will he forgive you if you don't let him come along?"

"Probably not." I imagined the outrage on Ansel's face if I were to tell him about the club and his exclusion from the outing.

"His name will be on the list, but he's your brother. Your call, Lily."

"Will you please stop calling me that?" I snapped.

"Never."

"Uh, hi." A new voice sounded just behind me. Ren's brow furrowed and I turned to face our visitor.

The hiker hovered at the end of our lab station.

Oh God.

"Can I talk to you?" Shay asked.

"Why?" My retort was knife sharp and harder to spit out than it should have been. I wanted to talk to him, but that wasn't an option. I could sense Ren's surprise at my hostility without looking at him. The force of my question drew the alpha near. I couldn't decide if I felt grateful or offended. After all, I was an alpha too.

The new boy's gaze moved to Ren. I could see his menacing expression reflected in the stranger's eyes. No human could withstand a Guardian's warning glare, especially one that emanated from an alpha. I almost felt sorry for him.

"Nothing. Never mind," Shay murmured as his nervous gaze darted from me to Ren, whose hands now rested on my hips.

My instincts battled back and forth between the desire to tear Ren's fingers off my body and relief from his closeness. I reveled in the strong, soft pressure of his hands, but I resented his attempt to possess me. I glanced up at him, filled with a nagging irritation. And then it hit me as my eyes returned to our uninvited guest. *This isn't how I want Shay to see me.*

Shay shook his head as though he'd been caught in a disorienting fog. The bell rang and he hurried away.

"Weird kid," Ren murmured, dropping his hands from my hips. "He's new, huh?"

"I guess. He was in homeroom with me and Bryn. Got stuck in the seat next to me, probably just wanted directions." I tried to look bored. "He hasn't figured out the rules yet. No mixing."

Ren returned to putting away our lab materials. "Right, *that* rule."

"Just 'cause you have boundary issues doesn't mean everyone else does. The rest of us respect the Keepers' wishes." My voice dripped honey sweet.

He just shrugged.

Damn it, stop being so arrogant.

"Look, I'm starved. You got that?" I gestured to the remaining beakers and bottles that needed to be reshelved in the classroom's cabinets.

"No problem."

"Thanks." I grabbed my bag, walking swiftly from the room.

The Guardians always ate lunch on the far side of the cafeteria. While the two packs sat at different tables, we still hovered near each other. Across the room were the Keepers' children, decked in Gucci and Prada, looking put out to be anywhere near the rest of us. The human students sat sandwiched between the wolves and our masters' children. Sometimes I felt sorry for the mortals. In their own world they wielded immense power. But not here. At the Mountain School, the humans knew they were at the bottom of the food chain.

Ansel and Mason already occupied our usual table, and I pulled up a chair next to my brother.

"So what did Ren want?" Ansel's eyes were bright with anticipation.

Mason leaned forward, interested, but he didn't speak.

"Let's wait until everyone is here." I pulled the turkey sandwich out of my bag.

Ansel growled impatiently and I shot him a warning glare. Steel legs screeched against the tile floor as Bryn took a seat close to me. Fey dropped into the chair beside Mason.

My gaze swept over my now-circled packmates before flickering to the next table, where the Banes sat. Sabine drummed her long vamp-painted nails on the table and whispered in Cosette's ear.

The younger blond girl pursed her lips. Her skin was so pale it was like you could stare right through her, and her constant fidgeting made it appear that she wished everyone could.

Dax and Neville began an arm-wrestling match. Though Dax— clad in a Broncos jersey and baggy jeans—clearly outweighed the lean junior, beads of sweat began to appear on Dax's forehead. Neville, head-to-toe in beatnik black, slowly began to push Dax's arm toward the tabletop. Ren perched on the edge of the table, laughing at his friends' antics, but his eyes darted frequently toward us.

I swallowed a mouthful of turkey and wheat bread. "Okay, listen up."

In a single movement the Nightshades leaned forward. Except Mason, who tipped his chair away to balance on its back legs and crossed his arms behind his head. He glanced at the Banes and then winked at me. I laughed.

"Ren's watching. Be cool. Be Mason."

The rest of the pack mumbled embarrassed excuses, trying to assume more casual poses with varying levels of success.

"The Bane alpha made an interesting suggestion." I chewed on my sandwich, ignoring my lurching stomach.

Bryn twirled her spaghetti around the tines of her fork. "And what was that?"

"He wants us to start hanging out." I tried not to cringe as my pack struggled to hold their composure.

Ansel sent corn chips scattering across the table. Fey's lips curled up in disgust and she threw an incredulous look at Bryn, who had drawn in a hissing breath. Only Mason remained unruffled. He stretched his arms languidly, looking pleased. My low growl made the pack settle.

Bryn spoke first, in a hushed voice. "Do you mean he wants to date you?" I winced at her incredulous tone.

"No, *us*." I swept my hand around the circle of the table. "Our packs. He thinks the Banes and Nightshades should start to merge now. Before the union."

"Oh, come on." Fey was livid. "Why would we want to do that any sooner than we have to?" She shredded a napkin that had the misfortune of resting on her lunch tray.

Mason rocked back and forth in his chair. "Could be interesting."

"Bryn?" I turned to face her.

"What's his motivation?" Her eyes darted to the Bane table.

I followed her gaze. Dax looked crestfallen, while Neville pulled his tweed cap over his eyes, dropping his head back against his chair to nap. Ren had taken a seat near Sabine, who leaned into him, her lips moving rapidly as she spoke. Cosette's head bobbed in affirmation as she listened.

"The same as mine," I murmured. "Efron's riding him. And Lumine's doing the same with me. She had wraiths in my house last night."

My pack bristled at the mention of the shadow guards.

"Ren thinks that if we show our compliance to the union early," I continued, "you know—follow orders before they are orders—that the Keepers will give us a break."

"What do *you* think?" Ansel had gathered the scattered Fritos back into a pile in front of him.

"I think we should try it. One step at a time," I said. "If it sucks, we'll separate and wait until the order is given in October."

Mason dropped his chair back to the floor. "What do you mean one step at a time?"

"We're invited to a party at Eden on Friday night."

"Whoa." Mason elbowed Ansel, who grinned.

"But . . ." All their eyes were on me. "I don't want the Banes to call the shots. Eden is Efron's turf. Their turf."

Bryn leaned closer to me but looked at the other Nightshades, baring her teeth. "She's right. Ren can't control the merge."

"He won't," I said. "I'm going to keep him guessing. He's always been too sure of himself."

My packmates laughed, nodding.

"I need you guys to follow my lead and play nice," I said. "Even if what I do is somewhat . . . shocking."

Mason drummed his fingers on the table. Ansel cocked his head. Bryn just nodded. I stared at Fey, who chomped at her apple before speaking.

"You're the alpha, Cal," she said, mouth full of fruit flesh. "But for the record, I hate Sabine. She's a heinous bitch."

"Maybe she's nice when you get to know her," Ansel said. He shrank away from Fey's withering glare.

"So we're agreed, then?" I straightened in my chair, waiting. They all nodded, Mason eagerly, Fey last.

"Okay, guys. Here comes the cannonball." I turned to face the Banes.

"Hey, Ren!" I called.

He broke off his conversation with Sabine, whose face contorted with outrage. His eyebrows shot up, but he quickly composed his face into a picture of disinterested but respectful regard.

"Yeah?"

"Push our tables together?"

I heard Fey swear under her breath. My smile broadened when Ren couldn't suppress the startled twitch of his limbs.

"Of course." He shot a quick look at Dax and jerked his head toward us.

The bulky senior walked over and gripped our table with one hand. He pulled it along the ground, which caused a horrible screeching of metal on tile, until it bumped up against the Banes' table. Heads all over the cafeteria lifted and turned toward the teeth-grating sound. The Keepers' faces registered shock and murmurs of interest drifted toward us.

Good. Let Lumine and Efron hear about this as soon as possible.

Mason was already on his feet; he dragged his chair over to Neville, who looked surprised but smiled and pushed his own seat back to make room. Mason waved Ansel over. My brother trotted happily to his friend's side, and Neville extended a welcoming hand.

Huh. I hadn't expected such an easy melding of our packs.

Sabine scooted backward when Fey carried her chair to the united tables. Fey stared back at the Bane girl, positioning her own seat as far from Sabine as possible.

Maybe not so easy.

"Calla?" Bryn waited beside me.

"Fey needs some moral support. And maybe restraints. Sit with her."

I kept my gaze on Ren. He leaned over to Dax. I saw his lips move though I couldn't hear the words. Dax stiffened. Ren put a hand on his shoulder, which Dax shrugged off as he stood.

The broad-shouldered wolf sauntered past me, picked up the chair I had been sitting in, and carried it over to Bryn and Fey. I nodded and they adjusted their chairs with some reluctance to make room for the imposing Bane. Ren gestured to the chair next to him and raised his eyebrows at me.

I grabbed my lunch and moved to the empty seat. Sabine sulked. Cosette offered a nervous smile as I sat down.

"Hello, ladies," I said.

Sabine grunted, tightening the lock of her arms around her body.

"Hi, Calla," Cosette murmured, toying with the meatball atop her plate of spaghetti. Her glance darted uneasily from me to Sabine.

"Interesting move, Lily." Ren took a swig from his bottled water.

I resumed chomping on my turkey sandwich and shrugged. "I thought it might save us from random acts of violence at Eden. I'm sure Efron wouldn't enjoy pulling rival teen wolves off each other in the middle of his party."

Ren laughed, tilting his chair on its back legs, but Sabine glared at me.

"So you're coming?" Her nails dug into the flesh of her arms, leaving bright red welts.

"Of course. We can't wait," I said. My voice dripped saccharin.

"Whatever." She pulled out an emery board and began filing her nails.

Ren brought his chair back to the floor with an abrupt clatter. "Knock it off, Sabine. Now."

She dropped the emery board and cast a pleading glance at Cosette. The younger Bane girl bit her lip, scooped up the board, and handed it back to Sabine.

A trill of wicked laughter came from the other table. Fey grinned as her eyes followed Dax's wildly gesticulating hands.

"Well, that is a strange sight," I said. "Smiling ranks at the top of her seven deadly sins."

Ren leaned toward me. "Dax is a funny guy. Great storyteller. Your pack will like him."

"That seems to be the case."

Mason, Neville, and Ansel remained so engrossed in their conversation—which from snatches I caught seemed to be about whether Montreal, Austin, or Minneapolis produced the best indie bands—they didn't even glance at the rest of the wolves. I leaned back in my chair, feeling rather pleased with myself.

This is easy.

The mouthful of turkey sandwich I'd bitten off caught in my throat when Ren rested his hand on my leg, his fingers exploring the curve of my thigh. I coughed and snatched the bottle of water from his other hand, taking several desperate swallows before swatting his fingers from my leg.

"Are you trying to kill me?" I choked the words out. "Keep your hands to yourself."

Ren opened his mouth as if to respond, but he suddenly jerked upright, looking behind me. I turned in my seat.

Shay stood in the middle of the cafeteria, staring at our two tables, a mixture of curiosity and fear playing over his face.

"I think you're right, Lily," Ren said. "That boy needs directions. He looks like he wants to come over here."

Shay took a hesitant step toward us. His eyes fixed on me, mesmerized. I shuddered and shoved the remainder of my sandwich into the brown paper bag.

Sabine snickered. "My, my, that's a love-struck gaze if I've ever seen one. It looks like the newbie has a crush on Calla. Isn't that sweet? Poor little human."

It was becoming too familiar, this mixture of fear and pleasure whenever I thought about the new boy and wondered what he might be thinking about me.

A low rumble stirred in Ren's chest. "Maybe I need to have a chat with him about how things stand with us . . . and where his place is at this school."

He started to rise. I couldn't let him get to Shay.

"No, Ren. Please. He's just a human. He doesn't know any better." I grabbed his arm, pulling him back into the chair. "Give it a day; he's bound to figure it out. They always do."

"Is that what you want?" His voice dropped low. "For me to leave him alone?"

"We're not supposed to mix with the humans," I said. "It will only draw attention if you confront him."

He pulled my hand off his forearm, threading his fingers through my own.

I tensed but didn't attempt to free my hand from his clasp.

Okay, we can hold hands. This is okay. This will be okay.

But my heart felt like I was trying to finish a marathon. I hated that I couldn't control myself around him—and that I had to.

The rest of the pack, attuned to the sudden bristling of their two alphas, dropped their conversations and turned to the stranger. A rippling snarl emerged from their throats and my spine prickled. Their defensive reaction was the first unified act of the young Nightshades and Banes.

We are *a pack.*

With ten pairs of hostile Guardian eyes fixed upon him, Shay began to quiver. His glance shot around the cafeteria, settling on his lab partners from Organic Chemistry. He hurried over to their table with a quick, regretful glance back at me.

A dark laugh rolled out of Ren's throat. "Guess you were right, Lily. There's the learning curve in action."

I smiled weakly and crumpled my lunch bag, too aware of the disappointment still pinching me from the moment Shay had walked away.

FIVE

LAMELY TITLED "BIG IDEAS," MY ONLY AFTER-

noon course surveyed philosophy from the classical era through the present day. Despite its vague theme, the class had become my favorite, but when I saw Shay sitting in a desk near the tall windows of the room's outer wall, my heart tripped over itself. I headed to the back of the room, as far away as I could get. Shay's eyes were on me as I took my seat. I pulled out the thick binder that contained our readings for the entire year and flipped to the homework from the previous night. As I tried to review my notes, the words blurred before me.

Who is he? Why is he here?

A low, husky laugh drew my attention to the door as the three Bane seniors entered the room. Sabine smiled up at Ren. My jaw clenched to see her arm threaded through his. Dax bounded in just behind the pair. Ren scanned the half-filled seats, his grin fading the second he saw our new classmate.

Ren pulled his arm free of Sabine, turned toward Dax, and jerked his chin in the stranger's direction. The two Banes swaggered shoulder to shoulder up to Shay, whose eyes widened as the wolves approached. I gripped the sides of my chair, ready to throw myself between predators and unwitting prey if things got out of hand. Ren's lips curled back in an expression that could hardly be called a smile. I fought back a snarl as I watched the alpha close in.

If you hurt him, I'll kill you. I swallowed my own gasp at the unbidden thought, glad we weren't in wolf form. Ren was the last person I could threaten. He was the pack's future. My future.

He extended his hand. "I'm Ren Laroche. You're new here. I saw you in Organic Chemistry."

Shay frowned and slowly reached out, wincing when Ren grasped his fingers. But instead of shrinking down into his desk, as most humans would have, the stranger glared at Ren and ripped his hand out of the Bane's grasp.

"Shay. Shay Doran." He flexed his fingers beneath his desk.

"Good to know you, Shay." Ren glanced at his hulking companion. "This is Dax."

Dax made a show of cracking his knuckles. "Hey, man. Hope you make it here. Tough school."

In a swift, unison motion Ren and Dax slid into the desks on either side of Shay. I clutched my pencil so tightly it snapped in half. From his newly selected seat, Ren winked at me. I sent him dagger eyes, but it only widened his smile.

The bell sounded and our teacher, Mr. Selby, began to write on the whiteboard. The scrawled question: WHAT IS THE TRUE STATE OF NATURE? filled the blank space.

"Before we launch into today's discussion topic, I want to bring your attention to a new member of our class." He turned and gestured to where Shay sat, tense, between the lounging Bane boys.

"Mr. Doran, would you say a few words about yourself?"

Shay shifted in his seat, glancing around the classroom.

"I'm Shay. I just moved here with my uncle. I was in Portland for the last two years. And then before that, well . . . I haven't ever stayed in one place for very long."

Mr. Selby smiled at our new classmate. "Welcome to the Mountain School. I understand that you may not have had time to catch up on all the assigned reading for this course yet, but feel free to join the discussion if you'd like."

"Thanks," Shay said, before muttering something under his breath that sounded like: "I'll try to keep up."

Mr. Selby turned back to the board. "From the reading: philosophers' ideas about how the natural order of the world operates. Where it all began, what it looks like?"

"*In paradisum*. Paradise. Eden." Ren flashed me a wicked smile.

"Very good, Mr. Laroche. The state of nature as paradise. Lost forever—maybe, maybe not? Enlightenment philosophers thought the New World might be the new Eden." Mr. Selby recorded the response on the whiteboard. "What else?"

"*Tabula rasa*," I answered. "The blank slate."

"Yes. Every person born with endless possibility inside them. Locke's theory gained quite a following. We should talk about whether you think it's viable in contemporary society. Other ideas?"

"*Bellum omnium contra omnes.*"

All the non-humans in the room stiffened in their seats, heads turning toward the speaker. The rest of the students looked impressed by all the Latin phrases being thrown around, but no comprehension dawned on their faces.

"The war of all against all." Shay frowned when Mr. Selby didn't copy the words onto the board.

"Thomas Hobbes is often considered a foundational theorist about the state of nature," Shay continued, though his voice had become more hesitant. Mr. Selby turned, face paling as he stared at his new pupil.

Shay's mouth flattened at Mr. Selby's expression. "I do a lot of reading on my own."

"Hobbes wasn't in our readings," a cold voice said.

I drew a sharp breath. The speaker was a Keeper boy with a crown of golden casually spiked hair. Logan Bane, Efron's only son, threw a spiteful look at Shay. I stared at the young Keeper. Logan never participated in discussion. He usually slept through class.

"That doesn't make any sense." Shay twirled a pen in his fingers. "He's in all the standard philosophy texts."

Mr. Selby glanced at Logan, who tilted his head at the teacher and raised his eyebrows.

"The, um, Mountain School curriculum doesn't include Thomas Hobbes." Mr. Selby's eyes bulged, still fixed on the young Keeper.

Shay looked ready to stand on top of his desk in protest. "What?"

Logan turned to him. "It has been concluded that his ideas are somewhat banal for our consideration."

"By who?" The Keepers' and Guardians' eyes were focused on Shay. The human students looked as though they wanted to hide beneath their desks until this line of discussion was dropped.

Logan pulled off the sunglasses he always wore, no matter the weather nor the time of day.

I watched, amazed. This must be a big deal.

"The Regents," he said, as if correcting a child's mistake. "One of whom is your uncle, Shay. Also my father and several other significant men who protect the reputation of this institution."

My jaw dropped. Uncle?

"And they've censored Hobbes?" Shay said. "I've never heard anything so ridiculous."

"Let's move on, shall we?" A sheen of sweat appeared on Mr. Selby's forehead.

"Why? Why wouldn't you study Hobbes? He's arguably the founder of this subject of discussion," Shay blurted.

My fingers gripped the edge of my desk. He might as well have walked in front of a firing squad wearing a target. *I can't believe I have to help him again.*

"Because we know better." I spit out the words. "We can evolve from Hobbes's disastrous world and not wallow in violence. War is a savage schoolmaster, right?"

Mr. Selby gave me a grateful smile, wiping his brow with a handkerchief. "Thank you, Ms. Tor. Nice use of Thucydides. The theorists we study in this class have a more hopeful outlook on the world than did Mr. Hobbes."

Ren beat pencils on his desk like drumsticks. "I don't know. Savagery seems okay to me."

All the Guardians in the class burst into laughter, including myself. The human children shrank into their seats looking terrified, except Shay, who wore an expression of utter confusion. The young Keepers smirked, throwing disdainful glances at the wolves.

Shay's next words were frustrated but insistent. "Hobbes isn't talking about savagery. It's about the ceaseless struggle for power. Strife unending that makes the world go round. That's the true state of nature. You can't just ignore it because some stuffed shirts call it vulgar."

Ren turned to face Shay, regarding the new student with a gaze that was almost admiring, if still wary. Dax glanced from his alpha to me and then to Shay. He looked like he was waiting for one of us to spontaneously combust. Sabine stared at Shay as if the boy's skin had turned inside out. Logan sighed and began to examine his fingernails.

Shay threw a pleading look at Mr. Selby. "Can we please talk about the war of all against all? I think it's the most important idea I've come across in philosophy."

The sweat on Mr. Selby's forehead formed droplets that trickled down his temples.

"Well, I suppose . . ." He raised the marker to begin writing on the whiteboard. A spasm jerked through his fingers and the dry-erase pen dropped to the floor again.

"You need to work on your reflexes, Mr. Selby," Ren teased. A nervous titter moved through the classroom.

Our teacher didn't respond; the quaking of his fingers moved up his arm. His entire body convulsed. He bent backward, flailed, and collapsed to the floor twitching violently. White spittle collected at the corners of his mouth, spilling down his jawline.

"Oh my God, he's having a seizure!" shrieked a human girl, who I thought was called Rachel. I'd never bothered to learn most of their names.

Dax bolted from his desk and crouched beside Mr. Selby's tormented body. He shouted at the still-screeching human girl, "Shut up and go get help!"

She scampered from the classroom. Several human children had pulled out their phones.

"Phones away now!" Logan's sharp command filled the room.

"Just get Nurse Flynn, Rachel," he called to the girl in a loud but rather lazy voice. The golden-haired Keeper looked bored. I stared at him. Nurse Flynn was a Keeper who oversaw the small infirmary in the Mountain School, but I wasn't sure she had any real medical training.

Dax, who had stilled our teacher's convulsions through sheer brute strength, frowned. "He needs an ambulance."

"No, he doesn't. When Flynn arrives, our dear teacher will be fine." Logan's cold response was accompanied by a sweep of his eyes across the room. He raised his crystal-clear voice, addressing the class.

"In case you hadn't noticed, we're finished here. Go find someplace else to be."

Most of the human students bolted from the room. A few stared for another minute at Dax, who still pinned Mr. Selby against the tile floor, then slunk off whispering to each other. The other Keeper children nodded at Logan and moved quietly out the door. The Guardians, and Shay, hesitated. Our eyes fixed on Logan, who gazed back at us with smug confidence. An ebony-haired woman, with a stunning figure marred by the large, misshapen hump on her back, appeared in the doorway. She was followed by two men who pushed a gurney.

"We'll take it from here, Dax."

Dax released Mr. Selby, who immediately began to flail again. Nurse Flynn withdrew a syringe from the pocket of her lab coat, knelt down, and plunged the needle into his neck. Mr. Selby's spasms eased and he moaned once before dropping into unconsciousness. Nurse Flynn nodded to her two companions, who lifted Mr. Selby onto the gurney and wheeled him from the room.

She turned to Logan. "Thank you for sending Rachel to alert me, Mr. Bane."

The golden-haired boy made a dismissive gesture with his hand.

"Your prompt attention to the matter is noted, Lana."

Nurse Flynn dipped into a curtsy and left the classroom.

Logan sauntered over to Shay. "Let's take a walk."

Shay slowly rose to his feet. "What the hell just happened?"

"Mr. Selby is epileptic. It's a shame, really. He's a fine teacher," Logan replied, the hand that he still held behind him jerking rapidly in odd flickers of his fingers.

Shay's eyelids fluttered as Logan smiled, sliding his arm around the boy's shoulders. He drew our new classmate, who stumbled forward in a near stupor, toward the door.

"I'll give you a ride home. I'm sure Bosque is eager to hear about your first day at our school."

The two boys walked away. Logan turned once and flashed a smile at the Guardians, who were now the sole occupants of the classroom.

Ren leapt to his feet and swore. "What was that?"

I thought about standing but decided against it. My limbs seemed to have transformed into Jell-O. Ren's gaze moved over my face. He crouched beside my desk, folding my shaking hands in his own.

"Calla," he said. "Are you all right?"

I pulled out of his grasp. "His uncle. Logan said Shay's uncle is a Regent. That's just not possible. God, Ren. Why would the Keepers have anything to do with a human boy? Who is Bosque?"

"I don't know. I've never heard of them adopting a human. If that's even the right word." Ren shoved his hands in his pockets. "Efron hasn't said anything about it. At least not to me."

"And what happened to Mr. Selby?" Dax wandered over to Ren's side. "I didn't know he was epileptic."

"When did you all become idiots?" Sabine's voice was jagged as broken glass. "He isn't epileptic. You know the phrase that stupid boy kept repeating is forbidden. He triggered one of the Keepers' spells. Selby was being punished for discussing a censored subject. The Keepers don't tolerate such behavior."

Dax turned toward her. "So no ambulance?"

"A doctor couldn't do anything for him," she said. "Flynn's obviously the spellwarder at our school. Don't you know anything?"

She stood up and, with a final withering glare, flipped her long hair and strode from the classroom.

SIX

"YOU CAN'T BE SERIOUS." I PULLED THE

corset from Bryn's hands. The velvet slid enticingly over my fingers, but I cringed at the thought of wearing it in public.

"Brutal truth time." She walked to my closet and began shuffling through clothes. "You own nothing that will work. Just pretend it's Halloween."

"Yeah, that makes me feel much better." I turned toward the mirror and held the corset against my body. "And who knows what I'll be wearing on *that* day."

Bryn shut my closet door, cutting off all fashion escape routes. "Since it's up to Naomi, probably something with puffed sleeves."

"Ugh. I can't think about the union now." I handed the corset back to her.

"You'll look amazing tonight at least," she said. "Get out of that shirt so we can get you into this."

I looked her up and down. She was striking in her formfitting black satin dress and brass-buckled combat boots.

"You're sure about this?" I sighed.

She bobbed her head with a little too much enthusiasm. "You have to look fierce, Cal. You're our alpha. Make an impression."

"Fine. I'll wear it. But only with a jacket," I said. "And I'm still wearing my jeans."

Bryn frowned for a moment but then shrugged. "I guess that works. Suit yourself."

She sat on the bed while I stripped off my T-shirt and bra and wiggled into the corset.

"I'll lace it up," Bryn said. "Just tell me when you can't breathe."

"Great," I said.

"Say uncle!" She jerked the stays.

"That's tight enough!" I choked, glancing down. *Oh my God.*

"I'd kill for your boobs," Bryn said to my reflection.

I snatched my leather jacket from the back of a chair, pulling it tight around my body.

"I didn't have *these* boobs until you cinched it up."

She laughed. "Ren's going to turn inside out when he sees you."

"Stop."

"Well, that's the point, isn't it?"

I didn't answer. Maybe that wouldn't be a bad thing. The union was getting so close. I wanted him to want me, even if we couldn't act on it.

She was quiet for a minute. "He hasn't bothered you again, has he?"

"I wouldn't say he's bothering me," I mused. "Ren's just being Ren."

"I wasn't talking about Ren."

"Oh." I frowned. "No. Nothing else. He hasn't tried to talk to me since Logan pulled him out of Big Ideas." I fiddled with the embroidery on the corset's hem, thinking about how I wished he would try, even if I shouldn't want him to.

"And Mr. Selby?"

"Back in class like nothing happened."

"Well, maybe everything will get back to normal now." She smiled.

"Nothing will be normal if I have to keep wearing stuff like this."
I rapped my knuckles on the corset's boning. "At least it might be
able to double as armor."

A gasp followed by several coughs came from my bedroom door.
I turned to see Ansel, ashen-faced, staring at us from the doorway. I
quickly buttoned my jacket, but his eyes were locked on Bryn.

"Are you feeling okay?" I frowned at my little brother.

Ansel seemed to have lost his ability to blink.

Bryn smiled at him. "What's up, Cub Scout?"

"Come on, Bryn." He kicked at the door frame. "I'm a sophomore now."

"Yep, and we're seniors. Which makes you a cub as far as I'm
concerned."

"Whatever. I just wondered when you guys were gonna be
ready." Ansel stared at his shoes. "Mason said he'd drive—his parents gave him the Land Rover for the night. Fey is already at his
house. He wants to know when he should pick us up."

"Half an hour, tops," I said. "Bryn, do you have fashion tips for
my brother too?"

She wandered over to Ansel, who stood transfixed in the doorway. She tugged at the collar of his black silk shirt, deftly unfastened
one button more than Ansel had left open, and eyed his jeans criti-
cally. After a moment she smiled, patting his cheek.

"Nah, he's adorable."

Ansel swallowed and then bolted from the door frame.

"I'll yell when Mason gets here!" he called without looking
back.

The bouncer, a Titanesque Bane elder, took our names and jerked
his thumb toward a stairway cordoned off from the main floor of
the club.

"VIPs head upstairs." His eyes were respectful but wary as they moved over our party.

"Thanks." I led the Nightshades up the steel staircase to the second level of the warehouse-like club. Eden throbbed with a mix of industrial beats and dark trance. Humans packed the main dance floor, pulsing and swaying with the heavy bass. Bryn elbowed me. Compared to the other women in the room, I could have been mistaken for a nun.

"Are you going to say I told you so?" I glared at her as I pulled off my jacket, baring my arms, shoulders, and far too much else.

"I don't think I have to."

"You're not gonna fall out of that, are you?" Ansel laughed.

"Shut up or I'll make you wait in the car."

Mason darted forward, wrapped his arm around my shoulders, and pecked me on the cheek. "You look fabulous. Ignore them—go forth and conquer."

I squeezed his hand but wrinkled my nose when we reached the second floor. Mason frowned when he caught the scent in the same moment. We both glanced up at the ceiling. No less than six wraiths floated in and out of the scaffolding above us.

"Tight security," he murmured.

"No kidding." I fought to keep my eyes off the shadow guards who hovered fifteen feet over our heads.

Bryn flinched when she saw the dark figures skimming along the ceiling. Ansel twined his fingers through hers and tugged her forward.

"Come on, we're on the list, right? Efron's guests. No trouble."

Bryn let my brother guide her onto the dance floor. Fey brought up the rear of our pack. Her lips half curled in a snarl as her gaze darted up at the wraiths. She took a few quick steps forward to catch us.

"So what do we do now?" she asked. "Just shut up and dance?"

I shook my head. "We need to find our hosts and thank them for inviting us."

Fey put her hands on her hips. "You're trying to kill me from prolonged Sabine exposure, aren't you?"

"Just say hello. Then shut up and dance."

"Deal." She shook her red hair so that it fanned around her shoulders, making her look like a lioness.

The dance floor gleamed, shimmering colors running across the black surface like it was a pool of oil. Bodies pulsed, pressed together, in rhythm with the throbbing bass line that shook the entire club. A sleek silver bar extended along the far side of the room. Dark velvet couches ringed the dance floor.

Professional dancers, scantily clad and wielding whips, writhed on platforms scattered throughout the room. Broad, leathery wings sprouted from some of the dancers' backs. Given Efron's reputation, I couldn't be sure if they were part of the dominatrix costumes or the real thing.

Most of the guests were Keepers. I saw Logan Bane dancing amid a crowd of his peers and, surprisingly, Lana Flynn. A few Bane Guardians, adults, stalked through the club, their eyes darting throughout the space, muscles tense.

Mason tightened his grip on my shoulder, steering me toward the bar. He walked confidently toward a young man who was laughing with the Bane Guardian pouring shots behind the bar. The bartender looked as though he'd been molded into his clothes, but that wasn't a bad thing.

Bryn leaned over, whispering in my ear. "Forget drinks. I'll take a double of him."

"Just behave." I giggled.

"Hey, man," Mason called, and Neville turned to face us, a wary smile sliding across his mouth.

If a band had been playing at Eden that night, I would have assumed Neville, dressed in a T-shirt and leather pants, was with them. I cast my eyes around, attempting to search the club in a casual manner. Neville watched me with a knowing smile.

"We have a table at the back," he said softly. "He's been waiting for you."

Neville led us away from the dance floor to a secluded corner of the room where the young Banes lounged on couches. Cosette and Dax sat opposite Ren. The alpha grinned at his packmates while one of the leather-clad dancers, draped across him like a cloak, nuzzled his neck. An unfamiliar, painful gnawing began in my stomach.

Bryn leaned into me. "I wouldn't let a succubus get that close, if I were him."

A shiver moved up my spine. *She thinks the wings are real.*

I looked closer and saw that the coquette whose lips were latched on Ren's cheek did not have wings. She sat up, smiling at Ren, who glanced at her with a disinterested expression. My eyes widened. It was Sabine. I could barely recognize her in the mirror-shine black leather hip-huggers and studded bustier.

Fey coughed: "Slut."

Bryn giggled. Ansel choked on his drink when he caught sight of Sabine.

"Hey, Ren." Neville squeezed himself on the couch between Sabine and his pack leader. "Look who I found."

A warm tremor bubbled up through my veins as Ren's eyes moved over my corseted body.

I stole a glance at my newly generous curves. *Maybe there's something to this outfit after all.*

"You guys look great." He gestured to the couch where Dax and Cosette sat and the other, still-empty couch next to them. "Please join us."

He turned to Neville and Sabine. "Make room for Calla."

Sabine rose with some reluctance while Neville eyed the near-empty glasses on the table.

"Looks like you're ready for another round anyway." He looked at Mason. "Make a bar run with me?"

Mason shrugged, trailing after Neville. Dax frowned as he watched the two boys move off. I caught Fey eyeing Dax's biceps and a smile twitched at the corner of my mouth.

Ansel took a seat on the empty couch, pulling Bryn along with him. Ren stretched his hand out to me. I hesitated but then took his fingers in my own, letting him draw me down onto the sofa next to him.

"Let me get that out of the way for you." He took the jacket I'd slung over one arm and draped it along the back of the couch. From behind me I heard Sabine sigh.

"I think there's a platform missing its go-go dancer, Sabine." Fey's brutal tone cut through our courtesies.

"Play nice," I growled.

"It's fine." Sabine held Fey in a steady gaze. "Talk bores me." She glanced at Ren.

"Go dance," he said. "Try to stay out of trouble."

With a toss of her hair, which shone like vinyl under the flashing club lights, Sabine turned on a needle-sharp heel and trotted away.

I patted the empty space on the couch next to me. "Fey?"

She lowered herself onto the velvet cushions.

"It's a party. Have fun." I flashed fangs at her, making sure she knew it was an order, not a request.

She settled for drawing patterns in the plush velvet with her sharp nails.

My hand still lay enfolded in Ren's grasp. His thumb slid up and down the back of my wrist, taking my mind off Fey completely. It was dangerous to be around him.

"Sorry, guys." Bryn suddenly jumped up. "As much as it pains me to agree with Sabine about anything, I'm here for the dancing. Who's with me?"

Ansel was on his feet immediately. "I am."

"Great!" Bryn dragged my brother away.

Fey watched them depart and pointed at Dax. "Do you dance?"

"Do you?" he replied.

"Why don't you find out?"

She rose, wandering past the Bane, whose eyes went wild when she trailed her fingertips over his broad shoulders. She laughed and darted away. Dax looked at Ren, who twitched his wrist, and Dax went after Fey.

I eased back into the cushions. "She's like Jekyll and Hyde."

"She's your best warrior, right?" Ren asked.

I nodded.

"That's Dax too. It makes sense that they'd be drawn to each other. Like attracts like."

"I thought opposites attracted," I countered.

Ren shook his head. "No. That's pop culture drivel. If you're a *real* student of literature, and I mean the good stuff—Chaucer, Shakespeare—you figure out that only souls who truly reflect each other make good love matches." He paused and a smile pulled at one corner of his mouth. "If they can find each other, that is."

I blinked at him. "You're talking about soul mates? When did you become a romantic?"

"There's a lot you don't know about me." Something in his voice made me quiver.

I sought a safe place for my eyes and then realized that Cosette still sat, abandoned, on the other couch.

Ren's gaze followed mine. "Cosette, why don't you go join the others?" She bolted from the couch.

I frowned, suddenly aware of the cloak of darkness that covered Ren and me in the solitary corner of the nightclub. "You didn't have to send her away."

"Are you afraid to be alone with me, Lily?" His voice looped over me like a rope, pulling me toward him.

I tried to sound strong. "I'm not afraid of anything."

"Anything?" he asked. "That's an impressive claim. Even for an alpha."

"Are you suggesting there is something you're afraid of?"

My chest tightened when Ren flinched.

"Yes, one thing." I could barely hear his murmured response.

His retreat drew me forward. "One thing?"

When he looked at me, his troubled expression faded.

"That would be my secret. I won't give it up without getting something in return."

His hand slipped over my shoulder beneath the cascade of my hair, his fingers pausing to cup the nape of my neck. He pulled me close; the strength of his arms set my blood on fire.

I twisted out of his grasp. There were Keepers everywhere. "You can keep your secrets." As much as I wanted his touch, I didn't trust him yet. I'd heard too much about his other conquests. Besides, he knew better. The alpha female was supposed to be pure at the union. And that meant no romance before the ceremony.

As if he'd read my mind, Ren's mouth slid in a wicked grin, eyes fixing on my curves. "Be honest. Can you breathe in that thing?"

My nails dug into the sofa cushion. *Watch yourself, Ren. Two can play hardball.*

"So you and Sabine?"

"Huh?" He lounged back into the cushions, drawing away from me into the shadows.

"Oh, I see. Do all the Bane girls suck on your neck as a matter of course?"

"What?" His face twisted, angry. "No. Efron has a thing for Sabine. Favors her. Something about her attitude he finds appealing. He gave her some X when we got here. She's been rather, um . . . playful since she took it."

"Uh, okay."

Her attitude? You mean Efron enjoys spiteful bitchiness?

He began to slide his arm around my waist.

"Jealous?"

I locked my fingers around his wrist, stopping the progress of his hand.

"Don't be ridiculous." But my skin crackled at the renewed touch.

Heavy footfalls nearby announced the approach of a massive Bane elder. We jumped apart.

"Efron's asking for you." The guard stared at Ren. "He's in his office."

"Of course. I'll be right down." Ren glanced at me. "You want to find the others? I don't know how long this will take."

Efron's guard shook his head. "He wants the Nightshade alpha too. Both of you."

Ren wrapped both his arms around my waist and I didn't resist.

What does Ren's master want with me?

"All right." Ren swallowed hard, gesturing for me to follow him. "Let's not keep him waiting."

The elder Guardian grunted in approval and faded into the darkness.

Ren led me along the edge of the shimmering dance floor and

back to the staircase. I gripped his fingers hard until I could feel each heartbeat throb in my veins. Efron Bane. The name made my spine curl up. I was trusting Ren to keep me at a safe distance.

We snaked through the claustrophobia-inducing crowd of humans on the first floor of the club until he stopped in front of a tall wooden door. The face of the oak surface had been intricately carved. I stepped back to examine the image. It depicted the archangel Michael barring a downtrodden Adam and Eve from entering the Garden of Eden.

"That's an interesting choice." I jerked my chin toward the door.

"Efron has an unusual sense of humor." He squeezed my hand and the icy chill on my skin thawed a bit.

He rapped sharply on the wooden door. A moment later it opened and I blinked in surprise.

Lumine Nightshade stepped back from the door, beckoning us to enter. "Welcome, children. So lovely to see you."

The air smelled of cigar smoke and sherry. Wall-length murals hung throughout the room. Each painting depicted a scene from Dante's *Inferno*. I quickly looked away; the images of hell were much too graphic for close scrutiny.

Lumine turned her eyes on the Bane alpha. "Renier Laroche. It is such a pleasure to meet you. I'm Lumine Nightshade. Efron has nothing but praise for you, dear boy." Her smile was like a string of pearls.

Ren inclined his head. "Thank you, Mistress Nightshade."

"There is someone newly arrived to Vail that Efron and I have been eager for you both to meet." Lumine led us toward two high-back leather chairs and a couch that faced a roaring fireplace. "Efron. They're here."

A man sat on the couch, one arm draped along its back; his other hand clasped a snifter of brandy. He had pale skin and the same golden halo of hair that graced his son's head.

"It's good to see you, Renier." Efron took a sip of brandy. "And the lovely Calla. We meet at last."

He stretched his hand out, hooking a finger at me. I hesitated, but Lumine pushed me toward the couch. My body went cold the moment Ren's fingers were wrenched from my own. I tried to keep from shaking when the Bane master took my hand in his, pressing my fingers to his lips. His eyes mirrored the bright amber of the flames that leapt in the nearby fireplace. My chest contracted and it took every ounce of my self-control to keep still.

"Please take a seat." He kept my hand in his grasp and pulled me onto the couch.

I cast a desperate glance at Ren, who wore an agonized expression.

Lumine touched Ren's shoulder. "Why don't you join them."

It was one of the only times I remembered feeling grateful to my mistress.

Ren came to my side, and I sidled closer to him, trying to put as much distance between myself and Efron as possible, which was difficult considering he wouldn't let go of my hand.

"Come now, children," Efron chided. "We're all here to have a good time, aren't we?" He released my hand, but only to run his fingers along my collarbone. My mind reeled.

Efron has a thing for Sabine. Favors her.

I pressed closer to Ren. He put his arm around me, glaring at Efron, who only raised an eyebrow at his alpha.

"You'd best remember your place, Renier."

"And you should remember yours, Efron. Let her be." Lumine's silky voice cut toward her counterpart. "Calla belongs to me for another month. If Logan doesn't object to your dallying with his pack, then so be it."

"Logan?" Ren's head whipped around to face my mistress.

She nodded curtly.

"Yes." Efron snipped the tip of a cigar. "It has been determined that Logan should inherit the new pack. He's just come of age. I couldn't be more pleased; such an appropriate gift for his eighteenth birthday. My son will be your master after the Rite of Union."

"It's true. But the decision didn't rest with us." Lumine leaned over Efron, lighting his cigar with a flame that jumped from the tip of her fingernail. "It came from—"

Her words cut off and her eyes flew to the office door, which had abruptly swung open.

A tall, elegantly dressed man swept into the room. He had his arm around the shoulders of a weary-looking teenage boy. I almost fell off the couch. *I must be dreaming; this cannot be happening.*

My nails dug into Ren's thigh.

"What?" He kept his voice low, turning toward the door. "Ugh, not this kid again."

Shay Doran appeared as shocked as we were. He halted, staring at us until the tall stranger guided him forward and gestured to one of the leather chairs opposite the couch.

"Have a seat."

Efron rose and Lumine bowed to the newly arrived man.

"May I get you anything?" She smiled sweetly.

He looked at Efron's glass. "A brandy would be fine. Thank you, Lumine."

The man unbuttoned his suit jacket, settling into the leather chair. When I met his eyes, they were an inhuman shade of silver that pierced my body like a sword. My hands began to shake.

"Thank you for inviting them to join us, Efron," he said.

"Of course." Efron bobbed his head.

Lumine returned with a crystal snifter of brandy.

"Ah, good." He took a long whiff of the liquor. "Fine indeed."

The two Keepers hovered near the man, watching his every gesture intently. I followed their movements with increasing alarm.

The stranger leaned forward, smiling. "Renier, Calla, my name is Bosque Mar. Your families and mine have a long history, though I've been away for some years now. I asked my dear friends to bring you here this evening so I could introduce you to my nephew."

He gestured to Shay, who still stared at us in mute bewilderment.

Our families?

Bosque Mar had aquiline features, olive skin, and deep brown hair that was slicked back helmet-like against his head. Like Efron's, his eyes danced as though alive with flames. My gaze moved to Shay. The boy's golden brown hair and tawny skin bore no resemblance to the man who claimed to be his uncle.

Why would the Keepers have a human child living among them?

Shay looked from his "uncle" to the other Keepers, then he glanced at me. He met my befuddled gaze, offering an uneasy smile.

"Perhaps you've already seen each other at school?" Lumine watched me expectantly, her tongue running over her ruby-painted lips.

"Yeah. We have a couple of classes together." I spoke carefully as I kept my eyes on my new classmate. I could barely hear myself over my shrieking nerves. "Hello, Shay. I hope you've had a good first week at school. Sorry we haven't had the chance to be properly introduced *until now*. I'm Calla Tor."

I could see a question forming on Shay's lips. I glared at him and his mouth snapped shut.

My mistress smiled, exposing her bright white teeth. "Excellent. We wouldn't want poor Shay to be isolated, now, would we? Life can be so hard for transfer students."

I stared at Lumine. *What?*

"The Mountain School is a tightly knit community." Efron leaned casually against the mantel, cigar smoke curling around him. "We just want to be sure that you know Shay is part of our family. You should keep an eye out for him, the way you would your own."

Ren watched his master, though he spoke to Shay. "Of course. You can let us know if you need anything."

A dry laugh escaped Shay's throat. "Thanks."

"If you'll excuse our brevity, I have more friends at the party I'd like my nephew to meet." Bosque took another sip of his brandy and then handed the glass back to Lumine.

"Shay." He rose, gesturing for the boy to follow. Shay glanced at me once more before trailing after his uncle. I watched them go, wishing I could follow and puzzle out Shay's place in my world. *Who are you?*

An imposing ebony grandfather clock in a corner of the room began to chime. Midnight. Efron's lips hooked upward.

"Ah, the witching hour. Best time for dancing. Go enjoy yourselves. I'm sorry I can't join you." He winked at me and my blood went cold. "Lumine and I have some business to discuss."

Ren grasped my arm, drawing me from the couch. I fought the urge to run from Efron's office. When the massive oak door had closed behind us, I convulsed with the shudder I'd been holding back.

Ren glanced at me. "Are you all right?"

I rubbed my arms, trying to shake the creeping discomfort from my skin. "I think so."

He placed his hands on my shoulders, turning me toward him. "I'm sorry about Efron. I didn't think he'd be that way with you— since you're a Nightshade."

"I'd heard about his habits but never took the rumors seriously," I said. "I can't believe Sabine encourages him."

"You shouldn't judge Sabine." Ren's hands dropped. He started to walk away.

"Why not?" I called, chasing after him through the tangle of bodies on the main dance floor. "Ren, wait!"

He finally paused at the bottom of the staircase, but he didn't look at me. "Sabine keeps Efron entertained so he won't go after Cosette. Cosette is young and terrified of our master. Sabine is very protective of her, and she's sacrificed a lot to keep Cosette out of Efron's sights—so she's jaded. I'd say it's understandable."

His fists clenched and unclenched at his sides. "She can help Cosette . . . in a way I can't."

"Oh God." My stomach rolled over. "I'm sorry, Ren. I shouldn't have said anything."

"Don't worry about it," he said quietly. "You couldn't have known."

He started up the staircase. "I'm just glad you've been under Lumine all this time."

When we reached the second floor, Bryn darted from the crowd. "Calla!"

Ansel followed just behind her; he was beaming.

"Where have you been?" She wrapped her arms around my waist. "You're missing such a great party."

She caught the expression on my face. "What's wrong?"

I can't seem to keep Ren at bay even though I have to, I'm terrified of Efron Bane, and I can't stop thinking about a boy who's even more of a mystery now than before I knew his name. I plastered on a smile. "Nothing. We'll talk later."

She hesitated, unconvinced.

I hugged her. "Come on, Bryn. Just show me a good time! Do I have to get my brother to dance with me?"

Ansel grinned, took my hand, and dragged me to the center of the pulsating crowd. He lifted me up, whirling us in rapid circles. When my feet touched the floor again, I spun on my own, letting the frenzied pace of the music push away everything else.

Fog filled the room, swirling at our feet. It wrapped silk-like around my limbs and shimmered in a vivid kaleidoscope of colors. It smelled sweet, like honeysuckle and lilac. A pleasant melting sensation traveled through my body.

Musical laughter caught my attention, drawing my eyes to the platform dancers, who moved in rapid synchronized steps as they turned in ever-swifter circles, tilting their heads back and blowing through full bloodred lips. The mist poured from their throats and wafted toward us. I blinked at the strange sight, wondering how safe it was to inhale the breath of a succubus.

The pulse of the music slowed, became dark, throbbing. Bryn's eyes closed; she twirled in slow circles, her arms weaving smooth, intricate patterns in the air. Ansel watched her, mesmerized.

My eyelids dropped low, lashes brushing my cheeks. I let the vibration of the floor flow up the muscles of my legs, guiding my hips in circles and dips as the liquid darkness of the music wrapped around me. I gasped when hands came from behind to encircle my waist.

"The way you move is incredible." Ren drew me back to press against him. His fingers slid down to the curve of my hips, rocking our bodies in rhythm with the heavy bass. The sensation of being molded against the hard narrow line of his hips threatened to overwhelm me. We were hidden in the mass of people, right? The Keepers couldn't see?

I tried to steady my breath as Ren kept us locked together in the excruciatingly slow pulse of the music. I closed my eyes and leaned back into his body; his fingers kneaded my hips, caressed my stomach. God, it felt good.

My lips parted and the misty veil slipped between them, playing along my tongue. The taste of flower buds about to burst into bloom filled my mouth. Suddenly I wanted nothing more than to melt into Ren. The surge of desire terrified me. I had no idea if the compulsion to draw him more tightly around my body emerged from my own heart or from the succubi's spellcraft. This couldn't happen!

I started to panic when he bent his head, pressing his lips against my neck. My eyes fluttered and I struggled to focus despite the suffocating heat that pressed down all around me. His sharpened canines traced my skin, scratching but not breaking the surface. My body quaked and I pivoted in his arms, pushing against his chest, making space between us.

"I'm a fighter, not a lover," I gasped.

"You can't be both?" His smile made my knees buckle.

I pulled my eyes away from him, trying to focus on the lace-like patterns created by the flashing lights on the dance floor. It didn't help. My body felt alien, hot and wild. Even if we were hidden, I didn't want that. Not now. I would not swoon for Ren. If we were going to lead the pack together, I needed his respect.

"I am not just another one of your groupies, Hefner." I shoved him back a foot.

Ren stalked toward me. "Of course you're not. You never could be." His words wrapped around me, low and soothing.

He trailed his fingertips along my cheekbone. His other hand slid around my waist, caressing my lower back where a sliver of bare skin lay exposed between the hem of the corset and my low-slung jeans. A sudden quivering filled my limbs. I hated how weak I felt.

Ren leaned forward, his thumb tracing the line of my lower lip. I was almost drowning in the heat and mist when I realized he intended to kiss me.

"No." I darted out of his reach. My body ached for his touch, but my mind was in a frenzy. "Seriously. We can't."

My heart slammed against my rib cage as I pushed through the intoxicating mist and the wall of dancers to escape his advances. I glanced back once, cringing at Ren's thunderstruck expression. I was about to turn back when I saw arms slink up his chest. Sabine curled her body around him, pulling him into the swaying crowd.

That is exactly why you can't have me yet, Ren. I'm not going to share.

I turned away from the press of bodies, slinking back to the couches we'd occupied. I snatched my jacket and made a break for the stairs.

SEVEN

I COULD STILL FEEL THE BASS VIBRATIONS

from the club as I stood on the sidewalk, wondering if I should just call a cab and go home.

"Um, hi. Calla?"

Shay Doran emerged from Eden's doorway wearing a shy smile. The cold night suddenly felt balmy. I thought about bolting.

The Keepers want you to take care of him. Don't freak.

"Hey," I said, returning his smile. "How are you, Shay?"

"Good. I'm good." He pulled nervously at the lapel of the slim-cut blazer that covered his white T-shirt. "Do you hang at Eden a lot?"

"Not really. My friends and I were invited tonight. I'm mostly here out of obligation." I wished I were at home in bed, instead of standing outside with this strange human.

A relieved laugh emerged from Shay's throat.

"Yeah, me too. This isn't my scene. Bosque thought I'd have a good time, but I'm not really a club kid."

"No?" I asked. "What are you?"

"Well, I think I have my uncle convinced that I'm a wannabe Greenpeace member." He flashed a grin, then he sighed. "I'd always rather be outdoors. I hike. But I guess you know that."

He suddenly looked fearful. I ran my tongue along my lips but didn't reply. He hurried to speak again. "And I like to read. Lots of philosophy, history, comics."

"Comics?" The unexpected image of Shay surrounded by volumes of Plato, Aristotle, Augustine, and Spider-Man amused me.

"Yeah." His eyes brightened. "Sandman has always been my favorite, but that's really more of a series of graphic novels. I like a lot of Dark Horse stuff: Hellboy, Buffy: Season 8 . . ."

He trailed off when he caught my blank expression.

"You have no idea what I'm talking about, do you?"

"Sorry." I shrugged. "I read novels."

"Works for me." He grinned. "What's your favorite?"

I watched a cab pass us on the street. *I really should just get out of here.*

"Ah. Too personal." He raised his eyebrows. "The relationship of a girl and her favorite novel can be complex indeed."

The cab turned down the next block. *So much for escaping.* "No, it's just strange to talk like this outside of the club."

"Agreed." He looked back at the massive bouncer who hovered by the door. "Wanna go get coffee?"

I wondered if I'd heard him right. *A boy just asked me out; that can't be right. No one asks me out. It's forbidden.* I felt warmth creeping up my cheeks. Then I remembered that he didn't know any better.

He spoke again. "I've been making a habit of finding the best late-night reading spots in Vail. There's a twenty-four-hour Internet café two blocks from here."

I nodded. "I know the place." *If I'm supposed to watch out for him, then this wouldn't really be breaking the rules, would it?*

He shifted back and forth on his feet as he waited for my answer.

I considered Ren and the dance floor one last time before saying, "*Watership Down.*"

"What?"

"My favorite novel."

He snorted. "Isn't that about rabbits?"

"It's about survival," I said. "I'll tell you about it over coffee."

I began to walk down the street, hearing the clatter of his shoes on the pavement as he rushed to catch up with me.

"Well, bunnies aside, at least you're original."

"I'm sorry?" I didn't look at him but continued at a fast clip along the deserted block.

"Every girl I know says *Pride and Prejudice*. Or some other Jane Austen tale of class-obstructed love, conflict, and—insert longing sigh here—marriage."

"I'm not the Jane Austen type." I slowed my steps so he didn't have to work to keep pace with me.

"No, I didn't think so." I heard the smile in his voice and felt a grin tug at my own mouth.

Shay kept his hands shoved in his jeans pockets as we walked.

"You know." He cleared his throat. "Grizzlies are supposed to be extinct in Colorado."

I kept my eyes on the sidewalk, pulling my jacket tightly around me. *Nothing is the way it is supposed to be up on that mountain. The world's natural laws don't apply.*

"I like to hike. Pretty good at it, actually," Shay continued. "And I read about the terrain when I moved here. Mountain lions maybe, but no grizzlies."

I shrugged. "Maybe they're coming back. Conservation movements are making significant headway these days."

"No, I don't think so. Wannabe Greenpeace guy here, remember? I can tell you think I'm an idiot, but I'm not. I'm pretty competent when it comes to backpacking. There should not have been a grizzly where I was hiking." He paused and then plunged on. "Or werewolves."

I bit my tongue and quickly swallowed down blood. "Is that what you think I am?" *He's only interested because he thinks I'm some kind of freak.* Disappointment gnawed at me.

"Let me see: super-strong girl who can turn into a wolf and hangs out with a bunch of other kids who act like a pack of animals at our school and are pretty damn scary. Do I have the definition wrong?"

"It depends on what you think werewolves are." I glanced at him.

He ran a hand through his already-mussed hair. "I think you should tell me. The rules of the world I'm used to don't seem to apply here. Lately it seems like I can't be sure of anything."

He stopped abruptly and I turned to face him. My breath caught in my throat when I saw the desperation in his face.

"Except that I should be dead." He shivered. "But I'm not. Because of you."

He took a step closer, his gaze moving over my face, searching. "I want to know who you are."

I could smell his fear but was intrigued by the other, more-alluring scents beneath it. Clover, rain, sun-warmed fields. I leaned toward him, taking in the shape of his lips, the light in his pale green eyes. He wasn't looking at me like I was a freak. His eyes were full of fear and wanting. I wondered what he could see in my eyes.

And I'm beginning to think what really matters is who you are.

Unable to resist, I reached out, curling my fingers around a tendril of hair that fell in his eyes. He took my hand, turning it over in his, tracing my palm as if I might not be real.

"You're so much like a normal girl." His eyes moved over my face and shoulders. He tried to hide his quick glance at my corset.

Man, this thing really does work.

I thought about new places his hands might wander but instead drew my lips back in a warning snarl, shaking free of his grasp.

He looked startled for a moment. "See, you have fangs when you're angry. You're a werewolf for sure."

When he rubbed his eyes, I noticed how deeply shadowed they were. "Or else I'm going crazy."

Sympathy tugged at my chest. *I want you to know me, Shay. To really know me.*

"You're not crazy." I kept my voice low.

"So you are a werewolf," he whispered.

"I'm a Guardian." I glanced around the street, worrying that we might be overheard.

"What's a Guardian?"

I spoke in a hurried whisper. "I need to know if you've said anything to your uncle or any of his friends, like Efron, about what happened on the mountain."

Shay shook his head. "Like I said, I thought I might be crazy. I didn't want to say anything about it. Things have been too weird ever since I moved here."

He shoved his hands back in his pockets. "And I was trespassing on that hike. I had my own reasons for being up there, and I didn't need my uncle to know about it."

Relief spilled through my body. "All right, Shay. I'll make you a deal." I hesitated another moment, knowing I shouldn't tell him anything. That I should leave him alone on the street right now.

But I didn't want to. I wanted something that was just mine.

A thrill coursed through me when I whispered, "If you swear that you won't speak to Bosque or anyone else, and I mean anyone—school, home, online Dark Horse fan group, whoever—about what I tell you, I'll let you know why things seem so weird in Vail."

He nodded with a little too much enthusiasm and I wondered if I was about to make the biggest mistake of my life.

"Let's get to the café and I'll start explaining after you buy me an espresso."

I was about to return his smile when I saw them. Two men across the street, a few yards behind us. They leaned against a building taking nervous, short drags off their cigarettes. I frowned. Though the pair chatted casually, I was certain that a moment ago, they'd been watching us.

"Come on."

I crossed the street onto the next block. Shay fell in step, oblivious to my sudden wariness. I glanced over my shoulder. The men trailed behind us. I sniffed the air, but the pair of strangers walked downwind of me, making it impossible for me to know if they were human . . . or something else. I flexed my fingers as I worked through a map of the area around Eden in my mind's eye.

I tilted my head and listened; it was easy to pick up their gruff whispers.

"We can't be sure without getting a look at his neck."

"You gonna ask him to roll back his collar to give you a peek?" the second man said. "He fits the description and he just came out of the warlock's club. Let's grab him and ask questions later."

"He's not alone."

"Are you afraid of a girl? Probably some tart our golden boy pulled off the dance floor. Just knock her down, snatch the kid, and we're out of here."

With a languid stretch I draped my arm around Shay and curled him toward me. A curious, flirtatious smile appeared on his lips. He glanced at my bursting cleavage again. A sudden low ache made me stumble, sending hot blood up my neck to scorch my cheeks. Then one of the men uttered a low, lewd sound, bringing me back to the street. I shook my head and dug warning nails into Shay's shoulder, trying as much to focus myself as distract him.

"There's trouble. Those guys are following us."

I took care not to say "you." It was still unclear to me what this boy did and did not know about his connection to our world.

"What?" Shay pulled his eyes off my curves and began to turn his head.

"No!" I hissed. "Keep walking. Look straight ahead."

When I pulled him tight against my body, his heart fluttered. So did mine; my eyes found his lips, tracing their shape.

Stop it. Stop it. Stop it. My blood was boiling.

I murmured in his ear: "When we get to the end of the block, I want you to run. Get back to the club. Tell the bouncer there's a problem out here. He'll send help."

"I'm not leaving you alone," he protested.

"Yes, you are." I smiled at him, letting my sharp canines catch the glow of the streetlamp. "I can handle myself but not if I'm watching out for you at the same time."

"I have a cell; shouldn't I call 911?" he asked.

"Absolutely not," I said.

"I won't leave unless you promise me something," he said. It took all my will not to nip his shoulder like I would a misbehaving pup. *Why isn't he afraid of me?*

"What?" My heart was pounding, both from the heat of his closeness and the possibility of an attack.

"Meet me tomorrow morning," he said. "On the mountain. You know where."

"That's not a good—"

"Meet me." He cut me off. "Promise or I stay."

We were almost to the corner. "Not tomorrow! Sunday morning. I'll be there."

"Sunday?" He clasped my fingers.

"Promise," I whispered, squeezing his hand briefly, and then I shoved him forward. "Get out of here. Now!"

He grinned before dashing around the corner. The rush of footsteps came from behind me. I whirled and spread my arms wide, obstructing their path.

"Out of the way," the first man said gruffly.

He raised a hand to shove me aside. I whipped my fist low, catching him with a sharp jab in the stomach. The air whooshed from his lungs and he doubled over in pain. Now that he was close, I caught his scent: not human. *Searchers.*

All the heat in my body gave way to an icy flood. I couldn't believe I'd let them get so close. My distraction could have cost me my life. Shay was even more dangerous than I'd imagined.

The second man lunged at me. I dived for the sidewalk, rolling out of his reach, and shifted into wolf form. A string of oaths rippled off his tongue.

"They've got Guardians watching the kid, Stu."

The first man recovered from my blow; his hand dipped into his long leather coat, and he moved into a crouch. His lips curled in disgust. "Let's see what you've got, fleabag."

Something glinted in his hand. I caught the twitch in his wrist just in time to dodge, and the dagger clanged along the sidewalk. I bared my teeth and leapt on him. His scream cut off as my jaws closed, crushing his windpipe. His blood poured into my mouth, molten copper. When I felt his heart stop beating, I raised my muzzle.

The other Searcher stared at me, his face contorted in horror. I dropped my nose low and stalked toward him. He made the mistake of turning to run. I hunched and then rocketed from the pavement. My teeth tore into his hamstring. He fell to the ground, shrieking, before he rolled over and brought his hand up. I yelped as brass knuckles drove into my shoulder. The blow was enough to bruise and enrage me but not to cripple. I barreled into him, pinning him against the sidewalk, eyes fixed upon the throbbing pulse at his throat.

Stop!

I froze at the sharp voice in my mind. Two Bane elders loped up beside me.

Efron wants him alive, if that's still possible.

It is. I shifted forms, catching the startled Searcher in the jaw with

90

a heavy blow. His head dropped to the sidewalk; his eyes lolled back unseeing.

The Banes shifted back into their imposing human shapes. I recognized one as the bouncer from Eden.

"Impressive," he murmured.

I shrugged, wincing at the throb of pain in my shoulder. The bouncer took a step toward me.

"Injured?"

"It's nothing," I replied, though the lingering pain from my opponent's blow was more intense than I'd expected.

The Bane frowned. "Did he hit you with his flesh or a weapon?"

"Weapon." My eyes darted to the unconscious Searcher's hand. "Blunt, not sharp."

"You'll want Efron to take a look at you. Searchers enchant their weapons. Could be more damage than you think."

The other Guardian gathered the Searcher's limp body in his arms. The bouncer nodded at him. "Let's go. Back door. Get word to the front office: we'll need someone to dump that other body. I'll get the Bane heir; Efron wants him to see this too."

I followed the hulking men through Vail's deserted streets to an alley that ran between Efron's nightclub and the other businesses on that block. The pulse of music and rush of heat made my shoulder throb. We moved through darkened back halls lined with storage closets but ended up outside a door I recognized from earlier in that night. Efron's private suite.

"Wait here," the bouncer ordered.

The door opened once again and the bouncer's head poked through the slight opening.

"Efron wants you inside."

He opened the door just enough for me to pass by him and stepped out, closing the door behind him.

Efron Bane stood at the center of the room talking on his cell phone. Logan hovered over the unconscious Searcher; a cruel smile floated on the young Keeper's lips. The Bane elder who'd carried my attacker back to the club stood just to the side of the couch. Lumine sat nearby in a high-backed leather chair and sipped a glass of sherry. The oak doors opened once more and the bouncer, followed by Ren, entered the room.

"Heard you bagged a Searcher." Ren came to my side.

I nodded, running my tongue along my teeth as a reflex. I could still taste the man's blood.

"Sorry I missed that." His gaze became troubled. "Are you hurt?"

"A bad bruise," I said. "Nothing to brag about."

"Ah, Renier. Thank you for coming so quickly." Efron slipped his phone into his pocket. "That should do it. We can begin."

"Where's Shay?" I hadn't seen the boy anywhere in Efron's office.

"Bosque drove him home. The encounter with your assailants—um, I believe he referred to them as 'muggers'—shook the poor child terribly. Best to get him safe in bed."

"Of course." I tried to keep the confusion out of my eyes. So the Keepers wanted to keep Shay ignorant. I couldn't puzzle out what the boy's place was in all of this. I wished I could see him to be certain he was safe.

Efron moved close to me; I fought to stay calm. "My guards say the Searcher used a weapon against you."

I nodded.

"Where is the injury?" His eyes narrowed.

"My shoulder."

"Take off your jacket," he ordered.

I swallowed my fear and complied, letting the leather jacket slip from my shoulders. The movement shot pain deep within the bruised muscles and along my spine. He took my arm in a rough grasp. I gasped as the wound throbbed again. Ren stiffened next to me, a growl rippling from his chest.

Efron's glance flickered to the alpha, a disdainful smile ghosting across his lips. He examined the dark purple splotch on my shoulder, muttered a curse, and hooked his finger at my mistress. Lumine rose from her seat and walked over. When she looked at the wound, her lips curled back. Efron nodded.

"Their enchantments are getting better. This won't heal on its own."

Lumine caught my chin in her slender fingers. "You need pack blood. Where is Bryn?"

Ren spoke before I could. "She can have mine."

Lumine's eyes widened. "Well, well. How very gallant."

She smiled at Efron. "It seems our young alphas have already bonded, my dear. That's encouraging." Her eyes moved over Ren. "Though I hope you haven't been . . . inappropriate with my girl," she said, licking her lips.

"Of course not, mistress." Ren's dark eyes sparkled.

Logan abandoned his watch over the Searcher and wandered over to his father.

"What's this?" His gaze flickered from Ren to me, and he raised an eyebrow.

"Your alpha has offered to heal Calla by gifting her his blood." Cold amusement trickled through Efron's voice.

"Oh, I've always wanted to see how this works." Logan's lips split in a mocking grin. "Such an unusual ability you Guardians have. I almost envy it."

I trembled with humiliation. Ren glowered at Logan but kept silent.

"Are you sure this is necessary?" I fixed my eyes on the Persian rug beneath my feet.

Even as I asked, I knew it was. The pain had begun to make my arms quiver. I felt nauseated; it was as if the wound were full of venom that wormed from my shoulder into my stomach.

"The Searchers have obviously used their seclusion to hone their skills, which is unfortunate. Now it seems they've found a way to undermine our finest weapons." Efron smiled. "That means you and your pack, Calla dear."

Ren rolled up the sleeve of his shirt. "It's all right, Cal."

But I don't want to be a spectacle for them! I racked my brain for any other solution, coming up with none.

Before I could object, he raised his bare arm to his lips. When he drew it back, crimson rivulets slid along his skin toward his wrist. Ren stretched his arm out to me. I turned my back on the three hovering Keepers. I drew a quick breath, took his arm in my hands, and covered the wound that marred his pale skin with my mouth. His blood ran over my tongue, down my throat. The liquid was hot, sweet as honey but with a smoky bite. Sparkling warmth traveled through my veins. The throbbing pain in my shoulder subsided and then disappeared.

Ren's hand cradled my head. His touch brought me back to the room. My cheeks flamed as I turned back toward my mistress. She nodded in approval, eyes flickering over my now-unmarked shoulder.

"Lovely," Lumine murmured. "Such a perfect match. We've outdone ourselves."

Efron put his hand on Logan's shoulder. "A fine inheritance indeed."

The boy smiled at his father and then glanced at Ren and me, assessing us.

The bouncer appeared beside Ren and handed him a first aid kit.

"Thanks." Ren tore open a wrapped square with his teeth and slapped a bandage over the puncture marks on his arm.

"Since that's been taken care of." Efron swept back through the room to where the limp form of the Searcher sprawled. "Lumine, would you like to do the honors?"

She had taken a few steps forward when Logan darted toward the couch.

"May I?" he asked.

My mistress blinked at the boy but then smiled.

"Of course." She gestured for him to approach the unconscious man.

Efron snapped his fingers. The Bane elders moved into watchful stances on each side of the Searcher.

Logan placed his hands on the sides of the man's temples. The boy's lips moved rapidly, murmuring an incantation that I couldn't understand.

The Searcher's eyes fluttered open; he drew a ragged breath and sat bolt upright. Logan smiled and backed away. The man searched the room wild-eyed.

"Where am I?"

"I think we'll be asking the questions, friend." Efron stepped forward.

The Searcher cringed back into the couch. The Banes snarled, and he whimpered like a caged animal. "Stay away from me."

"Is that any way to treat your host?" Efron continued toward the trembling man at a measured pace. "After all, you are in my home. You've violated my territory."

"It's not yours, warlock." The Searcher spat; his fear seemed to give way to outrage. "Where is the boy?"

"That is not your concern."

"He doesn't know, does he? Who he is? That you took Tristan and Sarah? What you're going to do?" The man's gaze continued to travel with desperation through the office, at last falling on me. "So it was *your* slave bitch who killed Stuart."

Ren snarled and leapt forward, shifting in midair into a dark gray wolf. He crouched low and stalked toward the couch.

"No," Efron said. Ren stilled but continued to glare at the Searcher.

Efron smiled coldly. "You'll soon wish a Guardian had taken your life as well. But I think we can find a more interesting end for you. My apologies, Renier." He waved the alpha off. "I'm sure you'd love a taste of our friend's flesh. I promise you'll have the chance to avenge your mother another day."

Ren shifted back into his human shape and returned to my side; a haunted expression shadowed his face. Lumine crossed the room, smiling at the prisoner.

"I'm not afraid of you, witch," the Searcher hissed, making an obscene gesture.

"So crude." Lumine drummed her fingers on the back of the couch. "Time to teach you some manners."

She raised her hand and drew an intricate pattern in the air. When she finished, a flaming symbol hung suspended before her. The design contracted, pulsed twice, and then exploded outward. The shadowy incarnation of a wraith hovered before Lumine.

My stomach flipped over and I shrank back, grabbing for Ren's hand. His fingers wound through mine, gripping them tightly.

The Searcher scrambled backward from the couch onto the floor. "Oh my God."

Lumine smiled. "He's not taking calls right now."

She flicked her wrist. The wraith slithered forward. Its body wrapped like bands of dark cloth around the Searcher. He shrieked, limbs convulsing as the shadow creature engulfed him.

"Now, let's talk about your friends in Denver, shall we?"

Efron cleared his throat. "Logan, why don't you show our faithful Guardians to the door so they can return to their friends. They've done more than enough for us tonight."

He smiled slowly. "You have our thanks, young alphas."

Ren nodded at Efron and then pulled me toward the door. Logan stepped ahead of us, unlocked the door, and swung it open.

"Enjoy the club," he said. "We'll have to chat about the new pack soon."

From within the room the Searcher screamed again. If it hadn't been for the deafening pulse of music, his cry of agony would have filled every corner of the cavernous nightclub. Logan winked before closing the door.

Without looking back at the office, we hurried to the second floor. When we reached the top of the stairs, I searched for my Nightshades and spotted them at the very center of the throng of swaying bodies. Ansel and Bryn whirled in dizzying circles, hands clasped. Neville and Mason were in the midst of a dance-off, while Cosette and Sabine cheered them on. Dax and Fey stood slightly apart, watching the others. Dax's head was bent near Fey's ear. Her face twisted into a smirk as he whispered. I started toward them, but Ren pulled me back.

"Are you okay?"

"Yes." I felt a light touch on my shoulder where the bruise from the Searcher's weapon had been. Ren's fingers caressed my skin in slow circles. The sensation of his subtle strokes moved out in ripples through my body. I closed my eyes, willing my heart to slow from its breakneck pace. *Why does this happen every time he touches me?*

"Are you sure, Lily?" he teased.

The hated pet name drew a rough laugh from my throat. "I'm sure. You took care of that."

He pulled me closer. "Will you dance with me now, or are you going to run away again?"

My fighting instincts kicked in. "If you'd give me a second to breathe, maybe I wouldn't have to run away!"

Ren's hands dropped from my shoulders. "Why do you hate me, Calla?"

I shook my head. "What are you talking about?"

"I've never encountered a girl so averse to my company." He looked away from me; the muscles in his jaw tightened.

"Maybe that's your problem." He jerked as if I'd hit him, and I regretted losing my temper. "I don't hate you. I'm just trying to follow the rules."

"Look, I understand. This situation isn't ideal," he said. "But I thought maybe things between us . . ."

His words ebbed away like fog caught by a stiff breeze. He shifted his weight and then spoke again, forcefully.

"You're right. I'll back off. I still think our packs need to be together. Particularly with Logan taking over after the union. He's unpredictable. We need to be strong. And they seem pretty okay with this new arrangement." He gestured at the dance floor.

I nodded, not sure what else to say. His eyes met mine. I stepped back, startled by his hard glare. "I won't bother you anymore. When it's time for the union, we'll figure it out."

My gut twisted as I dropped my gaze to the floor. I didn't want him to give up that easily. "Ren." I lifted my eyes to meet his. But he had already turned his back on me. My hand shot out, reaching for him a moment too late as he disappeared into the crowd.

EIGHT

I BARELY SLEPT. CHAOTIC DREAMS AS-

saulted me through the night. Sometimes the visions teased me: Ren's fingers on my bare skin, his lips moving close to mine, and this time I didn't turn away. Shay pulling me into an alley, holding me against a building while his kiss burned through me until there was nothing left but fire. Other images lashed me with cruel force: I was pinned to the ground; Efron hovered over me. Then it was no longer Efron but a wraith. I heard the Searcher screaming and then the screams became my own.

When morning arrived, I shuddered, overwhelmed by exhaustion. I hid in my room, burying myself in all the pillows and blankets I could find. I hunkered down in my cotton fortress until there was a knock at my door. I peeked at the clock from beneath the layers of warmth; it was almost one in the afternoon.

"Yeah?"

My father entered the room, closing the door behind him. His fists were clenched at his sides.

"Haven't seen you all day," he murmured, looking over my pillow turrets and quilt walls.

"I'm not feeling great," I said, and pulled a blanket up to cover my nose and mouth. Only my eyes peered out at my father. My response made him jerk awkwardly. He gripped the doorknob, twisting it back and forth in his hand.

"Ansel said you were with the Banes at Eden last night." His wary voice made me prop up on my elbows.

I nodded.

"Did you meet Efron?" The skin around his eyes tightened.

"Yeah. I did." I heard the revulsion in my voice.

"Are you okay?" My father suddenly couldn't look at me.

"Yes." I sat up with alarm as I realized what kept him hovering in the door frame. I wrapped my arms around a pillow. "Lumine was there too."

His eyes flicked up to me. "She was?"

I nodded, sliding back down beneath the covers. "Has it always been like that?" I stared at the ceiling. "Keepers have Guardians for whatever they want? Not just as their warriors."

"It depends on the Keeper. Efron has exotic tastes. I'm sure you saw that last night." His answer was gruff but resigned.

"Yeah." I closed my eyes.

"But it's our duty to serve them. The sacred sites must not be taken by the Searchers. The world depends upon that, and the Keepers give us the power to defend the sites." His voice was low. "We cannot question the Keepers, Calla. Even when we see sides of our masters that we may not like."

"I know." I turned my head toward him, wanting to voice the questions I couldn't ask.

What if Efron were our master and not Lumine? What if it were me or Mom and not the Bane girls who he asked for? What would you do then?

Horrifying thoughts rushed up to overwhelm me, so I grasped for another subject. "There was a Searcher attack last night."

"We received notice this morning," he said. "Congratulations on your first kill. Your mother and I are very proud." He smiled briefly and I shrugged.

My father looked pleased at my cool acceptance of his praise. "It's likely that our patrols will be intensified soon. I think they'll consider putting your new pack out even before the union is official."

I guess everyone wants a head start on the new pack. "Logan Bane has been given control of our pack as part of his inheritance."

He folded his hands in front of his chest. "That's unexpected. Though I suppose Efron's son will be of age soon."

"Do you know who Bosque Mar is?" I frowned.

He shook his head. "Who?"

"He's a Keeper. He was at Eden last night." I mulled over my memory of the bizarre encounter. "I think he gave the order for Logan to take our pack. Our mistress deferred to him. I've never seen her do that."

"We don't deal with the hierarchies of the Keepers' world," my father snapped. "That's their business. I answer to Lumine and no other Keeper."

He paced in front of the door. "When your new pack forms, you'll be accountable to Logan only. Don't become involved with the Keepers' affairs. You're a warrior, Calla. Remember that and keep it close. Distractions will only hurt you."

"Yes, of course." I shrank further beneath my blanket defenses. *I was stupid last night; my father is right. What I want doesn't matter. I have to be strong. Nothing more.*

I bit a pillow. *I hate boys.*

He watched my retreat, frowning. "Your mother is making lunch. Will you join us?"

"Okay." No matter how thick my cotton fortress might be, it wouldn't change anything. Besides, I was a warrior; it was time to act like one.

The chiming melody echoed in my ears before my eyes opened. Bell-like notes seeped in through my bedroom window, which I'd left cracked open the night before, along with a steady stream of cool, biting air. Frost. The first hard frost of the year. I glanced at the clock. Bryn would be outside in an hour for our weekly patrol.

How am I going to get rid of her? I chewed on shredded wheat and wondered if Shay would actually make the hike up the mountain this early in the morning.

"Hey, sis." Ansel appeared at the bottom of the stairs.

"What are you doing up?" I asked, suddenly worried that I was late. But it was 6:30 a.m. Our weekend patrols began at 7:00.

"I wanted to see if I could come along today." He tried to sound casual, but his hand trembled as he poured coffee. Black liquid splattered on the counter.

"You just patrolled with Mason yesterday." I watched as he wiped up the coffee with a paper towel.

"I know," he said quickly. "I just think the practice is good for me. I mean, with the attack and all."

"Oh." I chewed my lip. "I actually was going to give Bryn the day off. I'll patrol alone."

"Why?" Ansel sat at the table, fingers tapping the sides of his mug.

"I just need some time to think." I made up an excuse on the spot. "And I think best when I run alone."

"Are you okay, Cal?" Ansel shoveled spoonful after spoonful of sugar into his coffee.

"How can you drink that?" I shuddered.

"Just answer the question." He raised the cup to his lips.

"I'm fine."

"Mom said you spent half the day in bed while I was on patrol." He picked up the sugar and added another tablespoon to his coffee.

"We were out until four in the morning on Friday."

"Tell me about it. I was the one who had to get up two hours later.

And Mason is not pleasant to patrol with when he's tired. Cranky as hell. He snapped a rabbit clean in half when it startled him."

Ansel tasted his coffee again; this time he smiled and began to gulp it.

"Seriously, though, Calla," he said. "Did killing that Searcher freak you out?"

"No." He looked doubtful and I sighed. "Killing the Searcher was my job. He tried to attack Shay."

"You mean that new kid everyone's been talking about?"

"Yes." I got up to refill my mug. "The Keepers have some sort of interest in his well-being. He's living with them."

Ansel held his now-empty coffee cup out to me. "That's weird. And the Searchers tried to attack him?"

"Yes. I killed one. The other one—" I hesitated before pouring coffee into his mug. "Do you want only half a cup to leave room for your sugar?"

He didn't take the bait. "What happened to the other Searcher?"

"The Keepers used a wraith on him."

I watched Ansel pale. "What did it do?"

"I don't know exactly." I set his mug in front of him. "Efron sent us out. But it seemed like the wraith would make their interrogation pretty effective."

"I'm glad I didn't have to see that." He began his sugar ritual again.

"I wish I hadn't seen what I did," I said, and his eyes narrowed. "And yes, that did keep me in bed yesterday."

"What else?" Ansel pressed.

I stared at the dark surface of my coffee. "I'm worried about Logan."

"What about him?" He got up and went to the pantry to refill the now-empty sugar bowl.

"He's going to take over the new pack."

I heard a clatter from the pantry. Sparkling granules covered the floor.

"Ansel!" I went for the broom.

"Sorry," he muttered, pushing the spilled sugar into a pile with his hands. "Seriously? Logan? Not Efron or Lumine—or both of them taking turns or something?"

"Be glad it's not Efron," I said, handing him the dustpan.

He caught the dark expression on my face. "Why?"

I swept slowly, tightening my grip on the broom.

"Because of Sabine?" he asked in a low voice.

I froze. "You know?"

"Neville told Mason, and Mason told me." He stared at the pile of sugar.

"Ren told me," I said softly, and began to sweep again.

Ansel maneuvered the dustpan to catch the sugar. "Mason said Ren is really broken up about it. I mean that's third-hand info, but I believe it. He can't protect Sabine from Efron. I can't imagine what that feels like for an alpha. Master or no, it has to go against Ren's instinct to protect his packmates."

I didn't respond but continued pushing the sugar toward Ansel.

"What do you think about it?" he asked.

"For the first time I was glad Lumine is our mistress," I said. "And I hope Logan is different. Ren said he's not like his father but that he's unpredictable."

He shrugged. "Well, Logan would be different no matter what. I mean he wouldn't want—"

The front door banged open and Bryn bounced into the kitchen.

Ansel straightened abruptly, dropping the sugar in his dustpan back on the floor. I groaned.

"Oh. Sorry." He threw me an apologetic glance, taking the broom from me.

"Ready for the great outdoors, Cal?" Bryn smiled and then looked at the floor. "What happened?"

"Ansel believes that coffee should be drunk in equal parts with sugar." I smiled at my still-blushing brother. "He got a little enthusiastic about it."

Bryn laughed, turning to head back out the door.

"Hey, wait a sec," I said, catching her arm.

She raised a surprised brow.

"I'd like to make a solo run today. Do you mind?" It was hard to keep my voice even.

"What?"

"I'd prefer to do the patrol alone," I said, fumbling for a reason and finding nothing. *Lame, Calla, so lame. She'll never buy this.*

"I see." She wandered to the kitchen table, settling into a chair. "So you're meeting Ren?"

"What?" I blurted.

"What?!" Ansel jumped up, spilling the sugar again. He swore, but he didn't bend down to resume his cleanup.

My eyes darted from Bryn to my brother. "I am not meeting Ren." It wasn't what I'd expected but I realized it might be enough to keep Bryn away from patrol. Even if it meant suffering a week or more of teasing from these two.

"Really?" Bryn fingered the empty sugar bowl on the table. "I thought you two seemed to be getting along rather well at Eden. He's a great dancer. Isn't he, Ansel?"

She winked at my brother, who snickered.

I glared at each of them in turn. "I am NOT meeting Ren." I knew if I didn't protest, she wouldn't invest in her new conspiracy theory.

"Fine." She smiled, her eyes telling me she didn't believe me at all, which in this case worked in my favor. "That's good because it's technically against the rules for two alphas to patrol together. You know, in case anything were to happen and both of you were killed."

"*Technically* we're not alphas of the new pack yet. We're still a Nightshade and a Bane," I snapped.

"So you *are* meeting him, then." Her grin became so broad I thought her face would crack.

"I am not!" I snatched the sugar spoon from Ansel and threw it at her, but she dodged it easily.

My stomach tied itself into painful knots. I was fairly certain that over the course of our night at Eden, I'd succeeded in pushing the Bane alpha away.

Bryn laughed and went to the cupboard. "Whatever." She grabbed a coffee mug. "If you want to go alone, that's fine with me. No matter what you plan to do up there."

Still glaring at her, I returned to the kitchen table to finish my coffee.

Ansel finally managed to get the spilled sugar into the trash can.

"So, Bryn." He grabbed the empty sugar bowl and went back to the pantry. I was surprised there was any sugar left considering the amount we'd swept from the floor. "If you're not patrolling today, would you mind doing me a favor?"

Bryn took a sip of her coffee, squishing her face up. "If you can bring me sugar for this bitter stuff." She looked at me. "I don't know how you drink this straight. You're badass."

"That's why I'm your boss."

Ansel swept back to the table brandishing the refilled sugar bowl.

"Stop swinging that around; you'll spill it all over again," I muttered.

"Good man." Bryn grabbed the bowl.

He opened a kitchen drawer and tossed her a spoon.

"Thanks." She began to shovel granules into her mug. "What's the favor?"

I shook my head. "If you guys were humans, you'd already be diabetic."

Ansel laughed, but his gaze fell on Bryn. "Uh. You had Ms. Thornton for English as a sophomore, right?" He sounded nervous.

"Everyone has her." Bryn stirred her coffee. "She's the only English teacher for sophomores."

"Oh yeah, right," he mumbled. "Well, we're at the poetry unit now, and I'm just not getting it."

"Uh-huh." After one taste of her coffee, she wrinkled her nose and reached for the sugar once more. After a quick glance at the clock, I got up and carried my mug to the sink.

"So I know you *write* poetry," Ansel continued, his eyes fixed intently on the depths of his mug. "And I thought maybe you could help me out."

Bryn shrugged. "Sure. Since Calla's dumped me for her new boyfriend, I'm free."

My mug clattered into the stainless steel basin. "He is not my boyfriend!"

She ignored me. "You know, An, if you really want help with poetry, you should talk to Neville. From what I hear, his poetry is much better than mine. He's even had some stuff published."

"Yeah, yeah," Ansel said quickly. "I'll do that, but the assignment is due tomorrow and you're here now."

"Okay. Good point," she said.

"I'm glad you're doing something useful today." I stormed from the kitchen.

I could hear their laughter trail after me as I shifted into wolf form and bolted into the woods behind our house.

I ran up the eastern slope of the mountain. The frosted earth bit into my paws. I knew where I was headed and didn't pause until I arrived at my intended destination. When I reached the ridge, I dropped onto my haunches. He was there, quietly waiting for me, and I wasn't as surprised as I thought I would be. I watched him from my elevated vantage point for several minutes and considered my options. Finally I rose and leapt from the ridge, landing just a few feet away from him. He yelped in surprise, scrambling to his feet.

I stared at him, silent, unmoving. He blinked at me. Then he slowly stretched out his hand, taking a few steps forward. He bent down. When I realized what he was about to do, I snarled, snapping at his fingers. He jumped back and swore. I shifted into human form.

"You're like a dead man walking." I pointed an accusing finger at him. "Don't ever, ever try to pet a wolf. It's just insulting."

"Sorry." He looked chagrined, then he laughed. "Good morning, Calla."

"Good morning, Shay."

NINE

"I'M SURPRISED YOU SHOWED UP. YOU MUST

be an early riser." I paced back and forth uneasily, scanning the edge of the forest that surrounded us. "Why did you want to meet me here?"

I was more worried about why I'd *wanted* him to be in the clearing.

"Not so much an early riser as a non-sleeper. I'm trying to figure out what all this crazy I've fallen into is," he said. "Besides, I wanted to keep our coffee date."

He reached down and unzipped his bag, withdrawing a slender stainless steel thermos and a small tin cup.

"Date?" I shivered, but not because of the chilly morning air.

His playful smile didn't fade as he poured a cup of tar dark liquid from the thermos and stretched it toward me. "Espresso."

"Thanks." I laughed, taking the cup. "That's some high-class hiking."

"Only for special occasions," he said.

I looked at his empty hands. "None for you?"

"I thought we could share," he said. "I promise I don't have cooties."

I smiled, mesmerized for a moment by the way the morning

sunlight pulled golden threads through Shay's soft waves of brown hair.

"Calla?" He leaned toward me and I wished he would grab me the way he had in my dream. "You okay?"

I moved my eyes off him, taking a sip of my coffee. It was incredibly strong and absolutely delicious. "You know, most people don't return to sites of their near-death encounters. You might even say that wiser people would avoid them."

I stretched the tin cup toward him. His fingers brushed against mine as he lifted it from my hands and my skin crackled, warm and alive, at the contact. When his lips touched the metal, I shivered, as if he'd kissed me rather than the edge of the cup. *Is that what a kiss would be like? That electricity I feel when our hands touch, but on my lips?*

"I'm not most people." He dropped into a cross-legged position.

"No, you're not." I sat down opposite him.

"I am wise, though." He grinned. "I think that bear will stay away from here for a while. You're a pretty scary wolf."

"And that doesn't bother you?" I asked.

Shay leaned back on his elbows, stretching out his legs. "If you were going to eat me, you'd have done it already."

I shuddered. "I do not eat people."

"I rest my case." He lifted his face, letting sunlight wash over him.

I studied his features, wishing I could trace the shape of his mouth with my fingertips.

"Still," I murmured. "You should be afraid of me."

He plucked a faded wildflower from the ground. "Why?"

"Because I could kill you," I said.

"That bear *would* have killed me." He curled the flower's stem around his fingers. "You stopped it."

I shouldn't have. The words stuck in my throat. I looked at the soft curls of his hair, the sweet smile that played on his lips. *How could I let him die? He's done nothing wrong.*

He took my silence as a need for more explanation. "You saved my life. In my book that earns you a lot of trust."

"Fair enough." I managed a nod. "Still, you shouldn't be up here."

"It's a free country."

"It's a capitalist country and this is private property."

He stared at the small flower for a moment and then crushed it in his fist. "Your property?"

"Not exactly," I said. "But I'm responsible for it."

"Just you?"

"No," I said. "And that's why—among other reasons—after today you cannot come up here again. I'm not usually alone."

"Who would be with you?" he asked.

"Bryn." I stretched out on the ground. The early-morning sun brightened, throwing streams of light along the frosty ground. "Short, bronze ringlets, sharp tongue. You've seen her at school."

"Yeah." He nodded. "She sits behind you in first period."

"Yes." I hooked my finger at him and he handed me the cup. I tried to ignore my disappointment when our fingers didn't meet.

"And she's a werewolf too?"

My mouth paused on the rim of the cup.

"Sorry, sorry." He ducked his head. "I mean . . . uh . . . Guardian?"

"Yeah." I sipped the espresso, looking away.

"But you can turn into a wolf? Whenever you want . . . I mean. No moon necessary?" He held up a hand as if to ward off an antici-pated blow. "I don't mean to insult you. I'm going completely on pop culture references here."

"Yeah. That's fine," I said. "And the answer is yes. We can change whenever we want. The moon has nothing to do with it."

He looked impressed. "And you just kind of shimmer when you change, which is interesting. I mean, your clothes don't go flying off in shreds." The moment the words were out of his mouth, he flushed.

I nearly spilled the rest of the coffee. "I'm sorry to disappoint you," I murmured, feeling my own cheeks redden.

"I just meant . . ." He flailed, grasping for his question.

"It's complex magic," I said, hurrying past the awkward exchange. "Technically I'm both the wolf and human all the time. I choose what form my soul inhabits and I can move freely between the two. Whatever form I'm not in is still there, just invisible—in something like another dimension—until I occupy it again. My clothes, supplies, whatever was with the human form the last time I was in it doesn't alter. And I can pull on components of either form if I need them. Like the way I can make my teeth sharp even when I'm in human form."

I paused and thought for a moment. "I probably could make it so I had clothes on when I was a wolf if I really wanted. But there would be no utility in something like that. It would just be silly."

"Hmmm." He stretched his hand toward me. "I need more coffee before I can process that."

I gave him the cup, letting my fingers brush over his before I let go.

"Do you know where you come from?" His eyes stayed on my hand even as I let it fall into my lap. My pulse skipped. I thought about my father's words, wrapping my arms around my knees.

What am I doing up here? I'm risking too much.

Shay watched me, calm, but curious. I met his eyes and knew I didn't want to leave.

"Legend has it that the first Guardian was created by a Keeper who had fallen in battle. The wounded Keeper hid in the forest, terribly weak, close to death. But a wolf appeared and brought the Keeper food, kept the other predators of the forest away. The Keeper was able to bind his wounds while the wolf continued to provide sustenance. When the Keeper healed, he offered to transform the wolf into a Guardian. Part human, part beast, full of Old Magic. In exchange for the wolf's loyalty and eternal service, the Keeper would always provide for the Guardians and their kin. That was the first Guardian; we've been the Keepers' warriors ever since."

He stared at me, face blank. "What's a Keeper?"

I groaned, realizing just how dangerous this conversation could be. It was much too easy to be comfortable around Shay. I was giving things away without intending to.

He leaned forward. "What's wrong? Are some questions still off-limits?"

"I'm not sure." I liked it when he was closer to me. I could smell the excitement jumping from his skin, a wild scent of approaching storm clouds.

Delicious warmth swirled in my body. I dug my nails into my jeans. *It's the coffee. It's just the coffee.* My body curled in on itself.

He watched my taut limbs retreat from him. "Take your time. I want you to trust me."

You aren't the problem. I can't seem to trust myself.

I didn't want to leave, but I was starting to feel afraid. Maybe if I could control the conversation, I could keep us both safe. "For now let's just say the Keepers are who I have to answer to. Now can I ask you questions?"

"Of course." He looked delighted that I'd want to know anything about him.

I laughed. "Can I have some more coffee first? We've already finished this off."

"Sure." He refilled the cup I extended toward him.

"Where are you from?" I started with what I thought was an easy question.

"Everywhere," he grumbled.

"Everywhere?" I stared into the blackness of the espresso. "I don't think I've been there."

"Sorry. I was born in Ireland. Some tiny island off the west coast." His voice softened. "My parents died when I was an infant and Bosque took me as his own."

"And he's your uncle?" I watched him carefully.

Shay nodded. "My mother's brother."

That's a lie, but I wonder if he knows it. I just smiled, gesturing for him to continue.

"Bosque has some investment job. Government consulting, I don't know exactly what. He has lots of money but has to travel all the time. I haven't been at the same school for more than two years my entire life. We've lived in Europe, Asia, Mexico, and several cities in the U.S. I was in Portland for the last two years and then Bosque brought me to Colorado."

"That sounds very lonely."

He shrugged. "I've never really made friends, at least not close ones. I think that's why I read so much. Books have been my real companions."

He shifted onto his side, stretching out along the ground. "It's also why I backpack so much. I prefer isolation to crowds. The wilderness appeals to me."

Then he shuddered. "Except when I encounter a grizzly where there aren't supposed to be any." His eyes fell on me, sharp and interested. "Can I ask a question now? A different one?"

I took a large, final swallow of espresso. "Sure. But I still have more."

"That's fine. There's just something I really want to know." He rolled onto the balls of his feet and straightened. The sudden movement startled me. I jumped up, dropping the cup.

I stepped back when Shay shrugged off his North Face jacket and pulled his shirt over his head.

"Look." He swept a hand along his chest.

"Yes, very nice. You must work out," I murmured. The warm flow of blood in my veins suddenly burned.

His teeth clenched. "Come on. You know what I mean. No scars. Not here, not on my leg. That bear tore into me. Where are the scars?"

I returned his steady gaze. "Put your clothes back on. It's too cold for sunbathing."

I'd always thought my body was my greatest weapon, strong and unyielding as iron. Now my limbs were melting. I couldn't look away from the curve of his shoulders, the way his hips sharply cut into a V where his jeans rested precariously across them, and the maze of lines that carved muscles from his sternum to his abdomen.

"Are you going to answer my question?" Goose bumps popped up on his arms, but he remained stone still.

I wanted to step forward and put my hands on his skin, to feel if his pulse was rising like mine, to experience the intoxicating rush of heat his closeness provoked.

"Yes." I pointed at his discarded jacket, too afraid to move toward him. "Please get dressed."

"Start talking." He turned away from me, threading his arms back through his T-shirt sleeves. When he lifted his arms to pull the shirt back over his head, my eyes fixed on the dark pattern on the back of his neck. I hadn't thought of the tattoo since the day I'd saved Shay's life. But there it was, sharply etched in the shape of a cross.

I frowned. *We can't be sure without getting a look at his neck.*

"I'm waiting." He picked up his jacket and slipped it back on. His words pulled my thoughts back to the present moment.

"I healed you." I laced my fingers, hoping it would quash my desire to touch him.

"I know."

He took a step toward me. "I could feel it happening when I—" He broke off, his wonder-filled gaze moving slowly over my face. "I drank your blood."

My heart picked up speed and I nodded. He reached out and took my arm. My skin prickled as he pushed back the sleeve of my jacket and my sweater. His fingers ran lightly over my forearm, sending warm threads spiraling through my body.

The sensation was familiar and strange at the same time. I felt a thrill as if I were beginning a hunt. With Ren my desire came suddenly, like anger or a challenge. Shay evoked the slow burn of passion, an insistent, lingering white heat. Here there was no pack, no master or mistress. Just me and this boy, whose touch made me ache in places promised to someone else.

"Here," he murmured as his hand traced over the spot where I'd bitten myself. "You don't have scars either."

He raised his eyes to mine, his fingers traveling gently over my skin. I returned his gaze for a moment, then pulled my arm away, shoving the sleeve of my sweater back down over my still-tingling skin.

You can't do this, Calla. I dug into the dirt with my toe. *You know you can't. No matter what you feel up here, you are not free.*

"I heal very quickly," I murmured. "My blood has exceptional healing properties. All Guardian blood does."

"It didn't taste like blood." His tongue moved over his lips as if he could still taste me.

I wrapped my arms around my waist. I wanted him to taste me again, but not my blood.

"No, because our blood is different. It's one of our greatest assets.

Guardians can instantly mend each other on the field of battle. It makes us close to unstoppable."

"I believe that."

"That's its purpose, but as you've seen, we can heal anyone." My toe found a stone and I kicked it across the clearing. "We're just not supposed to."

He watched the stone bounce along the ground. "Then why—"

"Shay, please listen to me." My words spilled out, cutting him off. "Guardian healing is sacred to us. We are only meant to heal each other. What I did . . . when I saved your life, it was a violation of our laws. One that would make my life forfeit if any others in my world were to learn about it. Do you understand?"

"You risked *your* life to save mine?" He took a step toward me. I watched him move closer, blood roaring in my ears.

When his hands cupped my face, closing in so his lips almost touched mine, I shivered. Looking into his eyes, feeling the warmth of his breath on my skin, I knew I'd do it again, no matter the price.

"I would never want to put you in danger, Calla. Never." He breathed the words. My hands came up to cover his.

His fingers grasped mine. "But the other wolf? Bryn. She was here. She knows."

"She is my packmate, my second," I said. "Her loyalty is absolute. Bryn would never betray me; she would lay down her own life first."

"I won't betray you either." He smiled weakly, still shaken.

"You can't tell anyone. Please." I fought to keep my voice steady. "It would cost me everything."

"I understand," he said.

We both fell quiet. The silence of the meadow amplified our stillness. I wanted him to kiss me—wished he could smell the desire that I knew was pouring off me the way I was inhaling the heady scent of his own passion. *You can't, Calla. This boy isn't the one for you.* I closed my eyes, which made it a little easier to pull away from him.

"So since I drank your blood . . . am I going to turn into a were—, uh, Guardian?" he asked in a hesitant tone. "Is that why it was a violation of your laws?"

I shook my head. Was that a flash of disappointment in his eyes? "You've been reading too many comics, Shay."

His lips cut into a thin smile. "So then tell me what makes a Guardian. I mean besides your origin story."

"Well, we can be made the usual way. I have parents and a younger brother." He looked surprised and I laughed. "But our families function differently. There isn't a fall in love, get married, have children formula. New Guardian packs are planned well in advance. But if there is a sudden call for Guardians, they can be made. Alphas can turn humans."

"An alpha?" He wandered back over to his pack, searching through it until he pulled out a granola bar.

"Pack leader." I stood still, watching him.

"Are you an alpha? You act like you're in charge. And you referred to Bryn as your 'second.'"

"I am." His careful observations pleased me.

"How do you turn a human?" He beckoned to me again, patting the earth next to him.

"A bite and an incantation." I walked slowly toward Shay.

He glanced up at me, his eyes filled with a mixture of fear and interest.

"Don't get any ideas. I only bite to kill." I shook my head, smiling when he recoiled. "Turning a human only happens if there is a dire need for Guardians and there isn't time to wait for a pack to raise their young. Guardians who are made, not born, don't have innate comfort in both their forms. It takes a while for them to make the adjustment. But if they're needed, they're needed."

"What do you mean 'if they're needed'?"

I settled on the ground near him. "We're warriors. Wars make casualties. But there hasn't been that desperate a situation for several centuries."

"Who can order you to make new Guardians?" he asked.

I bit my lip. "My mistress."

"Your mistress?" He stopped unwrapping the bar.

"Lumine Nightshade. You know her. She was with Efron on Friday night, in the office."

Shay nodded, but his eyes were troubled.

"She has authority over my pack," I continued. "The Nightshades."

"Your pack?" he murmured. "Is there more than one?"

"There are two," I said. "The other is Efron's pack. The Banes."

"How many Guardians are there?" he asked.

"Fifty wolves in each pack, more or less," I replied, and he whistled, leaning back on his elbows. "The packs always start small and are allowed to grow over time if the alphas prove capable warriors and leaders."

"Do I know any of them?" He gave up on the idea of a snack, shoving his granola bar back into his bag.

"You've probably seen some of the adults around, but you wouldn't be able to recognize them unless they shifted in front of you, and that isn't allowed," I said. "The younger wolves all go to our school. The Nightshades are my friends, and lately we've been hanging out with the younger Banes."

Pieces of knowledge locked together, transforming his expression. "Ren Laroche and his gang."

"Gang?" I tore a fistful of grass from the earth and showered Shay in dirt and decaying greens.

"Well, you guys all kind of act like it." He brushed debris from his sweater, shook soil from his hair.

"We're wolves, not a gang," I said. "Besides, Ren's friends and mine—the Nightshades—we're just the kids. Our parents and the other mature wolves are the true packs. They run all the weekday and night patrols of the mountain. We just take over day shifts on the weekends."

He paled. "So that's why if I'd been up here any other day of the week . . ."

"You'd be dead," I finished.

"Right." He leaned back, watching clouds move above us. "So why two packs?"

"The Banes patrol the western face and we patrol the east," I said. "But the patterns will change soon."

"Why is that?" He didn't look at me.

"The Keepers are sending a third pack into the mix."

Shay sat up. "A third pack? Where are they coming from?"

I looked away, suddenly self-conscious. "Not from anywhere else. It's going to be a union of the young wolves from the two packs that already exist. The next generation of Banes and Nightshades. We're the new pack. Right now it's just the ten of us. Like I said, the packs always start out small; we'll have to prove ourselves before new wolves are added to our ranks."

"Calla." The ferocity in his tone drew my gaze back to him. He'd pressed his fingers into the earth, whitening his knuckles. "Why do you keep saying 'we'?"

"Ren and I are the alphas of our generation. We'll lead the new pack."

His brow furrowed. "I don't understand."

My cheeks grew hot. I reached for my braid, twisting it in my hand. "What do you know about wolves?"

"Bigger, stronger dogs?" He blanched at my baleful stare. "Sorry. I know nothing."

"Okay," I said, fumbling for the simplest explanation. "So, our social bonds are incredibly strong and revolve around loyalty to the pack alphas. Two alphas mate and rule over their pack. Each alpha has a beta, which is like our second in command. Bryn is mine. Dax is Ren's. The rest of the pack falls in line accordingly and follows our orders. The bonds of affection within the pack make us fierce, the warriors we need to be. That's how we move through the world and how we fulfill our duties to the Keepers." I smiled wryly. "And probably why you think we act like a gang."

Shay didn't laugh. "So how did you decide to make this new pack?"

"I didn't. The Keepers are the only ones who can order the formation of a new pack."

"But you just said that two alphas mate to create a new pack?" His voice quaked.

I nodded, feeling the heat in my cheeks spill down my neck and arms. *I have to tell him; he has to know.* But I didn't want to. I was sure he'd stop touching me as soon as he knew the truth, and that thought made me feel empty.

"You can't tell me that you're going to . . . *mate*"—he choked on the word—"with Ren Laroche because you've been ordered to."

"It's more complicated than that." I drew my knees up to my chest, anchoring myself to the earth. "The only reason that Ren and I, or any of the young wolves, were born was to form the new pack. It's what the Keepers brought us into the world for. They made matches for our parents, just like they've paired us as they see fit. Our union is a legacy of the alliance between Keepers and Guardians."

He was on his feet. "Are you even dating Ren?"

"That's not how it works." I stood up. "You don't understand. We're not supposed to . . . come together until the union."

"The union?" He turned away, muttering and shaking his head. When he faced me again, his lips thinned. "Are you trying to tell me you're getting married? To that jackass? When?"

"At the end of October." I put my hands on my hips. "And he's not a jackass."

"Could've fooled me. How old are you?" He peered at me. "Eighteen?"

"Seventeen."

He lurched forward, grasping my shoulders. "That is insane, Calla. Please tell me you're not just going along with it. Don't you care?"

I knew I should shake him off, but his eyes were so bright with concern that I remained still.

"I care. But it isn't my decision." I couldn't pull my gaze from his. "I serve the Keepers as all Guardians always have and always will."

"Of course it's your decision." His face filled with pity, and I was suddenly furious.

I shoved him away. He lost his footing and fell to the ground.

"You know nothing about my world." I spat the words.

He jumped to his feet with surprising agility. "I may not, but I do know that telling people who they can and cannot love is absurd." Despite my hostility, he walked toward me and took my hand. "And cruel. You deserve more."

My fingers trembled in his grasp; unwelcome searing liquid pooled in the corners of my eyes. Tears streamed down my face, blinding me. *Why is he still touching me? Doesn't he understand?* I ripped my hand from his and stumbled backward.

"You have no idea what you're saying." I wiped my eyes, but the salty torrent wouldn't stop.

"Don't cry, Calla." He was close again, touching my face, brushing away my tears. "You don't have to do this. I don't care who these Keepers are. No one can have that much control over your life. It's crazy."

I glared at him, flashing sharp fangs.

"Listen to me, Shay." My words lashed out. "You are a fool. You know nothing. You understand nothing. Stay away from me."

"Calla!" He reached for me, only jumping back when I shifted forms and snapped at his fingers. I could still hear him calling my name as I escaped into the forest shadows.

TEN

DARKNESS ENVELOPED THE SKY BY THE

time I wearily pushed open my front door. Tranquil piano nocturnes lilted through the house, the sound track of my parents' ritual on nights they didn't patrol the mountain. Chopin in the air, a glass of wine in my mother's hand or a tumbler of whiskey in my father's. Tonight my father would be nestled in his leather chair while my mother roamed the forests near Haldis.

My shoulders slumped as I climbed the stairs, feeling like a heavyweight's punching bag. All I wanted was to take a hot bath, to go to sleep, and to not wake up. Ever.

When I reached the top step, a strange series of bumps and shuffles came from behind Ansel's closed door. I paused outside my brother's bedroom and raised my hand to knock, but the door flew open.

"Hey, Calla!" Bryn emerged from Ansel's room, flushed. Her eyes met mine for the briefest moment. When she looked away, the muscles in her jaw jumped about in a furious dance.

"You're still here?" I swiftly did the math in my head. I'd left Bryn sitting at the kitchen table almost twelve hours earlier.

Her gaze darted along the hall. "Um. Yeah. Uh. I was . . . you know . . . helping Ansel with his poetry homework." She tapped her fingers on her hips and didn't raise her eyes to meet mine.

"Right." I peered at her. "I guess he's really fallen behind?"

A smile poked at the corners of her lips. "Oh, I wouldn't say that."

"Thanks for the help, Bryn!" Ansel called from within his bedroom.

"See you tomorrow, Cal." She flew down the stairs.

I followed her rapid exit with narrowed eyes before heading into my brother's room. Ansel lounged on the bed. He flipped over the pages of an English literature anthology with nonchalant sweeps of his fingers.

"How was patrol?" He continued his non-reading of the pages in front of him.

"Fine." I settled on the corner of his bed. "And how was your day?"

"Fantastic," he purred.

"And why is that, baby brother?" I asked, propping my chin in my hands.

He sat up, squared his shoulders, and shoved the book so hard that it careened off the bed onto the floor.

"Isn't that your homework?" I pointed at the discarded anthology. He ignored my outstretched finger.

"I need to talk to you," he announced, straightening even further.

"You do?" I rolled onto my side. "What is it?"

He continued to stare at me, eyes unblinking. "It's about me and Bryn."

"Yeah?" I raised an eyebrow at him and plucked at the coverlet.

A frustrated expression flitted over his face. "I mean, me *and* Bryn."

Oh dear. I'd been expecting this for some time. *Poor Ansel.* "That's what you just said. What about you two?"

"Come on, Cal," he said. "Are you gonna make me spell it out for you?"

"Obviously I am," I said, knowing what he was going to say and yet hoping it wasn't true . . . for all our sakes.

A rosy flush moved up his neck. He coughed. "I mean, haven't you noticed how I—?"

He shook his head and punched a pillow so hard its seams burst. Goose feathers floated in the air between us.

I sat up. "Tell me what's going on."

He moved his head up and down as though he was rehearsing a speech in his mind.

"I want to be with her." He drew a sharp breath and plunged on. "When the new pack forms, I want Bryn to be my mate."

"Ansel!" It was worse than I'd imagined.

"Look, Cal. I love Bryn. Totally. Utterly. Everything that you read about in books and watch in the movies. She is all I want in this life," he said. "I just needed to know if I had a shot. So I told her today."

The words I knew I should say ran through my mind, but they lost in the mental wrestling match to the question I wanted to ask.

"And what did she say?"

His face lit up. "She let me kiss her. I think she liked it."

I groaned but felt a spike of relief. Maybe this wasn't so serious after all. "God, An, this is Bryn we're talking about. You know she'll try anything once."

I gestured toward the hallway. "As soon as I got home, she couldn't get out of here fast enough. I'm sorry, hon, but I'm guessing she's mortified now."

"Nope," he said. "She's just worried you'll be mad. In fact, she's afraid you're going to bite one of her ears off."

"Look." I hoped he wouldn't take the letdown too hard. "I know you've been crushing on Bryn since you were a puppy, but don't get your hopes up."

"Gimme a break, Calla," he said. "I'm not your baby brother anymore. This is for real."

"You're awfully confident." I regarded his blinding smile cautiously.

His eyelids lowered, lashes veiling his gray irises. "What if I told you she let me kiss her for four hours?"

"What?" I nearly rolled off the bed.

"And it wasn't just kissing." His expression was positively devilish.

"Ansel!" I gaped at him, realizing I'd completely misjudged the scenario.

He bobbed up and down on the mattress, his eyes bright with mirth.

I rolled onto my stomach, grabbed a pillow, and sank my teeth into its cotton sheath.

"Come on, Cal. Be happy for us. We're in love." Ansel poked me in the ribs repeatedly.

I spit out the pillow and left the bed, pivoting to face him, fists pressed against my hips.

"That isn't how these things work for us. I don't care what books or movies say. We do not live the way humans do!" I snapped. "Ansel, you *know* that."

"I know, I know." He avoided my glare. "But Dad said that the Keepers take suggestions for matches from the alphas. So since you know how Bryn and I feel, then you can just pass that along."

"I can," I said. "But I cannot guarantee anything. Mating is arranged by the Keepers. They always have the final say."

"According to Dad, Lumine followed his suggestions to the letter." His eyes were so hopeful my heart somersaulted.

"I know. But Lumine won't be our mistress. Remember? I told you this morning, it's Logan." Knife-sharp jabs pierced my abdomen. "If he says Bryn and Mason have to pair up, there won't be anything I can do about it."

I expected an outraged protest from Ansel, but he burst into laughter. I frowned as he collapsed onto the bed in hysterics. "Yeah, that would be something."

"Uh—what's the deal, An?" I said. "I was being serious."

"Yeah, right, Calla."

When I remained silent, he gaped at me. "Do you really not know?"

"Not know what?" I asked, feeling like someone excluded from an inside joke.

Ansel picked up the only uninjured pillow left on the bed, squeezing it between his fists. "Mason is gay."

"You're not serious. Mason?" I said. "Mason is gay?"

Ansel sighed. "You know, this is the problem with you alphas, you're so concerned about taking over the new pack that you don't notice what's happening right in front of your face."

"Mason?" I repeated, embarrassed by the astonishment I heard in my own voice.

"He and Nev have been dating for the past year," Ansel said, flipping onto his stomach.

"Nev? Who's Nev?" I frowned.

Ansel just looked at me and waited. It only took a moment for me to understand.

"You mean Neville? Ren's Neville?"

"No, not Ren's Neville. Mason's Neville." He grinned. "And he goes by Nev."

"For a year?"

"Yes, they met in a support group for Guardians who are 'out.'" He hooked his fingers in air quotes around the last word. "Because you know, none of us could ever really be out in unapproved relationships. Straight or gay."

A wry laugh burst from my throat. "So you're telling me that Mason and Neville—er, Nev—are both in Gay Guardians Anonymous?"

He shrugged. I dropped back onto the bed.

"Wow." It wasn't so much of a surprise that Mason was gay as that he'd hidden it so well. Then again, it was a matter of life and death, but the thought that he didn't trust me enough to confide something so important made my chest burn.

Ansel stretched out beside me, his head resting on his folded arms. "It's all under the table, of course. Because of the Keepers. They aren't exactly tolerant of alternative lifestyles." He made a bitter sound.

I buried my hands in my hair, squeezing the sides of my head. "No, that's true."

Mason and Neville? It was hard to imagine. Mason was outgoing and hilarious, but Nev just seemed, well, quiet.

Ansel pulled the latest issue of *Rolling Stone* from his nightstand. "Which is ironic, considering Logan."

"Logan?!" I slapped my hand down in the middle of the magazine, forcing him to look at me.

"Yeah, Logan. At least that's what Mason says. But for him, or any Keepers for that matter, it's not an issue like it is for us. I mean, Logan will just get a witch trophy wife to pop out some heirs along the way and have as many incubi boy toys on the side as he wants." His eyes flashed wickedly.

"Ansel!" I shrieked. At least I won't have to worry about Logan acting like his father.

"Oh, come on, Cal. I know I'm your little brother, but it's not like I don't know about this stuff."

He threw the pillow at me. "In fact, this conversation makes it obvious that I know a lot more than you do."

Then his tone gained an edge of idealism. "But I hope that it means good things for us. I mean, what I said about Logan. He's still a Keeper, but maybe he'll be different."

"Yeah." I looked back at Ansel.

He chewed his lip, thoughtful but still optimistic. "I had to risk it, Calla. I love her. I've always loved her."

A shiver raced up my spine. "Okay, Ansel. I understand. But until there is an official order from the Keepers, you two are under the table as well. Please be careful."

"Thanks, sis." I could feel the flurry of his heartbeat as he nestled his head in the hollow between my shoulder and neck. I closed my eyes, knowing I'd help my brother and Bryn, but another, less-admirable emotion bit into me. As an alpha I could help my packmates get the things they wanted, but there wasn't anyone who could do the same for me.

ELEVEN

WHEN WE PULLED INTO THE SCHOOL PARKING

lot the next morning, Ansel turned to me.

"Bryn will want to talk to you, so I'm gonna make myself scarce."

I nodded, unfastening my seat belt.

"Please don't yell at her," he said. "And I really like *both* of her ears."

I glared at him. He gulped and fled the car.

When I reached my locker, Bryn was already there. I could practically see her wolf form, cowering, ears flat, tail between her legs, standing in the same space as the trembling girl.

"I swear I didn't plan for this, Cal."

"I know."

She danced uneasily around me as I opened my locker. "I'm so sorry. I know it's not the way things are supposed to happen."

I nodded, keeping my gaze on the stack of texts and folders.

"Please look at me."

I turned to face my best friend and found her sky blue eyes wide and fearful.

A lump formed in my throat. "I can't promise you anything."

She grasped my shaking hand. "I know that. Come on, let's get to first period."

As she led me through the classroom door and toward our desks in the rear of the room, she cast a sidelong glance at me.

"So did *you* tell Ansel I have a thing for John Donne?"

"You have a thing for John Donne?" I snorted.

"Wow," she murmured. "Your little brother is good."

As I searched my bag for a pen, I heard her murmur to herself: "Whilst our infant loves did grow, disguises did and shadows flow from us and our care; but now, 'tis not so."

I groaned. "That is so overwrought."

But my stomach tried to relocate somewhere near my ankles.

"You just don't have a romantic bone in your body, Cal." Bryn swatted the back of my head with her notebook.

I shrugged without turning to look at her. Bryn wasn't my only source of anxiety that morning. My eyes darted to the classroom door in anticipation of Shay's arrival, guilt over my harsh words on the mountainside weakening my resolve to shun him.

But Shay was dangerous; I knew I had to fight the attraction that seemed stronger each time I saw him. The decision provoked a dull ache that settled in my shoulders. I liked this strange human boy. His shockingly reckless approach to life and his disregard for its rules were welcome changes from the crushingly close world I was in.

Then he was walking through the door. Olive green henley, jeans, messy hair that kept falling over his eyes. He strode into the class without looking at me and took his seat in the desk next to mine. I followed his stiff movements, swallowing a sigh, relieved but also sad that he'd taken my warning seriously. I didn't just like him—I was fascinated by him. I'd never thought a human capable of capturing my interest. Shay's manner didn't mimic that of the boarding school sheep who scurried away when Guardians passed them in the halls. He was fearless and decisive, reminding me of a lone wolf, an alpha even, but without the bonds of a pack to root him in any one place.

I pulled out my copy of *The Great Gatsby* as Mr. Graham began his lecture on the politics of gender in the 1920s, and I tried to take notes, but my eyes kept flitting to Shay. His pencil scribbled furiously, and he paused occasionally to underline passages in the novel. Not once did he glance at me. I turned back to my own work, trying to convince myself that his changed behavior was a good thing.

Two down.

I'd gotten through the worrisome first encounters with Bryn and Shay. Now I only had one to go.

When I arrived in Organic Chemistry, Ren had already begun setting up our lab station for that day's experiment. I strode toward him, pushing back the unpleasant memory of our last encounter.

"Hi." I settled onto the stool in front of our table.

"Hey, Lily." He pulled his books out of my way. "Nice dress."

I bit back the knee-jerk desire to cuss him out, instead fishing my workbook from the bottom of my bag.

"What's on tap for today?" I asked without looking at him.

A quiet laugh traveled toward me. "Alchemy."

"What?" I asked. *He can't be serious.*

He pushed a dish of pennies toward me. "I think Ms. Foris is trying to keep us interested by pretending this isn't actually chem class. The experiment replicates the ways that classical and medieval alchemists tried to transmute metals into gold. We have to test a hypothesis about whether the process could actually be successful."

"I see." I began to read the instructions in the workbook and gathered several beakers that would hold the various liquids needed in the experiment.

"If it works, I'm taking the gold and running." He brought out more implements from our cabinet.

"Sounds like a plan." I searched for the long-stemmed butane lighter while he set up the Bunsen burner. "How was the rest of your weekend?"

Wrong question.

Ren stiffened. "Fine." He snatched the lighter from my hand.

The class period dragged by, tense and awkward, our conversation limited to abrupt questions and one-word answers. As we mechanically worked through the experiment, a sucking, hollow vacuum took up residence in my chest.

I was examining the penny clasped between the metal tongs, searching for signs of change, when a breathy voice came from behind me.

"Hey, Ren."

My grip on the tongs tightened as I glanced over my shoulder. Ashley Rice, leggy, brunette, and human, cocked her head at the Bane alpha. Her bubble gum pink lips parted in an inviting smile.

"Hey, Ashley." Ren set down his pencil, leaning casually against the lab station.

I turned back to our experiment as she batted her eyelashes. Ren's conquests fell into two categories: those girls who still pined for him and those who stuck pins into his voodoo likeness every night. Ashley ranked among the former.

I glanced at the clock. Our lab period was nearly over. I moved over to the sink and began to dump out liquids from our beakers.

"So, Ren." I winced at Ashley's smoky tone. "I know it's over a month away, but there's bound to be a line of girls waiting to ask you to Blood Moon."

My teeth ground together. I wiped out one beaker with a paper towel and grabbed another.

"We had such a great time at prom last year." Ashley's wistful sigh buried barb-like into my neck. "And we haven't hung out in a while. Would you like to go with me?"

"Sorry, Ash," he said. "I'm spoken for."

"You already have a date for the ball?" Her shrill voice was a little too loud.

"Yes."

I heard Ashley shuffle her feet. "Well, who is it?" she whined.

"Calla."

The beaker in my hand shattered. I swore as glass shards buried in my palm.

Ren was instantly at my side. "Come on, Cal. What did that beaker ever do to you?"

I shook my head, still cursing, and began to pull clear, razor-edged bits of glass from my skin.

"Are you okay?" Ashley managed to sound concerned as she leaned over our lab station. "Oh my God. There's so much blood."

Despite the pain in my hand, I smiled when she turned green and fled.

"I'll get the first aid kit." Ren left the station, returning a moment later with a red-cross-emblazoned white box.

"I told Ms. Foris it wasn't bad. If she saw your hand, she'd try to send you to the hospital for stitches."

I stuck my gushing hand under the stream of water from the faucet.

"Make sure you get all the pieces. The wounds will close fast, and you don't want glass trapped under your skin. I had that happen once; it hurts like hell."

"Thanks," I replied wryly. "I think I can manage."

He handed me a paper towel when I withdrew my hand from under the faucet. I checked the gashes for remaining shards and then pressed the towel against my palm.

"How did you break the beaker?" Ren leaned against the table, frowning at me. "I'd say you don't know your own strength. But you most definitely do."

"I heard some shocking news." I extended my uninjured hand toward him, expecting that he'd hand me the gauze.

"Let me." He took my marred palm in his fingers and began to dress the wounds. "What news?" he asked, gently taping squares of filmy cotton to my palm.

"That I have a date for the Blood Moon Ball." I tried to sound offended but was distracted by the soft touch of his fingers on my skin. "I didn't realize you were telling people we're dating."

He examined my bandaged hand and then stood up. "Yeah. It seemed like the appropriate response at the moment. It's not like I can send wedding invitations out to all my exes. Anyway, it will get the word out so I won't have to be turning girls down for the next three weeks."

I snorted. "You think more girls are going to ask you?"

He looked up at me, smiling. I pulled my eyes from his teasing face and glared at the floor.

Of course they would.

He walked to the trash can. When he returned to our lab station, where I stood with my hands on my hips, he abruptly tensed.

"Calla, did you honestly think I'd still be dating other girls between now and the union?"

I turned away, no longer able to meet his eyes. "I have no idea."

"Well," he growled, "I'm not."

He began to put our supplies into the cabinet, slamming the wooden door shut with such force that I jumped.

"I'm sorry to lay such a heavy burden on you," I said, clenching my fists and wincing as my injured palm throbbed.

"What are you talking about?" His head whipped around.

A loud clearing of someone's throat turned my gaze from Ren to the end of our station. Shay stood there, eyes burning with blatant dislike as they settled on my lab partner.

"Excuse me, Ren." He spoke through clenched teeth. "Would you mind if I spoke to Calla alone?"

Ren moved toward Shay, looking him slowly up and down. When

the other boy squared his shoulders, I could see the Bane alpha fighting not to laugh. "That's really up to Calla."

Shay glanced at me; the angry cut of his mouth dissolved into a grimace. I shifted uneasily, looking from Ren to Shay.

Ren suddenly grabbed his bag. "No problem. She's all yours."

My heart lurched. "No, wait!" I said, catching his hand in mine. The alpha stilled as I turned toward Shay.

"You and I have nothing to discuss." I watched my words cut him like the broken glass that had sliced my own palm.

Shay's fists balled up when I drew Ren's arm around my waist.

"Walk me to lunch?" The bell rang as the words passed my lips.

"Of course." He guided me away from our station, leaving Shay fuming at the table.

When we were out of the classroom, Ren glanced at me. "What was that all about?"

I felt a twinge of disappointment when he dropped his hand from my waist.

"Nothing." I had to fight not to tremble as I formed the lie. "He's just a little starstruck after the 'muggers' attacked us on Friday. Been hovering around me too much."

"Is he bothering you?" he asked.

"Come on, Ren." I lightened my tone. "He's the Keepers' boy; you can't bully him. Besides, you know I can kick his ass just as easily as you could. He's a little annoying, but it's no big deal.

"Anyway . . ." My heart picked up speed. I still didn't trust Shay's desire to get closer to me, but I couldn't deny that I enjoyed his attention. "He'll get the right idea now that the word's out that we're dating."

Ren pulled up, catching my upper arms in a gentle grasp. "You're going to start calling me your boyfriend?"

"If you think it's a good idea."

"If *I* think it's a good idea?" He ruffled his hair with one hand. "I just don't get you, Lily."

When we arrived in the cafeteria, our packmates had already congregated at our usual tables. Seven young wolves laughed at Neville, who stood on top of a chair singing "If I Were a Rich Man" at the top of his lungs. He was dressed in his regular open-mike-poetry all-black ensemble, making it one of the most bizarre scenes I'd ever laid eyes on.

Ren and I exchanged a puzzled glance. I couldn't imagine what Nev was doing; I'd always thought of him as one of the shyest wolves, with the exception of Cosette, who was so quiet she barely seemed animate.

"If I were a weal . . . thy . . . man!" Neville bellowed, and then jumped down from the table, collapsed into a chair, and buried his face in his hands. Mason, grinning like the Cheshire cat, leaned over and patted him on the head.

"What gives? Did Nev finally go off the deep end?" Ren caught the chair Dax slid toward him. He flipped it around, sitting in it backward.

"He lost a bet," Mason said. Neville raised his face and glared at him.

Mason sighed. "It's so sad to see an indie guitarist do show tunes. What have you been reduced to?"

Neville brushed off his arms as if to sweep away unpleasant remnants of his performance. "You know it was my personal hell. That's why you picked it."

"A bet?" I raised my eyebrows.

Mason grinned. "We got into an intense debate on Friday night at Eden. I was right, Nev was wrong."

"Your brother has better moves than I thought," Neville said, tipping his cap at me.

"What's this?" Ren popped open a Coke and looked at Neville, who jerked his head toward Ansel.

I wheeled on my brother and Bryn, who sat close together at the far end of the tables, dreamy expressions locked on their faces. Jealousy tightened my belly. Even if they were taking risks, they'd still been able to choose each other. And with Ren and me as alphas, their romance would probably be safe. Mason and Nev, Dax and Fey, they all had a chance at real love. Ren and I were the only ones who had no choice. Was that the reward for being an alpha?

Ren looked at the pair for a long moment and then a sharp laugh rolled out of his throat.

"I said to keep that quiet, you two." My teeth flashed in warning, knowing that envy as much as irritation made my canines sharpen.

Bryn cowered, but Ansel came to her rescue. "Of course, from everyone else, but it's not like we could hide it from our packmates."

I sat down in the chair that Fey pushed toward me, banging my forehead on the table. "You guys are killing me. We're at school. There are too many eyes to see you."

I cringed as I looked at Ren. "I'm sorry. I was going to tell you later today, I swear."

He just shrugged. "Your brother is right. You can't hide anything from packmates."

The Bane alpha spoke in a lower voice as he turned his eyes back on the new couple.

"Listen to Calla: keep it quiet outside our circle. Not a word to other Guardians. You don't want to step on the wrong toes." Then his lips split in a broad grin at Ansel. "Congrats, little man."

My brother beamed and looked at Bryn adoringly. She sighed, twirling her fingers through her ringlets.

I quickly looked away from her and focused on peeling my orange.

"Neville, I hope you're not thinking of leaving us to try to make it on Broadway," a cold, silky voice murmured from behind me.

All conversation at the table ceased. Bryn and Ansel jerked away from each other as if a geyser had erupted between them.

I turned in my chair to see Logan Bane smiling at his future pack.

"You have a wondrous voice, my friend," he continued. "My companions and I certainly admire it; you projected all the way to the other side of the cafeteria. Very impressive."

"Thanks." Neville threw him a nervous smile.

Logan circled the table to where Neville and Mason sat, stopping behind Mason's chair. The Keeper rested a hand on my packmate's shoulder. Mason tensed and glanced at Neville, whose face paled.

Ren began to rise, but Logan stilled him with a nonchalant wave of his hand. "No, please, just relax."

The Keeper leaned forward. "As no doubt your alphas have informed you, it has been decided that I will inherit the rule of your new pack come October thirty-first." He waited until each head bobbed in affirmation before slowly pacing back to Ren's side. "I'd like you to gather in the commons after school today. I'll meet you there."

"Of course." Ren inclined his head.

"Excellent." The young Keeper pivoted on his heel and walked back to join his companions on the opposite side of the cafeteria.

The circle of young wolves turned back to their lunches, though the mood at the table had become anxious and sullen. Mason sat very still, staring at nothing in particular. Neville leaned toward him, stretching his fingers toward Mason's. Mason took his hand, and they hid their clasped fingers beneath the table.

TWELVE

MY JAW CLAMPED SO HARD THROUGH THE

philosophy seminar I wondered if its dull ache would settle there permanently. The desk next to the classroom's tall windows sat empty. I hadn't seen Shay in the cafeteria during lunch, and now his regular seat in our afternoon class remained vacant.

I scribbled a few more notes and tried to tell myself that it didn't matter. My eyes traveled to the empty seat once again, my teeth grinding against each other with such force that the ache in my jaw flared into a sharp, searing pain.

I forced my gaze back onto Mr. Selby, who gesticulated wildly as he described arguments for and against the existence of God. He'd started the class out by showing us a bumper sticker that read: "God is dead—Nietzsche; Nietzsche is dead—God."

I tried to follow our teacher's enthusiastic lecture, but my thoughts were fractured. I glanced around the room. The rest of the class dutifully jotted notes and nodded along with Mr. Selby's comments. My gaze traveled to Logan. As usual, the young Keeper slouched in his desk, deep in slumber, Dior sunglasses hiding his eyes.

What will he say when we meet after school?

As the bell rang, I slowly unwound my wrapped limbs, wincing at my muscles' reluctant unclenching.

The three Bane seniors left class together. Sabine and Dax leaned close to Ren, murmuring quietly as they passed through the door. I wandered alone back to my locker, only to find my Nightshades already there. We moved down the hallway to the commons. None of us spoke. I could hear the collective rushed pace of our hearts as we waited.

Steady, sauntering footfalls along with the scent of cloves and mahogany announced Logan's arrival. He smiled at our huddled group; his perfectly tousled hair glowed like spun gold in the low, late-afternoon sun that poured in through the room's floor-to-ceiling windows. The Keeper grabbed a chair and sat on the back, his feet grounded in its seat, so that he stared down at us.

"Welcome." His gaze moved slowly over the tense young Guardians. "I realize that this meeting is somewhat unexpected, but things will change quickly now that the union is so close."

Logan rested his elbows on his knees. "In order for the alphas to proceed with the Rite of Union, they must be of age. For Ren and Calla that won't happen until Samhain, the day you both turn eighteen and the date on which the new pack will officially form."

He began drumming his fingers on a manila envelope. "In order to ensure a smooth transition, I've gathered some materials for you so that you'll know what the duties of the new pack will be, what the logistics of your new lives entail, and the timeline for the stages of the transition."

Logan nodded at Ren, who caught the envelope that sailed toward him.

Ren pulled open the flap and peered inside. "What's this?"

"Specs for the new development," Logan said. "Where you will live."

The young wolves stirred in their seats and exchanged wary glances.

Logan made a calming gesture. "Like I said, this change will occur in stages. Some of you—Ansel, Cosette—are quite young, and the Keepers understand that. The five houses of the new development are in the midst of construction. Of course, Ren and Calla's home is finished and they will be able to occupy it as soon as the union takes place."

I fought back the rising heat in my chest and neck, glancing at Ren, but his eyes remained locked on Logan.

"Bryn, as well as Sabine and Dax, will be the next to make the move, since they will also finish their schooling this year."

The two named Banes stiffened. Bryn shuffled her feet while Ansel gripped the sides of his chair. Ren cleared his throat. Logan arched an eyebrow at the alpha.

Ren looked at his packmates and then at the Keeper. "Are you pairing them up? Setting new matches now?"

Logan smiled slowly. "Would you have an objection to that, Ren?"

Ren stared at our master but remained silent. Logan's jaw twitched and then he laughed. "No. I'm not pairing them."

Dax and Sabine both relaxed, and Fey expelled a long, relieved breath. Bryn offered my brother a weak smile.

"The only mated pair as of this time will be Ren and Calla, your alphas," Logan continued. "You're free to live in the houses we provide in whatever arrangements you choose. Each house has multiple bedrooms and baths; the five homes are being constructed around a common garden space with a pool and spa. In the same way we've provided for your parents, you'll have a cleaning staff, gardeners, and full-time maintenance specialists so you don't have to focus on anything other than your duties. I'm sure you will find the living arrangements quite to your liking."

Quiet noises of approval sounded from the Nightshades and Banes. A sparkle of optimism lit my heart.

Logan smiled. "As I said, Ren and Calla will be the first to move.

The other seniors will follow. As to the rest of you, until you finish school, you are welcome to continue living with your parents should you prefer to, or you may move into the new development as the houses are completed. No matter where you reside, however, from this point forward you no longer answer to your former packs. You answer to Ren and Calla, and to me."

The Keeper stroked his chin. "My father has generously offered to assist with the oversight of the new pack. He seems to think that, as such a young group of Guardians, you might prove unruly."

His gaze fell on Sabine. "But I think that if we all show a commitment to our duties, then surely his involvement will not be necessary."

Ren glanced at Sabine, who had begun to tremble. "Of course, Logan," he said. "Whatever you ask."

A half smile pulled at Logan's mouth. "Excellent."

He pointed at the envelope once more. "You'll find in those papers the forms for any requisitions you'll need. Each of you can request a vehicle of your choice. The purchase orders are there."

Dax hooted, and Logan grinned.

"We'll also make arrangements for a weekly grocery delivery at your homes. Their location will make running errands into Vail something of an inconvenience."

"Where are our new homes?" I asked.

"At a much higher elevation on the eastern slope of the mountainside. Only one access road has been built for the site. The location of the development coincides with the primary objective of the new pack."

"And what will that be?" I leaned forward, interested.

Logan straightened, his eyes narrowed. "We have reason to believe that the Searchers will move against Haldis Cavern with whatever force they can muster within the next year. While the Nightshades and Banes will continue their patrols of the perimeters, the new pack will offer a second layer of defense at the cavern itself."

He broke into a grin once more. "Which brings me to another issue. Normally a pack is named after its Keeper, but a Bane pack already exists. The new pack will be named Haldis, after that site you are sworn to protect."

I glanced at my packmates and at the Banes. All their faces lit up.

"I'm glad the choice pleases you," Logan said. "While guarding Haldis will be the pack's key role, there is another matter that requires your immediate attention."

He looked from Ren to me. "Your alphas were introduced on Friday evening to a human boy by the name of Shay Doran. He is a senior at the Mountain School; he just arrived last week."

I shoved my hands underneath me. I couldn't afford for Logan to see them shaking.

"Shay represents a significant interest to the Keepers. His safety is our highest priority; it was this boy who was the target of the Searchers' attack on Friday."

"What do they want with him?" I blurted.

Several of the wolves gasped.

I dropped my gaze to the floor. "I'm sorry, Logan. I've gotten to know Shay; I was just curious."

"That's quite all right, Calla." He waved off my apology. "We are indebted to you for preventing his abduction. The truth is that we don't know what the Searchers want with Shay, only that they believe he is important to their success against us. Therefore we must keep him safe and out of their hands."

I kept my eyes averted, nodding.

"I have also had the opportunity to get acquainted with the human boy. It seems he's become quite infatuated with *you*. We need his trust, so I'd like to encourage that. Please befriend him. Think of yourself as something of a de facto bodyguard for the time being."

My head snapped up, eyes wide. Ren was glaring at the Keeper, who gazed calmly back.

"The boy knows nothing of our world, and it stays that way," Logan said. "The less he knows about the danger he faces from the Searchers, the safer he will be. Protect him, but do so without garnering his attention. He already knows Calla, so her interaction can be more direct."

I inclined my head to Logan, while Ren's face remained livid. The rest of the pack murmured acknowledgment of his orders.

"Very well, then. I believe that brings you up to date. Should any questions arise, your alphas should bring them to me. Lumine and Efron have agreed on this point."

Logan smiled, descending from his perch. The assembled wolves began to stir from their seats, but he snapped his fingers, commanding our attention.

"There is one last matter to discuss."

Ten pairs of eyes focused on their new master.

"Ren raised the very important question of how you will be paired in the future."

Ice-cold fingers wrapped around my throat as I waited for Logan to speak.

"Guardian mates have always been selected by Keepers so as to ensure the most beneficial outcome for our packs," he said. "I'm sure you can understand the utility of such a practice."

No one spoke. Logan's casual tone tore at me like barbed wire. "I will, as my ancestors did, seek the counsel of your alphas in such matters when the time arises. You are all very young; I don't anticipate making such decisions for some time. However, it is clear that you've already begun to form strong attachments to each other."

His slow smile revealed the gleam of perfect teeth. "This pleases me; it signals a strong pack whose loyalty will aid them in their duties. But I must remind you that the only sanctioned pairing in the Haldis pack is that between Ren and Calla, the alpha mates. Though you might be inclined to form your own matches, I hold the *only authority* to choose your mates. This law is one of our oldest and most important. Failure to respect it will be dealt with summarily and severely."

I couldn't breathe.

Logan reached into the pocket of his jeans, pulling out a pack of Djarum Blacks. He tapped the box on the back of the chair, withdrew a cigarette, and placed it between his lips.

"That will be all."

For a moment no one moved. Silence covered the room like heavy fog. Then Ren stood, jerking his head toward the door. The other Banes slowly rose. I hoped my legs wouldn't give out as I got to my feet. I couldn't look at my pack; my stomach slammed around inside me like a pinball. I had taken only a few steps when Logan's silky voice trailed after the departing wolves.

"Mason, could I have a moment?"

I froze. Mason stood just behind me, his body locked in place. I looked at Logan; his eyes gleamed in the red haze of the setting sun that filled the room. Smoke spilled from his lips and the scent of cloves wafted around us.

Mason's eyes met mine. A thin smile appeared on his lips and he began to turn. I stepped toward him, clasping his wrist.

"No." My whisper cut sharply between Mason and me. He tensed and gave an almost-imperceptible shake of his head, twisting out of my grasp.

"Calla!" Logan's whip-like exclamation lashed at me. "You have been dismissed."

An arm reached around my shoulders and I was pulled toward

the door. When I'd been led well away from the commons, I wrenched free of the strong arm that held me, glaring at Ren. Dax and Fey stood nearby, faces grim. Ansel and Bryn disappeared around a corner without looking back.

"I have to go in there." I tried to walk away, but Ren grabbed my upper arms, wheeling me around.

"You can't." He glanced down the hall.

I followed his gaze, watching Sabine lead Neville toward the school's main entrance. Her arms were around his waist. I could see her lips moving rapidly as she leaned against him. Cosette trailed after them, though she kept a respectful distance.

"I will not let this happen," I said. "He is in my pack, Ren. His welfare is my responsibility."

"He's in my pack now too," Ren murmured. "I'm so sorry, Calla. I wish you didn't have to go through this. I know how hard it is."

Dax made a disapproving sound and Ren threw him a sharp look.

"Don't let it eat you, Cal," Fey said, eyes bright and hard. "You haven't done anything wrong. This is Mason's mess."

"How can you say that?" I gasped.

She looked away. "Because it's true and you have more important things to focus on."

"She's right," Dax said with a rumbling growl. "We can't be mixed up with this nonsense. Let it go."

A stinging filled my eyes. I looked at the floor, digging my nails into my palms, reopening the wounds there. Ren watched the crimson drops hit the floor. He bared his teeth at Dax and Fey.

"Get out of here."

Dax bristled, but he jerked his head at the school entrance. Fey took his hand and they walked away.

"Calla." Ren's hands slid from my upper arms to my waist and he tried to pull me toward him.

"Don't." I squirmed out of his grasp. "Don't try to tell me it gets better."

His jaw clenched, but he didn't attempt to touch me again.

"It never gets better." A sheen of moisture covered his dark eyes. "It gets worse."

I wrapped my arms around my waist, not caring about the blood that stained my dress.

"Find Ansel. Please get him home. I need to stay here."

I heard him draw a sharp breath of protest and I held up my hand. "I'll wait for Logan to leave. I have to see Mason."

Ren shook his head. "I'll stay with you. We're in this together now. You can ask Bryn to drive your brother."

"Bryn needs to stay away from my brother! Or did you miss the lecture we just got?"

"Calm down." His voice dropped low. "Logan hasn't rung the death knell for relationships in the pack. He said he'd take advice from us, and we'll give it. Your brother and Bryn just need to be careful. We can help them."

"I can't think about that now," I said, staring at my hands, watching the punctured skin close up before my eyes. "Please, just go. I want to talk to Mason alone."

"Fine." He pulled on the leather jacket he had draped over his arm. "I'll make sure your brother gets back to your house."

He had already taken several long strides down the hall when I murmured, "Thank you."

I made my way to the girls' bathroom and turned scalding hot water on my palms, rinsing caked blood off the now-closed cuts. Steam rose around me as I gripped the sides of the basin. When grief's attack subsided, I walked slowly back toward the commons, pausing frequently to listen for approaching footsteps or voices. When I neared the double doors, I ducked behind a row of lockers and waited, my forehead pressed against the cool steel.

After what seemed like hours, but I knew had only been minutes, I heard the doors swing open. I peered around the row of lockers and watched Logan walk away in a smooth loping gait. When he'd disappeared around a corner, I left my hiding place. Once through the doors I paused, forcing myself to move with care.

Smoke tendrils twisted through the air, a heady mixture of cloves and tobacco. Mason sat in the center of the room. He leaned forward, his elbow propped on one knee, hand covering his eyes. A slender black cigarette burned in the fingers of his other hand.

I took slow steps forward and Mason lifted his face, smiling wearily. He slouched in the chair and took a drag of his cigarette.

"Hey, Calla." He tilted his head back, blowing rings of smoke into the air.

I opened my mouth to speak, but my throat closed. Mason watched me inch across the space between us. When I was close enough to touch him, I hesitantly stretched my hand toward his shoulder. I jerked back when he jumped to his feet, stepping out of my reach. He dropped the cigarette and crushed it out with his foot.

"Let's get out of here."

He swept past me and through the door so quickly I had to run to catch him.

"Mason." I at last found my voice.

"Don't say anything. It's not worth it." He stopped in front of his locker, rapidly turning the dial.

"Tell me what happened."

He swore as he missed a number in the combination and had to start over again. "Nothing happened. Not yet." The lock clicked and he flung the door open.

I took a deep breath, but my relief was quickly replaced by anger. "What did he want from you?"

A low sound, half laugh, half growl, emerged from his throat. "What do you think? He's Efron Bane's son."

"No." I closed my eyes, leaning against the locker next to his. "I just can't accept it."

He slammed the door shut, turning to face me. "Neither can I, Cal. Logan's had his eye on me for some time, but I didn't know if he'd make an issue of it. Now I have my answer."

"What are you going to do?" I asked, hating Logan and Mason's inability to disobey him.

He threaded his arm through the strap of his messenger bag, keeping his eyes averted. "I don't know. But I think I bought myself some time."

"Time?"

He ran his hands through his hair, pausing to rub his temples. "Logan might be inheriting our pack, but he's still young . . . and he's afraid."

I couldn't imagine any Keeper being afraid. "Of what?"

"Of his elders, especially his father. I said that if he pushed me, I'd get Ren to tell Efron about it."

I picked at the scab on my hand, ignoring the stinging it brought to my still-tender skin. "You think that will make a difference?"

"It will," he said. "This is the one time where the Keepers' 'traditions' might work in my favor."

"Traditions?" I frowned.

He struck the locker with his fist, leaving a dent. "It's a nice way of saying 'bigotry.' Until he has more power, Logan is still under the close watch of Efron and the other Keepers. Taking our pack on is like a trial for him—to see if he's worthy of the post. If I keep reminding him of that, I think I can stop him from . . ." He couldn't finish.

"You have to stop him. You can't—"

"I won't." He finally looked at me. "The Keepers tolerate a variety of tastes, but only in a recreational sense. Logan would never admit to his father or any of the rest of the Keepers that he's gay."

I bit my lip. "Mason, why didn't you tell me?"

"About me and Nev?"

I kept my eyes down. "You don't trust me."

He put his hand on my shoulder. "It's not that, Cal. I do trust you."

I raised my eyes to his, balking at the sadness I found there.

"But you're one step away from the Keepers," he continued. "Who I am, who I love . . . they'd never accept it. Neither would the elders in the pack, not my parents. No one. It would be the end for me and for Nev. And not just for our relationship. It would be *the end*."

He seemed so calm, I couldn't stand it any longer.

"How long can you stall Logan?" I blurted. "How long will you be safe?"

He pulled out his cell phone and sent a quick text. "What makes you think I'm ever safe, Calla?"

"Maybe I could talk to Lumine," I said.

"Don't go there, Cal," he murmured, reaching for my hand. "If you do anything, try to interfere at all, Logan will make an example of you. What good would it do any of us if you were handed over to a wraith? Or to Efron? You don't have a choice. None of us do. This is who we are. Guardians serve. Right?"

I couldn't answer, so I just gripped his fingers tighter.

For a moment, his voice trembled. "It isn't your fault. I'll be okay."

Then he pulled his hand from mine and walked away.

THIRTEEN

I SLID DOWN THE LOCKER AND TUCKED MY

legs beneath me.

Why is this happening? Isn't becoming the pack's new alpha supposed to make me stronger?

I wasn't sure how long I'd been sitting there when I caught the scent of unfurling leaves and clouds heavy with rain.

"Calla?"

I looked up. Shay stood a few feet away.

"Are you all right?" he asked, but didn't come closer.

I shook my head, not trusting my voice, certain if I tried to speak, I'd snarl at him. It wasn't Shay I was angry with. Not anymore.

He crouched so he was at my level.

"What are you doing here?" I managed to ask without growling.

"A hike sounded better than class," he said. "But I still need to grab my homework."

"Oh, okay." I started to rise, suddenly desperate to get out of the school, but in my haste my foot caught on my bag and I stumbled.

Shay darted forward, taking my faltering as a sign of imminent emotional breakdown. "Calla, what happened to you?"

"I don't want to talk about it," I said, feeling my outrage boil up again.

Shay's grip on my arms tightened. "Did someone hurt you?"

I shook my head, watching him, running my tongue over my lips. What if I didn't get mad but got even?

Shaking away the slight pinch of guilt, I took advantage of his assumption that I was ready to cry and let him pull me into an embrace.

"Can't you tell me anything?" he asked. "I'd like to help you."

I rested my forehead against his neck, knowing that what I wanted from him wasn't help. The cool scent of his skin soothed my temper, but I heard his heartbeat jump when I touched him. It only made me want him more. I let myself press into him, reveling in the way the tensing of his muscles ignited my skin.

"Want to take a walk?" he murmured into the crown of my hair. "I haven't been through the school gardens yet."

"Sure." I stepped out of his arms.

We left the building, crossing the parking lot to reach the Mountain School's collection of manicured hedges and flower beds. A few steps into the gardens, we surprised two boarders, a boy and girl, tangled up in each other's limbs beneath a vine-covered archway. They vanished like spooked deer.

I watched their retreat, wondering what it must be like to steal moments of desire and hide them from the world.

Shay walked beside me in silence. I turned my palms over. The scabs and puncture marks had disappeared.

"I'm sorry I was rude to you at school today," I said, reaching for his hand.

A mocking, crooked smile pulled at his lips. "You're always nicer without your bodyguard around."

"Who?" I frowned.

"Tall, dark, and rabid," he muttered, twining his fingers through mine.

"You mean Ren?" I didn't drop Shay's hand but wondered if I should.

He didn't answer, but his jaw twitched.

"How I acted had nothing to do with him," I said, unable to completely curb my temper. "I was angry at you."

"Whatever." He shook his fingers from mine. Apparently I wasn't the only angry one.

"Let's go this way." I turned down a small path. Unlike the others, this was untouched earth, not paved by round river stones like most of the garden's walkways. The trail passed beneath towering evergreens that filtered the late-afternoon sunlight. I stopped when we reached my favorite spot in the gardens, walked to the edge of the pine-ringed clearing, and dropped down, sitting half hidden among the tall ferns.

Shay paused to take in his surroundings. "Very nice."

"Yeah." I stretched my arms toward the sky, letting the sun warm my skin. "I come here when I want to be alone."

"It feels safe," he said, crouching near me. "Private."

The hem of my dress had inched up when I settled among the ferns and I caught Shay's eyes tracing the line where my skin disappeared beneath the fabric. I leaned toward him.

"Kiss me." It sounded like an order, and his shoulders tightened. "Please?"

I didn't know it would be so hard, asking for something I wanted. I wasn't used to making requests.

Just this once, screw the Keepers and their laws. That's what they got for ordering me to spend time with a boy this beautiful. My first kiss should be mine.

Shay stood up. "Don't take this the wrong way, Calla. It's not that I don't want to."

"You want to?" A rush of heat chased by emptiness swept through me. *But you won't.*

"Yeah, of course." His arms were folded across his chest, making the muscles of his forearms taut. "But you're upset and I'm not really sure why you just asked. Or whatever that was."

I pulled the hem of my dress down. "Never mind."

"I'll help you with whatever's made you so upset," he said. "But this morning you blew me off and I'm not going to kiss you today just so you can tell me to go to hell tomorrow."

An unsuspecting fern took the brunt of my humiliation when I pulled the plant up roots and all.

"I know, I know," I said, tossing leaves and dirt away. "I'm sorry."

"It's going to be dark soon." He stretched his hands toward me. "You might have wolf night vision, but I don't."

"Sometimes I forget about your flaws." I clasped his fingers in mine.

"Flaws, huh?" When he jerked me up, I was smiling again, surprised by how Shay's easy manner made all my irritation fade. Once I was on my feet, he kept pulling until my fingertips rested on his chest. His hands released mine and slid around my back, pressing between my shoulder blades so my body molded against his.

I could feel every contour of his chest, the press of his thighs against my hips. I lifted my chin and his lips were on mine. The light touch speared my body and exploded deep within me. I shuddered and took his lower lip between my teeth, biting gently. He groaned, digging his fingers into my back. His lips parted mine, exploring, lingering.

My eyes were still closed when he pulled away.

"I thought you weren't going to," I whispered.

I looked at him and he smiled shyly. "I couldn't help myself."

"I'm glad." I lifted my fingers to touch the throbbing pulse at my neck. "I didn't know it would feel like that. It was amazing."

"Wait a sec." He rested his index finger under my chin, turning my face up toward his. "That wasn't your first kiss, Calla. No way."

I retreated to the shadows of the circling pines, wanting to hide the hot flush in my cheeks.

He didn't follow. "Come on. What's wrong?"

"It was my first." I brushed dirt from the back of my dress. "That's all. Just drop it."

His hand followed the curve of a tall fern. "I'm having a hard time believing that. But if it really was your first, I'm glad it wasn't a disappointment."

"No." I could still feel heat pouring off my limbs. "No disappointment."

He started toward me, but I held up my hand. "But not something we can do again."

"Excuse me?" His eyebrow shot up.

"That was my first kiss," I said, "because I have to follow different rules than other girls."

"Kissing rules?" He looked ready to laugh, but when I nodded, he swore, kicking the ground with the heel of his hiking boot.

"I'm not telling you to go to hell." I came back to his side but didn't touch him. "But I'm not like other girls, Shay. I can't be selfish."

"And kissing me is selfish?" He stroked my cheek.

"Very." I turned my face, brushing my lips against the inside of his palm, reveling in his warmth, his scent.

"What if I want to kiss you again?" he murmured.

"Don't." I pushed his hand away from my face, wishing I didn't have to. "If you really want to help me, don't."

"I do have something that I think you might be interested in seeing." He reached for his backpack, unzipped it, and pulled out a book. "Something I found."

"You want to tutor me?" I glanced up at the darkening sky. "Remember that whole lack of night vision issue?"

"This will only take a sec." The book he held was thick and very old; its spine looked on the verge of crumbling. "I wanted you to see this."

"A book?"

"My excuse for trespassing on your mountain." He turned the front cover toward me.

The moment I caught sight of the title, black letters that looked as if they had been branded onto the front cover, I shifted into wolf form without thinking and backed away from him, wary, hackles raised. Shay stumbled backward, gaping at me. The book lay on the ground where he'd dropped it.

"Calla, Calla." He spoke my name like a chant, low and resonant. "What is it? What did I do?"

I kept my eyes locked on him, canines bared.

"Please turn back." His voice began to shake. "Whatever it is, I'm sorry."

I sniffed the air for the presence of others, signs of a trap. But there was nothing; we were alone. I scrutinized him, finding no hint of treachery in his fearful expression. With some reluctance I shifted forms. He let out an explosive breath, stepping toward me. I jumped back.

"Stay where you are."

He froze.

"Calla, what's going on?"

I shook my head. "My questions now."

He nodded quickly. I let my gaze fall on the book, pointing at the thick volume with a shaking finger.

"Who are you, Shay? Who are you really? And where did you get that?"

"You know who I am; I'm just me. I haven't lied to you about anything." A guilty flush crept up his cheeks. "And I got the book from my uncle's library."

I kept my hands outstretched, ready to hit him if I had to. "Your uncle doesn't mind you borrowing his books?"

He toyed with the zipper of his coat. "Not exactly."

I looked at him and saw how much he hated that he'd frightened me. I lowered my hands and crouched near the ground, my fingers moving over the soil in the hopes that the touch of the earth might calm me.

"What do you mean 'not exactly'?"

"Bosque gave me the run of his house but asked me not to go into the library. He's a rare book collector. He implied that a teenager might not take proper care of them."

"Like that?" I glanced back at the abandoned tome that lay on the soil. He grunted and snatched the book, brushing away dirt.

"That wasn't my fault. You scared me." He pulled the book close to his chest. "I usually take very good care of books. I wouldn't have taken it out of Bosque's house, but I wanted to show you. And I thought his ban on my use of the library was unfair." He rolled his eyes. "He even keeps the door locked."

"If the door is always locked, how did you get the book?" I traced my fingertip over the bark of a nearby tree.

An impish smile darted over his lips. "I don't read just philosophy. I went through a rebellious phase when I was pretty young and decided I wanted to be a professional thief. I was reading a lot of Thieves and Kings at the time."

He watched my eyebrows lift and he laughed. "It's a comics series. But anyway, I taught myself how to pick locks. I'm still pretty good at it. It was great to sneak in and out of my boarding school dormitories whenever I wanted to."

Despite my roiling nerves, I giggled at the image of Shay slipping out late at night from the sleepy halls of an elite prep school.

"But why would you move?" I asked. "If you were already at a boarding school . . ."

"That's what you'd think, right?" He began to pace through the clearing. "My uncle said familiarity breeds sloth, claimed I needed to see more than one part of the world. I think I've seen more than my share."

"Sounds like," I agreed.

"But moving is tough. I have no roots. No real friends. So I think he kind of owes me," Shay mused. "I also hold very strong personal convictions against censorship. I don't believe in forbidden knowledge." His words were so self-assured I felt queasy. He had no idea what thin ice he stood on.

"So you're a big fan of Eve?" I asked.

"She gets a bad rap. I'd take the Tree of Knowledge over Eden any day." He grinned. "I've been to Eden. I thought it was overrated."

"I have a feeling the original was better than Efron's version," I muttered, half shielding my body behind the tree trunk.

"But even with the temptation of breaking and entering aside," Shay continued, "I thought my uncle's request was ridiculous and kind of insulting. We'd been moving all over the world, I was always stuck in some lame dorm, and this was the first time we'd been in his family's original house—and then he set up this rule. I love books, especially old books. I wouldn't mistreat any of them. This one caught my eye. I think it's early modern, maybe late medieval, but I can't quite put a date on it; it doesn't have a publisher's imprint or anything."

"No, it wouldn't," I murmured.

"You've read this book?" he asked.

"No." My hands began to tremble again. "I have not."

"But you recognize it." He stepped toward me.

I flashed fangs at him. "Stay back. Don't bring that book near me."

He turned it over in his hands so that the cover faced him.

"You're afraid of it." He stared at the book and then looked at me. "Why are you afraid of a book you haven't read?"

Can I really tell him the truth? Too many pieces of a puzzle I had no idea how to put together were piling up all around me.

He opened the book. I whimpered and he snapped the cover shut again. "Okay, no looking at the book; I get it. I just wanted to show you the map."

"The map?" I asked.

He nodded. "There are four maps. They seem totally random, places from all over the globe." His voice grew wistful. "I'm sorry you won't look; they're unbelievable. You have no idea how surprised I was to find a map of the North American West in a book this old. I guess it's no wonder my uncle didn't want me messing with it; if there's evidence in this book that medieval Europeans knew about this continent's interior, that's pretty big stuff. This text is probably worth millions."

He hefted the tome as if weighing its value. I grimaced, waiting for him to speak again.

"Of course, it doesn't have any contemporary place-names. The whole book is in Latin. But the geography is recognizable. When you found me and that bear, I was looking for the cavern system. I've been toying with the idea of spelunking for some time."

My skin grew cold. He looked at my face, frowning. "Spelunking is cave exploration."

"I know what spelunking is," I said. "You were looking for Haldis?"

He blinked in surprise. "That's the name on the map, Haldis."

I thought about running.

"So if you haven't read this book or seen the maps, then how do you know about the cavern?" he asked. "I've read all the hiking guides and topographical maps, and the only place I've found a reference to this cavern—or this mountain—is in my uncle's book."

His gaze moved back to the book. I could see how much he wanted to open it, to review the images he had just described.

I didn't take my eyes off his face, making my decision, wondering what sort of fate I'd seal for myself. "My job, the duty of all the Guardians here, is to protect Haldis Cavern from our enemies. The Searchers."

I stared at the book's title, a single Latin phrase seared black onto the cover.

Bellum omnium contra omnes.

I closed my eyes, but I could still see the ebony lettering, as if the brand had been scorched on the inside of my eyelids. The forbidden words echoed in my mind.

The war of all against all.

FOURTEEN

SHADOWS POURED INTO THE CLEARING,

turning the bright green of the ferns to muted blues and grays.

"You thought it was Hobbes, didn't you?"

I glanced into the darkness of the trees, afraid that someone might be lurking there. "That's why you picked up the book."

I heard Shay's feet stir along the ground. "Yes. I thought I'd found an unpublished treatise." He sounded a bit mournful. "I was pretty excited, actually. But I have to admit I haven't read it yet. I got caught up in the maps. Plus my Latin isn't that great. Translating this beast is going to take a while."

I heard his fingers drum on the leather cover. "It's not Hobbes, is it?"

"No." I smiled in the growing darkness. "It is definitely not Hobbes. Put it away."

"So how do you know what it is?" There was an impatient edge to his voice.

"Because I'm forbidden to read it. On pain of death. Put it away now." My throat closed up.

"How could reading a book merit a death sentence?" he asked, stuffing the book into his backpack.

I reached for his hand. "We can't talk about this here. Come on."

"Where are we going?" He stumbled over a rock, bumping into me as I pulled him back through the garden.

"My car."

"You want to go to your car?" His fingers tightened on mine.

"Not for *that*," I said, but I didn't let go of his hand. "We have to be sure no one hears us."

When we reached the Jeep, I opened his door and went around to the driver's side. I climbed in and put my head on the steering wheel.

"What's going on, Calla?" I heard him unzipping his backpack. "What is this book?"

"It contains knowledge that is too powerful for anyone but the Keepers. It's their most hallowed text."

"So we're back to the Keepers again," he said. "Are you going to tell me who they are now?"

"I'm going to tell you about the war." I lifted my head, staring out the windshield at the darkened parking lot. "You seem to have fallen into the middle of it. But I don't know why."

"Is that why everything is so weird here?" He leaned from the passenger seat toward me. "Because there's a supernatural war that I don't know about? That humans don't know about?"

"Yes," I said. "But you're only caught up in the war because of who you're associating with."

"You?" I could hear a wry smile in his reply.

"Not just me. Your uncle."

"Bosque?" he blurted. "What does a millionaire business consultant have to do with your world?"

"Specifically, I'm not sure." I ran my fingers along the edge of the seat. "The first time I met your uncle was Friday night at Eden. But it was made clear to me that he is important in my world. He's a Keeper. A powerful one. Powerful enough to give orders to those who give *me* orders."

"What are you talking about?" I turned my head at the sound of his alarm. Even in the shadows I could see his face whiten.

I sighed. "I'm sorry, Shay. Your uncle. He's not human. And he is not your mother's brother. I don't know why you're with him. None of the Guardians have ever heard of a human living among the Keepers—until you showed up."

"You're wrong," he said. "I've known Bosque almost my whole life. He may not have been around much when I was growing up, but he's definitely human."

"I'm not wrong," I said. "Keepers look human, but they're not."

The veins in his neck stood out. "If they aren't human, then what are they?"

"Old Ones. Creatures who embody both the earthly and divine; full of magic. They are witches."

"Witches aren't human?" He stared at me. "I mean aren't Wiccans witches?"

"Humans are relatively new occupants of this world. And there are some who keep pagan rites, call themselves witches, but it isn't the same thing." I kept my eyes on him as I spoke. "The Old Ones have been in power much longer. Humans are mortal, fragile. The Old Ones are not. They were here before humans kept time or wrote histories. They move between worlds, this one and the spirit world. The Keepers are the wardens of the earth; they have the power to protect it. The witches rule the world, keep it from falling apart; they just let humans think they're in control now. The interests of the Old Ones lay in different places than human pursuits."

Shay braced his hands against the glove compartment. "Okay. For the sake of argument, I'm going along with this. You're calling them Old Ones, or witches, but you said my uncle is a Keeper. What's the distinction?"

"Keepers aren't the only witches. The war broke out, and still wages, because aeons ago the Old Ones split into factions. Keepers and Searchers."

"And the Searchers are your enemies?" He opened the glove compartment and began rifling through my CDs, as if seeking something normal to counter this strange conversation.

"Yes."

"Why?"

"When humans entered the world, the Old Ones were asked to protect them."

Shay dropped the *Sea Wolf* disc he'd pulled out. "Asked by who? God? Is there a God?"

"I really don't know," I admitted with a frown. "Theology isn't a big part of a Guardian's training. Maybe God . . . maybe gods or goddesses. All I know is that whatever force brought humans into being set up the Old Ones as their protectors, to guide them, help them thrive on the earth as part of creation."

"So the Old Ones were angels?" He sounded skeptical.

"No, not really. We're not talking choirs of heaven here. The Old Ones move between the material and spiritual dimensions, but their origin is a mystery . . . at least to most of us. Whatever religious traditions humans have invented throughout history, none of them can pinpoint the Old Ones and their place in the world."

"I'm not really buying this, Calla," he said, picking up the CD. "It sounds like muddy religious fantasy. Smoke and mirrors."

I reached up to toy with the seat belt. "I'm just telling you what I've always been told. And isn't this stuff always kind of murky?"

"If you say so," he grumbled. "So what was the problem? Why did things go badly?"

"Some of the Old Ones didn't want the job," I said. "They had other ideas about how they should use their power, and babysitting human beings didn't hold much appeal."

His brow furrowed. "See, this is exactly what I meant; that sounds biblical. Fallen angels, big egos, jealousy, and retribution against God—I know this stuff. Some of the boarding schools Bosque sent me to were Catholic."

"You already said you like Eve, which means you weren't a very good Catholic."

"I said he sent me to the Catholics." Shay went back to examining my music collection. "I haven't converted . . . yet. So fallen angels, war on heaven—am I on the right track?"

"I didn't say that humans haven't had some close ideas," I said. "But it's still speculation. I'm trying to tell you what's actually going on. And the war is here, not in heaven."

"So the Old Ones who didn't want the job . . . those are the Searchers? That's what the war is over?"

I glanced in the rearview mirror, still paranoid that we might be watched. "The Keepers watch over the sacred sites of the Old Ones. The sacred places of the earth grant the Keepers their power, and they use it to protect humanity. The Searchers want to control the sites, to take that power from the Keepers for their own gain. If they managed to win, humans would be subject to the whims and cruelty of the Searchers. They would be slaves while the Searchers dominated the earth, and the natural world would no longer be held in balance. All the good intention, the hope of creation would be unraveled and the world would be destroyed. The sites must be protected."

"And Guardians like you fend off the Searchers." He shut the glove compartment. His features were etched with weariness.

I touched his face in the dark cabin. "Shay, are you all right? Do you want me to stop talking about this?"

He shook his head. Stubble on his jaw rubbed my palm. "No. I want to know this, but honestly, it doesn't make sense. I sort of wish I could believe you were crazy or lying. And then I remember that I'm looking at a girl who can turn into a wolf whenever she wants."

I offered him a weak smile.

"So the Searchers are trying to get to the sites." He took my hand from his face, twining his fingers in mine.

It was easier to speak when he was touching me; I felt safer.

"Historically, yes. But they haven't been successful. About three hundred years ago there was a major turn in the war. We refer to it as the Harrowing. It was the last time that an army of Guardians was called upon to fight for the Keepers. We won, barely. Then the Searchers were hunted down and almost annihilated."

"Then why are you still here?"

"Our numbers are smaller now; the Keepers don't need an army of Guardians. But the Searchers represent a threat even though they are weakened. They attack in guerrilla fashion, ambushes, hit-and-run."

"Do you have to fight them often?"

"They actually hadn't made an attack on this site for almost twenty years." I bit my lip but forced myself to continue. "Until three nights ago."

"Three nights ago?" My fingers tightened around his and he took a deep breath. "You mean on Friday?"

I nodded. "The men who were following us outside the club. They were Searchers."

He dropped my hand, leaning against the passenger window. "What did they want?"

I hesitated. It didn't seem fair to tell Shay the Searchers had been hunting him until I knew why.

"I'm not sure."

He tapped on the glass. "My uncle said they were taken into custody. I thought he called the police."

"No." I gripped the steering wheel. "I killed one. The other went to the Keepers for questioning."

"You *killed* one of those men?" He shrank against the passenger door.

I glared at him, watching his hand move to the door handle. "I'm a warrior, Shay. That's what I do."

He became very still and stared at the book, which sat in his lap. His fear and judgment pricked at me. I crossed my arms over my chest and continued to watch him, my mood darkening with each passing moment.

"Look. I don't know why you're here, but it's clear that the Keepers want you safe. The Searchers may be hunting you, but now you have Guardians and Keepers watching over you. You're safe enough, but carrying that book around is very dangerous."

He pulled the text against his chest. "This book is the only source of information that I have about Bosque, who you have just pointed out *cannot actually be my uncle.* And it might contain all I can learn about you and your kind. I want to know what your world is. I'm part of it now."

"No." I loosened my grip on the wheel. "You can't be part of it. You're only a human. I don't want you to get hurt."

When he didn't speak, I looked at him. He was watching me, but the fear in his eyes was gone.

"It's not just about me," he said. "It just doesn't seem you know as much as you should about these masters of yours. The witches who rule the world."

Now it was my turn to stare out the window.

"That's why I wanted to show you this book," he said. "I wonder why they used Hobbes for the title."

I faced him, a cold laugh spilling from my throat. "They didn't. Hobbes poached the title from the witches."

"What?" I could tell he didn't believe me.

I shrugged. "The story, as I've been told, is that in earlier centuries the Keepers sometimes kept *philosophes* in their company as a form of entertainment. Sort of like holding court with the best and brightest of the human world. Hobbes was a particular favorite."

He leaned forward, interested.

"Okay."

"The Keepers liked Hobbes so much that they told him about their world. Offered to elevate him."

"Elevate him?"

"Make him one of them. Like turning a human into a Guardian."

Shay thumbed the book's pages. "That's incredible."

"But the revelations of the Keepers horrified him. He was too invested in the idea of human autonomy. He rejected their offer and began to write against them."

"Are you saying that Hobbes wrote *Leviathan* because he had a psychotic break about the existence of witches?" This wasn't going as well as I'd hoped.

"No, not psychosis. More like spite, or at least major-league denial. Hobbes wrote against witchcraft because he couldn't accept the reality of the witches' war. Of how much power the Old Ones *do* wield on earth."

Shay winced. "So what did the Keepers do to him?"

"Nothing. Hobbes was like a favorite pet to them who behaved badly. That's the way they treat all humans," I said. "Well, I guess they did something. He managed to get under their skin. They've made his name a dirty word among our tribes. His books are censored, like you've seen. The Keepers can definitely hold a grudge."

"So the war of all against all isn't a social theory?"

I tried to offer a sympathetic smile. His world had crumbled to pieces. I knew how he felt. My world didn't make sense anymore either.

"Hobbes stole the phrase to provoke the Keepers in his diatribes about natural order in human society. As far as I know, that book you have is the history of the world. *Our* world, not yours. *The War of All Against All* is the story of the Old Ones, of the Witches' War."

"If it's just history, why aren't you allowed to read it?" When he spoke, his breath materialized in the cold evening air.

I turned the ignition, fiddling with the heater. "I've never asked."

"Aren't you curious?"

I kept my eyes on the dashboard, staring into its dull glow. When I finally glanced at Shay, he bounced the tome up and down in a comical dance on his knees.

"Come on, let's read it together."

"It's forbidden."

Shay didn't back off. "That's what makes it interesting," he teased. "Plus I'm in the middle of your world and don't know why. Neither do you. Maybe this book will explain it to us."

I put my hand on his chest, pushing him against the passenger door.

"Listen to me, Shay. The laws in my world are final, punishments severe. I thought I'd made that clear. Forbidden means forbidden. If a Keeper found out that I'd read that book, they would kill me."

"Like they'd kill you if they knew you saved me from the bear?"

"Exactly. That's how serious it is."

"These Keepers sound like model citizens." He shoved the book in my face, making me shrink back.

"Don't!" I fisted my hands on my thighs, hating how uneasy I felt. I wanted to know more about my masters, but I was terrified of what it might cost me.

Shay covered one of my hands with his, pulling my fingers out of their tight clench. I shivered when his wrist brushed the bare skin of my leg. "Calla, there's a map of the cave in this book. It has information that can help us."

I watched his fingers stroke my palm. "We can't let anyone know that we're reading it."

His hand stilled. "Does anyone from school go to the public library?"

"No," I said. "We all use the school library."

"I like the Vail library; it's much better than the one at the Mountain School. Too many gum-snapping bimbos there more interested in gossip than reading."

"Don't knock gossip." I pinched his hand. "It makes the world go round."

"Too true," he said, laughing softly. "We can find out what's in this book. It might be slow, but we'll be able to pull a translation together."

"I can't read it," I said, twisting my fingers tightly around his. "I'm just too afraid. And I suck at Latin."

"So you want me to do all the work and just tell you what's in the book?" Shay said. "Nice try, grasshopper."

"I can still help," I said. "While you translate, I'll do research. Look up secondary materials that you need to understand the history. I can also answer questions about my world, things that might not make sense as you read them."

He nodded, sliding the Keeper's text into his backpack. "That would be helpful. But how are you going to manage to keep it quiet? I thought you weren't supposed to mix with humans."

I leaned against the headrest. "Well, one of the new orders I just received is to spend more time with you. The exact words were that I should be your 'de facto bodyguard.'"

His eyes lit up. "That doesn't sound bad at all." I stopped his hand when he began moving it up my thigh.

"I still have rules to follow."

"Your rules, not mine," he teased before I pushed his fingers onto the seat. "The library is open until 8 p.m. Monday through Thursday. As much as I'd like to cut school every day, I'll probably just work on this from four to eight on those nights. Can you meet me?"

"Yeah. I only have patrol on Sundays." I chewed on my lip as I committed myself to treason.

"Good. Then that's our plan." A devious grin split his face. "It's going to be fun."

"Risking our lives is fun?"

"Why not?" he said, opening the passenger door. "I'll start on this tonight and maybe I'll have some research questions for you tomorrow."

"Thanks, Shay."

"It's been a pleasure, she-wolf." He climbed out of the Jeep before I could hit him.

FIFTEEN

A SHINY BLACK GRAND CHEROKEE WAS

parked in our driveway. I frowned, wondering why Ren's SUV was still at our house. I walked in the front door and heard piano chords in a minor key lilting from the living room. Ren was seated at the kitchen table. He stood as I approached.

"What are you doing here?" The question came out more sharply than I intended; the Bane alpha had never visited my home before.

"I spent some time talking with your brother," he replied, glancing toward the stairs. "And then I waited for you to come home. Your parents said it would be all right."

"Why?" I rested my hands on the back of a kitchen chair. "I mean, why are you waiting for me?"

"I wanted to talk with you."

"About what?"

He looked back at the stairs. "Can we go to your room?"

I bit my lip, suddenly feeling a little dizzy. "I guess. It might be messy." I envisioned dunes of clothes we'd have to navigate. "Just let me check in with my mom and dad, okay?"

"Of course."

I rolled my tense shoulders back as I walked to the living room, trying to loosen the muscles.

I had paused in the hall, staying out of sight, when I heard their anxious voices. Something was up.

"The boy's nearly a man and built like the best sort of warrior," my father said. "There's no sense worrying over it. And Calla's always been a good fighter; she'll hold her own."

"Maybe," my mother replied. "But why the change? Neither of them will expect it. It's a harsh trial. They're so young."

"Only a few years younger than we were, Naomi. The point of the trial is to prove their ability to fight as a pair," my father said. I heard the clink of glass as he poured himself a drink. "It's still a kill like any other."

"It is *not*." My mother's voice shook. "She's never killed a—"

At the word *kill*, I dropped my bag. Their voices stopped when it thudded on the hardwood floor.

Great. No sense in hiding now. I kicked my bag toward the kitchen.

When I walked into the living room, my parents looked startled.

"Good evening, Calla," my mother said, working to compose herself. "We didn't hear you come in."

My father leaned back in his leather chair; his eyes were closed, but I knew he was awake. Chopin's notes trickled around me like a slow-moving stream under a moonless sky.

"Hi." I clasped my hands behind my back. "Ren and I are going upstairs to chat for a while."

"That sounds lovely, dear," my mother said. "Don't you think that will be nice for Calla, Stephen?"

"Should be fine." An uncharacteristic smile curved along one corner of my father's mouth. "Ren is an impressive young man . . . nothing like Emile. That was a pleasant surprise."

I blinked at him in disbelief. He continued to smile.

"Trust me, Cal. Your life will be much more pleasant than if you'd been mated to Ren's father."

"Uh, okay." I started back toward the kitchen, wishing I knew what they'd been talking about earlier.

"Calla." My mother's coaxing voice stopped me. "It is of course perfectly acceptable for Renier to call on you, but remember that you are a lady. Don't bring shame on yourself by making poor choices."

"No, of course not." I kept my eyes on the hardwood floor, thinking about Shay's kiss and how much more I'd wanted from him.

A sly smile hovered on Ren's lips when I returned to the kitchen table.

If he heard what Mom said, I'm going to kill her.

"Let's go, then." I waved for him to follow me upstairs. "So you talked to Ansel?"

"Mason called me while I was driving your brother home. He wanted to make sure Ansel didn't get any ideas about vigilante justice."

I paused in front of my bedroom door.

"Why did he call *you*?" The news stung; Mason really didn't trust me.

"You don't have to be territorial, Lily," Ren said with a quiet laugh. "He suggested that because you're Ansel's sister, the cub might not take your warnings to heart. Besides, I'm the alpha wolf of the pack now. It's protocol that they come to me first. Even before you."

"I guess." I felt a spike of resentment. With Ren as my partner, I could no longer claim final authority for my packmates. Alpha males had more clout than females. Ren ruled the pack. It was my job to support him and keep the others in line.

"It's not about you, Cal," he said. "It's just the rules."

I nodded, opening the bedroom door. "Oh no." It was much worse than I'd imagined.

He whistled. "If you hate clothes so much, why do you have so many? I can't see the floor."

"Give me a sec." I gathered clothes in my arms, throwing them at my closet.

"Don't trouble yourself on my account." When I'd cleared the bed, Ren stretched out on it, pulling over a couple of pillows so he was propped up.

He crooked his finger at me. "Come here."

My heart stuck in my throat.

"I won't bite, Lily." He flashed his teeth. No sharp canines in sight.

I walked slowly to the bed, pausing at its side. "Ren, did you know about Mason and Nev?"

He nodded.

"How long?"

"About six months, I guess." He shrugged.

"Is the rest of your pack okay with it?"

"More or less." He sounded uneasy.

"What does that mean?"

He sighed. "Sabine has no problem with it. She loves Nev, always has. And Cosette pretty much lets Sabine think for her, so she's fine too."

"So it's Dax," I said.

Ren didn't reply, but he rolled onto his side, reaching out to grab my wrists.

"Dax isn't okay," I pressed, even as he pulled me onto the bed next to him. My pulse went wild.

"Dax thinks it's too much of a risk to let Nev and Mason be together," he said as he tucked my body next to his. "He sees it as a weakness. A threat to the pack."

"That's too bad," I said, marveling at the steadiness of Ren's voice. *How can he be so calm?*

My stomach twisted. *That's right, he does this all the time.*

"It doesn't matter." I felt the muscles of his chest tighten. "Dax knows I'm the alpha, and I gave Nev the okay. He and Mason should be together if it's what they want."

"You and I are on the same page, then," I said, hiding my doubts. I had the feeling that Dax hadn't swallowed Ren's order happily.

"We are." His face hardened into sharp angles. "It won't be a problem."

"Good." I was pressed so tightly against him, I wondered if I'd ever be able to relax. "So what did you want to talk to me about?"

"I need to know that you're okay." His eyes softened and his voice became incredibly quiet. "So much has happened lately, it's been hard on all of us."

He paused, lowering his voice even further. "But it's different for alphas."

"It is." I held my breath when his fingers traced the shape of my collarbone.

Ren pushed his fingers through the waves of hair that spilled over my shoulder. "I can be here for you, if you let me."

He bent his face toward mine.

"What are you doing?" I tried to pull away, but his hand slipped from my hair to cup the nape of my neck.

When he whispered, his warm breath brushed over my lips. "Just let me kiss you, Calla. You don't know how long I've wanted to. No one has to know."

My lips parted as I drew a sudden, startled breath and in that instant his mouth was on mine, soft as velvet. I closed my eyes against the rush of a hundred wings that suddenly beat in my chest and soared through my body. His scent was all around me. Leather, sandalwood, bonfires in autumn. He pulled back, but only for the sake of moving his lips to trail over my neck.

My blood was on fire and I was shaking. *Is this really happening?*

I couldn't stop thinking about Shay in the clearing. About asking him to kiss me. The electric touch of his lips on mine.

But this is where I belong. I tried to push the memories back.

Ren stroked my knee, his fingers wandering up my thigh, sliding beneath the hem of my dress.

I grabbed his wrist. "Wait."

He didn't free his arm from my grasp but continued kissing my collar bone.

"Let's skip the waiting part," he murmured into my skin.

"Please, Ren." The frenzied beating of my heart was overwhelming. "It's too fast. We're supposed to wait for the union."

He rolled onto his side with a low growl. "I think you'll discover that delayed gratification is overrated."

"I'm sorry." I took his hand. "It's not that I don't want . . ."

I lost the words, realizing I didn't actually know what I wanted.

"I can help you with that." He reached for me and I jumped off the bed.

"I'm serious, Ren."

"Right." He slowly stood up. "This is new territory for you. Stupid sequestering, the Keepers better not have turned you into a nun or something."

I snatched a book off my nightstand and threw it at him. "Get out of my room!"

He caught the book in midair and laid it on the bed. "Easy, Lily. That was a bad joke. I didn't mean any offense."

I shook with humiliation. "You don't know what it's been like."

"I know, and I'm sorry." He came to my side and cupped my face. "I'm sure it hasn't been fun. You deserve better."

I nodded. He lowered his head, softly brushing his lips over mine. "I'll show you how much fun it can be. You need to trust me."

"I'm sorry I got angry," I murmured.

"It's okay. You're the boss," he said. "No pressure."

"I promise I'm not still mad, but I'm really tired." I sat down on the bed. "It was a hard day."

"It was."

"Can we just leave this for tonight? We've already . . ."

"Like I said." His smile was tight. "You're the boss. Until you're ready, I'll leave you alone. See you tomorrow."

He kissed my forehead and left the room. I fell back against the pillow, not feeling in control of anything, much less like anyone's boss. My lips still tingled from Ren's kiss, but when I closed my eyes, only Shay's face was there.

SIXTEEN

SHAY FLIPPED OVER THE PAGE AND SCRIBBLED

a few notes while I fidgeted in my seat.

"I can't believe they don't allow outside drinks in here," I said. "How am I supposed to read this much without coffee?"

"You haven't read anything, Calla," he corrected without looking up. "You've just sat there and watched me read."

"You haven't given me anything to look for in the stacks." My eyes darted toward the book that lay in front of him. "Have you come up with anything useful yet?"

His mouth flattened into a thin line.

"Look, I'm not being critical," I said. "I was just asking what you've got so far."

He leaned back in his chair. "Well, the book seems to be divided into three parts. *De principiis priscis,* which I'd guess is the origin story of your world. Then there's a section called *De proelio.* . . ." He paused, watching me expectantly.

"'Battle,'" I said.

Shay nodded, the corner of his mouth crinkling upward. "Somehow I thought you'd know that word."

I smiled, stretching my arms over the back of the chair. Even the suggestion of a fight made my muscles twitch restlessly. I'd been sitting for hours, first at school and now at the library. Shay watched me with amusement and then turned back to his notes.

"Maybe it contains the details of the Witches' War?" He glanced at the book. "I guess we'll find out."

"What's the third section?"

He frowned, pushing strands of golden brown hair off his forehead. "It's the one that makes the least sense. I can't figure what it is."

He opened the book, flipping pages until he had reached the end of the volume.

"It's the shortest section by far. *Praenuntiatio volubilis.*"

"An announcement?" I picked up a pen and began doodling on the notepad that lay in front of me.

Shay turned his attention to the Latin dictionary. "I don't think so. It's more like a prophecy or an omen. But the second word, *volubilis,* implies that it's not set in stone; you know, like the idea of fate or destiny. Whatever that section describes is something that can be changed, altered."

"So the book ends with a description of something that is supposed to happen in the future?" For some reason the hairs on the back of my neck stood up.

A disgusted grunt rose from his throat. "No. I skipped to the last page to see if it might have a conclusion that helped contextualize the rest of the book."

He turned the pages until he reached the final lines of the text.

The prickling at the back of my neck traveled over my shoulders and arms. "What does it say?"

His voice was laced with irritation. *"Crux ancora vitae."*

"What?" I stood up and paced alongside Shay's chair.

"I think it's a proverb or something. It means 'the cross is the anchor of life.' I didn't know that your witches were Christians." His finger moved along the lines.

I continued my restless path around the table. "They most definitely are not. And the contents of that book are not Christian. Whatever that proverb is, it isn't Christian; it means something else."

"You must be wrong, Calla," Shay said. "If you take into account the form of the Latin and what I've been able to discern about this text by comparing it to other rare books: the script, the illuminations, all that stuff makes it fairly easy to date. It's a late-medieval, early-Renaissance book, so it could definitely have a Christian influence. And then there's the cross thing."

"The book may have been created in the Middle Ages, but its contents were not. The Old Ones predate Christians."

"But if this book is pre-Christian, not medieval, then what the hell does that mean?" Shay shoved the tome away from him with a disgusted snort. "Someone needs to talk to this fool about how to end a narrative. No conclusion, some lame proverb," he said. "And a picture."

I stopped just short of his chair. "A picture?"

"Yeah. A picture of a cross." He pulled the book back toward him, staring at the final page. "I guess it does lend some credence to your idea that it's not Christian. It definitely isn't like any crucifixes I've seen."

I inched closer, my heart fluttering. "What do you mean?"

"Why don't you take a look?" He raised his eyes to mine. When he saw the fear there, he stood up and moved close to me.

"Calla." He took both my hands in his. "I understand why you're afraid of this book. But you've come this far. I think you have to look at it."

I began to shake my head, but he gripped my fingers tightly. "I need your help."

His eyes held mine, kind but challenging.

I wanted to object, but I knew that from the moment I'd committed to meeting Shay at the library, there was no point in turning back. "Okay."

He drew me back to the table. My hands began to shake as he turned the book to face me. Shay sat down in the chair, crossing his arms behind his head.

"Weird, huh? I mean, the way the bars are different on two of the ends. It makes the cross seem asymmetrical even though the pieces are the same length."

I stared at the image and then at Shay. "Don't you recognize this?"

"Recognize it?" He glanced down at the cross. "What do you mean?"

"Shay, this is the tattoo that's on the back of your neck." I tapped the image with my finger.

He laughed. "I don't have any tattoos."

I blinked at him. "Yes, you do."

"I think I'd remember if I'd gotten ink," he argued. "I've heard it's fairly painful."

He flinched when I reached around his neck, pulling back the collar of his shirt. The tattoo was there, just as I'd remembered it. The cross, an exact likeness of the one that stared back at me from the Keeper's text, lay etched in black ink on the golden skin along the nape of Shay's neck.

"See, I told you. No tats." He tried to twist out of my grasp, but I stilled him by gripping his shoulder.

"Shay—you do have the cross inked on your neck. I'm looking at it right now."

A shudder passed through his body. I relaxed my hold on him, giving his tense muscles a gentle squeeze.

"Calla," he whispered. "Are you serious?"

"Yeah." I crouched beside his chair. "I have a hard time believing that you've never seen the back of your own neck."

His forehead wrinkled. "I must have at some point. And I don't remember ever seeing a tattoo. Is that where it is?"

He shivered as my fingers traced the lines of the cross on his neck. "Yes, right here."

"Give me your compact; I'll go check it in the bathroom mirror." He jumped up from his seat and then looked at me, waiting.

"I don't have a compact."

"You don't?" Shay frowned. "I'll figure something out." He dashed away and I lowered myself into his chair, returning to the book I'd been reading.

A few minutes later, I looked up from the page to find Shay glaring at me, wary and nervous. "So are you pulling my leg or what?"

"You found a hand mirror?"

"I borrowed one from the librarian at the circulation desk," he said. "I told her I was having a problem with my contact and the bathroom mirror didn't magnify enough."

"You wear contacts?"

"No." He pulled up another chair. "You haven't answered my question."

I squared my shoulders. "I have no reason to lie to you, Shay. Are you saying you looked at your neck and saw nothing there?"

"That's exactly what I'm saying. I saw my neck, the bare skin of my neck. No tattoo. And definitely not a weird cross tattoo."

"I'm sorry. The cross is tattooed on your neck," I said. "I don't know much about the Keepers' magic, so I can only guess. But they must have cast something on your sight so you can't see it."

I looked at the image once again, my fingers tracing over the page. "They've instructed the Guardians to keep our world hidden from you, even though we've been asked to protect you. For some reason they don't want you to know anything about this."

His face went white. "You're saying my uncle put a spell on me so I wouldn't know about the tattoo?"

"He's not your uncle." I tried to make the reminder gentle but firm. "And yes, I think he must have."

Shay put his elbows on his knees, hiding his face in his hands. I hesitantly rose from my chair. My limbs quivered as I stretched my arms around his shaking body, drawing him against me. My heart was racing. As much as I knew I should maintain some physical distance from Shay, seeing him like this and not doing anything was too cruel.

His hands dropped from his face, encircling my waist. Warmth seemed to slide from his fingertips over the length of my body. He leaned into me, resting his cheek in the hollow between my neck and shoulder, sending electric tendrils like vines over my skin. I gently brushed his messy golden brown hair, biting my lip so I wouldn't kiss his forehead.

"Thanks." His quiet murmur was strained. He cleared his throat. "It's a little hard to cope with the growing realization that I have no idea who I really am."

I laughed quietly.

Shay tensed. "Is that funny?"

I twisted my fingers through his hair. "No. It's just that to me, it sounds a little interesting. I've always known exactly who I am and what I would be."

He straightened and I released him from my arms though I remained crouched next to his chair.

"Do you wish you were something other than what you are?"

"No," I said quickly. "We are who we are. I have no desire to be something else. But right now I'm afraid of what it means for those who I care about."

Shay looked at me, slowly lifted his hand, and caressed my cheek. Looking into his eyes felt like stumbling upon a hidden garden.

I quickly returned to my own seat, short of breath, my heart pounding.

I could feel his eyes on me as I scratched shapes on my notebook page. "I wanted to learn what was in the book because I needed to know more about the Keepers and Guardians."

I turned to face him. Shay watched me curiously. I was relieved to see that he didn't appear offended by my abrupt retreat.

"But it's clear that everything that's happening here is about you, Shay. We need to find out who you are."

He didn't speak, but nodded once.

I pointed at the leather-bound tome. "So we know that cross is on your neck. But we don't know what it means."

Shay turned back to the image. "Are these triangles on my neck too?"

"No." With some reluctance I dragged my chair close to his so I could look at the book.

"But you think they're important?" He pointed at my notebook. I glanced down and was shocked to see that I'd drawn at least ten triangles across the white page.

"I can't shake the feeling that I've seen them before, but I don't know where." I chewed on my lip for a moment, letting my mind wander.

"Oh!"

I rummaged through my bag and pulled out my Organic Chemistry lab workbook.

"Are you having trouble in chem?" Shay frowned as he watched me flip through the pages.

I shook my head and kept turning through the book until I found the introductory notes from Monday's experiment.

"Look. I knew I'd seen this. It's in the historical introduction to the alchemy lab." I pointed at the triangles. "These are alchemical symbols."

Shay rose and came to peer over my shoulder. "It's a good thing you read the introduction. I just skipped right to the experiment."

I smiled and continued to read. "These four triangles represent the four elements: earth, air, fire, and water."

I looked at the image in the Keeper's text and then back at the workbook.

"But I have no idea what that has to do with a cross."

"Looks like you just found your first research question, Cal." He tapped me on the shoulder.

"Fine. But is there anything else for me to work with besides that proverb? What is it again?"

"The cross is the anchor of life," he intoned in mock solemnity. "That's the last line of the book. Then the picture."

I jotted the phrase down amid the scattered triangles on my notebook page.

"What comes before the proverb?"

"More nonsense." His frustration trickled out with the reply. "There are two lines set apart from the text at the very end of the book. The last line is the proverb and the other is 'may the Scion bear the cross.'"

"May the Scion bear the cross. The cross is the anchor of life," I murmured, then looked at Shay and saw comprehension dawning in his eyes even as a chilling wave poured down my spine.

"What does *Scion* mean, Shay?" I whispered.

His Adam's apple moved up and down as he swallowed. "It means 'descendant.'"

"Descendant of whom?" *I was right, he is someone.*

"It isn't specific; it can be a descendant of anyone. Sometimes it's used to mean 'heir.'"

"Shay—" I reached for his shoulder, hoping to turn him. I was afraid to touch him, but I wanted to look at the tattoo again.

"No," he said sharply. He pulled away from my hand, pacing toward the tall bookshelves that surrounded us.

I jumped up. "That has to be you. You bear the cross. It's on your neck. You're the Scion."

"No, no, no." He backed away as I approached him. "This is all—it's some kind of trick. Or sick joke." His face was drawn. He glared at me accusingly.

"I have a tattoo I can't see. My uncle isn't a person, but a witch. And now I'm some special descendant who is mentioned in a book that was transcribed hundreds of years before I was born? I don't think so."

When I realized he was about to bolt, I did the only thing I could imagine would stop him.

"Shay." The razor-sharp edge in my voice locked him in place.

In that instant I leapt forward, shifting into a wolf in midair, and knocked him onto the floor. My forepaws dug into his chest, pinning him to the ground. I shifted back into human form.

"You may wish I was lying, but you're looking at a girl who can turn into a wolf whenever she wants. Remember?" I brushed his cheek with my fingers, too aware of the way my body melted against him. I closed my eyes, taking in his scent, the heat of his body.

Shay reached up and wrapped his arms around my neck. One hand cupped the back of my head. He pulled me toward him. Before I could react, his lips were on mine.

The kiss started slowly, a sweet, tentative searching. The soft touch of his mouth mesmerized me. I parted my lips for him, letting desire draw me down.

Shay's kiss deepened; his hand ran along my back, tracing the length of my braid, sliding beneath my shirt to stroke my skin. I felt like I was drinking sunlight. My fingers moved from his chest to his neck and stroked the line of his jaw. I pressed into him, wanting to know more of the mysteries he pulled so easily from my body. More of this freedom, this wildness.

Shay grasped my hips and in a swift motion turned us, pinning me to the floor. His hands moved beneath my shirt, his body pressing hard against mine. I could smell his rising desire mixing with my own, our feverish need infusing the air like lightning about to strike. Instead of being pulled down into him, I was rising up, legs wrapping around him. His fingers moved carefully, tracing my curves, lingering in places that stole my breath, binding me to him and yet setting me free. My own gasp of pleasure against his mouth brought the world hurtling back.

The room spun as I pulled out of his embrace, stumbling toward the table. My heart rammed against my ribs, insistent and painful.

I can't do this, I can't. But I wanted to. More than anything.

He scrambled to his feet, smiling at me. The warm light was in his eyes again.

"What's wrong?"

I stomped angrily back to my chair without speaking, hating myself, my body still aching from when I'd wrenched free of Shay.

"Oh, right." His smile flattened. "Kissing rules and your impending nuptials. When is that happening again?"

"Samhain." My heart cramped when I thought about how close it was.

"So—what?" He tried to sound out the word. "Is that supposed to mean something to me?"

I crumpled a piece of paper and threw it at him. "For someone whose name most people would read as SEE-MUSS, that's pretty pathetic."

He picked up my notebook missile, tossing it in the nearest wastebasket. "Just because I have an Irish name doesn't make me an expert in all old languages."

"You're pretty good at Latin," I countered.

"Which is why I don't have time to learn all the others," he said.

"Fair enough," I said. "Samhain. SOW-WHEN."

"Okay, Samhain." He pronounced it correctly. "Your wedding day. So when is it?"

"October thirty-first."

"Halloween?" He scowled. "How romantic."

"Halloween doesn't matter. Samhain does." I threw him a warning glare, which he ignored.

"And it's a big deal because . . ." He waved his hand to mimic smoke rising in the air.

"The Keepers can renew their powers that night. The veil between the worlds is thinnest at Samhain."

Shay's hand dropped. "What worlds?"

"This one and the nether."

"Sounds scary." He grabbed a pen and jotted some notes, but I saw his fingers shaking. I wondered if it was from actual fear or if his body was still taut with frustrated desire like mine.

"It probably is," I agreed. "Luckily the Guardians just patrol the perimeter. I've never had to see what they do."

I suddenly felt queasy.

"Whoa." Shay peered at me. "You're all green. What's up?"

I gripped the edge of the table, wishing the dizziness would subside. "I'll have to see it this year."

He leaned forward. "Why?"

"The ceremony is different this time." My nails took a thin peel of varnish off the table. "Because they picked that night for the union, I'll be there."

"Do you know what it involves?" His own face had whitened.

"No," I said. "The ritual of the union is a secret. I don't know much about it at all."

"Sucks for you," he muttered. "Like everything else about this."

"Stop it, Shay." I tried to start reading again.

"I don't see why you can't bend the rules," he pressed. "From what I've been told, Ren's dated half of Vail."

He looked at me as though expecting a shocked response.

"Everyone knows that. It doesn't matter. That was his choice." I kept my eyes on the table. "The rules are different for him."

"So, what, boys will be boys and girls have to behave?" he scoffed.

"I'm the alpha female." I hooked my ankles around the chair's legs. "No one can touch me. It's the Keepers' Law."

"But Ren can touch whoever he wants?" he asked. "'Cause it sounds like he does."

"He's an alpha male. The hunt is in his nature." My ankle lock on the chair legs was so tight I heard the wood creak. I didn't want Shay to ask the question I could see on his face.

He frowned. "But if you're an alpha too, wouldn't the hunt be part of your nature?"

I didn't answer. My legs felt like they were on fire.

"And I touched you . . ." His fingers twitched, as if he wished he were touching me now. *Does he want me as much as I want him?*

"I shouldn't have let you." My body went limp. "Can we talk about something else, please?"

"But it's not fair—" He reached for my hand.

I leaned away from him. "Fair has nothing to do with it. It's about tradition. Tradition is important to the Keepers."

"But what about . . ." His words trailed off.

"The union is too close." I slipped my hands under the table. "I'm not free. And for your information, Ren is not dating anyone else now either."

"Is he dating *you*?" Shay slammed his laptop shut.

"It's complicated." *Actually, it's simple. I belong to Ren, not you.*

He dropped into his chair. "I can't stand that guy. He acts like he owns you."

"You don't understand him." I squirmed at the futility of the conversation. "And you will not kiss me again, Shay Doran."

"I won't promise that," he said.

I turned away, hoping he wouldn't notice the warm blush that had crept over my cheeks. I didn't want his promise, but that choice wasn't mine. *I have to stop this, now.*

"Fine." I tried to make my voice cold. "I'm sure you'd go through life ably enough with only one hand."

He jerked his hands from the table. "You wouldn't."

I laughed. "You'll just have to decide if you're willing to risk it."

He shuddered, muttering something unintelligible under his breath.

"I didn't catch that." Frustration snaked through my belly, making it tighten. I wanted him to touch me again, and I was furious with myself for it and with him for making me feel like this.

"Just nice to know I'm falling for a vestal virgin," he said, anger clouding his own face.

"A what?"

"Fun history trivia." His smile was cold enough to make me bristle. "Another set of highly desirable but untouchable girls. If they broke their vow of chastity, they were buried alive."

"Buried alive?" I shuddered. *Is that what would happen to me if the Keepers found out about Shay?* I knew there would be consequences if anyone but Ren touched me, but I hadn't thought about how bad they might be.

"And the lucky guy who'd tempted a sacred virgin from her duty was flogged to death in public," he finished.

I suddenly felt hollow inside. My own punishment might be frightening, but the thought of what could happen to Shay was much, much worse.

"I guess we should take our lessons from history, then," I murmured, trying to hide the trembling in my voice.

"We aren't living in ancient Rome," Shay snapped.

"Since that subject is closed," I said, ignoring his livid expression, "let's please get back to what's important."

He stared at me.

"Please," I murmured.

"Okay," he said, opening his laptop again. "So if we accept the idea that I'm this Scion, what does that mean?"

Thank you.

"I'd imagine somehow it matters who you are descended from," I mused.

He nodded and shrugged. "No one famous."

"You don't remember your parents?"

"No. They died in a car crash when I was two. I don't remember them at all, not even what they looked like." He pulled the Keeper's text into his lap, fingers tracing an outline of the cross. "I don't have any pictures. Uncle Bosque always said it was best to leave the past in the past."

I frowned. "You don't have anything of your parents? Nothing to remember them by?"

"Just a blanket my mother knitted for me." He offered me a sheepish smile. "I carried it around when I was a kid."

I toyed with the end of my braid, trying not to laugh. "What were their names?"

"Tristan and Sarah Doran."

I jerked so forcefully in my chair that it almost tipped over. *Oh God, those names. No, no, no.*

His head snapped up. "What is it?"

"Tristan and Sarah?" I repeated, fresh horror nestling in my belly.

"Yes. Calla, what's wrong?" he said. "More bad news?"

"I don't know what it means. Please keep that in mind. But the night we were attacked outside Eden . . ." The face of the captive Searcher loomed large in my mind. "The Searcher who we took alive." I wanted to erase the sickened hue of Shay's skin. "He spoke their names, Tristan and Sarah."

"One of the men who jumped us knew my parents?" The veins in his neck throbbed.

"I'm not sure." I was trying to be truthful, but every word I spoke seemed like a stray thread that could unravel my life.

"What exactly did he say?" Shay leaned forward, watching me intently.

"He asked where you were . . ." I said, pausing to dig up the memory. "And then he said: 'He doesn't know, does he? Who he is? That you took Tristan and Sarah? What you're going to do?'"

Shay gripped the arms of his chair. "I thought the Searchers were trying to destroy the world. Aren't they the bad guys?"

I nodded, not having any explanations to offer.

He rose, shutting his laptop and picking up his backpack. "I'm sorry, but I need to leave. There's too much . . ." He shook his head. "I need some time alone. But I'll be back here tomorrow."

I stayed still as he moved past me, wanting to go with him.

"And Calla." He bent down for a moment, whispering into my hair. "I don't think I'm the only one who's being lied to."

SEVENTEEN

SHAY WASN'T IN FIRST PERIOD. A WAVE OF

nausea swept over me.

Could the Keepers have done something to him?

I gnawed on my fingernails through my next two classes. When I walked into Organic Chemistry and saw him already seated at his lab station, I had to fight the urge to run across the room to embrace him. His two human lab partners caught sight of me and shrank to the other end of the station. Shay observed their swift retreat from the corner of his eye.

"Do you always have that effect on humans?" he asked, a smile hooking the edge of his lips.

"Usually, yes. All Guardians do. You're a freak for not being terrified of me." I leaned against the table, trying to keep my voice even. "Where were you this morning?"

"Worried about me?" His smile broadened. "Your very own freak?"

"Oh, please," I lied.

"I cut." He twirled a pencil between his fingers. "I didn't feel like getting out of bed this morning."

"I think your attitude about cutting class is a bit cavalier," I said, annoyed that I'd been working up an ulcer while he slept in.

He lowered his voice, leaning toward me. "Well, according to you, my uncle is some kind of super-powered warlock, and according to Logan, he's a Regent of this school. What are they gonna do, kick me out?"

"That may be the case, but I'd appreciate a little consideration," I said. "For all I knew, the Keepers had given you to a wraith for breakfast."

He frowned. "What's a wraith?"

A chill ran down my spine. "Never mind. Just call next time, okay?"

"Are you giving me your phone number?" He flashed a teasing grin.

I couldn't stop my own smile. "I guess I am."

He pulled out his phone, punching in my number as I rattled it off.

"Want mine?" He raised his eyebrows and watched me, his face hopeful.

"Sure." I drew out my own phone and entered the number he recited for me.

"Your sweetheart isn't too happy about this," Shay said, still smiling.

I looked toward the back of the room. Ren watched us as he leaned casually against the table, holding a pair of scissors. I'd never seen a classroom tool look so dangerous.

"Enjoy your lab," I murmured, and headed for my usual seat, wanting to kick myself for being so openly friendly with Shay.

By the time I reached our table, Ren had busied himself setting up for the day's experiment.

"Hey Ren." I could barely hear myself over my racing pulse. When I looked at him, all I saw was my bed. All I felt was the heat of his body next to mine. All I heard was my shallow breath while his hands moved beneath my dress.

When I tried to fight those memories off, images of Shay took their place. I couldn't shake the feeling that I'd betrayed Ren in some unforgivable way. But that very thought provoked my temper, conjuring up images of all the girls who'd happily accepted Ren's kisses and more. Both impulses converged violently inside me, making it impossible for me to look at him.

But Ren didn't seem inclined to look at me either.

"Calla." He greeted me coldly. For the first time I could remember, I missed my much-hated nickname.

Is this what he means by no pressure? Or is he mad I was talking to Shay? God, I'm messing up everything.

I muted the sigh that welled in my chest and began digging for my lab workbook.

"So I see you've taken Logan's orders to heart." Ren's growl sounded much closer than I'd expected. When I turned to face him, I almost jumped. He hovered over me, his body only inches from mine.

I shrugged. "Orders are orders."

"Well, that should make him happy." He placed one hand on the lab station, shifting his weight uneasily, standing so close my body could have nestled in the curve of his own if I only took another step forward.

I tried to focus on the conversation. "Logan? Yes, I'd imagine he'll be pleased."

"I meant Shay." Ren glared at the front of the room.

My head was suddenly filled with lovely sacred virgins thrown into open graves, screaming as dirt was shoveled onto their still-living bodies. *I have to fix this.*

I placed my hand on his wrist. His gaze flitted back to me, softer now and curious.

"About the other night—" *I am an alpha female. He is my mate. Why is this so hard?*

He straightened, stepping away. My stomach knotted as I watched his retreat.

"Ms. Foris said this lab will take up the entire period," he said. "We need to get started."

"Ren—" I began, but his obsidian glare stopped me in my tracks.

"Just drop it."

I strode forward, grasped his elbow, and turned him to face me.

"Listen to me, Ren. Everything is a mess right now and it's been hard on all of us. Like you've said."

He tried to turn away, but I growled, holding him still. A thin smile broke his stony expression.

"You need to know . . ." My courage faltered for a moment, but I drew a quick breath and plunged on, "That I don't want you to leave me alone."

The alpha tensed, eyes wary, as if he was waiting for my next qualifying statement. When none came, he carefully extricated his arm from my fingers. "I'll keep that in mind."

We carried out our assigned lab work in uncomfortable silence. By the end of the class I was miserable. Ren left the room without so much as a wave.

When I entered the cafeteria, I found the Haldis pack gathered around our two tables yet again, chattering contentedly. Dax, Fey, and Cosette sat in a group. The large senior gesticulated wildly while the two girls beamed at him. Bryn and Ansel sat close together in quiet conversation, but I was relieved to see that they had managed to curb their love-struck gazes at least a little.

I tripped over my own feet when I caught site of Sabine—smiling. She had taken a seat next to Mason and Neville. Mason was demonstrating some questionable uses for a banana, and all three of them burst into fits of laughter.

"Hey Cal," Ansel said when I sat beside him. "Wanna trade an apple for an orange? You took the last one before I packed my lunch."

"Sure."

He immediately began digging in my lunch bag.

"You feeling better, Cal?" Bryn asked. "You seemed really out of it in first period."

"Uh-huh." I snatched my oatmeal cookie back from Ansel. "I just didn't sleep well. I'm fine."

When Ren approached our tables, I angrily pulled my sandwich from the paper bag, trying to remember what my appetite was. I'd taken a single bite of roast beef when I heard a familiar voice.

"Hey guys." It sounded like Shay was right behind me. "I wondered if I might join you."

The bite of sandwich caught in my throat. My eyes watered as I coughed. Ansel slammed me on the back until I could breathe again.

I cleared my throat, turning to face him. *Don't, Shay. Don't do this. You don't understand what it means.*

"Are you okay?" His tone was serious, but his eyes were laughing.

"You want to sit with us?" As each word of the question left my mouth, my disbelief rose. I had no idea what he was playing at.

"Yes. If that's all right."

Conversation at the table had ceased. All the young wolves stared silently at the human boy who was either brave or crazy enough to step into their social space. I glanced toward the Keepers' tables across the cafeteria. Sure enough, Logan had pushed his sunglasses up on his forehead to watch the exchange. A lazy but somewhat interested expression hovered in his eyes.

"Of course."

I blinked at the speed with which Ren had covered the space between himself and Shay.

"We've all been wanting to get to know you better, Shay. Please join us."

We have?

Ren slid into the chair on the other side of me, pulling my lunch bag in front of him. One corner of his mouth curved into a smile.

"Calla, would you mind giving up your seat so Shay can sit here?"

Shay frowned. "I'm sure I can find a chair to bring over."

"That's not necessary." Ren's voice was icy; he kept his eyes on me.

I wasn't sure what was happening, but I didn't want to push him any further when it came to Shay. If I had to stand through lunch, so be it. I shoved my chair in Shay's direction.

Fingers circled my wrist. My head whipped around to see Ren's eyes dancing with dark mirth while he drew me toward him like he was reeling in a prize catch.

"So what's for lunch?" He pulled me onto his lap.

"I really could get another chair." I could hear the fury in Shay's words.

Ren's charcoal irises glowed with a challenge, and I was determined to meet it.

"No." I fought to keep my voice steady. "This will be fine."

"It really doesn't look very . . . comfortable."

I turned and saw Shay's jaw twitch as he watched the alpha's arms slide around my waist.

"Oh, I'm finding it very comfortable," Ren purred. My cheeks ignited when his lips brushed my neck. "Aren't you, Lily?"

Shay cringed at the sound of Ren's nickname for me. It took all of my will not to crack the alpha across the jaw. He was simply being cruel.

"It's fine."

I glared at Bryn, who was fluttering her eyelashes at me. Ansel had a foolish grin plastered on his face.

"Awww, look at that. It's just the most adorable thing I've ever seen." Mason dropped his chin into his hands. "What have you two been up to when the rest of us aren't around? Naughty, naughty."

Dax eyed us, a growl of pleasure rumbling in his chest. Fey winked at him and licked her lips. Nev looked up from the notebook he was scribbling in, raised an eyebrow, then went back to writing.

Bryn and Ansel were both making faces at me. Even Sabine giggled. Cosette glanced at her but fidgeted in her seat and couldn't manage a smile. Defeated, I leaned back against Ren, whose arms tightened around me, making me think about how low his hands were on my waist, the way his touch lit fires in places that, until recently, I'd hardly been aware of. Then I caught sight of the pain etched on Shay's face.

"Shut up, Mason."

I snatched the orange from my lunch and whipped it at him. He laughed as he caught it in midair.

"Don't mind us, Shay." Mason flashed him a smile. "We're just a bunch of wild animals."

"No joke." Dax flexed his arms.

A nervous titter rolled through the pack, but Shay smiled at Mason. "I've noticed, but some of you are more well mannered than others."

He glared at Ren, who returned the look with equal malice. Dax stopped smiling and Fey's lips curled back. I shot her a warning glare when I saw her sharp canines. She gave me hard, steel gray eyes but flattened her lips to hide her teeth.

"Well, this will be interesting." Mason pulled something silver from his pocket and tossed it to Shay. When Shay opened his palm, a Hershey's Kiss rested in his hand.

Mason winked at him. "Welcome to the table, man. I hope you survive."

"I think I'll manage." He turned the silver-wrapped chocolate in his fingers. "Thanks for this. There's nothing quite like a really good kiss."

His mouth crinkled in a smile and he cast me a sidelong glance, making my toes curl.

"You've got that right." Mason laughed, leaning back in his chair. "Now, then, for introductions . . ."

He grabbed Nev's hand, stopping him from writing. "Do it."

"Do what?" Nev asked, looking irritated at the interruption.

"The limerick." Mason grinned.

"No way." Nev scooted his chair back.

"Come on," Mason said. "It's great."

"There's a limerick?" Shay looked at Nev.

"It's not any good." Nev jerked his hand free.

"Nev's a poet." Mason pulled the notebook out of Nev's hands. He kept it out of Nev's reach while the other boy grabbed for it. "This is his collection. Shall we read it?"

Nev pointed his pen at Mason as if it were a knife. "If you show that to anyone, I will kill you."

"Once you do the limerick, I'll give it back." Mason sat on Nev's notebook. "I know you have it memorized."

"I have no idea why I'm nice to you," Nev muttered.

"My relentless charm," Mason said.

"Your relentless something," Nev replied.

"I'd like to hear it too," Ren said. He began to stroke my thigh. His scent was warm and soothing, but his touch made me tremble. *Please, please don't look over here, Shay.*

Nev tossed his pen down. "Fine. Here goes:

Ren and Cal's lives may be torrid
for the young ones in Vail are quite horrid
Bine and Cos aren't too frail

Dax and Fey never pale
while Ansel and Bryn might get sordid

Bryn spit Diet Coke all over the table. Mason and Ansel clapped. I was too dumbfounded to react.

This is what quiet Nev does in his spare time?

"'Bine'?" Sabine frowned while Cosette mopped up the soda that flowed to their end of the table. "Since when am I 'Bine'? And we never call Cosette 'Cos.'"

"It's about cadence," Nev said. "Sorry. I said it wasn't very good."

"Why aren't you and Mason in it?" Ansel asked.

"Oh, he has another one about us." Mason wiggled his eyebrows.

Nev pushed him out of his chair, and Mason hit the floor laughing.

"It was great," Shay said with a grin. "Can you say it again and I'll practice matching names to faces? It would help if you'd raise your hand when Nev says your name."

Nev looked at Ren, who nodded.

With a little less reluctance, Nev recited the limerick a second time. Each of my packmates raised a hand when his or her name was sounded, except Sabine, who just sniffed, and Fey and Dax, who gave Shay the finger when their turns came.

"Thanks." Shay inched his chair toward Bryn's, now knowing where his likely allies were sitting. Bryn smiled at him. Ansel shoved a handful of Fritos in front of our lunch guest.

Shay returned Bryn's smile, popping a corn chip in his mouth.

"Calla's told me a lot about you," he said between crunches.

"Has she?" Bryn cast an alarmed gaze at me. I gave a brief shake of my head, and she relaxed.

"It's 'cause we're so awesome." Ansel gave him a thumbs-up.

"Nice, baby brother," I muttered. "Very cool."

He blushed and Bryn kissed his cheek. "Ignore her. We are awesome. What's your story, Shay?"

"Not much of a story." He glanced at me and winked. I glared at him.

If you wink at me again, I'll be forced to pull your eyelashes out.

"I'm a senior," he said. "I live at Rowan Estate with my uncle."

There was a collective gasp around the table. Visions of empty halls and cobwebs filled my mind. I almost fell off of Ren's lap, but he caught and righted me with a chuckle. I bit my lip and glanced at Shay. I'd never given any thought to where he was staying in Vail, but now I couldn't believe what I was hearing.

It must be some mistake. That's an institution, not a home.

"Rowan Estate?" Ansel repeated. "I thought that was a museum or something. You live there?"

"Yes. My uncle owns it; he just doesn't live there very often. His job takes him around the world. I pretty much have the run of the house," he said. "I think he does have it open for historic tours when he's not in residence. You'd be welcome to come visit, if you'd like to see it." Shay flashed a bright smile at Ansel, who paled.

"That's very kind, Shay," I said. "But I'm sure your uncle would prefer to keep a rowdy crowd like us *away* from all those priceless antiques."

I would never let my brother pass through those doors. I didn't wish that on anyone.

"Whatever suits you." He turned his attention to his lunch, which as far as I could tell consisted of four granola bars and a Sprite.

"So what's it like to live there?" Bryn settled her chin on Ansel's shoulder. I smiled as my brother's eyes began to glow from her closeness.

Shay popped open his Sprite. "I can't complain about being cramped. It's gigantic, opulent. But kind of creepy, to be honest. Bosque, that's my uncle, is gone most of the time on business, so I'm there alone a lot. There's staff that comes in to clean a couple times a week. There are hundreds of rooms."

I shifted uneasily in Ren's lap, hating the thought of Shay alone in the enormous manor.

Shay lowered his voice, as if he were telling a ghost story. "It's the sort of place where the shadows seem to follow you around."

"Shadows?" Ansel asked.

I shook my head at Ansel, but I knew his worry was the same as mine.

Wraiths. The dark thought sent a shiver through my limbs.

Ren turned his face toward me. "You okay?"

I looked at him and my breath caught in my throat. Our faces were only inches apart; I could see each tiny silver fleck in his eyes, a swirling galaxy set against black depths. I felt myself getting lost in the velvet darkness of his irises.

"Calla, you're trembling. Are you all right?" His worried voice shook me out of the heady trance.

"I just remembered that I didn't finish the reading for Big Ideas today." I slid off his lap. "I've gotta run."

Without looking back at my packmates, I hurried in the direction of my locker and dove into the nearest girls' bathroom. I wasn't sure why my heart raced, nor why I felt so short of breath. All I knew was that I couldn't stand another moment balanced on the tightrope between Ren and Shay at that lunch table.

I checked the stalls to make sure I was alone. They were empty. I went back to one of the sinks, turned on the cold tap, and bent down to splash water on my face.

The bathroom door creaked open.

I guess two seconds of privacy was worth something.

"Calla." A strong hand gripped my shoulder, turning me around.

"Get out of here!" I shoved Ren back. "This is the girls' bathroom."

He grinned. "If anyone comes in, we'll tell them I got lost."

I scowled, trying to wipe my face with the back of my hand.

"You're really pale," he said. "What's going on?"

Water still dripped from my chin onto my neck. "Nothing. I just have work that didn't get done last night. I said that." I went to the paper towel dispenser.

A quiet growl stirred in his chest. "Nice try. You never forget homework."

Busted.

"Why did you follow me?" I turned to face the mirror, making a show of straightening my blouse. "I said I was fine."

An amused smile hovered on his lips. "You said you didn't want me to leave you alone."

I tossed the crumpled paper towel into the wastebasket. "Speaking of that, did you enjoy yourself today?"

His sharp laugh bounced off the bathroom walls. "Do you mean having you in my lap or the look on his face?"

"He knows about us, Ren." I leaned against the basin. "You don't need to be cruel."

"I think I can judge his level of respect for our relationship on my own. Are you aware of the way he looks at you?"

"Don't be silly," I snapped, but my cheeks grew hot.

"I'm completely serious," he said quietly. "He's not afraid of us the way humans should be. I'll tolerate him because of the Keepers' orders, but he's testing the limits of my patience when it comes to you."

I poked him on the chest. "You're jealous."

He didn't respond but instead covered my hands with his, welding them to the sink.

I bared my fangs at him. "When I said I didn't want you to leave me alone, I didn't mean at all times. And I'd like to be alone now. This isn't my idea of a romantic setting."

He shook his head. "Three things."

"What?" I frowned.

"One: what's really bothering you?" The worried lines around his eyes dissolved my anger.

"Wraiths. What Shay said about thinking shadows followed him around. I'm afraid they might be in that house, watching him when Bosque is away. He doesn't know about them." I shuddered. "It's so dangerous."

"You're worried about him." His eyes flickered with emotions too rapid for me to follow.

"We're talking about wraiths," I said. "Of course I'm worried. You know what they could do to him."

There was no use lying to him about my instinct to protect Shay. I couldn't hide it. Luckily, since it was also Logan's order, I didn't have to. At least not yet.

Ren's jaw clenched and he was silent for a moment. But then he seemed to make a decision, his conflicted expression fading.

"It is dangerous, if that really is the case. But we don't know. Plus the Keepers want Shay safe. It seems unlikely that they'd willingly endanger him. An untethered wraith would go after any human."

His grip on my hands relaxed. "I wouldn't worry. He's a strange kid. Probably just imagined the shadows."

"I hope so." I glanced at the door, worrying that someone would walk in on us. "Three things?"

"Two: would you like to go hunting with me after school?" He leaned closer, one corner of his mouth curving up.

"Hunting?"

"There's a deer herd that's getting too large on our side of the mountain."

My muscles twitched eagerly at the invitation, but I shook my head. "Thanks, that sounds great, but I can't."

"Why not?" Disappointment flickered across his face.

I bit my lip and decided to be honest. Sort of.

"So you know how Logan asked me to spend more time with Shay?"

He didn't speak, but I heard the rumbling, deep and menacing, in his chest.

"I'm helping him with homework every afternoon."

The growl erupted in sharp, biting words. "Every afternoon?"

"Orders are orders," I offered lamely.

"Right." The defeated note in his voice made me cringe.

"What's three?" I asked, hoping to move away from this uncomfortable topic.

The smile pulled at his lips again.

"Three." One of his hands cupped my face and the other slid around my back. He pulled my body against his and my heart began to pound. I took advantage of my free hand and pushed at his chest.

"I don't think so, Lily," he said. "If you want to get rid of me, you'll need to do better than that."

I drew a sharp breath and tried to wiggle away, but he held me firmly in place, watching me struggle. He grinned as he lifted me up onto the sink.

"What are you doing?" I started to panic. "Someone could come in!"

"If they see us, they'll just turn around and get out of here," he murmured, lips touching my ear. "No one crosses me."

His hips pressed against my knees, opening them, pushing my

skirt up my legs. I gripped his shirt, clinging to him so I wouldn't fall into the sink. His hand pushed into my lower back. I gasped as his body fitted against mine. Heat flooded my chest, my pelvis. I thought I would drown in it.

"We can't—" His lips stopped my words. The kiss just made me dizzier. I dug my fingers into his shoulders.

"You said you didn't want to be left alone." His tongue flicked over my cheekbone. "This is me pestering you."

"Aren't you breaking the rules?" I could barely get the words out. "What about the union?"

"I'd rather have you on my own terms." His hand slipped between my thighs.

All strength fled my limbs. "I can't breathe."

"That means you like it." He kissed me again.

A passing shadow caught my eye. "Ren, wait," I whispered against his lips. "I think—"

The bathroom door swung open.

"Oh my." Nurse Flynn didn't sound startled at all. "Am I interrupting?"

Ren swore under his breath. This was someone *he* couldn't cross. "Sorry, Ms. Flynn. I was just leaving."

I blushed when he rebuttoned my shirt. I hadn't even realized the blouse was hanging open. "Thanks for the chat, Lily. I'll see you in class."

He leaned in, brushing his lips along my forehead, and then flashed a winning smile at Nurse Flynn as he left the bathroom.

I squeezed my eyelids shut and gingerly slid off the sink. Somehow I managed to support my own weight. I'd been certain I would just puddle on the floor. In the darkness of my mind's eye I could still feel Ren's embrace, but then the image blurred and instead of the alpha, Shay smiled back at me. *I can't live like this.*

Rippling, musical laughter brought me back to the bathroom.

Nurse Flynn walked toward me, letting the door swing shut behind her.

"Poor, poor dear. Waiting must be so hard for you. I've heard Renier is an exquisite lover. All the Keepers gossip about him—the young Guardian who haunts their dreams."

The smile on her glossy red lips was teasing and cruel. "But rules are rules. He's an alpha male, so his . . . eagerness can be excused. Yours, however, is a disappointment."

I grabbed the sink when my stomach lurched.

"Careful now, little girl. Or I'll tell Logan how your union is progressing a little *too* well. You'd be wise to keep him happy. Those lovely legs of yours should be closed until Samhain." With slender, chalk white fingers she reached up and stroked my cheek. "I'll excuse your behavior this time. Don't stray from your path."

Her nails dug into my face, forceful enough to make me draw a sharp breath but not enough to break my skin. In a mockery of Ren's tenderness, she leaned in, pressing her lips against my forehead.

Lana Flynn's laugh became more of a cackle as she walked back out the door. I stared after her. When she'd turned away from me, I thought I'd seen the hump on her back twitch.

EIGHTEEN

SHAY SLAMMED THE LIBRARY BOOK SHUT,

giving it an abrupt shove. It sailed over the edge of the table, hitting the floor with a dull thud. It was the fifth time he'd done that since I'd taken a seat next to him at four o'clock.

"Do you want to have a fight now or are you just trying see how many book bindings you can break before we get kicked out of the library?"

His only response was a ferocious clicking on the keyboard of his laptop.

"Come on, Shay. Knock it off."

He leaned back in his chair. "Are you honestly all right with being treated that way?"

"What way?" I asked.

"Like a piece of property." The veins in his neck throbbed.

"That's not how it is." I got up and began restacking books on our table. "You just don't understand the way we interact. We're both alphas; we're always challenging each other."

"Of course," he said. I put my hand on top of the book closest to him so he couldn't throw it off the table too. "And how exactly do you challenge him?"

"That isn't any of your business." I pulled the book out of his reach. "Besides, none of that would have happened if you hadn't provoked him by insisting on sitting with us today. Ren only responded to your encroachment on his territory. What were you thinking?"

"See, you admit it!" he said. "You just referred to yourself as his 'territory.'"

"It's an expression, Shay," I countered. "And you have no business acting like the wronged party here. You're not innocent; you were challenging Ren about me and you know it."

He scowled, giving his full attention to his computer.

"Look." I buried my hands in my hair. "I've explained to you how things are. You can't change it."

"That's where you're wrong," he snapped. "On two counts. First—I don't know how things actually are—just how you say they have to be because of your Keepers' orders. I have no idea what you really feel about your little arranged marriage deal because you won't tell me."

I almost knocked the books back off the table.

"Second—I think it can change." The determination in his eyes terrified me.

"You're wrong and you need to stop pushing this issue. The kisses, then the lunch table. You don't know how dangerous what you're doing is. Ren is already jealous—"

"You *asked* for the first kiss and obviously wanted the second." He rocked back in his seat. "If he's jealous, that's fantastic. He should be."

I grabbed a book, retreating to my chair. "That is not a good thing. He's an alpha. You're acting like an interloper—a lone wolf. If he thinks you're interfering with his pack, his instinct would be to kill you."

A haughty smile slid across his mouth. "I'd like to see him try."

I was instantly at his side, leaning over him, my fingers digging into his shoulders. "Have you completely lost your mind? Ren is a Guardian; you could never fight him."

"Lost my mind?" he murmured. "Yes, sometimes I think so."

He lifted his hand and touched my face tentatively. His fingers trailed along my cheekbone and then gently moved over my lips.

"I've never felt this way about anyone before."

I haven't either. My lips parted under his touch. *I didn't know I could feel this way.*

When Ren touched me, it was like being swept up in a tornado of sensations, tossing my body into a wild abandon with no sense of control. Shay's gentle caress was different and somehow more addictive. The way his fingers lingered at my mouth seemed to ignite a flame that burned slowly, building heat, spreading through my cheeks, down my neck, finally consuming every inch of my skin with a fire so intense I didn't think it could ever be quenched. I knew if I stayed a moment longer, I'd let him kiss me again. Or I'd kiss him. I darted back to my seat, drew my knees against my chest, and hoped he wouldn't see that I was trembling.

"I've asked you not to do that," I said. "I don't want to be buried alive. And I don't think a public flogging is what you're after either."

He opened his mouth as if to protest, but then he shrugged.

"Fine. But if you could at all tolerate my presence, then I'd like to keep sitting with you at lunch. I actually had a really good time after you and Ren took off. I like your friends—your pack—Ansel and Bryn are great. And Mason, well, I've never met anyone like him. He's fantastic."

I didn't speak, but I nodded.

"Neville doesn't say much, but whenever he does, it's brilliant. The big guy, Dax, and the two mean girls, Sabine and Fey, they're a little scary, but still interesting," he mused.

"Dax is Ren's beta, like Bryn is to me," I said. "Dax, Sabine, and

Fey are just reacting to you the same way Ren is. You aren't afraid to challenge their alpha. It makes them instantly defensive. Not to mention that in a human, that kind of behavior is unheard of. The pack pretty much thinks you're crazy. Don't be surprised if they're making bets about how long it will be before Ren rips your throat out."

"Well, I don't exactly fit in with the other humans anymore," he said. "Not that I ever did."

He looked away. "That's the real reason I asked to start having lunch with you."

My chest contracted as I thought about how lonely Shay's life must be, probably more so now than ever.

"You can still sit with us. The pack is supposed to watch out for you anyway. Just watch yourself. If you don't provoke Ren, he won't strike back at you, like he did today."

"You know, you talk all the time about how strong you are—the Guardians, I mean," Shay mused. "I don't understand why you don't just fight back."

"Fight back?" I frowned at him. "Against who?"

"The Keepers. I don't know what happened that made you want to read this book, but you said you got orders you don't like. Why do you even follow orders in the first place?"

"It's our duty. The work we do is sacred." I tucked my legs beneath me. "And we're rewarded. The Keepers provide for our every comfort. Houses, cars, money, education. Anything we ask for, we're given."

"Except your freedom," Shay muttered, and I shot an angry glance at him. "So what would happen if you refused to follow an order?"

"That never happens," I replied. "Like I said, our duty is sacred. Why would we refuse?"

"In theory?" He gazed at me steadily. "I mean, it sounds like you're stronger than the Keepers."

"Physically stronger, yes." My voice trailed off as icy fingers crawled over my skin.

"Shay, when you said that you thought shadows followed you around at Rowan Estate," I said. "Did you mean that literally?"

"How could a shadow follow me literally?" He pointed at a medieval history text and I slid it over to him. "I mean, other than my own."

"Have you seen shadows, dark shapes that don't seem to be attached to regular objects in the house, moving around—above you, alongside you?" I tried to keep my voice steady.

"No. It's just a really old, creepy manor." He opened the book. "Why are you asking me this?"

"We can't fight the Keepers because they wouldn't fight us alone," I said.

He looked up. "What?"

"The Keepers have other allies, not just Guardians," I said. "We serve as their soldiers, and we protect the sacred sites. But the witches rely on wraiths to act as their personal guards."

"Wraiths?" I could see the fear abruptly born in his eyes.

I nodded. "Shadow guards. They aren't of this world. The Keepers can summon them at will. Nothing can fight a wraith, and they can be controlled only by Keepers. If, in theory, a Guardian disobeyed an order . . ." My voice quaked. "Or if they knew that I was here with you and this book, a wraith would be dispatched to deal with the situation."

"I see," he said slowly. "And you thought there might be wraiths in my uncle's house?"

"I thought it was possible that Bosque had summoned them to guard you while he was away. But it would be risky; without a Keeper there the wraiths could act unpredictably. You'd be in danger. I was worried." I twisted my fingers together nervously.

"All right." He shook his shoulders as if to brush away unpleasant thoughts. "If you're risking your life, we might as well be sure it's worth it. Let's get back to work."

I threw him a grateful smile. "Deal."

"I think I may have come across something interesting." He pulled the Keeper's text in front of him, flipping to its early pages.

I leaned forward but then stiffened and sat up. My eyes flickered to the tall bookcases that surrounded us.

"What's wrong?" Shay asked.

I waited and listened. Nothing.

"I thought I heard someone in the stacks." I shook my head. "Never mind. What did you find?"

"According to the history you've learned, when did the Witches' War begin?"

I frowned. "Before people even recorded history. Like I said, the Keepers are both earthly and divine, much older than the world we know."

"Not according to the book." He ran his finger over a passage.

"What?" I straightened.

"According to this text the first battle of the Witches' War took place in the late Middle Ages, around 1400," he said.

"That can't be right," I said.

"Do you want me to read it?"

I nodded.

He smoothed the page of notes in front of him. "'Anno Domini 1400: With the Rise of the Harbinger and the quickening of our power began the great schism and trials of our people.'" He paused. "Any of this familiar?"

"Not at all."

"That's too bad," he said, letting the book's cover fall shut. "I was hoping the Rise of the Harbinger would ring a bell. Sounds intriguing."

"I have no idea what a harbinger is," I said. "Or the quickening of power."

"I'd guess it means the Keepers got their magic in 1400."

"That doesn't make any sense." I turned his notes toward me. "The Keepers didn't get magic; they've always held great power."

"Unless . . ." He scooted his chair back an inch.

I eyed him warily. "Unless what?"

"Unless the story they told you isn't true."

"Why would they make up their own origin story?" I asked.

He looked relieved I hadn't pounced on him. "I don't know. You tell me."

"I have no idea," I said. "The story I told you is the only one I've ever known—that any of us know."

"I guess there isn't much to go on from here, then." He sighed.

I caught the scent a moment before something flickered on the edge of my vision.

"Calla!" Shay shouted, but I'd heard the buzz of the crossbow bolt and tipped over my chair. The bolt lodged in a book spine on the shelf that had been level with my chest a moment earlier. I sprawled on the floor, rolling just in time to see the Searcher taking aim again.

"No!" Shay shouted, jumping on the table and launching himself at the stranger. The Searcher grunted when Shay slammed against him, their entangled bodies tumbling along the floor.

"Shay, don't! Just get out of here!" I shifted into wolf form, muscles tensed.

"Over here, wolf girl." I turned to see another Searcher emerge from the stacks, a sword grasped in each hand. The blades flashed as they whirled in a lethal flurry of strokes.

I glanced toward Shay, still locked in combat, and then back at my new adversary. Both of the Searchers were young men, no more than twenty-five, and they seemed to be alone. Even so, they looked deadly: hardened faces, rough with shadows from lack of shaving, tangled nests of hair, and a feverish desperation in their eyes. I backed against the bookcase, snarling.

Shay struggled with the other Searcher. They wrestled on the floor, each straining for the advantage. The Searcher muttered unintelligibly, gritting his teeth as he attempted to overpower Shay, but he didn't reach for a weapon.

"Come on, kid," he hissed. "Ease off. I'm not going to hurt you. Just give me a chance to explain. Connor, get over here and give me a hand!"

Shay responded with a fist to the Searcher's jaw. And then another to his face.

"I'm serious, kid." The stranger spit blood, voice thick and suddenly nasal, and I guessed Shay had broken his nose. "We're here to help you."

"Stop messing around, Ethan, there's no time to get chatty. Fight back. One blow to the head won't kill him." Connor took his eyes off me for a second and I threw myself forward, sliding along the wooden floor beneath the sweep of the sharp blades.

Connor swore, turning to track me, but I raced around the table toward Shay. Ethan threw his arm up so that my jaws locked around his biceps instead of his throat. He shrieked, trying to rip his arm from my mouth, but I dug my fangs in deeper and pulled against him. Shay leapt to his feet and dashed around the other side of the bookcase.

"Get off him, bitch!" Connor shouted.

I jumped away from Ethan when Connor lunged at us. His momentum brought him down hard on top of his companion. Ethan yelled, but the sound cut off as breath whooshed from his lungs.

"Run, Calla!" Shay cried. I bolted to the side and an avalanche of books crashed down on the two Searchers. A rush of air passed through my fur as the shelves smashed against the floor, inches from my body.

I looked up to see Shay standing in front of the next row of stacks. I shifted forms, darted to him, and shook my head when I caught sight of the smirk on his face.

"Are you hurt?" My eyes flicked over him.

"What? No kiss?" He pointed at the motionless pile of books, wood, and Searchers. "I'm a hero."

"You're impossible," I said.

"Just trying to prove I'm as worthy as your wolf boy," he said. "Let's get the book and get the hell out of here."

Shay took two leaps across the jumble, swept the Keeper's book into his backpack, hooked his arm through the strap of my bag, and hurried back to me.

I gazed at the rubble of books and saw limbs peeking out; one of the Searchers' fingers twitched.

"I really should kill them," I murmured.

"I don't think that would be a great idea," Shay said, jerking his thumb toward the main area of the library. "We're about to have an audience."

"There was a horrible noise a moment ago. It came from back here." A startled patron appeared from around the corner with the reference librarian in tow.

"Oh my God!" The patron dropped his reading glasses. "Is someone trapped underneath all that?"

"Call 911! Did you two see what happened?" The librarian clutched at her chest and I worried she might be having a heart attack. "Do you know who it is?"

The patron had pulled out a phone but stared at the mound of paperbacks and hardcovers in mute disbelief. The librarian snatched the cell from his hand and began punching buttons and muttering. No heart attack, just a drama queen.

"No, ma'am," Shay said in a serious voice, offering wide, innocent eyes. "We just needed a quiet place to study. It didn't work out so well."

I couldn't stop the smile that pulled at my mouth when I grabbed his hand and we ran from the library.

NINETEEN

BLOOD MOON. SAMHAIN. BLOOD MOON.

Samhain. I made my way to class, unable to think of anything else. They were so close now, and I felt less certain than ever about both.

When I walked into Organic Chemistry, Ren flashed a broad smile.

"Lily."

I couldn't resist the challenge in his eyes. I aimed a kick at his shin, and he darted out of the way.

As we set up the lab, I glanced at the alpha. "Ren, what do you know about Samhain?"

He put on an overly thoughtful expression and wandered toward me. "Let's see, it is my birthday and yours. But of course, you already know that."

I blushed when he stepped behind me, encircling my waist with his arms.

His lips brushed against my ear. "I believe the answer that will not get me in trouble with you is: the happiest day of my life. Or something along those lines. Definitely not the end of my carefree days or when I get a ball and chain. Hmmm, I'm just realizing that I'm going to have to buy you birthday and anniversary presents at the same time. What a pain."

"Oh, please." I pushed him off with sharp jabs of my elbows.

His smile remained impish as he sidled back to the table and began to measure tea leaves. I flipped open my workbook.

"So we're extracting the caffeine from tea?"

"Looks like." He pulled out a set of scales.

I handed him a beaker and toyed with the pleats of my skirt. The folds kept rippling against my knees in a distracting way. It was one of Naomi's additions to my wardrobe. I quickly decided that I hated it.

"I was being serious. Samhain. Do you know anything about the rites?"

"Nothing besides the usual stuff," he said. "Spirit world, veil thins, blah, blah, blah." I ignored his wink. "But my father did say it's a dangerous night, that spirits are unpredictable when they have so much power."

I shuddered, wondering what sort of spirits might be present at the union.

He reached for the calcium carbonate.

"It was the day my mother died," he said quietly.

I froze in the midst of my attempt to light the Bunsen burner. Ren remained focused on the lab. Other than the tightening of his jaw, he gave no indication of distress.

"Your mother was killed on Samhain?" I breathed the question, thunderstruck. I had no idea that our union had been arranged to take place on the anniversary of Corinne Laroche's murder.

He kept his eyes on the scales. "It was a Searcher ambush . . . You know the story. An attack that successful hasn't occurred since."

I did know the story; all the young wolves did. It was the stuff of legends. The Searchers had attacked the Bane compound on the west side of the mountain. The ambush had occurred before dawn, while Corinne was home alone with her infant son. Several Bane Guardians, including Ren's mother, had been killed before the Keepers realized what was happening. The counter-assault against the Searchers had been brutal: the Keepers waged a six-month campaign to seek out and destroy the insurgents, who they'd discovered in various camps near Boulder. Before the incident outside Eden had occurred, the Searchers' blow against the Banes had been the last major attack in the region.

I felt goose bumps rising on my arms.

Ren glanced at me and smiled when he saw I was shivering. "It's all right, Calla. I barely remember her. And my job is to kill the people who took her away. Not a bad deal. That's justice, in a way."

I bit my lip, waiting for him to continue.

"Why are you trying to ruin the big surprise?" His lighthearted tone surprised me. "I thought you were a fan of the Keepers' rules."

"It would be nice to know *something* about what we're supposed to do," I muttered.

He pointed at the Bunsen burner. "Are you going to light that? We have to heat this for twenty minutes"—he looked down at his workbook—"while stirring."

"Yeah. Sorry." I grabbed the lighter, hurrying to start the flame.

"Do you want to stir?" He placed the beaker over the wire gauze.

"Sure," I said. He handed me a glass rod.

Stirring proved rather dull. I sighed, leaning against the lab station. Ren reached out to catch one of the many pleats of my skirt between his fingertips.

"This skirt kind of looks like an accordion." He laughed. "Not that it isn't lovely on you."

"Thanks," I replied drily. "I believe they are actually called 'accordion pleats.' At least that's what my mother tells me."

"So I've been thinking about how we're supposed to be officially dating now."

"What about it?"

"Would you like to have dinner with me?"

"You mean go on a date?" I focused on stirring instead of my suddenly racing heart. "When?"

"Before the union. Have dinner with me and I'll take you to Blood Moon for a couple of hours until it's time for the ceremony." His fingers moved from the pleats to the hem of my sweater, his hand slipping under the pale blue cashmere to stroke the skin of my lower back.

I gasped, caught his wrist in my fingers, and pulled his hand away from its provocative exploration.

"We are in class," I hissed at him through clenched teeth.

I glanced around and noticed several pairs of eyes quickly averted. Ashley Rice kept her glare on me. I couldn't bring myself to look in Shay's direction.

Grinning, Ren tried to free his hand from my fierce grip. "You're supposed to be stirring."

"Behave yourself." I released his wrist, giving him a final warning pinch before I returned to my task.

"Not likely," he answered, but contented himself with clasping my free hand. A warm glow spread from my fingers to the crown of my head.

"So would you like to have dinner and go to the ball? I thought it would be nice to have some time alone." His thumb stroked the back of my hand and my knees buckled.

I cleared my throat. "Alone?"

"Yes," he said. "I had to live with Dax as a hunting partner after you shot me down. Though I can't claim the hunt itself was disappointing—he took down a twelve-point buck on his own."

I raised an eyebrow. "That's impressive."

"Definitely," he said. "All the same, Dax wasn't the partner I was hoping for. You've been so busy taking care of Logan's boy that I haven't had any time with you at all."

"Be nice."

"I just think we deserve a real date, don't you?"

"I suppose we do." I could hear the strain in my own voice; I was already anticipating Shay's reaction to this development.

"You wouldn't like that?" The playful note in his voice began to fade.

I fumbled for a response. "No. I mean—yes, I would like to have dinner with you. I'm just surprised. I thought the whole pack would go to the ceremony as a group."

He leaned toward me, murmuring, "I think one-on-one sounds better, don't you?"

His teeth gently caught my earlobe. All my muscles turned to liquid. I dropped the stirring rod and grabbed the edge of the table so I wouldn't collapse.

Ren straightened in alarm. "Are you okay?"

I just nodded, not trusting myself to speak. He smiled, turning back to the workbook. "Okay, what's next? We're supposed to have a cheesecloth. Where's our cheesecloth?"

He searched the table while I tried to remember how to breathe.

I kept a safe distance from the alpha for the remainder of the lab. He was in a dangerously playful mood, and my reactions to his attention were erratic enough that I worried he'd startle me into spilling flammable liquid and igniting our entire station.

When I was walking from class to collect my lunch from my locker, Shay fell into step beside me.

I glanced at him. "Are you walking with me to the cafeteria?"

He kicked a discarded Coke can, sending it clattering down the hallway. "Ren was friendly today, wasn't he?"

Great. "You don't have to watch us all through chemistry."

"I didn't have to be watching to notice." He made a disgruntled noise. "He was all over you."

I blushed. "Ms. Foris didn't say anything, so I think you're exaggerating."

"Ms. Foris would never say anything. She's terrified of both of you."

I shrugged. He was absolutely right.

An awkward silence descended as we walked to my locker. I was relieved when Shay finally spoke.

"Do you want to go to a coffee shop or something tonight? I assume the library is out."

"Definitely out," I said. "But I can't get coffee."

"Why not?"

"My mother is having a thing," I mumbled. "Some union stuff I have to do."

"Oh." He leaned against the locker next to mine while I hunted for my lunch. "What kind of stuff?"

I wanted to crawl inside my locker and hide. "Girl stuff."

"Sounds enthralling," I heard him say, though I'd buried my head in my jacket.

I stopped imitating a frightened ostrich and grabbed my lunch bag. "Okay. Let's go eat."

Shay strolled alongside me, humming "Here Comes the Bride," until I punched him in the kidney.

TWENTY

"OW!" I JERKED AWAY FROM SABINE'S PIN-

filled fingers. It was the third time she'd stuck me and I was convinced she was doing it on purpose.

"Sorry," Sabine said, not sounding sorry at all.

"Calla, you must keep still," my mother muttered. "Sabine, be more careful."

"Yes, Naomi," she replied, bowing her head, but I saw her smirk. If I hadn't been weighed down by fabric, I would have kicked her.

Bryn stood in front of me, assessing the progress of the gown. "I think it needs to be gathered here." She pointed at my left shoulder.

My mother stood up. "Good eye, Bryn. Sabine, we'll need more pins up here."

I grabbed Sabine's shoulder. "If you stick me again, I'm going to make your head my personal pin cushion."

"Calla, that is no way for a lady to address her liege," my mother clucked. "Cosette, how is that hem coming?"

"Nearly there," Cosette said from somewhere beneath me. I couldn't see her for all the swells of taffeta.

"Damn it, Sabine!" I rubbed the new stinging spot at my shoulder. "If I bleed all over this gown, you'll be sorry."

"I'm not breaking the skin." Sabine didn't cover her smile.

"You'll probably end up with blood all over it anyway," Fey said from the corner she'd tucked herself in. She'd stayed as far from the dressmaking activity as she could, acting as though touching silk might infect her with the pretty princess virus.

My mother bared fangs at her. "Fey!"

I swayed on the pedestal that Mom had brought to my room for the dress fitting. Bryn grabbed my waist to keep me from falling.

"Ow," I said weakly as more pins pushed into my skin.

"Sorry," she said, loosening her grip.

"What is she talking about?" I looked at my mother, who was shaking her head.

"How do you know about the ceremony?" She glared at Fey again.

"Sorry, ma'am." Fey stared out my bedroom window. "Dax overheard Emile talking about it with Efron."

"Dax should learn to use more discretion," my mother said.

Bryn stayed where she was, seeing that I was still unsteady.

"Mom, please," I murmured. "Can't you tell me anything?"

My mother ran her tongue over her lips, looking over the anxious girls in the room.

"I can tell you a little," she said quietly. "And I assure you, there will be no blood on this gown."

I started to breathe again. "Oh, good."

"Because you'll be a wolf when you make the kill," she finished.

"Kill?" I caught my reflection in the tall mirror. I looked like one of Henry VIII's wives who'd been told she'd soon be replaced.

"Come on, Cal." Fey grabbed a tattered teddy bear from my dresser, and I worried she'd rip its head off. "The kill is probably going to be the only fun part of the night."

"Until Ren takes her to bed," Sabine purred.

Fey's laugh was like a roar. Even Cosette's muffled giggles floated up from under the layers of fabric.

"Shut up, Sabine." Bryn kicked her and I grinned.

"Honestly, girls." My mother put her hands on her hips. "You're acting like barbarians."

She reached up and held my face between her palms. "Calla, the ceremony is beautiful. We'll wait for you in the sacred grove—except for Bryn, who will guide you to the ritual site. She'll leave you alone. Drums will raise the forest spirits, and the warrior's song is the last thing you'll hear before you're called to join us."

"Who calls me?"

"You'll know," she murmured, smiling. "I don't want to give everything away. The mystery of the ritual makes it special."

Special? I stared into her misty eyes, not feeling special, only anxious. "What about the kill?" *This is what my parents were worried about.*

She took her hands from my face, folding them in front of her. "It's a trial, a public demonstration that you and Ren have the mutual skill to lead your pack."

"We hunt together?" I couldn't imagine how that would work. "And the Keepers watch?"

"Your prey will be presented at the end of the ceremony," she said, smoothing the front of my gown. I winced when another pin pricked me.

"What's the prey?" Bryn took my hand, her own fingers shaking.

"You won't know until that night," my mother said. "The surprise is part of the challenge."

"What was it when you were united to Stephen?" Sabine asked. I was startled to see her fingers laced tightly together, as if the news about a kill frightened her as much as me.

My mother walked to the dresser and picked up a brush. She was quiet as she came behind me and began pulling the bristles through my hair.

Just when I was certain she wouldn't tell us, she said, "A Searcher. One we'd captured."

"Oh," I said. The face of the Searcher I'd fought outside Eden flashed in my mind. I remembered his screams in Efron's office. *Could he still be alive? Would the Keepers drag him out of some secret prison only to throw him at our feet at the ceremony?*

A buzzing sound came from my bed. Fey dug under a heap of crinoline until she found my phone. "Should I answer it?"

"Who is it?" I asked.

She glanced at the screen. "Shay."

The brush stopped mid-stroke. "Who's Shay?" my mother asked.

"The human kid we're babysitting for Logan." Fey tossed the phone to me.

"Mom!" I yelped, barely managing to catch my phone as she jerked a fistful of my hair.

I heard the brush hit the ground, and in the next moment my mother stood before me. Her face was paler than the rumpled sheets on my bed. "The Keepers' human is calling you? Why?"

"You know about Shay?" The phone was still vibrating in my hand.

"I—" She bent down, picking up the brush. "I may have heard something from Lumine. I didn't know the boy's name."

"What did Lumine say about him?" I watched as she busied herself tidying my nightstand.

"It's not important." She didn't look up. "I didn't realize you were on familiar terms."

"Too familiar," Sabine muttered.

"What do you mean?" My mother looked at her and then at me. "Are you fraternizing with young men other than Ren? That's shameful!"

I tried to kick Sabine and would have tipped over if Bryn hadn't caught me.

"Of course she isn't, Naomi," Bryn said. "Logan has asked Calla to watch over Shay. Keep him safe."

My mother's face went even whiter. "Why would he—"

She fell silent and started to fluff the pillows. I glanced at my buzzing phone, unsure what to do.

"Naomi, didn't you say we'd have dessert and presents soon?" Bryn asked. "I think we could use a break."

"Yes, yes!" My mother looked relieved, heading for the door. "I've prepared tea and petit fours. We'll enjoy refreshments in the parlor."

"Thanks, Bryn," I whispered as the other girls followed my mother out the door.

She squeezed my arm before running to catch Fey, who turned to her with a frown. "What the hell is a petit four?"

I flipped open the phone. "Hey."

"Calla." Shay sounded surprised. "I didn't think you'd pick up."

"Yeah." The sound of my mother giving instructions on the correct placement of china and silver drifted up the stairs. "I only have a couple minutes."

"This will be quick," he said. "I think I realized why we can't find anything useful in the library."

"Why?"

"Something was bugging me about those alchemy symbols," he said. "You know the ones in the picture with the cross?"

"Uh-huh."

"So I did some hunting, and that's not the only place they are." I heard the rustling of pages. "There's a triangle on the map. The one I used to get up the mountain. Right on the cave."

"There's a triangle on Haldis Cavern?"

"Yes," he said. "An upside-down triangle cut by a single line."

"That's earth," I said, mentally reviewing the alchemy symbols. "The cave must have something to do with the elemental power of earth."

"You don't know what's in the cave?" Shay asked.

"*In* the cave?" I repeated. "I assumed it was the place that mattered. The Keepers have always referred to it as a sacred site. You think there's something inside?"

"I think we should find out."

"You're serious?"

"We can't go back to the library after the Searchers attacked us there," he said. "You've already pointed that out. But we have to try something."

"I'm not sure." My mouth went dry. "The cavern is at a high elevation. There will already be a lot of snow up there."

"I'm a good climber. I'll manage," he said. "I know I can do it, Cal."

"It would have to be on a Sunday, when Bryn and I patrol," I mused. "Getting rid of Bryn isn't a problem. She'd jump at the chance to spend the day alone with Ansel. But we might not be able to make the climb quickly enough to get to the cavern and back before the next Nightshade patrol showed up. Well, I could do it . . ."

"Don't think for a sec that I'll let you go without me."

My mother appeared in the doorway, waving a doily at me. "Calla, time for presents and games! Do you need help getting out of your dress? Be careful not to lose any pins."

"Games?" I felt a little sick.

"Games?" Shay's laughter crackled in my ear. "Are you having a bridal shower over there? No wonder you wouldn't tell me what you were doing. You must be miserable."

I put my hand over the phone. "I'll be down in a sec, Mom."

"It's rude to keep guests waiting," she said sourly before she disappeared back down the stairs.

"Calla?" Shay said. "Are you there?"

I stared at my reflection, imagining how much fun it would be to shred the dress into the world's most expensive confetti. "I'm here. Sorry."

"So when are we going?"

Shay's eager tone made me want to laugh and cry. Samhain was only a little more than a week away. Once the union took place, there would be no sneaking off with Shay. I wondered if I'd be able to see him at all. "This Sunday. We're going to the cave this Sunday."

"In three days?" he said. "Oh, man, I was excited about my brilliant plan. Now I'm just nervous."

"You should be. I'll see you tomorrow."

"Aren't you going to tell me about your dress?"

I hung up on him.

"I'm coming, Mom!" I shouted, hopping off the pedestal.

I'd made it two steps out of my room when my foot caught on the hem of my dress and I tumbled forward, falling flat on my face. I tried to right myself but couldn't find my way out of the endless pink, gold, and ivory layers that cocooned me. With every movement, pinpricks stung me like a swarm of angry bees.

When Bryn finally dug me out of my silken prison, I was still screaming.

TWENTY-ONE

"SO WHAT ARE YOU DOING TONIGHT?" SHAY

asked as we walked out of Big Ideas.

"Outlining this essay." I tapped my notebook. "I'm starting to fall behind because of . . . everything."

"Can I come over?" he asked, holding up his full page of notes. "We could do it together."

"I don't think it would be a great idea for you to be at my house."

"Why not?" He held my books while I opened my locker.

"My mother wouldn't like it."

"But I'm such a nice boy."

"That doesn't—ouch!"

Ansel had nailed me in the back with a soccer ball. "Score!"

I grabbed a water bottle from my locker, squirting him in the face.

"Good comeback." He grinned, wiping his face. "But you shouldn't shoot the messenger."

"You're still breathing," I said. "What's the message?"

"Nev's playing at the Burnout tonight. He asked us to come."

"What's the Burnout?" Shay asked.

"It's a bar just west of town." I slipped on my jacket. "More of a shack than a bar, really."

"Come on, Cal. You love it there," Ansel said, bouncing the soccer ball on his knees. "Don't pretend dive bars aren't up your alley. Besides, we haven't done anything with both pa—, er, all of us since Eden. We need to blow off steam. Together."

"What time?" I asked.

"Ten."

"I don't know." I glanced at Shay. Ansel followed my gaze.

"You should come too, Shay. Hang out with us tonight," he said. "We have a good time even when we're not eating lunch."

"How will you guys get past the doorman?" Shay asked. "Or do you all have fake IDs I don't know about yet?"

"Nev's got an in with the owner," Ansel said. "No IDs needed."

"Sounds great." Shay threw a wicked smile at me.

"Uh, yeah." I swallowed a groan. "That sounds just great."

Ansel beamed. "Mason's gonna pick us up after nine. It's just off Highway 24, Shay. There's a gravel road on the right. Follow it and you'll get to the bar."

"I'll be there," Shay said.

I rummaged through my coat pocket, tossing Ansel keys. "You can drive us home, An. I'll meet you at the car in a sec."

"Really? Cool!" He made a dash for the parking lot before I could change my mind.

Once he was out of earshot, I glared at Shay. "Are you insane?"

"For wanting to hear Nev play?" Shay smiled placidly. "I don't think so. I hear he's good. Though I suppose Mason's opinion might be biased."

"You know what I mean." I didn't smile back. "Ren will be there."

"That seems likely."

I couldn't stop thinking about both boys in the same dark, cramped bar. The night spelled disaster in garish neon lights.

"He'll want . . ." I bit my lip.

"To be your boyfriend?" Shay's eyebrow shot up. "In public?"

I dropped my gaze and nodded.

"I understand."

"Thanks, Shay," I said, relieved he wasn't putting up a fight. "I do wish you could come hang out."

"Really?" He grabbed the top of my locker door, swinging it back and forth. "And why is that?"

I frowned. "Can't you just take it at face value?"

"I don't think so." His lips curved playfully. "No."

"Why are you always so difficult?" His smile made my chest ache, reminding me of how much his mischief could make me laugh. It would be a stressful night without his company to take the edge off my anxiety.

"Just tell me."

"I don't know if it matters, but I'll miss you." I edged closer to him. "Sunday feels like a long time from now."

The minute the words were out of my mouth, I bit my lip.

Why did I just say that? I should never say anything like that.

"That's nice to hear." Shay's smile was dangerous. "But I'm still coming tonight."

"What?" My heart skipped a beat. "But I just told you—"

"I know, Calla," he said, squeezing my hand. "See you tonight."

I stared at him. He just laughed and walked away.

Mason turned his Land Rover up the gravel drive. The imposing vehicle looked out of place next to the motorcycles and muscle cars that belonged to the bar's regulars.

Bryn unbuckled her seat belt. "I don't know why we had to come here. I'd much rather be at Eden."

"Nev doesn't play at Eden," Mason said. "Besides, it's good to be well rounded."

"Trust me, this is better than Eden." My gut knotted at the

thought of returning to Efron's club. Mason and I exchanged a glance. We didn't say it, but I knew what we were both thinking. Logan would never show his face at the Burnout.

Ansel slid his arms around Bryn's waist, pulling her from the car. "You'll have a good time and you know it."

She pouted until he kissed her, and then she beamed.

The Burnout had been built on the remains of a roadside café ravaged by fire a decade earlier. Rather than tear out the ruined building, the new management had simply built the bar around and over the old site. Charred, smoke-stained wood appeared throughout the small space like misplaced modern art. The hardwood slats that composed the floor had a definite upward slope, so sharp at some points that it was easy to trip over.

The only light in the bar flickered from the variety of neon beer signs that hung along the walls. A haze of smoke hung in the air like a veil, filling my nostrils, masking other scents. A collection of grizzled regulars perched on mismatched stools along the bar, and leather-clad bikers clustered at tables in the more-shadowed corners of the room. A squat platform that served as the stage faced the bar.

Neville sat on the edge of the stage with his legs dangling off, guitar at a casual angle across his lap. Shay leaned against the platform. Nev caught sight of us and gave a brief nod. Ansel and Mason immediately headed for the stage.

Bryn laced her fingers through mine. "Their music talk gets pretty intense. Want to grab a seat?"

I followed her gaze to the opposite side of the room, where Ren, Dax, Fey, Sabine, and Cosette sat together.

"Sure."

As we approached the table, Ren got up, stretching his hand out to me. "Glad you're here."

My pulse stuttered, but I walked to him, letting him tuck me into the curve of his body and lead me to the chair beside his.

"Thanks," I murmured into the folds of his leather jacket before we sat down. Bryn sank into the chair on the other side of me.

"Hey guys." I smiled at the other wolves. "Good to see you."

"Hey Calla," Dax said.

Sabine smiled briefly. Cosette spoke too quietly for me to hear her over the buzz of the bar crowd.

"Fey." I glanced at my packmate as I settled into the chair. "Mason said Dax gave you a ride here."

"Yeah." She edged her seat closer to Dax.

I opened my mouth but thought again and kept quiet. *Better to see how this plays out.*

Ren looked toward the stage, his eyes settling on Shay.

"Your fan club arrived earlier. He's been waiting for you."

I bit the inside of my cheek. *It will be a miracle if I make it through this night.*

"Ansel invited him."

"I'll have to thank him for that," Ren said with a smile full of knives.

"I think it's a good thing," Bryn said, sounding a little defensive. "Logan wanted us to look out for him. Calla shouldn't have to do all the heavy lifting. It's a pack responsibility."

"Of course." Ren's irritated tone faded. "We should help her take care of the kid."

"We'll see if he can hold his own outside of school." Dax grinned.

Fey whispered in his ear and he laughed loudly.

"Something you'd like to share?" I leaned over, catching her wrist in a vise grip.

She tried to twist out of my grasp. "Not really."

Bryn drew in a hissing breath and Fey stopped struggling.

"Sorry, Cal. I didn't mean any disrespect," she said quickly. "It was an inside joke."

"I understand." I stared her down until she looked away. I dropped her wrist when Ren squeezed my shoulder.

"Easy now," he said. "It's our night off. Dax, go get another round for the table."

Dax nodded, patting Fey's thigh before he went to the bar.

Ansel, Mason, and Shay settled into the other chairs at the table.

"Hey guys." Ren offered them an easy smile. "Glad you could join us, Shay." I tried not to notice the sudden sharpness of Ren's expression, that of a wolf on patrol.

"Isn't that the bartender from Eden?" Bryn's eyes were on the stage.

Two men had ascended the platform with Neville. I recognized the Bane from the club, but now he had a bass slung over his shoulder.

"That's Caleb," Mason said. "And yeah, he works at Eden. He's a good friend of Nev's."

"Who's on the drum kit?" Ansel asked.

"Tom," Mason said. "He owns this place, and he likes to sit in with the local musicians who play here."

Neville spoke into the mike. Even amplified, it was tough to hear his quiet voice over the din.

"Sabine. We could use you. Why don't you get up here and bring your chair."

My packmates all looked at her with surprised expressions, while the Banes just smiled at each other. Ren dragged my chair even closer to his, slipping his arm around my waist. I met Shay's eyes for a moment before looking back at the musicians, feeling like I might as well be the rope in a tug-of-war.

Sabine went to the stage, dragging her chair along. Nev handed her a tambourine and put a mike in front of her.

"What's going on?" Bryn asked.

"Sabine sings backup for Nev. Sometimes they do duets," Ren said. "She's got a great voice."

"Really?" Bryn said, grabbing a handful of peanuts. "Who'd have thought?"

Cosette glared at her.

"Evening." Nev's voice drew our attention. "I'm Nev. Caleb's on bass, you all know Tom, and the lovely Sabine is gracing us with her presence tonight."

The only applause came from our tables. Apparently the other bar patrons weren't here for the music.

Neville nodded at Tom. The bar owner and Caleb exchanged a quick glance and in the next moment, bass and drums had set off at a slow, grinding rhythm. A smile ghosted across Neville's lips; his fingers moved over the guitar strings, and he began to sing.

Mason flashed a grin at me and I nodded. *Yeah. I get it now.*

Sabine took up the harmony. Her voice was sweet and dark like the first shadows of twilight. The music poured into my veins, a mixture of grit and silk. Subtle and intoxicating.

The Banes leaned forward in unison, drawn into the pulse of Neville's song. My own limbs felt like they were humming with the bass line.

I could see Bryn's feet sliding over the floor, moving along an invisible river of sound. She looked at Ansel, eyes alight. "So I was promised there would be dancing."

"Already?" Ansel objected. "I'd kind of like to just listen for a while."

Her lips cut into a thin line, but Shay spoke up.

"I'll dance." He turned to my brother. "If you don't mind."

"Ladies' choice." Ansel gestured to Bryn.

Bryn couldn't quite hide her startled expression, but she quickly offered Shay her hands and a playful smile. "Let's go, then."

Shay led her onto the uneven floor. A few interested glances from bikers passed over the two of them as they began to move together in front of the stage. Neville nodded, smiling as Shay slipped his arms around Bryn and guided her body with his.

"Huh," Ansel murmured. "He's good."

"Nervous?" I laughed.

He grinned at me. "Hardly. She's not the one Shay's after."

"I wonder where you got that idea." Ren's hand tightened on my waist.

Ansel cowered. "Sorry, man. I wasn't thinking."

"I suppose he's a decent dancer." Ren's dark eyes flashed. "But I think we should show him how it's really done."

I tensed but was more than surprised when he turned to Cosette. "Feel like dancing?"

Her large eyes went even wider, but she smiled shyly and nodded. He took her hand and they left the table. Dax grabbed Fey's arm and they followed the other couple.

I couldn't stop my frown.

"That was weird," Ansel said. "You okay?"

"Fine," I said, trying to ignore my irritation at Ren's sudden departure with Cosette.

Is this what it will be like after the union? Will he go off with other girls whenever he feels like it?

"Don't worry about it, Calla," Mason said. "Shay's a thorn in his paw and he's trying to make you think he doesn't care."

"Never mind," I said, embarrassed by their concern. "I don't need to dance with Ren."

Mason tapped out a quick rhythm on the table with his knuckles. "But you do need to dance."

He stood up, offering me his hand.

"Great, the only one without a partner," Ansel said as I rose. "Where's Sabine when I need her?"

"I think Sabine might bite you before she danced with you," I said.

"True enough." He grinned. "I'll just wait for Bryn to remember she likes me."

"Good plan," Mason said, pulling me away from the table.

We'd barely made it alongside the stage when the music took a decidedly slower turn.

"How romantic." Mason kissed me on the cheek.

I laughed, following his slow circles over the bumpy floor.

Mason's arms suddenly dropped from my waist, and another set of hands moved along my hips.

"I'll take it from here, Mason," Ren said from directly behind me.

"Of course." Mason inclined his head.

Ren turned me in his arms.

"That was rude," I said, more irked by his earlier abandonment than the interruption. "You could have waited."

He just smiled. "No. I wanted to dance with you now."

"Fine. We're dancing. Are you happy?"

"Almost." He brushed his lips against my forehead. I focused on not tripping over the slanted floor.

"Don't you want to know what would make me happy?" he teased.

"I'm not sure." The stormy darkness of his irises made my skin crackle, electric.

"Let me give you a ride home tonight." He reached into his pocket. "I want to show you something."

"What?"

There was a flash of silver before my eyes. Keys.

"Our house."

I stared at him and then at the keys again. "Our house?"

"At the new compound. It's ready. I asked Logan if I could take a look and he just handed the keys over. I'm sure I could get you a set if you want."

"Our—*Our* house?" I stammered again.

"Yes, Calla." He grinned. "It's that place we'll be living together after the union. When we're the alpha pair. Remember how that works?"

"You want to go there tonight?"

"Just to check it out."

"And Logan said it was okay?"

"Logan doesn't have to know I brought you along." He jangled the keys in front of me. "Besides, aren't you curious?"

"A little." I was even more curious about what Ren wanted to *do* when we got there.

He smiled, sliding his arm back around my waist.

My eyes narrowed. "And you'll take me right home after we see it?"

"If that's what you want," he said softly, running his thumb along my cheekbone. "But I'd be tempted to see if I could convince you to stop acting like the proper lady your mother wants you to be."

"So you did hear her." I groaned, blushing. *As if I want to be a lady. All it means is that I have to pretend I don't feel anything but a sense of duty.*

"I can't blame her for wanting to protect your virtue," he said, grinning. "I'd like to be in her good graces, but maybe I could have a little slumber party with you at our new house. It would be our secret. I promise I won't kiss and tell."

I kicked his shin lightly. "I can't believe you. Just stop it."

"Or maybe that would spoil the anticipation," he continued, eyes merciless. "I'm pretty limber. I'm betting I could get onto the roof, swing down, and sneak in through your bedroom window. Surprise you some evening in the near future."

I froze in his arms. "You wouldn't."

"No, I wouldn't." He laughed. "Only if you asked."

My heart's rapid drumming countered the slow rhythm of Nev's song.

"This is where you belong, Calla." He pulled me closer, tilting my chin up. "Be with me. Tell me it's what you want."

I couldn't tear my eyes from his. "What I want?"

"Yes. Anything, everything you need, I'll give you. Always. I promise. Just tell me one thing."

"What?"

"That you want this, us." His voice dropped so low I could barely hear him. "That someday you'll love me."

My hands began to tremble where they rested around his neck. "Ren, you know we're going to be together. We've both known that for a long time."

He gave me a hard look. "That's not what I'm talking about."

"Why are you asking me this?" I tried to pull back, but he held me against him.

The glimmer of a smile appeared on his lips. "Why not?"

My temper flared. "Are you trying to say that *you* love *me*?"

I meant it as a challenge rather than a serious question, but his eyes seemed to catch fire.

"What do you think?" He touched his lips to mine, softly at first, gradually building pressure, parting them. Startled, I stiffened in his arms. But he continued to caress my lips with his own, gentle and measured, but insistent. I sank into the kiss, drowning in Ren's warmth, moving slightly against the weight of his hands on my waist, knowing it would make him pull me closer to his body.

The crash of wood and shattering glass brought me back to the room.

Damn it. I knew this was a terrible idea.

I whirled, expecting to see Shay charging toward us. But he wasn't looking at us. No one was.

The music had stopped. The table where the young wolves had been sitting was turned on its side. Glasses lay broken on the floor; those that remained intact were rolling along the slanted hardwood into the far corner of the room. Dax held a fistful of Mason's shirt and stood snarling at him. It looked as though Mason had caught Dax's other fist mid-swing, and he now grasped the larger boy's hand in his own, pushing it away from him. Fey stood alongside Dax. Ansel's hands dug into Dax's forearm, and he struggled to pull the Bane away from Mason. Shay stood just behind Ansel, muscles tensed. Bryn had half risen from her chair and glared at Fey.

Ren pulled away from me. "What the hell?"

He bolted toward Dax, with me at his heels.

Mason's face was twisted in a scowl. "You have no right."

"And you need to learn to keep your mouth shut."

"Stop being an ass." Ansel tugged on Dax's arm but didn't manage to move him an inch.

"He's right, Dax," Shay said. "What's your problem?"

"Shut up and stay out of it," Fey snapped.

Neville shoved his guitar at a startled Sabine, jumped off the stage, and came to Mason's side. He glared at Dax. "Knock it off, man. What do you think you're doing?"

Dax ignored him.

I glanced around the bar, worrying we were about to get booted. But the rest of the patrons had returned to their drinks, unconcerned by a run-of-the-mill brawl.

Ren gripped Dax's shoulder. "Let him go, get outside, and wait for me. Now."

Dax released his hold on Mason's shirt, throwing one last angry glance at him before turning and walking out of the bar. Fey took a few steps after him.

"Where do you think you're going?" I blocked her path.

"Sorry, Cal." There was a flash of steel in her eyes. "I'm with him on this one."

"Watch yourself, Fey," I growled.

She didn't balk. "Do you have a problem with me?"

"I'll let you know when I've heard what happened."

"Fine." She stepped around me, running after Dax.

Neville started to follow them, his eyes livid.

Ren grabbed his arm. "Get back onstage and start playing again. Whatever just happened, it's over."

"But—"

"I'm fine, Nev." Mason put his hand on Neville's shoulder. "We'll sort this out. Go play."

With some reluctance Nev headed back to the stage, and a moment later, the music picked up again, though on a noticeably angrier riff.

"Someone want to tell me what's going on?" I asked.

"It was nothing." Mason helped Cosette right the table. "Like Ren said, it's over now."

"It wasn't nothing," Ansel protested.

"What happened?" Ren asked.

"Really, let's not make a big deal out of it," Mason said, his face drawn. "He lost his temper, that's all."

"I don't think you can just drop it, Mason," Shay said quietly. "It is a big deal. Dax was out of line."

I turned to Bryn. "What did Dax do?"

She glanced at Mason and Ansel. "He didn't like something Mason said . . . about Neville."

Ren's jaw tightened. "I see."

He started toward the door, and I was right behind him. We were halfway across the room when he turned abruptly.

"I'll take care of it, Calla."

"I should be there," I said. "This affects both of us."

He shook his head. "I can handle this. Dax already knows he's in for it. It would be better if you stayed here and tried to convince the rest of them that it's going to be okay."

"All right." It was already happening. Ren was in charge now.

I watched him leave the bar.

How am I supposed to convince anyone that things will be okay? Nothing feels okay.

I was so angry my muscles began to ache from tension. I hated being treated like an inferior. I'd always led my pack and suddenly it was as if all those years of being their alpha meant nothing. I was only Ren's mate. I felt a hand on my shoulder and turned to find Shay standing beside me.

"That was pretty intense."

I nodded. "It's a problem. Dax and Fey aren't handling Nev and Mason's relationship very well."

"I noticed that." He glanced at the door. "What do you think Ren's going to do?"

"I'm not sure," I said. "But I trust him." *Like I have any other choice.*

"You must," he said, the corners of his mouth crinkling. "Well?"

"Well, what?"

"May I have this dance?"

I blinked at him. "Excuse me?"

"Ren had his turn on the dance floor," Shay said. "Now it's mine."

"I don't remember agreeing to that arrangement." I stepped back. "Besides, I have to talk with the others. Get things back to normal."

"That's what I thought," he said. "I'm going to help you."

I frowned at him, puzzled, as he put one hand at my waist and grabbed my other hand. He pulled me close while stretching our arms out, straight as an arrow.

"What the hell is this?" I asked.

"The tango," he replied, guiding me across the floor with melodramatic, sweeping steps.

"How is this helping?" I glanced at my packmates. They were all watching us, looking befuddled.

"Music doesn't soothe the savage beast, Cal," Shay said, dipping me so low my hair brushed the floor. "Laughter does."

I looked toward our tables again, startled at what I saw. Shay's plan was working. Ansel and Mason were already chuckling. Bryn giggled madly and even Cosette couldn't stop smiling.

Shay sighed and spun me away from him before jolting me back as if I'd been a coiled spring. "It would be much better if I had a rose between my teeth. Wouldn't I be dashing?"

I started to giggle. "That would be ridiculous."

"Ridiculously dashing." He grinned. Even the bikers around the bar were laughing now, morphing their hardened faces from Sid Vicious to Santa Claus.

I leaned into the warmth of Shay's body. When he held me close, I could actually believe everything would be okay. I wondered if he knew how happy he could make me, despite my constant fears about the future. Regret suddenly constricted my chest, cutting off my laughs. Seeing me lip-locked with Ren earlier must have hurt Shay so much. He deserved better, more than I could ever offer him.

"So you're not angry with me?" I asked as he made me pirouette like a ballerina.

"About what?" he asked. "You aren't the bigoted one. Fey and Dax can go to hell as far as I'm concerned."

He didn't see the kiss.

Cool relief spilled through me, followed by a nip of guilt.

Why don't I want him to know? Hiding the truth isn't fair.

Nothing could change what lay ahead for Ren and me. Shay needed to understand that more than anyone. But looking at his smile, the warmth in his eyes, I couldn't bring myself to say anything more about the kiss.

"I think you'd better share this brilliant plan of yours with Nev," I said. "I wouldn't want him to think we're mocking him."

"Nev's got a great sense of humor," Shay replied, dipping me again. "I think he'll get it."

"If you're sure." I glanced at the stage. Shay seemed to be right. Though Nev looked a bit thrown, he was also grinning from ear to ear.

"You know, if I kissed you at the end of this number, it would be a real showstopper," Shay said, keeping me tipped upside down.

I couldn't stop my smile at his devilish grin. "If you kiss me now, Ren will kill you."

"All's fair in love and war," he said. "And at least I'd die happy."

"You're terrible." I dug my nails into his shoulder. "Pick me up again!"

"I just don't want to disappoint our audience," he said.

"They'll have to live with disappointment, then." I was getting woozy from all the blood rushing into my head. "I've been very clear about what will happen if you kiss me again. I think you'd miss your hand."

He lifted me upright only to dip me low again on the other side. "Do you solve all your problems with threats of violence?"

"No."

"Liar." My head was spinning when he set me on my feet, but my body felt light as air.

I broke down into a fit of giggles as Shay began to polka. Neville shook his head, but he was laughing too. The music stopped; Nev said something to the rest of the band I couldn't hear, but in the next moment they broke out a punk-rock cover of "Roll Out the Barrel."

Shay turned us in circles, faster and faster. "I told you it would work!"

I collapsed against him, dizzy but ecstatic, resting my cheek on his shoulder. Then I caught sight of Ren. He stood just inside the door, eyes fixed on us. He was so still he could have been carved from stone.

I pulled out of Shay's arms. "I think the show's over."

"Great," he muttered, following my gaze. "Go talk to him."

"I'm sorry," I said as I took unsteady steps away from him, still unbalanced from all the twirls and dips.

"I know you have to." His smile was flat. "I'll go hang out with Mason and Ansel, see if anyone wants to know where I got my badass polka moves."

I started to turn toward Ren, but my stomach lurched violently. He crossed the dance floor, his scowl making my own temper flare. I hadn't done anything wrong. I thought about the drive home, our new house, the union, suddenly wanting to do nothing that Ren had asked of me.

"What was that all about?" Ren snarled.

"We were just trying to break the tension." I kept my own voice steady, waving toward our tables, where the pack sat laughing. "It was a joke. Behold our success."

"Could you have thought of a way to settle them that didn't involve having Shay's hands all over you?"

"It wasn't like that," I snapped. *I wish it had been like that.*

"Fine," he said, taking my arm. "Try not to do that again. I don't like to see another man touch you."

Another man? Ren had pointedly been referring to Shay as "that kid" since we'd first met him. Jealousy really was eating at the alpha.

"Of course, Ren." I shook him off. "But if you'll excuse me, I think I've had enough of this for tonight."

"What are you talking about?"

"I'm leaving," I said. "I did what you asked. The pack is happy. Now I just want to get out of here."

"Don't be like that." Ren sighed, tucking a lock of hair behind my ear. It only made me feel like a child, and I swatted his hand away.

"I wasn't trying to come down on you." He tried again. "You're right, that kid bugs me. I don't like feeling jealous. It's not your fault."

He seemed sincere, but I was too angry to let it go. And there it was again, "that kid"—only now he was scolding *me* like a little girl too.

"Thanks for being honest," I said. "But I don't want to stay. Please don't make me."

I knew he could and I hated it.

"Where are you going?" he asked.

"I'm going to the woods. Where wolves belong at night." I flashed a sharp-toothed smile at him. "Maybe I hear the moon calling."

"I'd like you to stay with me," he said slowly. "But I'm not going to force you."

"Great." I walked away before he could speak again.

I slammed my way out of the bar, breaking a chair that I kicked a little too hard. Outside, cold night air bit my skin, taking long pulls of tension out of my limbs. Fey and Dax were still standing in the parking lot, heads close together, speaking in low tones.

Dax looked surprised and annoyed. "Did Ren send you out to give us another round of scolding?" he asked, flexing his broad shoulders as he faced me.

"I have nothing to say to either of you," I snapped, walking past them and then breaking into a run. I shifted forms and plunged into the forest without looking back at the Burnout.

TWENTY-TWO

SHAY LEANED AGAINST HIS FORD RANGER.

He waved briefly when I loped up and then reached into the bed of his truck, pulling out a pair of ice axes, which he tied onto his back.

I shifted forms when I saw him trying to hide his smile. "What?"

"I was just thinking about the last time I was here," he said, tightening the laces on his hiking boots. "I woke up in my truck. I thought I'd fallen asleep before I'd even managed to get a hike in and that the whole thing was a dream."

I bent forward, stretching my back muscles. "Yeah, that was what I'd hoped would happen."

"You knocked me out and then dragged me back here. Didn't you?"

"I didn't drag you," I said. "I carried you."

He laughed, shaking his head. "Well, thanks for that. Ready?"

Shay proved an adept climber, moving up the slope with steady grace as I bounded through the woods just ahead of him. Only once did we have to pause so he could strap crampons to his boots before we scaled a particularly icy face, which I launched myself up in two giant leaps. His pair of ice axes remained strapped across his back for the duration of our climb.

I darted in front of him as we approached the cave. My head

dropped low to the ground and I paced back and forth. I couldn't stop the plaintive whine that spilled from my throat.

Shay trudged up behind me. "It's going to be okay, Calla."

I shifted into human form, stomping the snow restlessly while staring at the cavern, a dark opening in the mountainside that looked too much like a gigantic mouth ready to swallow us.

"I'm not entirely convinced of that," I said. "What if someone finds out we've been here?"

"How would that happen?" Shay asked.

"My scent, Shay," I said. "Any Guardian who comes to the cave will know I've been inside."

"But you said none of you can go in the cave," he said. "I thought it was forbidden."

"It is, but—"

"Do you want to go back?"

I looked at him and then at the cavern. As far as I knew, no Guardian had ever set a paw beyond its entrance. Why would that change now?

"So are we doing this or not?" Shay asked.

"We're doing this," I said, pushing away my doubts.

He shrugged off his pack and pulled out a headlamp. We moved slowly into the cave, the light from his lamp dimly illuminating the blackness. The tunnel seemed to lead straight back, but there was no indication that it ended.

When the light from the entrance was little more than a glimmer behind us, I froze. A strange scent hit me. I shifted into wolf form, testing the air again. It was there, distinct but unfamiliar, like a mixture of rotting wood and gasoline. I lowered my head and crept forward. Shay took a tentative step alongside me, sweeping the headlamp along the cavern floor. We both saw the bones at the same time. My hackles rose as I hunched closer to the ground.

Scattered across the cavern were the whitened remains of animals, mostly deer. I looked more closely at the piles of bones and shuddered. The immense skull of a bear grinned at me from one side of the tunnel.

"Calla." I heard Shay's fearful murmur just behind me at the same time that the scrabbling noise reached my ears.

My eyes darted around the space, but I couldn't see anything moving in the blackness. The scratch of something hard on stone was getting closer. I whimpered and bristled. My eyes followed the light of Shay's lamp as it moved back and forth along the tunnel floor.

I'd just taken another step forward when Shay's cry of alarm pierced the tunnel. "Calla! Above you, move!"

I launched forward into the darkness, hearing something massive hit the floor of the tunnel behind me in the very space I'd stood just a moment before.

"Oh my God." I heard Shay's choked exclamation and I whirled around, snarling.

The brown recluse stared at me with three pairs of eyes that shone like pools of oil. Its long, thin legs were covered in silky, fine hairs and they quivered as the spider focused on its prey. I backed away, teeth bared, attempting to appear menacing despite my terror. The spider was enormous, almost the size of a horse.

Its abdomen pulsed as it watched me. I stalked from side to side, wanting to hold its attention. The spider skittered forward with startling speed. I felt the brush of one of its eight legs against my back as I barely darted out of its way. I circled, knowing that the arachnid was just behind me. I could hear the scraping of its limbs along the stone surface of the cavern. Heart pounding, I racked my brain for an attack plan. Wolves had no natural instincts about killing mutant insects. This creature bore no resemblance to the opponents I'd faced in the past.

I whirled to face the spider, having settled on an attempt to maim it until I found some way to strike a fatal blow. My abrupt about-face startled my attacker. Its first two legs reared up and I leapt, catching one of the limbs between my teeth and jerking hard. The spindly leg snapped in my jaws and I tore it away. When I hit the ground and faced it again, the six dark eyes glittered with agony. I stared at the immense beast, which twitched and quivered as it prepared to attack. Its silence was more terrifying than if it had been screaming at me.

The spider reared again, launching itself at me. I jumped to the side, but not quickly enough. I thrashed against the cold stone floor as the recluse pinned me down with two of its legs. I wrenched my neck, trying to fight back, snapping at its limbs and shuddering when the spider's head descended toward my shoulder. The sound of my desperate struggle became a whimper when I saw its fangs. My jaws locked around one of its legs at the same moment the spider's bite pierced my side.

A horrible thud was followed by a tearing sound and the squelch of gore. The spider bucked, releasing me, and I scrambled away. Pale, bluish liquid poured from large punctures Shay had made with his ice axes. With furious, determined strokes he brought the sharp spikes down on the spider's unprotected back again and again. Maddened by pain, the recluse tried to turn on its attacker. I rushed forward and tore off another of its legs. The spider faltered. Its blue blood gushed along the cavern floor. The creature's legs splayed and it collapsed. Shay ran to the front of its convulsing body, his jaw clenched as he brought the ice axes down between the spider's center pair of eyes. The spider jerked one last time and then became still.

Shay drew a long, shuddering gasp and backed away from the corpse. His fingers wrapped tightly around the ax handles, veins bulging along his arms. I sniffed the air again and listened, but the signals of imminent danger had dissipated. I shifted forms and turned toward Shay.

His eyes widened as I abandoned my defensive stance. "Are you sure there isn't another one?" he asked.

"No, it was alone." I rubbed my back where the spider's fangs had punctured my skin. I could feel a trickle of blood, but Shay's attack had disrupted the bite. It wasn't deep, but it ached.

"What is it?" He shuddered, gazing at the immense spider.

"A brown recluse," I murmured. "You can tell because it only has six eyes."

His eyebrows went up.

I shrugged. "We just finished a unit on arachnids in AP Biology."

"Calla. That is not a spider," he moaned. "Spiders do not get that big. What is that thing?"

"It *is* a spider. But it's been changed by the Keepers. They have the ability to do something like this. Alter the natural world. The recluse must be the last line of defense for Haldis should something get past the Guardians." But which Keeper had created this beast I didn't know—or when they might come to check on it.

"Killing it might have been a mistake," I said. "It's another sign that we've been here."

"Are you insane? What did you want to do with it—grab that bear skull and try to teach it to play fetch?" Shay asked.

"Good point," I said. "But that doesn't solve the problem."

He didn't reply, staring at the lifeless arachnid, face ghost white.

"Are you all right?" I took a step toward him.

"I really, really hate spiders." He glanced at his shoulders, as if expecting the offending creatures to be crawling there.

A wry smile tugged at one corner of my mouth. "For someone who claims arachnophobia, you dispatched that thing quite nicely."

I glanced at the axes that hung from his hands; blood dripped from the sharp steel picks. "Where did you learn to do that? You moved like a warrior."

Shay's pale face brightened a bit and he flipped the ice picks in the air, catching their handles easily when they dropped back down.

A sudden throb took my breath away. I put my hand on my side, surprised to find blood still flowing steadily from the wound.

"Let me guess," I said, trying to ignore the pain. "You went through a phase where you wanted to be a ninja or something?"

He shook his head, blushing. "Indiana Jones. I liked how he could use whatever was around when he got into trouble. You know, versatile."

"There's an Indiana Jones comic?" I raised my eyebrows at him.

"Yep." He kicked the corpse of the spider.

"Ah." I fixed a teasing smile on him. "So you're also handy with a bullwhip."

He gave a noncommittal shrug.

I turned back toward the dark tunnel ahead of us. "Well, I guess that's good to know for the future."

With wary steps we moved forward; I kept my eyes off the bones that lay scattered along the floor. My hand massaged the spider bite at my waist. The blood had finally stopped, but the ache at the puncture sharpened and seemed to be spreading. I stumbled on loose stones and Shay caught my arm.

"You okay?"

"Yeah. It's nothing, just hard to see." I rolled back my shoulders, trying to focus on our progression into the darkness. The air in the cave seemed colder; it wormed beneath my skin. Even with the aid of Shay's headlamp I was finding it difficult to see, my vision blurring more with each step. The ground beneath my feet lurched and I stumbled again.

"What's going on, Calla?" Shay asked. "You're not this clumsy. You're not clumsy at all."

"I'm not sure." The darkness swam and I dropped to my hands and knees.

"Are you hurt?" Shay asked.

My limbs trembled. I was getting colder by the moment. "Maybe. The spider bit me, but I didn't think it was deep enough to matter."

"Where did it bite you?" He crouched next to me. "Show me."

I opened my jacket and started to lift up my shirt but then bit my lip, hesitating.

He laughed. "I'm not trying to make a move, Cal. We need to see how bad it is."

I nodded, pulling up the shirt. The bite was level with my lower ribs on the right side of my body. I strained my neck, but I couldn't get a good look over my shoulder.

Shay gasped.

"What's wrong?" I twisted further and caught a glimpse of my flesh. Bile rose in my throat.

"How can it do that?" His voice was tight.

I shook my head. "Damn. That's right . . . I forgot."

The trembling of my body had become shuddering jerks. "The recluse has a necrotic bite."

"Necrotic?" Shay breathed. "It kills your flesh?"

"Looks like. I remember reading something about rapid tissue breakdown." I closed my eyes against the wave of nausea that crashed through me.

"Oh God, Cal. It's spreading; I can see it happening," he groaned. "It's like it's eating away at you."

I tried to smile but only managed a grimace. "Thanks for the update. I feel much better."

"Why aren't you healing?" He sounded panicked. "I thought that's what Guardian blood does."

"My own blood protects me . . . but not from everything," I gasped. "Venom is tricky, and venom from an enchanted spider is something I've never had to deal with before. I might not be able to heal fast enough without help."

"What can help?"

"Only another Guardian," I said. "Pack blood."

"Can we call Bryn? Or Ansel?"

"How fast is it spreading?"

He didn't answer.

"I guess the answer is no, then," I said. My arms couldn't support my body any longer. I rolled back against the cave floor.

"Calla!" Shay wrapped his arms around me, drawing me against him. "Come on, there has to be something we can do."

I shook my head. "There isn't. Just get out of here."

"No."

"Shay, you need to get off the mountain. If anyone finds you up here, they'll kill you."

"I'm not going to let you die in this cave," he snapped.

"You don't have a choice. There's nothing you can do." The pain that racked my muscles began to subside but gave way to a creeping numbness all the more terrifying.

"Yes. There is." I tried to focus on Shay; even through the fog of sickness his fierce tone startled me.

He shrugged off his jacket, pulling his sweater over his head and ripping off his white T-shirt.

"What are you doing?"

"You have to turn me, Calla," Shay said. "Hurry, before I lose my nerve."

He shivered and I knew it was as much from fear as the chilly air.

"No."

"We don't have time to argue." He repositioned himself so my head was cradled against his neck. My body had grown so cold that his warm, bare skin felt like it was searing my own flesh. "Make it so my blood can heal you."

"You're insane," I murmured. "I can't do this. It doesn't matter what happens to me. Leave now. Just make a run for it. You'll be okay."

"Yeah, right. If you die, I'm as good as dead," he argued. "You know that. I need your help."

"I haven't ever turned anyone," I said. "It could go badly."

"Come on," he snapped. "A bite and an incantation, that's what you said. How hard can it be?"

He cupped the nape of my neck, pressing my face into his shoulder.

"Please, Calla."

The scent of his skin, crisp and sharp as a glacial pool, wrapped around me and cleared the haze of my mind. My flesh suddenly shrieked with renewed pain, desperate for healing. I dug my nails into his bare chest, drawing blood. He tensed but didn't pull away. My canines sharpened. Shay gripped my shoulders and molded my body against him. He gasped when his hands dug into fur, his arms around a white wolf. I sank my teeth into his shoulder. He drew a sharp breath. His muscles tightened, but he remained still.

Blood gushed from the deep punctures in Shay's flesh. He moaned and his eyes rolled back. He swayed a bit as he clung to me. I shifted into human form, raised my trembling arm to my mouth, and bit into the soft skin. I pressed my wound against his parted lips. My strength was sapped; I could barely hold myself upright. I struggled to keep my mind clear and my body from shaking as I chanted in an ever-weakening voice.

"*Bellator silvae servi.* Warrior of the forest, I, the alpha, call on thee to serve in this time of need." The cave floor seemed to be rolling beneath me. Shay's face blurred and contorted as I tried to focus on him, hoping I'd gotten the incantation right.

A ripple of energy passed through Shay. His arms dropped from my waist and he fell back against the cave floor. He became very still, drew a shuddering breath, and in the next moment his entire body convulsed. He screamed.

No longer able to control my limbs, I dropped to the ground alongside him, trembling and fighting to remain conscious. Muscles quivering, he twisted and writhed next to me. His face contorted as he was slowly divided from one essence into two. Once only human, Shay's being parted into wolf and mortal: two selves, fully Guardian.

Another minute passed, and then another. My eyes were open, but I couldn't see anything or move. Breathing had become difficult; dark waters rose up to swallow me. The silence of oblivion pooled in the cave.

It's too late. I let my heavy eyelids close.

A quiet whimper echoed in the blackness. Fur brushed against my skin; nails scraped on the stone floor.

My lips parted and I tried to speak. No sound would come.

Something warm and soft pressed against my open mouth. Hot liquid trickled along my tongue, gathering, pouring into my throat. It had a sweet bite, like wild honey.

Pack blood.

"Drink, Calla," Shay whispered. "You have to swallow or you'll choke."

I forced the muscles of my throat into action, struggling to get the blood down.

"That's it," he said, stroking my hair. "Don't forget to breathe."

After a few painful swallows I could drink steadily. Sensation returned to my limbs. First came the pain, but it slowly ebbed. My vision cleared and the cave stopped vibrating beneath me. I pushed his arm away and sat up.

He clamped down on his punctured skin. "Is that enough?"

"I think so," I said. "Take a look."

I lifted my shirt again and he nodded. "Yeah. It's definitely healing up."

He swallowed, looking away. "Not pretty to look at yet, though."

I quickly pulled my shirt down. "If the healing has started, I'll be fine."

"Good."

"Are you okay?" I inched closer to him, peering at his face.

"Yeah." He rolled his neck back and forth. "It hurt. A lot. But I feel okay now." He frowned briefly. "Different, though. I think I like it."

"You are different. You're a Guardian."

He shifted and a gold-brown-furred wolf blinked at me with moss green eyes, wagging his tail. Then Shay was smiling at me.

"So how do I look as a wolf? Good? Badass?" he asked. "How strong am I now?"

"Oh God." My heart skipped a beat. "This is very bad. This is a disaster."

"Why?" His smile vanished. "Don't you think I can cut it?"

"That's not it, Shay," I said. "I can't believe I did this. What was I thinking?"

"You weren't thinking," he said. "You were dying. We didn't have a choice."

"I might as well have died. Now I'm dead for sure." Not one wolf in Haldis Cavern, but two. Me and this strange, new wolf.

"No," he said. "You're not dead. But you would be if you hadn't turned me."

"Your wolf scent will be all over the cavern now too, Shay. How are we going to hide it?" I stared at him. "What I did is forbidden . . . twice! I can't be here, and turning you should have been out of the question!" I thought about the spider carcass, my blood pouring over the floor—there was nothing I could do to erase the evidence.

He offered me a lopsided smile. "Just add it to your list of things you weren't supposed to do but did anyway. It's starting to get long."

"Could you please be serious?"

"I am, Calla." His voice was firm. "You turned me. I'm happy about it. I thought I'd already convinced you that no one is going to come to the cave to smell our wolfy crimes. As far as school goes, we'll figure out a way to hide it. Will anyone be able to tell?"

I wanted to argue but forced myself to consider his words. "As long as you don't give it away. You'll have to be careful."

"What would give it away?"

"You can't shift forms when anyone can see it."

"That's easy enough."

"Not as easy as you think," I said. "Anytime you get angry or feel threatened, the predator instinct of the wolf will push to take over your body. Don't let your teeth sharpen. Don't growl, and for God's sake don't lose your temper."

"So avoid Ren at all costs?"

I let it pass. "You'll have heightened senses now. Smell, hearing."

"I noticed." He laughed. "I thought that spider smelled bad when I was human."

"Exactly," I said. "You can't react to things you notice that a human wouldn't."

"I'll be fine," he said. "I'm a good actor." He stretched his arms before him, as if checking for any lingering signs of wolfishness. "So are you going to teach me how to be a wolf?"

I nodded slowly.

"Great!" He shifted forms several times in rapid succession.

"What are you doing, Shay?" I rose, brushing dirt from my jeans.

"I just can't believe how easy it is," he said. "To go back and forth, I mean. I'm a werewolf . . . It's so cool!"

I couldn't help myself, laughing until my sides hurt. Maybe it would be okay. Shay's delight made me fearless. I knew it was dangerous, but it was also addictive. He smiled sheepishly.

"I have never, ever heard a Guardian say anything like that." I wiped tears from my face.

"Well, I am one of a kind." He grinned.

"You certainly are." I shook my head but smiled. "Come on, special boy. Let's go find out what the monster spider was protecting."

Shay nodded, pulling his shirt back on. The wound where I'd bitten his shoulder had already closed, and we continued to pick our way through the darkness. I frowned as we made our way deeper into the tunnel. Maybe it was my eyes simply adjusting to the darkness, but the cave seemed oddly brighter. Shay reached up and switched off his headlamp. The cavern remained alight with a warm, reddish glow. He pointed ahead to where the tunnel abruptly turned right. The source of light seemed to emanate from around that corner.

We exchanged a puzzled glance and continued our cautious progress. The crimson haze intensified as we drew closer to the turn in the cavern. The air around us grew warmer, almost hot. Shay shrugged out of his jacket. I unzipped my coat, glancing around nervously as I stepped toward the curving wall. I was about to pass the threshold into the next chamber when I felt his hand grab mine. When I looked at Shay, he smiled.

"We do this together." He drew me alongside him so we moved lockstep around the bend.

The curve of the tunnel opened into a broad space. The walls of the inner chamber undulated with waves of rust, ochre, and crimson light. As my eyes moved along the cavern walls, I realized that they were covered in crystals reflecting the infinite shades of red, which emanated from the center of the chamber.

In the middle of the spherical room was a woman. She floated rather than stood, her ghostly form shimmering with warm light. I tensed when her eyes found us. But she smiled. Her gaze focused on Shay, hands stretching toward him, beckoning. I gasped and had reached out to grab his arm when he dropped my hand and walked swiftly toward her. He was out of my reach before I could pull him back. When he reached out and took both her hands in his own, I wanted to scream a warning, but my body, tongue to toes, was suddenly paralyzed.

The light in the cavern wavered and then intensified so quickly that I covered my eyes. All at once it blinked out, plunging us into darkness. I jumped when Shay switched his headlamp back on. I rushed forward, terrified that he'd been harmed.

"What happened?" I searched his body for signs of injury. "Why did you just run up to her like that?"

He blinked at me. "Couldn't you hear her?"

"Hear what?" I asked, unconvinced that the strange woman hadn't hurt him.

A wondrous expression moved over his face. "It was so beautiful. She sang, and the melody was like a song I've always known but hadn't heard in years."

"What did she say?"

"May the Scion bear the cross," he murmured. "The cross is the anchor of life. Here rests Haldis."

"Here rests Haldis?" What he'd just said made no sense.

He glanced down and my eyes followed. The light from the headlamp shone directly on his hands. They weren't empty. Lying on his palms was a long, narrow cylinder that curved up at the ends into slightly raised edges. In the light the object reflected the multitude of red hues that had sparkled on the walls of the cavern.

"What is it?" I frowned at the strange cylinder.

"It's Haldis," he replied in a hypnotic tone.

"Uh, sure," I said. "But what is it?"

"I don't know," he said. "It's not heavy, and it feels warm. Like it's full of energy."

"Really?" I reached out and had barely touched the object with the tip of my finger when I jerked my hand back and swore.

"Calla?" His voice was full of alarm.

"That hurt." I stared at the cylinder, fingers still throbbing. "A lot. Like it bit me." I turned my eyes on Shay. "I guess you're the only one who gets to touch it."

"Only me?" His fingers curled protectively around Haldis, turning it over in his hands, examining it. "Interesting."

"What is it?" I leaned over his shoulder.

"It has an opening on one end. Like a slit." He angled the cylinder to show me.

"Is there something inside it?" I peered at the narrow slash.

He shook it, holding it up to his ear. "No, and it's not completely hollow either. I don't know what it is."

"Well, we need to figure that out later. Right now we have to get back down the mountain before the next patrol comes out." I threaded my arm through his, pulling him back out of the chamber.

"Will they track us?" he asked.

"Not likely," I said. "Now that you're a Guardian, they won't recognize the scent. They'll think it's a normal wolf that strayed into this range."

"Cool."

When we reached the mouth of the cave, I shifted into wolf form; Shay followed suit. He shook his ruff and gazed at me, eyes questioning.

Come on, it's time to run. I playfully nipped at his shoulder.

He barked and jumped away; his ears flicked as he gazed at me. He whimpered, pawing the snow.

I watched him for a moment and then understood. *If you need to talk, focus your thought and send it toward me.*

His tentative response quietly entered my mind.

Okay.

My tongue lolled out in a wolf grin before I spun around, bounding away from the cavern into the cover of trees. I glanced back once to be certain he followed and saw Shay close at my heels. We burst into the forest, plunging through the deep, fresh powder. We sped down the hill as though we had wings, leaping over icefalls, churning snow in our wake. It was as though we traveled backward through time, from winter to fall, as we streaked down the mountain.

I feel like I could run forever. Shay's awed voice rang in my mind.

I yipped and put on another burst of speed, reveling in the power of my limbs.

Night cloaked the base of the mountain when we arrived at Shay's truck. Silver wisps of cloud barely veiled bright moonlight, which shone down in ghostly beams through the pine trees.

He shifted forms and headed for his Ford Ranger, shoving his hand into his coat pocket to rummage for the keys. The keys jangled in his hands when he turned, watching me. I shifted into human form and walked up to him.

"Can I give you a ride home?" he asked.

I gazed up at the moon, swallowing a sigh when I remembered Ren's invitation to cull the local deer population. "I'd rather run. All our time in the library has kept me indoors too much."

Shay smiled. "Yeah. That was incredible. You must want to be outside all the time."

"I'm glad you liked it." I moved closer to him. Despite the change, he still had the same scent I'd come to love, the smell of new leaves striking a sharp contrast to the heady incense of the autumn night. "I didn't thank you for saving my life."

"Well, you saved me twice, so I'm still one behind you." He laughed. "But I don't know that I'm looking to even the score. I'd rather you didn't almost die again, if you can help it."

"That makes two of us." I lifted my eyes to his. He was watching my face, his green irises swimming with moonlight. He reached out and stroked my cheek.

"Do you want to go home?" I caught his fingers in mine, letting my face press against his palm, taking in his scent again, shivering with excitement that I had an entire world to share with him. "Are you tired?"

"Not really. I'm pretty wired from all of this."

My lips curved into a wicked grin. "Are you hungry?"

TWENTY-THREE

STOP WHINING; YOU'RE EIGHTEEN YEARS

old and you keep acting like a puppy.

Though my complaint carried a teasing note, the irritated edge behind it was real. The focus required by the hunt made me tense.

It's not my fault. His plaintive reply came back. *I've never had a tail before. I can't figure out what exactly it's supposed to do. It's so distracting.*

I halted on the top of a ridge, eyes tracking over the broad meadow before us. The small group of deer I'd scented grazed a half mile below us, upwind and completely unaware of our presence, their brown coats transformed to slate gray in the moonlight.

You'll need to figure it out now if you want to do this. My snapping thought raced toward him.

He loped up beside me and then dropped to his haunches, his tongue lolling out in a wolf grin. *I'll be fine.*

We'll see about that. I lifted my muzzle, testing the air again. *Do you remember what I taught you? A deer is different from rabbits. We need to coordinate the attack to take one down.*

The brown wolf, whose thick fur glinted with golden streaks, pawed at the snow-covered ground, clearly irritated by my patronizing tone. *Yeah, I know. I get the hamstring, you take the throat.*

Right. My gaze moved back over the herd. *The yearling on the far right. That's the one we'll separate for the kill.*

He took a step forward, making his own assessment. *It's a little scrawny, isn't it?*

There are only two of us, Shay. We don't need a fully grown deer. We just ate that rabbit. How hungry are you anyway?

He threw me a reproachful glare. *So long as you're not implying that I can't take down a buck.*

I flicked my ears irritably. *It's not a competition; we're just trying to get some food.*

He bared his teeth, dancing in a playful circle beside me. *If it's not a competition, then why are you critiquing my wolf skills?*

I'm not critiquing, I'm teaching. I turned to watch him weave slowly around me.

Could I get a gold star once in a while, Miss Tor? He darted forward, nipping at my shoulder.

Shut up. I snapped at him, but he jumped out of my reach.

He cocked his head at me, filling his eyes with shock and sorrow.

I sniffed the air disdainfully. *You're impossible.*

Awww, you love it. He stretched his front legs.

I attempted to bare my teeth at him, but my effort rapidly devolved into a wolf grin. *Come on, Mowgli. Let's go kill Bambi.*

He sent a haughty laugh into my mind. *You do realize you just mixed Disney metaphors, right?* Disney *metaphors. Wow, Calla, now I'm just sad for you.*

I pivoted and began a stealthy descent along the ridgeline. Shay followed close behind; his careful foot pads matched my own silent steps as we wove through the trees. We stalked through the shadowed cover of pines that encircled the small glen. The deer remained ignorant of our presence, striking at the snowdrifts with their hooves in search of buried roughage.

Ready? I didn't look back at Shay as I sent the thought to him.

Always.

I lunged from the forest. The startled deer scattered. I focused on the yearling, driving it away from its companions. I nipped at the terrified animal, turning it sharply left. Shay darted in from behind me. With a sudden burst of speed he launched into the air, sinking his teeth into its hamstring. The deer cried out and faltered. Crimson blood poured into the snow as the yearling futilely struggled to continue its flight despite the crippling wound. Focused on the golden brown wolf, the deer failed to see me dart past. The yearling's next cry died in a gurgle as my teeth tore through its throat. Hot copper liquid filled my mouth and I clamped my jaw down more ferociously. The young deer shuddered, dropping to the earth.

Shay trotted up to the carcass, tail wagging.

Nice work. The deer's blood was still hot in my mouth; my stomach rumbled. I glanced at Shay.

Ladies first. He lowered his head respectfully.

My tongue lolled out and then I tore into the carcass. Shay settled down on the opposite side of the deer and began ripping the warm flesh from its body.

After a moment he licked his lips.

It's good.

Better than rabbit? I tore out another mouthful.

Shay cocked his head for a moment, ears flicking back and forth. *Better than dinner and a movie.* He bared his teeth at me in pleasure before he went back to gulping down hunks of venison.

He'd balked when I first suggested that we hunt together. But as I'd predicted, it had only taken one rabbit for him to realize that as a wolf, the instinct to kill for food and devour raw flesh was natural.

When we'd both eaten our fill, I glanced around. Traces of dawn slipped over the glen, tingeing the night's last shadows chalky pink.

We should think about heading back. I danced in nervous circles around the picked-over carcass.

I suppose it's getting pretty late. Shay scrambled to his feet.

More like early; the sun will be up in a couple of hours. Let's get back to your truck.

We were still a good distance from the trailhead when Shay shifted into human form. I followed suit, startled by his decision to change. Our wolf forms offered much more protection from the elements than human skin and clothing ever could. I frowned at him, pulling my jacket more tightly around me when an icy gust of wind crept beneath my clothing.

"What is it?"

"I've been thinking." He zipped and unzipped his coat, clearly nervous. "Haldis. We need to know what it is."

I looked at his pocket, where the strange object was tucked away. "The library isn't safe. The Searchers clearly were watching us there before that ambush."

I shuddered, rubbing my arms.

"I'm sorry, I know it's cold," he said, green eyes darkening, full of wariness even as he watched me shiver. "But I need to be able to read your facial expressions. I'm not great at wolf body language yet."

"Why do you need to know what my facial expressions are?" I started to walk toward him, stopping when he backed off.

"'Cause you're not going to like this plan, and I need to know if you're going to attack me. So I can get out of the way."

I laughed, but his face was serious.

"You think I'm going to attack you?" I regarded him curiously.

He drew a slow breath.

"So we need to do research, right?"

I grimaced and nodded.

"But the public library is out, and so is our school library . . ."

"Yep." My interest grew as his expression became calculating.

Shay backed as far from me as he could without having to shout for me to hear him.

"This must be some plan," I muttered.

"Just promise you'll listen to the whole idea before you lose your temper." His eyes darted toward the trail that led back to the parking lot, as if to gauge how much time it would take for him to make a run to his truck.

My lips curled into a dangerous smile. "I promise."

"Great." He didn't sound convinced at all. "What if we could get all the Keepers' information from the source?"

"The source?"

"Their books."

I frowned. "I'm not following you."

He squared his shoulders. "We need to use the library at Rowan Estate."

It was no longer the wind that made me shudder. "Please tell me you're joking."

"You know I'm not."

"I am not going to Rowan Estate."

"Why not?"

"I can't believe you're even suggesting this!"

He inched toward me. "Listen, Calla. My uncle travels constantly; he's never home. We won't get caught, and we need the information that's in the library. I don't think *The War of All Against All* is the only book he didn't want me to see."

"Which is exactly why it's too dangerous for us to snoop around there," I countered.

"Bosque doesn't know I can pick the lock to the library," he said. "I'm always alone. The staff only come to clean on Tuesdays and Sundays. We won't go on Tuesday, and you patrol on Sunday anyway. No one would know if we did our research there on the other days."

"I don't know—"

"Logan said you're supposed to hang out with me, right?" Shay interjected.

"Yes, but . . ."

"Don't you think it would seem more suspicious if I never invited you over to my house?"

"Maybe." I frowned.

He was grinning. "Definitely."

"You're not going to drop this, are you?"

"Nope."

I sighed.

"So what's the verdict?" he asked.

"I guess I'd better get my list out," I said. "It looks like I'm about to add another forbidden act."

"That's my girl."

"Alpha."

"Whatever."

TWENTY-FOUR

WE GOT THROUGH SHAY'S FIRST DAY AT

school since turning without incident, except for one close call in Big Ideas. As soon as Ren walked into class, Shay tensed up, the shadow of his wolf form sliding over his shoulders, making him bristle. I'd anticipated his reaction and glared at him until he settled down. By the end of the school day I almost shared Shay's confidence that our expedition to Haldis would remain our secret, but my optimism was short-lived.

I knew something was wrong as soon as I walked through the front door. The air stung my nostrils and I coughed out the wraiths' stench. I considered heading for the back door so I wouldn't have to pass the kitchen, but the thought came a moment too late.

"That must be our girl now." *Oh God, they know. This is it.*

My heart skipped a beat. That voice had never been in my house before. When I walked into the living room, the Keeper was sitting in my father's leather chair, smiling at me.

"We've been waiting for you, Calla," Efron Bane said. "You're a busy girl to come home this late. And on a school night. I hope you're not getting into trouble."

He wasn't alone. In addition to the wraiths that swirled behind his shoulders, Logan and Lumine sat on the couch. *Why are they all here?* I tried to think about anything but turning Shay, not wanting them to sense my fear.

"I've been following orders." I glanced at Logan, who nodded. "Like you asked."

"Yes, so I've heard," he said. "Our Ren thinks you've taken your orders a little too seriously."

Am I going to have to give up time with Shay because Ren is jealous? "If I misunderstood—" I began.

"No, no. I know you're the soul of innocence, dear Calla." Logan laughed. "Ren's hackles raise at the thought of any other male getting near you. But that's who he is, nothing more. Keep up the good work with our boy."

"Yes, Logan," I murmured.

"Here we are," my mother chirped, carrying a silver tray loaded with a tea service and miniature scones. "Welcome home, Calla. You'll notice we have guests. Your father is out on patrol, of course."

I nodded. My mother poured the tea. Maybe they hadn't figured out their spider had been killed after all. But if they weren't here to punish me, what was this visit about?

A car door slammed outside.

"That makes our company," Lumine said, selecting a porcelain cup. *More company?*

There was a knock at the door.

"Calla, would you please get that while I serve tea?" I watched my mother's nervous movements with growing anxiety. *Who else could be coming?*

I went to the door, letting it swing open to reveal two men. One I knew well, the other I'd only heard talk of. Talk that hadn't been favorable.

"This must be Calla." Ren's father took his time looking me up and down. "Well, at least they aren't giving you a horse face for a mate, boy. She's not half bad, is she?"

318

I couldn't help it; I snarled at him, showing my teeth.

He laughed, glancing at Ren. "And she's got spirit. That's good. Breaking her in will be all the more fun."

Ren didn't respond, keeping his eyes on our doormat. Emile Laroche shoved past me into the living room, taking in his surroundings like he was casing our house. It was a good thing my father was on patrol. I was trying so hard not to gape at the elder Bane alpha that I barely noticed when Ren came to my side, kissing my forehead in greeting.

"Nice to see you," he murmured, taking my hand.

I mumbled my hello, still staring at Ren's father. I'd never met Emile Laroche; until the recent melding of the young wolves, Nightshades and Banes had stayed clear of each other. The Bane alpha bore little resemblance to his son. Where Ren was strong but lithe, Emile was squat and broad, thick muscles straining against his clothes. Unlike Ren's dark hair and eyes, Emile's hair resembled matted straw, his eyes the pale blue of a frozen stream.

"Naomi!" Emile barked, grinning at my mother. "You're a sight for sore eyes."

"Emile." Naomi kept her eyes downcast. "Can I offer you something to drink?"

"Something stronger than that," he said, pointing at the tea.

"Of course." She hurried toward the kitchen.

"For me as well," Efron called after her before smiling at Emile. "Good man."

"You're welcome." Emile leaned against the wall near Efron. "Good evening, mistress, young master."

"Thank you for coming, Emile," Lumine said, stirring her tea. "I know a meeting like this is somewhat unprecedented."

My mother returned with drinks for Emile and Efron. She glanced around the room, pursing her lips. "I'll get more chairs."

"Aren't you going to sit on my lap?" Emile said, downing his drink in one gulp. I stared at him, but Efron laughed heartily while

Logan snickered. Lumine's mouth turned down, disapproving, but she continued to sip her tea.

"I'll just bring the bottle," my mother murmured when Emile thrust his empty glass at her, and went back to the kitchen.

I helped her carry the kitchen chairs into the living room, settling near Ren and wondering what the hell was going on.

"It's a shame Stephen isn't here," Lumine began.

"Yeah, a damn shame." Emile snorted, lounging in his seat. "It's been a few years since we've had a good fight."

"Easy, friend," Efron said. "We need both packs on this. You'll have to set your prejudices aside for the time being."

"What's happened?" Naomi asked, handing Emile a bottle of scotch.

"We think something has gone wrong up at Haldis," Lumine said. "We may have delayed putting the new pack out too long."

I fixed my expression into what I hoped was a blank stare while horror curled at the base of my spine. *They do know!*

"We haven't seen anything on patrols," Naomi said.

"The problem occurred within the cavern itself," Lumine continued. "One of the last lines of defense may have been taken out, but we can't be certain without an investigation. Logan?"

But they don't know everything. How soon will they put all the pieces together?

Logan turned to Ren and me. "You won't be going to school tomorrow. I need the new pack to check out the area around the cavern and just inside the entrance. Don't venture too far inside—you'll know if you've disturbed her."

"Her?" I repeated, trying to mask my astonishment.

"Unlike you, this beast is something of a pet." Logan smiled. "A very deadly pet that keeps the cave protected. Should anything slip past our faithful Guardians, that is."

"Will it attack us?" Ren asked.

"Without a doubt," Logan said. "That's why you make your observations and report back to me. She doesn't leave her lair. If you see her alive, just go; she won't pursue you beyond the mouth of the cave. If something has happened to her, we must find out how. Split your group. Send a few wolves to check the cave. The others should examine the perimeter to find out who or what has been near Haldis. We need to know if the Searchers have gotten close."

"What is she?" Ren asked. His grip on my hand had tightened.

"I wouldn't want to spoil the surprise," Logan said. "She's quite spectacular."

I returned Ren's hard grip but only so I wouldn't shudder. I had to be one of the wolves that searched the cave. In fact, I had to be the only wolf. Otherwise . . . I couldn't think about otherwise.

"And you want us to go tomorrow?" I asked, making sure to keep my voice steady.

"Yes," Logan said. "We must act now. If the Searchers have broken through our defenses, we need to make changes immediately."

"I'll call the pack when I get home," Ren said, looking at me. "Okay, Calla?"

Before I could answer, Emile scowled. "You don't need her permission, boy."

"There's nothing wrong with manners, Emile," Lumine chided. "Calla has been a fine leader of the young Nightshades. Ren is wise to ask her opinion."

Emile muttered something into his glass and Efron snickered.

"It's fine," I said. "Call them." I'd figure out how to get myself on the cave patrol tomorrow.

"We'll meet at first light, then?" he asked, squeezing my hand. "At the base trail?"

I nodded.

Lumine rose, smoothing her skirt. "Excellent. Your first trial. Don't disappoint us."

"Never," Ren murmured.

"Very good." Efron smiled. "We'll bid you good night, then."

"Thank you for the tea, Naomi," Lumine said. "Your hostessing never fails to impress."

"Mistress." My mother gave a little curtsy.

Logan paused in front of us on his way to the door. "Good hunting."

The wraiths floated soundlessly after them. The front door banged shut and Ren stood up, but Emile poured himself another drink. He extended the bottle to my mother.

"For old times' sake?"

"No, thank you," she said.

"Are we staying?" Ren frowned, looking from his father to my mother.

"It hardly seems polite to leave two lovely ladies on their own, seeing how Stephen can't be here to watch over them." Emile wandered to my mother's side, letting his fingers slide through her hair. She paled but didn't move.

"We can take care of ourselves," I snapped.

"Not like a man could," he said, fingers moving from my mother's hair to trace her jawline. "Naomi, what nonsense have you been filling that girl's head with? She's not about to give my boy trouble, now, is she?"

"She will be a fine mate," she said. "Deserving of your son."

I stared at her, not understanding why she didn't shove him away. I knew how strong my mother was; she might not be able to take Emile in a fight, but she could certainly fend him off.

"Fine indeed. Just like her mother, I suppose. You're a good girl, Naomi. You know your place. I've always thought it a shame we weren't better friends."

"Thank you," she whispered, but I could see her hands trembling.

"The night is young," Emile continued, leaning down so his lips touched her ear. "And full of possibility. We could make up for lost time."

"How dare you!" I was on my feet. "Get away from her!"

Emile whirled on me, snarling. "Renier, take your little bitch upstairs!"

"I'm not going anywhere!" Only Ren's grip on my shoulders kept me from flying at Emile.

"Father, we should go; it's late and we're overstaying our welcome," Ren said quietly. "Stephen will be coming off patrol soon."

"I suppose he will, won't he?" Emile's smile was like the light of an oncoming train. "I really should pay my respects."

"I have a lot of homework to get done and I still have to call the pack about tomorrow's run to Haldis," Ren added. "I'd prefer to go now. Please."

"I don't know where you get your work ethic, boy." Emile finished his drink, slamming the glass down on the arm of my mother's chair. "It's been a pleasure, Naomi."

"I'll see you tomorrow." Ren didn't look at me when he spoke, following his father out the front door.

I watched as my mother stood up, straightening her blouse.

"Well, we'd better get this cleaned up." She began collecting glasses, placing them on the tea tray.

"Mom," I said. "Aren't you going to say anything?"

"Whatever do you mean, dear?"

"Why did you let Emile do that to you?"

"He's an alpha male, Calla." She didn't meet my eyes as she continued to tidy the living room. "It's simply their way."

"Dad isn't like that!"

"No," she replied, lifting the tray. I followed her into the kitchen. "But Efron and Lumine prefer different characteristics in their leaders. Lumine encourages a stoic approach and of course—"

"Finesse," I finished. "How could I forget?"

She offered me a flat smile. "Efron thinks it's better to have alphas who use . . . a firmer hand."

"Is that what you call it?" I snarled. "Because I'd say Efron and Emile are both leches!"

"Don't be vile, Calla," she snapped. "It's unbecoming."

"Are you going to tell Dad?" I asked.

She piled dishes into the sink. "Of course not. He hates Emile enough, and you heard our masters say that cooperation is of vital importance right now. We can't have the men tearing at each other while we're trying to set up new defenses. They're so silly that way."

"Silly?! No one besides Dad is allowed to touch you!"

"No *inferior* man can touch me. This was about rival alphas. Something you'll hopefully never have to live with. Emile will take any chance he has to challenge your father. He's always wanted to prove he's the dominant alpha of the two packs. It's only gotten worse since Corinne was killed."

"But—"

She turned on me, holding up her hand. "Leave it, Calla. It's over."

"So this is what finesse is?" I couldn't hold back my outrage. "Acting like a whore for any man who visits your parlor?"

I was on the floor before I realized she'd hit me. My cheek throbbed from the blow.

"Listen very carefully, Calla." My mother stood over me, her fist still clenched. "I said it once, and I don't want to explain myself again. Emile is not any man. He is the Bane alpha. You cannot cross an alpha male, even when you belong to another. You risk your own life to do so. Do you understand me?"

Still dazed, I couldn't speak.

"Do you understand me?" I'd never seen such a hard look in her eyes.

"Yes, Mother," I whispered.

"You must be tired." She rearranged her face into a picture of kindness. "Once I've finished here, I'll make you some chamomile tea and draw you a bubble bath. You have a big day tomorrow."

I nodded, numbly climbing the stairs. Ansel's door was shut, music blasting from within. My mother must have sent him upstairs when the Keepers arrived. *He didn't hear any of that.*

I thought about knocking but headed for my own room instead, letting my baby brother keep his dreams about romance and true love a little longer. I closed the door and started to cry, wondering how much time I had before my mother would appear with tea and when the Keepers would discover how far my betrayal had gone.

TWENTY-FIVE

"YOU CAN'T ALL GO TO THE CAVE." I PACED

along the base of the steep slope. My packmates had pleading eyes locked on me. We were still waiting for the Banes to arrive. The bare light of dawn made the earth shimmer in rusty hues that reminded me of Haldis. I shivered, knowing that the mysterious object was the reason for this patrol and that none of my packmates shared that secret. None of them could go to the cave. They'd know I'd been there and with another wolf. I was desperate to keep them away.

"But Logan has some horrible pet in there!" Fey exclaimed. "It's not fair if we don't all get to see it. I'll bet it's monsterific!"

"Did you really just say 'monsterific'?" Bryn asked, garnering a stony expression from Fey. They'd been bickering more and more since the night at Burnout.

"This is not about fair, it's about our orders," I said. Their grumbling set my teeth on edge. "Just take it up with Ren when he gets here."

And I'll make sure Ren sends me *to the cave.*

A rustling in the underbrush announced the Banes' arrival. Five wolves emerged; seeing that we were still in human form, they shifted one by one. Ren last.

"What's up?" he asked.

"My pack is more interested in sightseeing than doing their jobs," I said.

"That's not what—" Fey began.

"Shut up, Fey," I snarled. Last night's visit from the Keepers and Ren's father had pushed me well past my normal line of tolerance.

Ren began to laugh, waving at the rest of his pack. "Don't worry, Lily. The thing in the cave is all this lot will talk about too."

"Perfect," I muttered. "Why don't I just go up there? The patrol route is more important anyway. We really need to know what's been sneaking around the slope behind our backs."

"Calla's right." Ren raised his voice. "The patrol is much more important than whatever is in the cave."

A few of them grumbled, only to be silenced by Ren's growl.

"Which is why I'll be going to the cave myself," he continued.

"But—" I tried to hide my panic.

"I'm not saying this more than once." Ren ignored me. "Calla looks for evidence of the Searchers along the cavern perimeter. Bryn, Ansel, you're with me—we're heading to the cave. The rest of you, do what Calla tells you, and if I hear complaints, you'll answer to me. We'll catch up with you after we've checked the cave and finish the patrol together."

No one spoke. I bit back my own startled response. *Bryn and Ansel?* I didn't understand why he'd take two of my packmates and not his own. At least I'd be able to talk to them afterward.

For their own parts, Bryn and Ansel looked stunned but followed suit when Ren shifted into wolf form. I did the same and the rest of the pack focused on me, though Dax glanced at Ren once, looking forlorn.

This is how it goes. I shared my thoughts with my assigned group. Even if my fear outweighed my strength, I still had to act like an alpha. *Sweeps in widening circles, starting with the inner perimeter, then moving south. Mason, Nev, Sabine, and I will take the east-west route. Dax,*

Fey, Cosette, you run west-east. We'll minimize overlap while covering maximum ground. Any questions? I felt a little guilty for snapping at Fey earlier and hoped putting her with Dax would make up for it.

They lowered their muzzles in compliance. *Good. Get going.*

Fey took the lead with Dax and Cosette following her up the western route.

I was about to lead Mason and Nev up the slope when Ren's voice entered my mind.

Calla?

What is it? I halted, ears flicking back and forth. It was clear he was sending his voice only to me.

Sorry if I threw you off, but it's important that they get used to new patrol patterns. I'll take good care of Bryn and Ansel.

Of course. Thanks.

I'm sure you won't miss anything too exciting in the cave. I'll let you know what we find as soon as I can.

And then his voice was gone. What was he going to find in there?

No dawdling. Fear and frustration drove me to nip at Mason's heels, but I let Nev and Sabine hear the thought too. *Let's go.*

Hey! he protested. *We were waiting for you.*

That's no excuse. I wagged my tail, wishing I could feel anything besides the twisting of my stomach.

I told you, man, Nev crooned. *I always knew she was a tyrant.*

Sabine sat quietly, waiting for her orders. I wondered what she was thinking.

Nev and Mason's laughter filled my mind as we raced up the hill, playfully biting at each other's flanks, flying past each other to take the lead. But the joy of running free had been sapped from my limbs.

It had only been a matter of days since Shay and I battled Logan's spider and took Haldis from its resting place. I'd lost so much blood, it could have seeped into stone, staining the cave walls. Maybe the spider's scent would cover mine? But what if it didn't? What would Ren do?

I snapped at a squirrel that darted in front of me. Mason nipped at my jaw. *You okay?*

Headache, I responded. *Let's slow up; we should start tracking here.*

We spread out, noses low to the ground, moving at an easy lope, searching for scents that were out of place, clues I knew we wouldn't find. Knowing that we had nothing to search for but evidence of me and Shay made tracking an exercise in tedium. I caught his scent early on our patrol, knowing it would be unrecognizable to my pack-mates. I dutifully led Nev, Mason, and Sabine through the motions of a hunt, all the while wondering what was happening in the cavern.

Can we grab something to eat? Mason's voice interrupted my own thoughts. *I saw a grouse back there and I'm starving. I don't think there's anything to find. Just a stray wolf who's been wandering in this range.*

Though I'd expected it, Mason's assumption about the unfamiliar wolf sent a wave of relief over me.

That's all I've got too. I vote for lunch, Nev answered. *Not grouse, though. I hate the way feathers stick to my tongue. What about rabbit? I love a fat rabbit.*

You two need to focus, Sabine snapped. *We should wait to eat until we finish patrol. If there's a new wolf pack coming into this area, we'll have to chase them out. It will get too confusing.*

It's just one wolf, Sabine. Stop showing off for Calla, Nev responded. *I've hunted with you. You'll go after the first rabbit we see.*

She sniffed the air disdainfully. *Hardly.*

My own stomach rumbled, reminding me that we'd been at our pointless task for hours.

I was about to answer them when a howl stopped me in my tracks. Ren's long, keening cry pierced the mountain air, summoning the pack to their alpha. All the ease I'd felt knowing that Shay's identity would remain hidden vanished. In a few minutes I'd face Ren, and I didn't know what he'd found in the cave.

Maybe that's the lunch bell. Mason wheeled in the direction of the howl.

Let's find out what he wants. I turned, leading the way back up the mountain.

Ren, Bryn, and Ansel were waiting when we arrived. I shook my ruff nervously when I saw the place he'd selected for our rendezvous—the very meadow where I'd first saved Shay's life. I pawed at the dirt, not wanting to share this place with others, suddenly wishing that Shay were here and my packmates weren't. Trying not to seem skittish, I approached Ren cautiously. He appeared calm, silently waiting for the rest of the pack to arrive.

Fey and Cosette darted out of the eastern forest.

Where's Dax? Ren's voice filled all our minds.

He got hungry, Fey answered, looking over her shoulder.

Dax appeared from the woods, dragging a freshly killed doe with him.

Three cheers for Dax. Nev darted forward, sinking his teeth into the deer's haunch to help Dax drag the carcass the rest of the way.

Ansel's tongue lolled out as he trotted toward our meal.

Alphas eat first. Dax lowered his muzzle, baring his teeth at my brother.

Ansel dropped to the ground, ears flat. *Sorry, Ren.*

Don't worry about it. Ren padded to my side, laying his muzzle atop mine. *Hungry?*

He nuzzled my jaw, giving no sign of hostility. Maybe he hadn't found anything. Reassured by Ren's easy manner, my stomach rumbled at the suggestion of fresh meat. *I guess.*

What's your favorite part? He nudged me toward the deer.

The smell of fresh blood edged out my irritation. *The ribs.* I licked my chops.

Have at it.

I tore into the carcass. Ren settled beside me, pulling chunks of flesh from its shoulder.

The rest of the pack joined us, keeping a respectful distance.

I know you're all enjoying the food. Ren's voice reached us even as he continued to eat. *But I need to fill you in on some things, so pay attention.*

What was in the cave? Dax asked, his muzzle crimson with blood.

You won't believe it, Bryn said, hackles rising.

A very big, very dead spider. Ren tore the deer's leg from the shoulder joint.

That sounds awful. Sabine strayed away from the gorging pack, either not hungry or put off her meal by the idea of a mutant spider.

How big? Mason asked.

Dax times three. Ansel licked Bryn's jaw.

That's Logan's idea of a pet? Nev snarled, tearing more ferociously into the deer's flank.

I think it was more of a sentinel than a pet, Ren replied.

Nice to know he has such confidence in our ability to defend the cave, Sabine sniffed.

Ren flashed his teeth at her. *Anyway, it's dead and Logan asked me to call him immediately if the cave was no longer guarded by that thing.*

When did he ask you that? I looked at him, not recalling any such conversation.

He called last night, after we left your house.

I laid my head on my paws, wondering how many times Ren would get orders that I didn't know about.

He wasn't happy, Ren continued. *My father, Logan, and Efron are on their way to the cave now. They wanted to look at something else, but it's something that doesn't involve us.*

Haldis. I rose, pacing around the group, trapped in my own thoughts. They were coming to check on Haldis. They had to be.

Did any of you find anything on patrol? Ren asked.

There's a lone wolf on the mountain. Fey stretched back, shaking her ruff. *I haven't seen it yet, but that's the new scent. Otherwise it's just us.*

Shay. They'd also found Shay's trail. My hackles rose.

No Searchers, though, Dax added, gulping down a massive hunk of venison.

We didn't find anything either. Nev rested on his haunches.

Not even a fat rabbit. Mason nipped at Nev's ear.

Let's keep tracking down the slope, just in case. Ren walked away from the deer, which had been reduced to bones. *Bryn, go with Dax's group; I'll join you too. Ansel, you track with Calla.*

You're the boss, Ansel replied, craning his head to scratch his ear with his back paw.

The pack split, moving off toward the woods.

We're right behind you. Ren sent the thought to the group. *I need to talk to Calla for a minute.*

I watched my packmates disappear among the pines before turning to face Ren.

What's up?

Ren came close to me, locking me in his charcoal eyes. *Why were you in the cave?*

My pulse jumped, but I sniffed at the ground, feigning disinterest. *I don't know what you're talking about.*

He lunged forward, knocking me onto my back. I tried to roll over, but he was above me, pinning me down, my belly exposed. His jaws locked around my throat, pressing on my windpipe, making it hard to breathe.

I know your scent, Calla. You'd been in there. Two, maybe three days ago.

I kicked at him, scraping at him with my nails. *Stop. Let me up!*

Bryn and Ansel must have recognized your scent, but they claimed not to notice anything, which means they lied for you too. Are you trying to divide the pack's loyalties? Do you really want to work against me? His teeth bit into my neck, forcing me to submit. I'd never thought I could hate Ren, but in that moment I was close. He clamped down harder, making me writhe from the pain. I kept kicking and he snarled. *Don't fight me. Just tell me the truth.*

I whimpered and went limp beneath him. *I'm sorry, I should have told you. I was curious, so I went in this weekend during patrol.*

A low growl rumbled in Ren's chest. *Did you kill Logan's spider?*

My mind raced as I weighed the risks of lying or stretching the truth; telling the real story was out of the question.

No, I replied, choosing the lie. *The cave smelled all wrong, dangerous. I didn't stay there long.*

I waited, hoping he'd believe me, wondering how closely he'd been able to track my progress through the cave.

Why didn't you say anything? He was still growling, but his grip on my neck loosened.

I whined again but remained still. *I'm sorry, Ren. I thought Logan would punish me. You know we're not allowed to go inside.*

You're braver than I am. I've wanted to sneak into that cave for years. His growling stopped and he released me, nudging my head up, helping me stand. *I didn't enjoy doing that to you, Calla. I will always protect you, but you can't keep secrets from me. And your packmates can't either— I'll talk to Bryn and Ansel about this later.*

I'm sorry. I couldn't meet his eyes.

He pressed his nose into my shoulder. *I need your trust. Do you understand?*

Yes. My limbs were shaking. *What do you think killed the spider?*

The only other scent was the lone wolf, Ren replied. *I'm guessing it's the same one your group and Dax's tracked on the slope. It's hard to believe* it could have taken Logan's pet out by itself—that wolf must be some fighter.

I thought of Shay wielding the ice axes, about how much I'd admired his courage, his skill as a warrior.

I'm only trying to keep you safe, Calla. Ren licked my muzzle. *Don't take unnecessary risks. You're too important for that. I need you by my side. I'm sorry if I hurt you.*

You didn't. I let him nuzzle me despite my humiliation, relieved that he didn't press the issue further.

Without another word he darted into the forest, leaving me alone in the meadow. When I closed my eyes, I saw Shay, felt his lips on my arm, those first sparks of desire when he touched me. I raised my muzzle, wanting to howl my frustration, hating the silence forced upon me. The Keepers would be hunting for Haldis's thieves soon. What would they do then?

TWENTY-SIX

I MADE IT HALFWAY TO THE STONE STEPS OF

Rowan Estate before terror locked me in place. Shay had to drag me the rest of the way.

"I've changed my mind." My feet skidded along the paving stones.

"Too late." He gritted his teeth and kept pulling.

"I never should have turned you," I said. "You wouldn't be able to drag me anywhere."

"You're not exactly making it easy." He strained to get me another foot forward. "You owe me, remember? You abandoned me at the bar last week. I think Ren spent the rest of the night planning the order in which he was going to break every bone in my body."

"He probably was."

"Exactly. You're lucky I'm even here to give you a tour of the place."

"You have my eternal gratitude for the offer. I'm sure it's a lovely house." I squirmed in his arms. "Now let go of me."

"Come on, Cal, go up the steps. You agreed to this. Are you really going to make me carry you inside?"

I gazed at the solid ebony double doors. "Maybe."

"If you do, I'll fling you over my shoulder caveman style." He grinned. "It won't be pretty."

My eyes narrowed. "You'd enjoy that, wouldn't you?"

"Wanna find out?"

I twisted out of his grasp, scurrying up the stairs. Shay drew an enormous brass key from his jacket. My gaze traveled over the face of the mansion while he unlocked the door.

The imposing manor cut a stark outline against the sky, its facade the lonely color of fog. The building stretched out for an incredible length to either side of the main entrance. Tall, mullioned windows lined each of the three floors. The gables were filled with stone creatures: coiled snakes, rearing horses, shrieking griffins, and roaring chimeras. Winged gargoyles crouched along the roof, as if prepared to spring from its eaves.

"Are you coming?" Shay held the door open.

I pulled my eyes from the statues, took a deep breath, and walked into the darkness of the mansion. Once inside, I gasped. The doors opened into an enormous hall. A balcony encircled the broad space. Two marble staircases rose in opposite directions along the far wall. An elaborate crystal chandelier was suspended from the ceiling. Its prisms caught the sunlight from the windows, throwing infinite rainbows along the stone floor. Though devoid of furniture, the room was ringed with art that ranged from exquisite porcelain vases that reached to my waist to full suits of armor grasping fierce halberds and wicked maces in their gauntlets.

"Like I said." Shay came up beside me. "Opulent." His voice bounced off the walls.

I nodded.

"The library is through those doors straight ahead on the second level," he continued. "The stairs lead to the east and west wings of the house. Do you want to get started on the research right away? Or do you want a tour?"

"I want to make sure it's actually okay for us to be here," I muttered.

"The tour, then," he said, heading for the stairs on the right. "I live in the east wing."

I cast glances over my shoulder as I followed him. Eerie silence shrouded the house; the strikes of our footsteps on the stone floor echoed around us.

"How do you get used to this?" I realized I was whispering.

"I haven't really." He shrugged. "Being alone all the time is pretty weird."

"I can't believe how quiet it is."

"Sometimes I blast music from my room and open the door so it fills up the halls," he said. "It helps a little."

We turned down a long corridor. Floor-to-ceiling portraits of life-sized figures hung from the walls at regularly spaced intervals. I glanced at one and froze. A man was suspended in a black void, face contorted by agony, his tormentors obscured by the dark hues of the canvas. I looked at the painting on the opposite wall. It was similar, but featured a woman.

"Can we walk faster?" I muttered.

"Sorry," Shay said. "I should have warned you about the paintings. Bosque's taste in art tends toward the morbid."

"No kidding." I kept my eyes on the floor as we walked forward. "What are they anyway?"

"I don't know," he said. "I thought they might be portraits of the martyrs, but they don't have labels, and the forms of torment don't correspond with those of any of the Christian martyrs I know about."

"So he just likes pictures of people suffering?"

"Maybe," he replied. "Lots of art is about suffering and death, though. Bosque's paintings aren't any different than stuff you see in museums."

"I guess."

He turned sharply to the right and I hurried after him down a side hall. When I came around the next corner, I almost collided with a man. A beautiful man with broad, leathery wings. I shouted in surprise, dropping to the floor as I shifted forms, baring my fangs.

"What is it, Cal?" Shay frowned, seemingly oblivious to the menace a few feet from where he stood.

I stalked past him, eyeing the tall winged creature that held a spear aloft in one hand, its point aimed straight at us. The incubus stood immobile, paused mid-action, ready to release its weapon.

"It's a statue." Shay laughed. "You're growling at a sculpture."

I inched forward, sniffing the marble foot of the incubus. Shay was still laughing when I shifted forms and glared at him.

"You could have warned me that there were sculptures of incubi in the house."

"There are tons of sculptures in this house. I don't think you can go more than fifty feet without running into one. There are even more in the gardens."

"Are they all like this one?" I eyed the statue.

"Lots of them," he said. "Some of them are winged women, not men, but all of them have weapons like this one. Some of them are animals—well, mythological creatures, not real animals."

I shuddered.

"Why did it scare you?" he said. "I thought you were worried about wraiths."

"There are other things to worry about besides wraiths," I murmured.

"Are you saying that this statue is modeled on something real?" He reached out, touching the tip of the incubus's wing.

"Yes."

He jerked his hand back. "Damn."

"So where are we going on this tour anyway?" I asked, wanting to get away from the statue.

"I thought I'd show you my room." He smiled shyly. "It's at the end of this hallway."

He led me down the hall, pausing in front of the last door on the right.

"Well?" I waited for him to open the door.

"I was just trying to remember the last time I cleaned my room," he said.

"Bosque's staff doesn't do that for you?" I poked him in the side and grinned.

He shook his head. "They would, but I asked them not to. I'd rather not have strangers rummaging around my things."

"Especially when you're reading a forbidden book as a bedtime story?"

"Well, that too." He smiled, opening the door.

Shay's room was halfway between messy and clean. The bed was piled with books, and a couple of discarded sweaters hung from a wooden chair. The Keeper's text lay open on an antique writing desk. Haldis rested beside the book, giving off a muted glow in the afternoon light. But you could see the floor, and there weren't any precariously tipping mountains of dirty clothes, which was more than I could say for my own room.

Shay glanced around. "Not too bad."

"For me this would qualify as a major improvement," I said.

"Well, it's good to know I'm not offending any obsessive cleaning standards you keep hidden."

When I laughed, he stepped closer, running a hand through his hair.

"So . . ." he murmured.

The air in the room suddenly felt electric. I was all too aware that Shay and I were alone in his bedroom. *Get a grip, Cal. Can you control your hormones for five minutes?*

I cast my eyes around the room, unnerved and desperate to break the tension. As much as I wanted Shay to touch me, my fight with Ren had made me less willing to take risks. My gaze fell on a large steamer trunk half hidden by a pair of jeans.

"What's this?" I walked over to it.

"Nothing, really," he said, following me. "Just stuff I've collected and carted around with me over the years."

I threw him a mischievous smile. "I don't believe you."

"Hey!" He didn't grab my arm quickly enough to stop me when I knelt beside the trunk and flipped open the latch, lifting the heavy lid.

I began to laugh immediately. "It's all comics."

"Well, yeah." He bent down, straightening the stacks. "But they're really good comics, and some are very rare."

I browsed through a few. As I lifted one stack, my fingers brushed against something soft. I frowned, pushed aside the comics, and buried my fingers in the plush material. I drew my hand from the trunk and saw that my fist clasped a fine wool blanket.

Shay cleared his throat. "My mother made that for me."

"I remember." I trailed my fingers along the soft cable weave. "It's the only thing you have of hers."

He pulled the blanket from my hands.

"Is something wrong?" I asked, worried I'd offended him by picking it up.

"I don't know," he murmured. "That's weird."

"What?"

"The blanket," he said. "It's like . . . I think it smells different. But I don't even have it close to my nose."

"Oh." I began to nod. "It doesn't smell different. You're different. And your sense of smell is much more keen. That will heighten your sense perceptions."

His brow furrowed; he lifted the blanket to his nose, taking a deep breath. I jumped to my feet when his eyes suddenly shut and he stumbled backward with a gasp.

"Shay?" I took his arm. "What is it?"

"I . . ." His voice was thick. "I remember . . . I can see her face. I remember her laughing."

"Oh, Shay," I murmured, drawing him toward me.

His eyes opened, full of memories. "It can't be real."

"Yes, it can," I said. "Scent and memory are completely tied up in each other. Your Guardian senses unlocked the memories for you."

He was frowning. "Maybe."

"Did it feel real?" I pressed. "Familiar?"

"More than anything," he said.

"Then it's your mother."

He twisted the blanket in his hands. "Wait a sec . . . no, no way."

"Shay?"

He grabbed my hand, pulling me back down the hall.

"What?" I asked as he dragged me at a run back to the broad landing in the main hall.

He didn't answer, stopping in front of the tall wooden door that led to the library. He drew something that looked like a Swiss army knife from his jeans pocket and fiddled with the lock. I heard a click and the door swung open.

He didn't say anything as he strode into the room. I followed hesitantly while my eyes took in the library. It was easily the largest room I'd ever seen outside of our school's gymnasium. The library rose through the second and third stories of the mansion. Three of the walls featured built-in shelves that stretched from floor to ceiling. A spiraling wrought-iron staircase on each wall led to balconies that ringed the upper tier of bookshelves. I'd never seen so many books. No wonder Shay had been dying to get in here. Beautiful and terrifying, the library seemed too perfect to be safe, like a carnivorous plant that used vivid blossoms to snare insects.

"This is amazing," I breathed.

Shay was staring at the outside wall. It was the only part of the library not filled with books. Tall, stained glass windows framed an immense fireplace that was large enough for two men to stand inside it. I followed Shay's gaze to a portrait that hung above the mantel.

Unlike the grotesque paintings that lined Rowan Estate's hallways, this portrait appeared more traditional, though its occupants' expressions were sober to the point of severity. A woman in a simple white dress sat in a chair. Her hair, the color of dark chocolate, spilled over one shoulder; her pale green eyes seemed to brim with tears. A man stood behind her, his hands resting on her shoulders. His face was stern but also terribly sad and was framed by softly waving golden brown hair that brushed his jawline.

Even though I stared at strangers, the portrait brought a lump to my throat. I'd never seen faces so filled with grief. I came to stand beside Shay.

"Why wouldn't he tell me?" he murmured.

"Why wouldn't who tell you what?"

"My uncle." He tore his eyes from the portrait. "That's my mother . . . and I think my father too."

I couldn't believe what I was hearing. "Are you sure?"

"If you're sure that my sense of smell triggered a real memory," he said. "That is the woman I saw when I smelled the blanket."

"But Bosque didn't let you keep any pictures of them," I said.

"Exactly. So why would he be keeping a portrait of them in his library?" he said. "And why wouldn't he want me to see it?"

"Maybe he was afraid you'd remember something if you saw pictures of your parents. Do you? Now that you've seen this painting?"

Shay looked at the portrait again. "No."

I reached for his hand. "Are you okay?"

"I don't know." He stroked his thumb over my palm. "It would help if something in my life made sense."

I squeezed his fingers. "I get that." We'd both turned over too many stones, revealing ugly secrets squirming beneath. "So now what?"

"Now we do what we came here for in the first place," he said.

"Research?"

"Research."

I glanced at the multi-storied bookshelves. "Any ideas about where to begin? Or if your uncle has a card catalog?"

"Well, that wouldn't offer much of a challenge, would it?" he quipped.

"I guess I'll just start browsing," I said, ignoring his taunting eyes.

He smiled wickedly. "There is one thing."

"What's that?"

"A locked bookcase."

"Sounds promising. Have you checked it out before?"

He blushed, rubbing the back of his neck. "As much as I hate to admit it, I felt a little guilty about breaking into Bosque's library. I thought leaving that bookcase alone made up for it . . . kind of. Karmic compromise."

"You are a strange boy," I muttered.

"That's why you like me." He flashed a grin and walked across the room.

The carved mahogany bookcase stood in the corner next to the outside wall alongside a tall, quietly ticking grandfather clock. Shay picked the lock and opened the case. It was filled with six shelves of black leather-bound volumes. He pulled a book from the top shelf.

"It's all handwritten. Like a journal."

"Does it have a title?"

He flipped to the front page. *"Haldis Annals."*

The title was familiar, and I had the feeling that these books weren't what we needed.

"And there are dates," he continued. "1900 to 1905."

I drew a volume from a lower shelf. "This book is dated 1945 to 1950."

I began to read, confirming my suspicions. It was a genealogy. The complete history of Guardian packs.

"I don't get it." Shay was frowning. "It's a list of names, almost like a family tree. And there are notes about the family members."

"This isn't going to help us." I shut the book, putting it back on the shelf. "We should focus on the other books in the library."

He looked at me, startled. "What are you talking about?"

"These books aren't about the Haldis we're looking for," I said.

"What are they about?"

"These are the Keepers' records of the Guardian packs."

"Really?" His eyebrows shot up.

I nodded, taking the book from his hands and reshelving it.

"Close this up and lock it again."

"Don't you want to read these?" he asked. "This is your history."

"I know this history," I said. "And it will only make us argue."

"Why?"

"Because the entries aren't just about what's happened to the packs," I said. "They're mostly about how the packs have been formed, who their masters will be, and the decisions the Keepers have made in the past about mates."

"About mates?" His eyes flitted to the lowest shelf. "You mean one of those books details the way you and Ren were matched up."

"Yes," I said. "And all the other pairings that were made in the pack's history. It is a family tree, among other things."

His gaze stayed on the books, fingers twitching.

"Just leave it, Shay."

"But—"

"There isn't anything you can do about it," I said. "You'll only get angry. Now close the case."

He muttered something under his breath, but he closed the bookcase and locked it.

"Do you have another order for me, O great alpha?"

"Don't be a jerk." I waved my hand at the floor-to-ceiling books that filled the library. "We have enough work to do without you turning our research sessions into a soap opera."

"A soap opera?" He stared at me and then darted forward, wrapping his arms around me. I could feel his body shaking.

"Shay?"

It took me another minute to realize he was laughing. A smile pulled at my lips and I began to laugh too. Tears dripped along my cheeks, my belly began to ache, but my smile widened. We lay side by side, the sound of our laughter bouncing off the stone floor and echoing through the immense space of Rowan Estate's library.

Before Shay, I'd never laughed like this, so giddy and free, my body shaking with joy instead of anger. But even as I let the laughs lift me up, I couldn't help wondering if the union meant he'd soon be gone and with him the chance of ever feeling this way again.

TWENTY-SEVEN

A STARTLED CLUSTER OF PIGEONS DROPPED

from the eaves above the stained glass windows. At the sudden rustle of wings and ripple of shadows against the colored glass, I jumped up, knocking my chair over.

Shay yawned, stretching. "Calla, you need to stop freaking out every time there's a noise."

"I'm just being cautious." I picked up the chair, waiting for my heart to slow.

"It's fine for us to be here." He turned a page. "I'd say my suggestion was brilliant if we'd actually found something useful."

I scanned the index of *Sign and Symbols in Human Culture*. "It is getting a little frustrating. Not one of the crosses I've read about sounds like your tattoo."

We both looked at the stacks of books strewn up and down the table. *Nothing. We're finding nothing. This is useless.* Frustrated and exhausted, I folded my arms, letting my forehead rest against them.

"I think we're back to square one." Shay slammed a massive art history text shut.

"And where exactly is square one?" I turned to look at him.

"Translating the book." He pushed the art book aside, pulling *The War of All Against All* back in front of him.

"You're probably right about the book." I rolled my head back and forth, working out the kinks in my neck. "But maybe you should skip ahead."

"Huh?" He was already flipping through the pages.

"Instead of the beginning, look at the end," I said. "You said the woman sang to you the last lines of the text and then sang 'Here rests Haldis.' So, maybe it's the final section of the book we should read and not the beginning. You said it was the shortest anyway, so at least it will go faster."

"That's not a bad idea," he said, opening the book from its back cover.

I went back to staring at woodcuts of medieval crosses on the page that lay open before me. Shay cleared his throat. I looked up, but his eyes were fixed on the Keeper's text.

"So there was something I wanted to ask you."

I frowned at the artificially casual note in his voice. "Yeah?"

"I've overheard a lot of talk at school recently about this thing called Blood Moon." He picked up the Latin dictionary, fiddling with its pages but not really looking at it. "I guess it's only a few days away now."

"Yep." *Don't go there, Shay. Please. Please.*

"What's it all about?" He leaned back in his chair.

"Oh," I said with a measure of relief. "Um, let's see. It's called the Blood Moon Ball, but everyone just says Blood Moon for short. It's kind of a weird event, like a Halloween party mashed up with a cotillion. The parents of the human boarders come in for the event before they drag their kids back home for fall break. There's always a chamber orchestra, lots of booze, and they don't ID anyone. It's ridiculous but generally fun. If you're connected to the school, student or parent, you're invited. The adults tend to drink a lot, talk about their stock portfolios, and write checks to the school. The students also drink a lot and dance in fancy clothes they'll never wear again."

"Why is it called Blood Moon?" he asked.

I flexed my fingers like talons. "Because it's held on the first full moon after the harvest moon. That moon is called the blood moon."

He stood up and walked to the window, watching leaves drop like rain. "But why blood?"

"Because the full moon gives the best light for hunting at this time of year." My limbs twitched at the thought of a hunt. "It's the time of the Great Hunt. The blood moon is also known as the hunter's moon. This year it's on October thirty-first. It's late for blood moon, but that's when it will happen."

He turned to look at me. "Wouldn't it be easier to just call it a Halloween ball? Or do your masters object to stashes of mini–candy bars?"

My mind stuck on the image of Logan trick-or-treating for a second; I wondered what he would dress as. "No. It's Samhain, remember. Halloween isn't the real holiday. The Keepers are suckers for the old ways, their traditions. So it's the Blood Moon Ball; it always has been." As soon as I mentioned traditions, my stomach cramped.

"And everyone goes? Not just the humans?" He sounded more nervous now.

I nodded and eyed him warily, suspicious of his changing tone. "It's a good party. Everyone goes. Blood Moon and prom are pretty much the only events that the entire student body socializes at together. I think they exist only to give the humans some marker of normalcy at our school."

He drummed out a quick rhythm on the tabletop, and then his words tumbled out. "So, I know it's *really* short notice, but I hope you'll forgive me for being a guy and not thinking about this stuff in advance. Would you like to go with me?"

My stomach toppled into my shoes. This was exactly what I'd been afraid of.

"Calla?" I didn't want to look at him. "Are you going to answer me?"

"I can't," I said quietly, glancing at him.

He leaned against the table, his mouth cutting into an unfriendly smile. "Why not?"

"I'll be with Ren. I'm going to Blood Moon with him, but only for an hour or two. That's the same night as our union." I concentrated on the page in front of me. "Just drop it."

"I can't take the union seriously, Cal," he snapped. "You and your wolf prince mated for all eternity because somebody else says it's the way things have to be. It's bullshit and you know it. And Ren doesn't even realize how lucky he is to have you; he's too busy screwing all the other girls at school."

"He is not! Would you lay off Ren for once?" I sat up, glaring at him. "You've been hanging out with us almost every day and he's been perfectly respectful, despite what you pulled at Burnout and the puppy eyes you constantly throw at me."

"Puppy eyes?!" Shay blurted, and lurched to his feet. He shoved his chair aside, slamming books into his backpack.

"Shay." I wrapped my arms around my waist, feeling sick again.

"At least I know how you really feel about me." His voice shook as he jerked at the zipper of the bag.

Then I was on my feet, my hand covering his. "Stop, please. That's not how I—" My voice choked off; I knew that sentence was impossible to complete.

"Not how you what?" He grasped my hand, pulling me close. His other hand cupped my face and his thumb stroked my cheek, sending curls of heat beneath my skin. I pulled back and fled to my chair, shaking my head.

"Please don't. I can't."

I swore as I swept away hot trickling tears from my cheeks. I didn't know what was wrong with me; I never used to cry and now I was constantly fighting off tears.

"Calla." When I looked up at him, I saw how horrified he was that I was crying. "God, I'm sorry. I shouldn't have said anything."

We returned to our work in strained silence. Shay put in earbuds, blasting music so loud I heard the scream of guitars from where I sat.

The sky behind the stained glass windows was ink black when Shay abruptly pulled the earbuds out. I looked up at him questioningly.

"The union is the night of Samhain?" he asked. "The same night as the ball?"

"Come on, Shay." I rubbed my temples. "I really can't talk about this anymore."

"No, it's not about you." He gestured to the Keeper's text. "It's about the date."

"Yes, the union will happen at Samhain," I replied with a frown. "October thirty-first."

The furrow of his brow deepened. "And why is it then?"

"Well, it's one of the eight Sabbats—the days of power for the Keepers," I said. "Samhain is one of the strongest Sabbats."

He tapped his fingers on the pages. "When the veil between the worlds thins. I remember you saying that."

I nodded and he looked back at his notes; his expression grew worried.

"What is it?"

"It's kind of ironic. There's a ritual involving the Scion that is supposed to happen the night of Samhain. I'm not sure what exactly it is, but it seems to be the event that this whole section, *Praenuntiatio volubilis*, is focused on. There's a word I'm having trouble with; it means 'gift' or something similar. The context it's in is really strange."

"Gift?" I repeated.

"Or something," he said, turning back to the dictionary. "Whatever it means, the Scion is connected to your holiday."

"It's not really my holiday, Shay, it's just the day the Keepers picked for the union," I said. "You're saying their book describes you being there too?"

"Well, that's the thing. What I'm reading here doesn't seem like it's about a union. I'm not sure what it is," he said. "A lot about two worlds and darkness. And there are several references to the Scion. It mentions some kind of gathering that has to do with this 'gift,' but I'm having trouble making sense of it."

"So how do we figure out what it means?" I asked.

"Maybe *you* need to dump the search for my tattoo and read more about Samhain, find out what other kinds of rites might take place other than your much-anticipated union."

"Ren said something interesting about Samhain last week," I said.

He glanced at me. "So we're sharing information with Ren now?"

"Not about our ... project; I'm just trying to find out more about the Sabbat myself," I replied. I felt like I was going into the ceremony blindfolded and I hated it. "Anyway, he said that it's a dangerous time. That the spirit world is unpredictable because it's more powerful when the veil thins."

"How does Ren know anything about that?" he grumbled.

"Lay off, Shay," I snapped. "His mother was killed by Searchers during an attack that happened on Samhain. That's why he knows."

"Oh. Sorry." He tapped his pen on the table. "Searchers killed Ren's mother?"

"Yeah."

"How old was he?"

"It was on his first birthday," I said.

"Man, that sucks," he said. "Though it does explain a lot about him."

"What is that supposed to mean?"

"Nothing," he said quickly, getting up from the table and heading for the stacks. "We should get back to work."

TWENTY-EIGHT

THE NEXT MORNING SHAY WANDERED INTO

homeroom with a haunted expression on his face. When the bell ending the period rang, I waved Bryn off, heading over to Shay, who remained at his desk and watched me approach.

"Hey, Cal." Dark shadows lay under his eyes; it looked like he hadn't slept at all. "Can I convince you to skip your next class?"

"If it's important," I replied, fear settling in my bones.

I walked alongside him to the school's student lounge, which was quiet and empty. He sat down, pulling up another chair next to him. When I sat down, he put his face in his hands and sat silently for a moment.

"What happened?" I could barely hear my own whispered question.

"You know how you told me that Searchers killed Ren's mother in an ambush?"

I nodded.

"Was her name Corinne Laroche?"

"Yes." *Why is he asking about this?*

His jaw tightened briefly. "I went through the *Haldis Annals* for the year after you and Ren were born. I wanted to know if anything had been recorded about that attack."

I watched him in silence, feeling a bit irked that he'd ignored my request to leave the books alone but curious about what he'd discovered.

"There was no attack," he said quietly. "Corinne Laroche was executed."

It felt like time slowed, as if the air had been sucked out of the room, making any reaction impossible.

"It's true, Calla." He spoke in hushed tones. "She and some of the other Banes planned a revolt against the Keepers. The Searchers were helping her. The Keepers discovered the plot and she was punished."

My muscles slowly came back to life, shaking.

"They killed her, Calla," Shay said. "And they laid a trap for the Searchers who were coming to aid the rebellion. When the Searchers showed up, the Keepers had a force assembled that slaughtered almost all of them."

"But Ren . . ." I choked, unable to finish the horrifying thought.

"They lied to Ren about what happened," he murmured, sounding like he might be sick himself. "From what the entry said, it sounds like they lied to all the wolves who weren't involved in the plot and eliminated those who were."

"It can't be true."

"There's more." He took my hand. "When I read about Ren's mother, I went back through the *War of All Against All* looking for other revolts. That's how I learned about your history. Your real history."

Clasped between his warm fingers, my skin felt cold and lifeless. "What do you mean my 'real' history?"

"I worked through the later sections of the *De proelio*, the part that described that last major conflict in the Witches' War, the one you call the Harrowing."

"But I know all about the Harrowing," I said, frowning. "It was a terrible time of bloodshed, many Guardians were lost, but it was still an important victory for the Keepers. One that almost rid us of the Searchers."

"No, Calla. That isn't what happened." He took my other hand in his, forcing me to meet his eyes. "The Harrowing wasn't the annihilation of the Searchers. It was when the Keepers quelled a Guardian revolt. The Searchers attempted to aid the rebellion, and the Keepers staged a devastating counterattack. They culled Guardians and Searchers alike. And the Keepers created a new weapon that helped turn the war in their favor, something called the Fallen. I'm not sure what it was, but it made the rebellion fall apart. Any Guardians and Searchers who managed to escape went into hiding."

I pulled my hands from his grasp, wrapping my arms around my chest.

"The revolt instigated a new policy with regard to Guardians," he continued, not taking his eyes off my face. "Smaller packs, no turning of humans, closer regulation, with more-severe punishments for disobedience and the production of strong family ties so as to prevent the likelihood of revolt. The Keepers believed that Guardians wouldn't risk their families, even for the cause."

"What cause, Shay? Why did so many Guardians revolt in the last century?" I couldn't believe what I was hearing.

"Freedom," he said. "The Guardians revolted because they could no longer bear to be slaves."

"We are not slaves," I whispered, digging my nails into my sides. "The Guardians are the Keepers' loyal soldiers. We serve and they provide everything for us, education, money, homes. Everything. Our calling is sacred."

"Open your eyes, Calla," Shay snarled, pacing through the room. "It's called hegemony. Antonio Gramsci. Look it up. A system of rule whereby the oppressed are convinced to support the system of oppression, to invest in it, believe in it. But it still means at the end of the day, you and the other Guardians are slaves."

"I don't believe you," I said, rocking back and forth. "I can't believe any of this."

"I'm sorry," he murmured. "But you can read about what happened to Ren's mother yourself the next time you come to Rowan Estate. As for the rest of it . . ."

I heard rustling. When I opened my eyes, he held out a stack of pages ripped from a notebook. "I knew it would be hard for you to hear. I stayed up all night and transcribed the entire section so you could see it word for word. I'm telling the truth."

I held up my hand. "I can't take those. Keep them."

"Why would I lie about something like this?" He pushed the papers toward me again, eyes filled with anger. "We already know they executed Ren's mother. It's who the Keepers are, Calla; this is what they do."

I opened my mouth, ready to scream at him, but then I was sobbing. "I know it's true, Shay. I know you're telling the truth."

He knelt beside me, pulling me forward into his arms. My body shook as tears seared along my cheeks. Shay cradled my head against his chest, stroking my trembling shoulders and back. His lips pressed gently against my hair.

"It's going to be okay, Calla. I'm going to find a way to get you out of here. I promise."

I laid my face against his neck and sobbed again. His arms tightened around me.

"What exactly is going on here?" Lana Flynn's voice lashed from the double doors that led to the commons.

My blood turned cold as her eyes moved over my tearstained face and then gazed at Shay, who returned her glare with a steady calm. He rose, clearing his throat, and stood just in front of me to shield me from her view.

"I'm sorry, Nurse Flynn. We had a fight. She's going to Blood Moon with someone I don't care for, but I handled the situation poorly. I owe Calla an apology."

I blinked in amazement at his smooth lie.

The nurse's lips parted in a smile that revealed her delight in our mutual agony.

"Ah yes, unrequited love is such a torturous thing. No wonder you despise Renier. That kiss I witnessed him bestow on this girl was quite stirring indeed. The passion of youth is just so . . . delicious."

The blood drained from my cheeks as I watched Shay take in her words. Flynn's smile widened when she saw the tense, throbbing vein in his neck.

Fear gripped me. *Don't change, Shay. Please don't change.*

She strode forward until she stood face-to-face with him, running a long-nailed finger along his cheek, down his throat, and then her entire hand trailed over his chest and abdomen. I stifled a gasp as she hooked her finger in the waist of his jeans and jerked him close so there was barely space for air to move between their bodies.

"Don't worry, my handsome, golden boy. There's still good work left for you in this place."

He remained stone still while she turned to face me. "Logan will hear of this, Calla. A lady of your stature should use more discretion."

She released him and strode from the commons.

Shay let out an explosive breath. "She's not just the school nurse, is she?"

I shook my head. "No. I'm not sure what she is. Sabine once referred to her as a spellwarder, but I don't know what that means."

I walked to his side and he stiffened. "You never told me that he kissed you."

"I also never told Ren that you kissed me." I sighed. "What do you want me to say? Do you really want to have the fight you just told Flynn we were having?"

"No." A quiet laugh escaped his throat. "Maybe later."

"Fair enough."

He turned to face me, his eyes worried but kind. "What do you want to do?"

I shook my head. "I have no idea. I can't just leave my pack."

"But you can't stay here," he countered.

"Shay, who are the Searchers?" I had more questions now than I'd ever had in my life.

"I don't know." He walked across the room, kicking chairs out of his way. "It's clear they allied with the Guardians who revolted way back when and they helped Ren's mother; both times they paid the price for plotting against the Keepers, but I haven't figured out exactly who the Searchers really are or what they're after.

"But I don't think they're your enemies, Cal," he said. "They're the Keepers' enemies, not yours."

"Right now I'm not sure that means anything." I shuddered. "I've killed a Searcher. The Keepers' enemies have always been mine. Maybe it's too late for anything else."

"It's never too late." He brought his fist down on a table. It splintered under his hand. "There must be answers in that book! I need to figure out the last section. It seems to indicate mutability, change. I think it's the key."

I could see the shadow of his wolf form swirling around him like a cloak.

"We'll keep trying." I put my hand on his chest, smelling the way his wolf scent mixed with his sweat. "You need to breathe, Shay. Push back the wolf. You're too close to changing."

"I don't know how to stop it," he growled.

"Just breathe." I laid my head against his neck, waiting for both our hearts to slow. "Today and tomorrow. I'll come to your house and work with you." His hand stroked up and down my spine.

Why can't it always be like this? Just us. Nothing else to shatter this stillness.

"And after that? What about the union?" His question made my chest ache.

"I don't know." I didn't feel like I knew anything anymore.

I steeled myself as I walked into Organic Chemistry, angry, frustrated, wanting desperately to control some aspect of my life. My new and terrifying knowledge about the Guardians and Keepers changed every feeling I'd ever held about my place in the world. Knowing what had happened to Ren's mother, how we'd all been lied to, I couldn't bear the thought of hours alone with him before the union. *How can I hide the truth from him?* I didn't think I'd be strong enough.

"Review session today," Ren said, indicating the notes that lay before him. "Ms. Foris is feeling benevolent, or else she doesn't want to lose any more lab equipment to your fury."

He grinned at me and I wondered if I'd be able to go through with my plan after all. Then I remembered his teeth digging into my neck.

"Ren, I have to change our date tomorrow night."

"How so?"

I laced my fingers together so he wouldn't see them tremble. "I can't have dinner and go early to the ball with you. There won't be enough time."

He turned to face me, eyes wary. "What do you mean there won't be enough time? Our time is whatever we want it to be."

"Bryn is really excited about helping me get ready. It's a girly-girl thing that she's pretty invested in. My mom too—you know how she gets." I produced a weary sigh. "I just think it's going to cut too much into the time we could be at the dance with the others."

"You want to just go to the union with the rest of the pack?" His fingers curled around his notebook, slowly tearing the paper.

It took all my will not to cringe as I spoke, flailing for a legitimate excuse. "Can I just meet you there? You live all the way on the other side of the mountain, so it's out of your way to come pick me up, and I'm supposed to work at the library with Shay after school anyway."

Ren's lips drew back. "You're meeting *him* right before the union? Instead of going to dinner with me?"

I made my tone as plaintive as I could. "I'm sorry, but Logan said I have to keep the boy happy and he was pretty devastated when I turned down his invitation to go to the ball. I thought if I agreed to spend time with him beforehand, it would keep the peace a little better."

He paled, eyes flashing as though a cold, silver fire had been ignited within them.

"He asked you to be *his date* for Blood Moon?" Each word was so low I could barely hear what he said.

I realized my incredible miscalculation a moment too late. My bones seemed to hollow and then fill with ice. Ren had pushed away from our lab station and was at the front of the room before I could open my mouth to answer. I heard the crash and shrieks from students around the class as I turned.

The stool that Shay had been perched on rolled away from his lab station. Ren leaned into Shay, pinning him against the tabletop. I couldn't hear his words, but I saw the alpha's lips moving rapidly as he bent over Shay. His two human lab partners were huddled in the corner of their station, crouched low to the ground as if trying to avoid attracting Ren's attention. But they stared at Shay with wide eyes, seeing his strength, sensing the dangerous animal that lurked beneath his skin. They knew. If I didn't do something immediately, they wouldn't be the only ones.

Ms. Foris stood by her desk, paralyzed by terror. Her hand covered her mouth, eyes bulging, as her chemistry lab devolved into a battle arena. A few human students bolted from the room. The Keepers exchanged worried glances, leaning across their tables and whispering to one another.

I ran toward the station. My breath faltered when I saw how close Ren was to losing control. His wolf form, dark gray, hovered like an aura all around him. His sharpened canines flashed as he gripped Shay's shoulders, holding him down. Shay's fingers dug into Ren's upper arms; he didn't look afraid, only outraged. The shadow of his wolf self slid over the table, stretching the length of his body. I held my breath, hoping Ren was blinded by rage enough not to notice. It was only a matter of seconds before they would both be wolves tearing at each other's throats.

"Ren, no!" I lunged forward, wrapping my arms around his chest. It took all my strength to pry him from Shay.

Shay leapt to his feet, his fists clenched. His lips curled back and I saw the glint of his sharpening canines. I sucked in a quick breath, desperately shaking my head at him. If he lost control and shifted into his wolf form, we were done for.

"Do not move," I hissed. "You have to calm down." His muscles twitched and his neck bulged, but he remained in place. I watched him struggle to hold back his fury.

I turned Ren in my arms, keeping his body locked against mine. His heart beat at a tremendous pace, and a steady, menacing growl rumbled in his throat.

"Please, Ren. Logan, you have to remember Logan." I pulled him tighter against me, pressing my cheek against the hard muscles of his chest.

Ren snarled once before going still. I felt his breath ease, his heartbeat slow.

"Let go, Lily." It was only the sound of my nickname that convinced me his fury had ebbed.

I released my locked arms from his body. My muscles shrieked in painful protest; I'd gripped the alpha so fiercely that every fiber ached as they slowly unwound.

Ren looked down at me, his dark eyes resigned. The slightest tug lifted one corner of his lips into a smile. Without looking at Shay again, he walked swiftly from the classroom.

I drew a long, shuddering breath.

"What a nice guy," Shay said.

Suddenly I was furious with him. This was all his fault. My world had made sense until I'd saved his life. Now everything was falling apart.

The slap made a sharp cracking sound. His eyes widened; his fingers touched the bright red print of my hand that had appeared on his cheek. Without speaking, I turned and followed the path of Ren's flight from our class.

I found no sign of him in the halls, nor was he in the commons or cafeteria. It appeared that he'd abandoned school. Shaken and sorrowful, I wandered to my locker with the faint hope that he might reappear to join our pack for lunch. When I reached my destination, I found a folded note shoved between the vents of the steel door. I bit my lip as I opened it. It was clear how angry he had still been from the hard press of the pen against the page; he'd nearly torn the paper as he wrote.

Calla. I won't be around today or tomorrow. I'll see you at the union.

I dropped into a cross-legged position and leaned against the cool steel, remaining there until the bell rang. I dragged myself to the cafeteria without bothering to collect my lunch from my locker.

Lunch had gone on without disruption for about ten minutes when Ansel frowned and glanced around the table.

"Hey, where's Ren? And Shay?"

My mood had been so dark I hadn't noticed that *both* boys were missing. The rest of the pack shifted in their seats, suddenly uneasy, as they also took in the absence of their alpha and our regular human companion. I looked around the cafeteria. Shay wasn't among the humans. The Keepers had bunched into a tight circle, heads bowed and close to one another, though I didn't see Logan in their midst. The young Keepers had been acting strangely since Logan and Efron went to investigate Haldis. The acrid scent of their anxiety filled my nostrils whenever I passed them in the halls or my classes.

Not finding Shay anywhere in the room, I glanced at Ren's pack-mates, expecting that he would have called Dax to fill him in on the incident in chemistry. But the hulking senior's expression was as blank as those of the other wolves around the table.

"There was a problem," I said quietly. "They got into an argument in class this morning."

"About what?" Ansel frowned.

I fought a rising, hot discomfort in my chest and throat.

A low whistle sounded from across the table.

"Damn." Mason leaned forward, his lips flat and drawn. "So that finally happened, eh?"

Dax glanced from Mason to me, laughing as he reached into his pocket. "Well, it's about time. I owe you ten bucks, man, he made it a lot longer than I guessed."

"Hang on." Mason grinned, looking at me. "Did Shay lose any fingers? Or an arm?"

I shook my head.

"You owe me twenty, Dax." Mason stretched his hand toward the now-glowering senior. "Your alpha has more self-restraint than you thought."

"No way, that's just what I said *I* would do if it were me, not what I thought Ren would do. The bet was ten." Dax pulled a crumpled bill from his jeans, slapping it into Mason's palm.

Fey ran her fingers through Dax's cropped hair. "Too bad. I thought you'd win."

"What's going on?" Ansel's confusion heightened as he watched their exchange.

Dax cracked his knuckles. "Ren taught that cub a lesson. Shay's been panting over Calla ever since he got here."

Ansel cast a worried glance at me. "What happened?"

"Ren found out that Shay asked me to Blood Moon, and he didn't take the news very well." I lowered my voice. "He slammed Shay across a lab station and I had to pull him off."

Dax and Fey erupted into laughter. Cosette paled, inching her chair closer to Sabine, who put her arm around the younger girl.

"Shay asked you to the formal?" Bryn murmured. "What did you say?"

"She said no, of course!" Sabine glared at her and then at me. "What an obstinate, foolish boy. Calla, how did this happen? I warned you. Did you keep leading him on?"

"Sabine, you were there when Logan ordered me to spend time with Shay! I didn't want any of this. He asked and I explained to him that I was already going with Ren."

Sabine rested a spiteful stare on me. Cosette watched her reaction and then imitated it. I slumped in my chair.

Ansel slowly turned an apple in his hands, looking at it but clearly not seeing it. Fey and Dax had abandoned their laughing fit in order to debate the terms of Mason's original bet.

"I still think you owe him the other ten." Neville was flipping a guitar pick in the air like a coin. "You definitely implied that limbs would be lost when Ren took Shay on."

"I knew I could count on you." Mason wrapped his arm around Neville's shoulders.

"Knock it off." Dax bared his teeth at them. "The bet was ten."

"What if we put them in a room together again without Calla there to interfere and then saw if Shay could keep his arms?" Fey rested her fingers on Dax's biceps. "Maybe you'd like the sight of him bloodied up so much you'd just give Mason the extra ten dollars."

"What is wrong with you?" I brought my fist down on the table, nearly tipping it over. "Don't you realize how serious this is? Ren attacked Shay in the middle of class and now he's left school. He could get into serious trouble with Logan for this!"

"Yes," a silky voice said from behind me. "He could."

I slowly turned to face our master. Logan's smile sliced through me, cutting my gut into ribbons.

"Calla." He turned slightly, beckoning someone to stand beside him.

I gripped the sides of my chair when Shay stepped forward.

"I was quite concerned to hear about the incident in your class this morning," Logan said. "As you can imagine, word reached me very quickly since Shay's uncle is a good friend of my father's."

I nodded, tightening my hold on the chair. The wood creaked in protest.

"According to Shay, the fault is solely his. Apparently he insulted you in such a way as to provoke Ren to defend your honor?" Logan tilted his head at me. "Nurse Flynn reported something similar about an argument between Shay and yourself that would have contributed to this . . . unpleasantness."

Shay's attempt to cover for Ren surprised me, but I nodded, masking my feelings. "Yes, that's what happened."

"I see." Logan nodded at Shay with an expectant glance.

Shay cleared his throat. "Calla, I'm so sorry that I lost my temper this morning. I was out of line. I don't blame Ren at all for coming after me when he heard about it. I hope you can forgive me."

Logan smiled, turning his eyes on me.

I barely glanced at Shay. "Thank you. It's fine."

Our young master's gaze moved over the rest of the wolves. "Quarrels between friends are so unfortunate and best quickly forgotten. It's been so heartening to see you welcome Shay. Let's not change a good thing. I'm *certain* Ren will find it in his heart to forgive him, as should all of you."

The pack's murmured agreement was barely audible.

Logan's cold smile reappeared. "Very good. I'll leave you to your reconciliations, then." His eyes lingered on Mason for a moment before he turned away.

"Do you want to sit down?" I asked Shay.

"Not today," he said. "Another day, I hope." He put his hands on the table and leaned forward, looking at my packmates.

"I realize this is a bad time, but I do want you to know that I'm sorry. I understand that by provoking Ren, I placed each of you in a really tough position. You've become my friends, and jeopardizing that friendship is the last thing I want. I'll be back here tomorrow, if you don't object."

There was no answer from the group, but I gave a brief nod.

"Thanks." Shay walked away and I put my forehead down on the table.

"That was decent of him. Maybe he's not such a cub after all," Dax grunted. He and Fey had begun to arm wrestle. "So long as he knows his place, I don't mind him being around."

Fey gritted her teeth. "I'd still like to see them fight."

Neville and Mason had turned away, whispering quietly to each other.

Sabine's narrowed eyes burrowed into me. "He seems to understand an awful lot about how our relationship to Logan works. More than he is supposed to . . ."

I had opened my mouth to fend off her speculation when Ansel's nervous response cut in.

"I don't think that's a big surprise, considering he sits with us every day. He's probably just picked up on the group dynamic. He's a smart guy."

He didn't look at Sabine as he spoke and he tried to give a casual shrug, but the movement was more of an awkward jerk. His fingernails tore into the skin of his apple.

I frowned at him for a moment but then looked at Dax. My mind was back in chem class, remembering the defeat in Ren's eyes before he left. "I'm worried about Ren. He left a note saying he wouldn't be around today or tomorrow. I have no idea where he's gone."

Dax glanced in my direction. The moment he was distracted, Fey slammed his arm to the table.

Dax rubbed his elbow, unfazed. "I'll track him down, make sure he hasn't killed off the entire deer herd. It should be fine. The guy has a bad temper but usually doesn't stay pissed off for that long."

He cast a sidelong glance at Fey. "Wanna help me find him, in case he's still in a bad mood and decides to take it out on me?"

"Cut our afternoon classes?" She flexed her fingers like talons. "Sure, I could use a good run."

"I want Ren found, but you shouldn't cut classes," I argued. "The Keepers don't approve when we miss school. We're already in enough trouble."

Fey banged her fists on the table. "Screw that; I say we go now."

Dax gave me an unfriendly look before grinning at Fey.

"Let's go." He grabbed her arm. She twisted out of his grasp, driving her elbow into his side. He winced as Fey laughed and dashed from the cafeteria. With a playful growl, Dax chased after her.

TWENTY-NINE

SHAY WATCHED AS I STRETCHED OUT ON HIS

bed.

His eyes moved over me like a tentative caress. "What made you change your mind?"

"No questions," I murmured. "Just kiss me."

He smiled and lay beside me; his hand trailed over the curve between my hips and waist.

"Are you sure?"

"Yes." I twined my arms around his neck, drawing him close.

His lips met mine and I sank into the embrace, pressing against his body. His hands stroked my throat, sliding down my chest; my heartbeat was deafening. His fingers moved to the buttons of my shirt.

One button unfastened. Two. Three.

His lips brushed against my ear. "Do you want me to stop?"

I couldn't find breath to answer, but I shook my head.

His mouth moved along my neck. Lower.

Somewhere outside the room, I heard a roll of thunder.

No. Not thunder.

The rumbling sound, though deadly quiet, was closer than any storm could be.

My eyes wandered to the hallway beyond the open bedroom door.

Something was in the shadows. Eyes like burning coals.

Ren's steady growling continued as he moved from the cloaking darkness that camouflaged his deep gray fur.

I tried to speak but couldn't. My fingers grasped Shay's arm; he looked up at me and smiled. "I love you."

In that moment, Ren crouched and lunged, slamming into Shay and knocking him from the bed.

As they tumbled along the floor, Ren's jaws locked around the other boy's neck.

I heard the tearing of flesh, the crunch of bone, and closed my eyes.

When I looked again, Ren was in human form crouched over Shay's unmoving body.

The alpha turned to face me.

"There was no other way," he said quietly. "You are mine."

"I know," I whispered, and didn't move as he came closer. "I'm sorry."

He bent down, kissing me with lips still lacquered by Shay's blood. The taste set my own veins on fire. I moaned, grasped his shirt in my hands, and pulled his body against mine. Out of the corner of my eye I saw Shay's corpse shimmer, shifting over and over. Boy to wolf, skin to fur, sinking into a pool of blood, the change never ceasing. Until, at last, he disappeared from sight.

My eyes fluttered open. I clutched my knotted stomach, forcing back the bile that rose in my throat. The room around me spun several times before it came into focus. I stared at my bedroom ceiling; my tattered copy of *Watership Down* lay open on my chest. Searching for comfort, I'd only gotten a few pages in before drifting off. My phone buzzed angrily on my nightstand. I picked it up, staring at the screen. Shay Doran.

I pushed the button to answer the call, muttering, "I'll be there tomorrow, Shay. I need a night alone," hanging up before he could speak. I didn't think I could handle hearing his voice when his words from the dream, *I love you,* still rang in my ears.

Is he in love with me? Do I want him to be?

The patter of tentative footfalls reached my ears. I flipped on my side to face the door and saw Ansel wander by. I rolled onto my back, rubbing sleep from my eyes. I'd crashed on my bed as soon as I'd gotten home from school, collapsing under the weight of the day.

The floorboards creaked as Ansel passed my door again. I caught his nervous glance in my direction before he hurried down the hall.

"Ansel, I'm not the sun; stop orbiting and get in here," I called. He reappeared in the doorway, and I frowned as I watched my brother inch nervously toward my bed.

"You're acting weird," I said, patting the coverlet. "Just sit down."

He perched on the corner, twirling silken wisps of hair that came down over his ears.

"You need a haircut," I said.

He shrugged. "Bryn has some idea of wanting me to style it differently, and she says it needs to be a little longer."

"You're the one who wanted to date her." I wagged my finger at him. "You are now subject to her constant makeover ideas. Thank God, maybe she'll finally give up on me."

He smiled shyly. "I don't mind."

"Just wait," I muttered, envying the simple intimacies they could share.

His smile faded. "I need to talk to you about Shay."

I sat up, suddenly wary, wondering if I'd cried out during my nightmare.

"What about him?"

He continued to avert his eyes. "You know how at lunch today Sabine said it seemed like he knew more about us than he should?"

He knows. Bryn and Ansel were in the cave with Ren—they figured it out.

"Well," he said, studying the embroidery on my pillowcases, "I may have let something slip when we went climbing a couple weeks ago."

I didn't know whether to be relieved or horrified. "You let something slip?"

"Actually, to be more accurate . . ." He swallowed a couple of times. "I may have explained some things to him . . ."

"Ansel!"

He finally raised his eyes to mine; they were huge and apologetic.

"I'm sorry, Calla, I couldn't help it. We've been hanging out a lot, and he's a great guy. But whenever he talks about you, it's like his eyes just glow. He's totally done for. And I felt so bad about it, since I figured he didn't have a chance in hell with Ren around."

My eyes narrowed and he rushed on.

"So I tried to explain that you guys have a long history and now you were getting together and he kept asking questions that I couldn't really answer without giving stuff away. The next thing I knew I was telling him about the Guardians and the pack and why it's important for you and Ren to go through with the union." He ran out of breath, tensing as he waited for my fury to unleash.

When I didn't start shrieking at him, he relaxed.

"You know, he wasn't nearly as shocked as I thought he would be."

"Well, he reads a lot." I pulled the excuse out of thin air. "I think he's more open to the fantastic possibilities of the world than most humans."

Ansel brightened, bobbing his head. "Yeah, he lent me Sandman; it's awesome."

I collapsed back onto my pillows. "I don't want to hear about comics. Did you tell Bryn about this?"

"No."

"Ansel?"

"Okay, fine, yeah. But can you blame us?" He stretched out on the bed. "It's not our fault, Calla. We both had a lot of questions after we went with Ren into Haldis. We know you were there, and there was another wolf's scent too."

I didn't respond and he wormed closer. "Bryn and I have been wanting to talk to you about this since we went to the cave, but it almost seems like you're avoiding us. She thought it might be better if I talked to you alone."

"About the cave?" I asked. "I didn't mean for you guys to get in trouble with Ren."

"Not just that," he said. "With all the time you're spending with Shay and the fact that he acts like part of our pack these days, we've been thinking something happened with you guys. Did it?"

I remained silent. My heart picked up speed.

Ansel became quiet. Then he expelled a long breath.

"When I heard about the fight today, some things fell into place. I mean, I don't know Ren well, but I'm good at reading people. He's not as confident as he puts on—especially when it comes to you."

I turned to look at him, startled. Ren not confident?

When he caught my surprised expression, he nodded. "It's true. Ren may be territorial, but he's also smart. He wouldn't have gone after Shay like that, in the middle of class and all, unless he thought there was the chance—" Ansel broke off, as if it was too painful for him to finish the thought.

"Unless he thought what?" I frowned; my heart was beating at a breakneck pace.

Ansel's voice dropped to a whisper; he watched me closely as he spoke. "That you might actually be in love with Shay."

My heart galloped right off the cliff it had been racing toward and I couldn't breathe. I closed my eyes. *Am I?*

"Calla?"

I could barely hear him over the roaring in my ears.

"Did you turn him?"

I sat up, nails digging into a pillow, shredding cotton.

"It would make sense." Ansel's voice had grown soft, and he traced a slow pattern on the coverlet with his fingers. "You wanted Shay to be one of us so you don't have to be with Ren. He was the other wolf in the cave, wasn't he?"

I didn't know what to say or do. The truth? More lies? I didn't want Ansel and Bryn mixed up in this. They'd already tried to protect me by lying to Ren. If they knowingly betrayed the Keepers, I couldn't imagine what it might cost them.

I shook my head furiously, fear for his safety pulling the lie from my lips. "No. That is not what's going on. You know that was just a lone wolf. I was in the cave by myself. I'm sorry you had to find out that way. I should've talked to you sooner. And thanked you. For not saying anything. Bryn too."

"Why were you in there?" he asked, doubt lingering in his eyes. "What kind of stunt were you trying to pull?"

"I know it was dumb," I mumbled. "I was just curious when I patrolled alone. I decided to sneak in—but I ran when I smelled the spider."

He shuddered. "I would have run too. I've never seen anything like that."

"I haven't either," I murmured, lost in memories of the fight, Haldis, Shay.

"You really should have told us." Ansel frowned. "Ren was pissed off. He's a good alpha. He wants us to work together."

"I know," I said.

"Don't you trust us?" Ansel asked. "I know a lot has changed because of the new pack, but we're still your friends. We wouldn't let you down, Calla."

"I'm sorry, An," I said, hesitating before I spoke again. "Why did you think I turned Shay? I mean besides smelling the other wolf in the cave."

Ansel raised his gray eyes to meet mine, his irises hard as flint. "Because I would have run away with Bryn if anyone told me I couldn't be with her. If she weren't a Guardian, I would've turned her, and I would've run for the rest of my life to keep her by my side."

I looked at him for a long moment and then nodded slowly. *He loves her. That's what love is. It must be.*

"Thanks for not yelling at me for saying that." He offered me a sad smile.

I nodded again, unable to push words past the lump in my throat.

"I wish you would tell me how you feel, Cal," he said. "I just want to help. Shay and Ren are both good guys; I'm not judging you either way. You have to follow your heart."

I winced. "It's not that simple."

"Sure it is," he said with a frustrated huff. "God, Calla, don't you love anything?"

I stared at the bed. *Maybe I don't. I'm only trying to be strong. What if being an alpha means I can't love anyone?*

When I looked at him again and he saw the bright sheen of tears reflected back at him, he cringed.

"I'm sorry. I'm so sorry. That was a horrible thing to say."

I smiled weakly. "I love you, little brother." I reached out, pulling him into my arms.

He nestled his head against my neck and I stroked the tousled mess of his sand brown hair. I wanted to tell him everything. I felt so alone. But I couldn't risk it. I was desperate to keep my pack out of this mess as long as I could.

"And I love our packmates," I murmured, trying out the words, feeling their truth, their strength. "Promise me, An. No matter what happens, you'll be strong. I need you to protect Bryn, to protect the pack."

He tensed. "What are you talking about?"

"I wish I could tell you," I whispered. "But it's too risky. There's too much I don't know right now. Please just promise me."

He nodded, his hair brushing against my chin. "I love you too."

THIRTY

"YOU DIDN'T SLEEP AGAIN LAST NIGHT, DID

you?" I asked, walking over to Shay's desk at the end of first period. He'd spent most of class using his forearms as pillows. Mr. Graham didn't bother him or hadn't noticed since Shay had been thoughtful enough not to snore.

"I was working on the last section. I think I made some headway," he said, pulling a sheaf of notebook paper from his pocket. "Take a look."

I took the paper, slipping it into my pocket. "I'll look at it later today and then we'll talk in the library this afternoon."

"Sure." He shuffled his feet. "Should I skip chem today? Would that make things easier for you?" He didn't say *and Ren,* but I smiled thinly as I watched the thought make him grimace.

"He won't be there," I said. "And even if he was, you'd be better off pretending nothing happened. The Keepers are all watching . . . They'd tell Logan if things were still strained."

"Ren won't be there?" Shay frowned. "He isn't—I mean, Logan didn't—"

"No," I hurried to reassure him. "Ren's just blowing off steam . . . I think. He wasn't specific, but he let me know he wouldn't be around until the dance tonight." I sighed, sinking into the desk next to Shay. "What you did yesterday . . . with Logan. I can't thank you enough.

You gained respect from the whole pack. It could have been awful for Ren, for all of us."

He started to reach for me but thought better of it, shoving his hands in his pockets. "Yeah, well, sometimes I can manage to do the right thing." One corner of his mouth crinkled. "Are you going to apologize for slapping me?"

"No."

"I didn't think so," he said.

The bell for second period rang. I stood up, hating that he'd stopped himself from touching me, knowing that if I didn't get out of there, I'd be the one reaching for him.

I tried to keep my thoughts neutral through the day. My nerves seemed to be on the verge of shattering, which I couldn't afford. It helped that Bryn passed me sketches of possible hairstyles for that evening all through our French class. The cold vacuum in my belly pulled at my stomach painfully when I sat alone at my lab station through Organic Chemistry. We had a substitute teacher, and I wondered if the stress of the previous class had caused Ms. Foris to avoid school or resign immediately.

Since there was no experiment, I turned my attention to the notes Shay had scribbled on the folded piece of paper. His frustration was apparent with the chaotic arrangement of words and phrases. *Scion, two worlds, gift?? What is the veil?* After the jumble of notes was a transcribed paragraph that while still confusing at least had full sentences.

> Those who waited for the harvest child
> must choose his fate
> To begin again, search for the cross
> To guard the power, make your gift (??)

Shay's punctuation betrayed his irritation.

Two worlds battle, the Scion lives between
When the veil thins, the gift (??) must be made
Lest one world fade while the other remains

The bottom of the page was covered with more questions and some choice rants about the confusing passage. I read it through again. Shay was right; other than the mention of the Scion and the indication that this choice took place at Samhain, the passage made no sense at all. There couldn't possibly be something happening at the same time as our union. I read the words once more, letting them float to the back of my mind.

At lunch none of the wolves objected when Shay pulled up a chair, especially since he made the politically astute decision to sit between Neville and Bryn rather than next to me. But even with Shay present, our entourage had a gaping hole.

"So, did you find Ren?" I asked Dax.

He made an affirmative grunt.

"And?" I frowned at his nonverbal response.

"And he's fine." Dax shoved a slice of pizza into his mouth. "You'll see him tonight."

I looked at Fey. She glanced at Dax, who shook his head. She turned to me and shrugged before becoming incredibly interested in her lunch.

I raised an eyebrow but decided to drop the subject.

By the end of the school day a gentle snowfall had developed. The pattern of swirling flakes behind the tall stained glass windows of Rowan Estate's library made the jewel tones ripple.

Shay drummed his pencil on the notebook in front of him as I flopped down into a chair. "So, are you going to be okay tonight?"

I focused on digging in my own bag for a pen, but I nodded. "I hope so."

"Calla." His voice grew tense. "There's something I need to say, and I'm only going to say it once. I really need you to listen."

My fingers gripped the canvas bag tightly. "Shay—"

He waved off the warning note in my response.

"Sorry, but I have to. Please look at me."

I lifted my gaze to meet his. Shay's jaw was set.

"I know I've really pushed you about your feelings for Ren and your loyalty to the Keepers. What happened yesterday, with Flynn and then in chem class, made me realize just how much what I've been doing puts you and the others in danger. I don't want that."

He stood up and walked to the massive fireplace, staring up at the portrait of his parents. "So I'm backing off. After tonight I'll leave you and Ren alone. You're going to be with him. I know that, and I know how much you have at stake now that you know the truth about the Keepers. I don't want to put you at risk any more than you already are."

"Shay, that's—" I began.

"I'm not finished." He stayed where he was, not looking at me. "You need to understand that in no way does this mean I'm—" I watched his shoulders slump. When he spoke again, his voice was thick, husky. "Conceding to him. You know how I feel about you. That won't change."

I pulled my eyes off him, faltering as my throat closed. "It's true that you'll keep us all safer by giving Ren and me some distance. Especially while you're adjusting to your wolf instincts. As for the rest of it . . ." I could barely hear my own voice over the pounding of my heart. When I turned to look at him, he was standing right behind me, eyes filled with that warm spring-like glow.

"I belong to Ren," I said, hating the words, wishing Shay could kiss me and make the rest of the world disappear. "There's nothing I can do to change that."

"You belong to yourself," he said quietly. "And I can wait for you to figure that out."

Shaken by his words, I pulled out the notes he'd given me that morning, not wanting to think about how little time we had left. He bent over my shoulder.

"So what did you make of that?"

"Nothing new." I handed him the piece of paper. "Except what you've already said."

"What do you think the 'harvest child' means?" He frowned at his own scribblings.

"I think it means more research." I slid back my chair.

"Hang on," he said, pushing a book along the surface of the table into my hands. "I thought you'd want to see this for yourself."

I opened the cover and stared at the handwritten title page. *Haldis Annals*. The years inscribed below were the first five of my own life.

"Ren's mother?" I murmured.

He nodded. I fell silent as I paged through the book until I found the entry. Shay sat quietly while I read, though he stirred when I closed the text, brushing tears from my cheeks.

"My parents were there," I said. "The Keepers sent the Nightshades after the Searchers. But the pack didn't know . . . no one knew what had happened to Corinne. The Keepers gave her to a wraith."

"Calla—" He reached for me, but I backed away, shaking my head.

"I'll be fine." I headed for the spiral staircase that led to the balcony. "We have work to do."

About twenty minutes later I returned with an armload of texts, dropping them on the table. I picked up the largest of the books, offering Shay a thin smile, and began to read.

We sat side by side, the silence of the library broken intermittently by the scratch of a pencil or the crackle of a turning page. Shadows poured into the room while the large grandfather clock in the corner chimed the passing of another hour.

I blinked at the paragraph I'd been reading about Sabbat rituals. "Hey." I read it again.

Shay rubbed his eyes, yawning. "Find something?"

I scanned another page of *The Great Rites*. "Maybe. When's your birthday?"

He didn't look up from his reading. "August first."

I clapped. The noise made him jump.

"What?"

I leapt to my feet, spinning in mini-celebration. "It's you! You're the harvest child. They're interchangeable terms—the Scion and the harvest child are the same person."

"What are you talking about?" he said. "My birthday is the middle of the summer; wouldn't the harvest child have been born in autumn, when people are actually harvesting?"

"No." My grin broadened. "This is where my research pays off. Since I was reading about Samhain, I decided to read about the other Sabbats. The first of August is the witches' harvest in the Wheel of the Year. *You* are the harvest child; it has to be you. We finally found something!"

He blinked at me and then looked back at the crinkled page we'd been handing back and forth all afternoon. "So it's all about me. This passage . . . whatever is supposed to happen at the Samhain rite."

My smile faded at the sight of his worried face. "Yes, yes, it is."

"Samhain," he murmured. "That's tonight."

"Yes." I chewed on my lip. "But nothing's happening with you tonight. There's no way. All the Keepers are focused on the union. That's where they'll be. It has nothing to do with the Scion—tonight's ritual is only about the new pack."

"Well, the prophecy just states the day, not the year," he said. "And prophecies are about the future, right?"

"You think it's a far-off event?"

"It must be." He nodded, but his eyes were still troubled. "At least that's some sort of progress," he said, glancing at his watch. "Didn't you say Bryn was coming over at five thirty to get you ready for your big night?"

"Yeah, why?"

"It's six." He turned the watch face toward me.

"She's going to kill me." I began stuffing my notes into my bag. "We won't have time to hang out at Blood Moon."

"I thought you were getting ready for the union." He frowned.

"We are," I said. "But the ceremony is near the site of the ball. Everyone involved gathers at Blood Moon to dance and drink for a couple of hours so they can all toast our health or something. But we'll leave and go to the Samhain ritual while the humans are still distracted by the party."

"I see," Shay murmured.

I didn't want to leave him, but there was nothing left to say. No shared laughter could dull this pain.

I pulled on my coat and he nodded. His smile couldn't mask the sadness in his eyes. "Good luck, Calla."

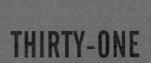

THIRTY-ONE

"THERE. THAT'S THE LAST ONE." BRYN

turned me around so she could make her inspection.

"Why are there so many buttons?" I asked, wondering how I would ever get the dress off again.

"They're called embellishments, Calla. Your mother loves them." She pointed an eye shadow brush at me. "Are you sure you don't want makeup? I could at least do your eyes. Really make them pop."

"No. No makeup." I wondered why I'd want my eyes to "pop"; it sounded grotesque. "I agreed to let you do my hair. But I do not wear makeup." I was trying hard not to be sick; if anything popped, it was going to be my stomach.

"You're going to ruin it." She slapped my hand away as I reached to touch the carefully pinned arrangement of curls she had expertly piled on the top of my head. "No touching. Are you sure about the eyes?"

I smiled at Bryn. She was stunning. More than stunning. Her chin-length ringlets were styled much in the usual way, but their bronze highlights shimmered in contrast to the inky shade of her silk empire-waisted gown, which skimmed her body like it had been spun from the night sky. It wasn't fair. Bryn and the other Haldis females would go to the union in subtle beauty, like priestesses of a dark goddess. I looked like a wedding cake, and I was sure it was my mother's fault.

"No eyes, no lips. Nothing." I gestured to my floor-length gown. "This is plenty. Any more and I will spontaneously combust."

"Fine." She packed her beauty supplies into what resembled a large toolbox.

There was a light knock at the door. Ansel's muffled voice sounded anxious from the other side.

"Are you guys done yet? Mason's already called twice. The rest of the pack thought we'd gone into a ditch or something."

I glanced at Bryn. "Do you have some sort of grand entrance planned?"

"Nah. He can come in."

"Okay, Ansel. We're ready," I called.

The door swung open and Ansel stepped inside. Bryn pivoted on her sharp heels, ambushing him with a devastating smile. My brother stopped in his tracks. He paled, then flushed bright red, and then paled again. His lips parted, but only a strangled sound bubbled from his throat, and he abandoned his attempt at speech for the sake of sighing.

Bryn crossed the room and took his hands. "Thank you."

She brushed his cheek with her lips and began to turn back to me. But Ansel grabbed her, kissing her full on the lips while she melted into his arms. I looked away, feeling foolish for the biting jealousy that struck me whenever Ansel and Bryn were together. *They found each other and they're happy. What if I've found happiness that I have to leave behind?*

After an uncomfortable period where I stared at my shoes, Bryn murmured: "We'll continue this conversation later."

"I didn't hear that, and I'm turning around now," I said.

Ansel grinned at me, lipstick covering his mouth.

"You need to go wash your face." I laughed.

"Oh, right. You look great by the way," he said before he headed for the bathroom.

Bryn bounced back toward me, fishing in her handbag for lipstick, skin flushed, nearly glowing, and I wanted to hit her out of spite. I doubted I'd be glowing from happiness during the ceremony.

Ansel reappeared at the door, jangling the car keys. "Let's get this party started."

The three of us stood watching dancers twirl on the other side of French doors that separated the ballroom from the garden terrace. Blood Moon was hosted by Efron Bane and took place at one of his five-star hotels on the outskirts of Vail, a palatial Victorian resort that rested on the edge of a dense forest. At the far end of the ballroom a chamber orchestra sent waltzes soaring through the air. Dark satin draperies, floor-to-ceiling stained glass windows, and hundreds of candelabras made the atmosphere appropriately Halloweenish. A near-translucent paper sphere, dyed red, cocooned the ballroom's chandelier, washing the room in ochre hues. Our very own Blood Moon.

An ornate table along one wall featured a huge cauldron, complete with dry-ice smoke spilling out and as many delectable hors d'oeuvres and desserts as one could imagine. Keepers, Guardians, and humans alike swirled to the music decked in their finest. Viewing them through the blur of the glass doors was like watching an array of brightly colored baubles float past.

"It's no Eden, but it looks nice enough." Bryn winked at me. "Too bad we can't join in."

"I said I was sorry about being late," I muttered.

"I can't believe you were tutoring on the night of your union," she said with a pointed stare, pulling me away from Ansel and whispering. "You and Shay must really like your classes. Care to fill me in on that? Do you have some tips you'd like to offer me and Ansel?"

"I already told Ansel you guys had the wrong idea," I said. "Didn't he fill *you* in?"

"I thought maybe you'd have a different answer for me," she said. "You know—girl talk. If you wanna spill before you walk down the aisle, now's the time."

"Drop it." The mere mention of Shay made me want to bolt. The union meant I was losing him, and that felt like losing everything. I was in no mood for teasing.

"I'd better go see if we're on schedule," Ansel said, turning away from the blurred colors of the ball. "Oh hey, there's Ren now."

"Oh!" Bryn hurried after Ansel. "I'll go with you, then."

I ignored the sudden wrench of my gut, walking to meet Ren at the edge of the terrace. His tuxedo skimmed close to his lean body; the dark jacket and pants contrasted with the gray vest and tie. I smiled at the sight. Those were Ren's colors when he was a wolf.

"That dress is a ceremony in itself, Lily. How long did it take you to get it on?"

"Too long." I reached for my braid out of habit. When it wasn't there, nervous energy pricked my skin. "Are you okay? I've been worried."

"Yes." He laughed, low and sharp. "As much as I will never like that kid, Dax told me what Shay did to keep Logan at bay. Classy move. I owe him; he's more perceptive than I gave him credit for."

I made a quiet, affirmative sound, rubbing my arms so I wouldn't shiver.

The harvest child, the Scion. Shay's face flashed before my eyes. *It's all about me.*

Ren's light touch on my arm pulled me out of my own thoughts.

"I know it's not your style, but you do look amazing," he said. "As long as you can walk under all those layers."

"Thanks." I ran my fingers over his tie. "You do too."

"So." He reached into his pocket. "I have something for you."

"What?" I was completely caught off guard. Why would he have brought me a gift? Was I supposed to have a gift for him?

The hint of a blush flitted over Ren's cheeks. His nervousness made my heart pick up speed.

"It's just . . ." he began, and then paused. He paced a few feet away and then returned to my side. Finally his eyes met mine, tender and vulnerable. My breath faltered at the unfamiliar mix of emotions on the alpha's face. Ansel's words echoed in my mind. *He's not as confident as he puts on—especially when it comes to you.*

Ren drew his hand from his pocket, his fist clenched tightly around something. He took my wrist, turning it so my palm offered a flat, level surface. Something cool dropped into my hand. He snatched his fingers back, moving away as if he'd placed a ticking bomb in my grasp. I glanced down and sucked in a startled breath.

In the middle of my palm lay a delicate ring. A smooth, polished oval sapphire gleamed up at me; the stone had been set in a silver band that was exquisitely wrought in a braided pattern. I stared in silence at the ring. My hand began to shake.

Ren kept his distance.

"The band is white gold," he murmured. "It reminds me of your hair."

I pulled my gaze from the ring and looked at him. His eyes returned to mine, questioning. I parted my lips, but a lump in my throat obstructed any words I willed to surface. The quivering in my hand spread through the rest of my body.

His charcoal irises flickered with disappointment. "If you don't like it, you don't have to wear it. I just thought you should have something before the union. My father said rings aren't usually a part of this, but I want you to know that I . . ."

He shook his head; a low growl rumbled in his chest. "Never mind," he said, reaching for the ring as if to snatch it from my still-open palm. I snapped my fingers shut and pulled my hand against my chest. He blinked at me, startled by the sudden, protective movement. I finally managed to clear my throat, though I didn't recognize the voice that escaped me, quaking, husky.

"It's beautiful. Thank you." *He does care about me. About us.* I wondered if I could get through this night after all.

Unwelcome stinging assailed my eyes and I dropped my gaze. I slowly unfurled my tightly clenched fist and slipped the ring onto my finger.

"I'm sorry I don't have anything for you."

He moved close to me and took my hand, running his fingertip over the ring. "You do."

Bryn reappeared on the terrace, this time with Dax at her side.

"It's time," Dax said. Ren nodded; he brushed his lips over my forehead before following Dax down the stairs.

"You ready for this?" Bryn asked. She offered me a bright smile, but I could hear an edge of fear in her voice.

"I'm not sure that's the right question," I said. I glanced at the ring again. *This is where I belong. I've always known my path. Now I have to walk it.*

"Just know that I'll be right behind you." Bryn took my arm. "None of the pack will let anything bad happen."

"You're not allowed to participate," I said, letting her lead me out, down the steps and into the forest.

"You think they'll be able to stop us if you're in trouble?" She elbowed me, making a smile pull at my lips.

"Thanks."

"And you look beautiful," she added.

"I look like a cake."

"But a beautiful cake."

Our giggles transformed into miniature clouds in the cold night air. We walked into the darkness, Bryn taking me along a path I didn't know, deeper and deeper into the forest, a thin layer of fresh snow glittering like a carpet of diamonds. The sounds of the ball faded and disappeared. I took in the serenity of the unblemished snowfall, knowing I'd soon mar it with some creature's blood. I glanced up at the moon, wondering again about the kill, what our prey would be.

Blood moon. The hunter's moon. *Tonight is a night for killing.* I let the moonlight pour into me, hoping it would summon my hunger for prey, but those instincts lay buried deep beneath my fear.

"How much farther?" I asked, but saw the torchlight before she could answer. Flames pulsed in the gaps between the tall pines, which circled the opening in the woods like the bars of a cage.

"I have to go in first." She hugged me, leaving me outside the ring. "Naomi said you'll know when to come. It's going to be fine. You're badass, remember?"

"Of course." My twisting gut didn't feel badass at all; it felt like pudding.

"And I hear brides get to go all diva at these sorts of things," she said, grinning. "So if you want, you can make Ren wait a little longer; it'll be good for him."

"Okay," I said. "I'll see you soon."

"I love you, Cal." She kissed my cheek and headed for the ring of torches.

I watched her go, fighting to steady my heartbeat, desperate to slow my breath. I didn't trust my limbs; my body felt strange and unbalanced, like a foal trying to learn how to walk.

Calla, you know you have to do this. This is what you were made for. This is who you are.

Then why did I want to run? Shouldn't I feel drawn to my own destiny?

I put my hands over my face, struggling for calm. A steady drumbeat rose from the circle ahead, summoning spirits to the ritual. Gathering my heavy skirts in my fists, I started toward the clearing, wanting to catch a peek of what I'd be walking into.

The scent stopped me in my tracks. I glanced around, alarmed. It couldn't be. But it was unmistakable—that smell of rainfall and plants straining for the sun. *Shay.*

For a minute my mind flashed to the ceremony. Efron speaking, "Whosoever objects to this union, speak now or forever hold your peace," Shay leaping from the shadows and tearing me out of Ren's arms.

I'm totally losing it. I tried to shake away the scent, the treacherous vision. It couldn't be real. Not only was I sure there was no place in the ritual at which anyone would ask if there were objections to the union, but Shay wouldn't be here to rescue me. There was no way.

But when I took another breath, the scent was still there, pulling me away from the grove toward the forest shadows. I hesitated, torn by the compulsion to go to the ceremony and the need to know where the scent was coming from, if it was even real. I didn't know how much longer I could put off my entrance.

A new sound wove between the trees. Sabine's voice, sweet and sorrowful, pierced the air. Another voice joined hers, Neville. Their harmonies entwined, singing of battle and sacrifice, one more re-minder that the union wasn't about romance, but duty.

The warrior's song. I had a little more time. Turning from the torchlight, I stole into the darkness, following the scent. It grew stron-ger as I moved through the trees farther into shadow and away from the flames.

I came upon a massive oak, its presence striking amid the galley of pines, and I was no longer alone. Someone was at its base.

Shay was blindfolded, his head bowed, hands tied behind his back, and he'd been left in a kneeling position beneath the gigantic tree. My throat closed up.

He lifted his chin, breathing deeply. "Calla? Calla, is that you?"

Air rushed back into my lungs. *He knows my scent too.*

I hurried forward, almost tripping over my skirts, and dropped to the ground beside him.

"Shay, what are you doing here?" I tore the blindfold from his eyes, cupping his face in my hands. "What happened?"

"She brought me here. I think I know why." The color leached from his face. "I just can't believe it."

"Can't believe what? Who did this to you?"

"That word in the prophecy." His voice shook. "The one I was having trouble with."

"You mean 'gift'? What does that have to do with anything?" *Why on earth is he talking about the book when he's tied up in a forest?*

When I said "gift," he shuddered.

"Yeah, that one." His face turned greenish, and I worried he would vomit. "It doesn't mean 'gift,' Calla."

"What does it mean?" I tugged the knots binding his wrists loose, wincing when I saw the rawness of his skin beneath the rope.

"It means 'sacrifice.'"

THIRTY-TWO

THE WORLD BLURRED AND I THOUGHT I

might pass out.

"Calla." Shay was holding my arms, keeping me upright. "Did you hear me?"

"Sacrifice?" I repeated, feeling nothing but the cold, black chasm of night that wanted to swallow me whole. "Who did this to you?"

"Flynn," he said. "She came to the house after you left. Knocked me out. Ether, I think it was ether."

"Yes." A smoky voice came from behind the tree trunk a moment before Lana Flynn stepped partly into view, still half cloaked by darkness. A wicked smile split her face, her teeth gleaming fluorescent in the pale wash of moonlight. "And now you've ruined the surprise, Calla. Don't you know it's bad luck for the bride to see her prey before the kill? Oh, wait, that's Ren seeing your dress, isn't it? Silly me."

Sacrifice. Our sacrifice.

"No." I shuddered, pushing Shay behind me, shielding him. "It can't be him. They wouldn't."

Her smile curved like a hooked dagger. "Well, well. It seems there is much more going on here than I first imagined. What a treat."

Flynn's eyes gleamed with pleasure as she absorbed my stricken expression.

"I warned you about straying from your path, Calla. Perhaps now you'll see how things really are. Renier clearly wants you. If you're willing to make the sacrifice with him, he might forgive the error of your ways."

"You're making the sacrifice?" Shay scrambled away, staring at Flynn and me, horror creeping over his face. "You and Ren?"

"Of course," Flynn said. "What do you think the fuss over this union is all about? You're the featured entertainment."

When I took a step toward Shay, he bared his fangs at me. "Stay where you are."

"I swear I didn't know," I whispered, the forest murmuring dark secrets that filled my ears, making me dizzy. My parents' conversation, my mother's insistence about the need for secrecy about what our prey would be, the way she'd paled when I said I knew Shay.

"I didn't know," I repeated, dropping to my hands and knees, head spinning. *It's Shay. The sacrifice isn't going to happen away from the union. It's part of the union. He's our prey.*

"Courage, little one," Flynn purred. "You won't have to bear this much longer. Be a good girl and go to the grove. They're waiting for you. I'll bring Shay along shortly. Right after Ren kisses his bride."

As if bidden by her words, the air swelled with a chorus of wolves' howls, calling for their alpha. My mother had been right—I couldn't mistake the meaning of the pack's cries. I was being summoned. But the sound didn't beckon me; it was only frightening, deadly. *I am no longer one of you. I will not let this happen.*

"No!" I drew a hissing breath and struggled to my feet. "We're leaving. Now."

Shay shrank from me, flattening himself against a pine tree. I caught the scent of his wolf form and knew he was struggling not to change, trapped between fear and fury.

"I would never hurt you," I said. "You have to trust me."

Please believe me, Shay. You have to know how much I care about you.

He scanned the forest, desperate, searching for an escape route.

"Shay, please," I whispered, stretching my hand toward him. "I love you."

He went completely still. I didn't know what frightened me most—what I'd said, what he would say, what was happening all around us. A minute passed where I couldn't breathe.

"I know," he finally said, reaching for me. "Let's get out of here."

A sound spilled from Nurse Flynn's throat, something between a shout and a hiss, like splintering bones. "You aren't going anywhere."

The shadows at her back began to move and my skin went icy. If wraiths were with her, we didn't stand a chance. But as I watched, I realized that the dark shapes moved with her, as if they were attached to her very limbs. Her shoulders shuddered when she stepped into full view, immense leathery appendages stretching out around her. Wings.

Shay's eyes bulged. "What the—"

I dropped to the ground, an angry white wolf, stalking around the succubus. She laughed and flicked her wrist. A long whip appeared from thin air and snaked from her hand. The length of the cord undulated as if it were made of shadows rather than leather.

I leapt out of the way as the whip cracked toward me. It struck my flank, making me yelp. The cut of the leather was nothing compared to the wave of despair that hit me along with the blow.

I was paralyzed by a vision of Ren attacking Shay. I heard my own screams and Efron's laughter. Sticky, tar-like emotions caught in my mind as they emanated from the gash that the whip had made. She laughed again, narrowed eyes moving to Shay.

"I may not be permitted to kill you, Scion, but we can still play."

She tilted her head back and I barked a warning. Shay rolled out of the way as a stream of fire shot out from her mouth, scorching the tree where he'd been standing.

My eyes fixed on the whip and its shadow aura. I crouched down and then lunged at her. She shrieked with agony as my jaw clamped down on her wrist, crunching through bone. I jerked to the side, ripping her hand away from her arm. Blood poured onto the ground. I rushed around her, smelling my singed fur as her spouting fire chased me. Flynn screamed in a language I'd never heard, and I was grateful for the deafening howls that filled the air; without them the sounds of our struggle would have led Guardians and Keepers straight to us.

I barked at Shay again, wishing I could shout at him. *Why isn't he shifting into wolf form?* I needed help in this fight.

Shay's gaze locked on the severed hand that I'd dropped from my jaws. He darted forward and grabbed the shadow whip. He pivoted, the long cord swirling in the air and then lashing across Flynn's chest. She screamed again. Her eyes bulged as she turned toward her unexpected assailant.

His cool, determined stare seemed to unnerve her even more than his skill with the filched weapon. The whip's length snaked back toward him and then flew out again, this time wrapping around her upper arm above the still-bleeding stump where her hand had been. She shrieked, clawing at the coiled shadow that latched leech-like onto her biceps.

Shay clenched his jaw, giving the whip a sharp jerk. Flynn lost her balance and tumbled to the ground. I flew at her. My fangs sank into her neck, tearing through soft flesh. There was a brief gurgling in her throat, a wisp of smoke rose from her parted lips, and then she was still. I backed off and shifted forms.

Shay stood in silence, staring at the corpse. I hurried to his side and gripped his arm.

"Are you okay?"

He nodded. "What was she?"

"That's a succubus, but a real one, not one of your uncle's statues. She's a netherworld creature that can be summoned by the Keepers, like wraiths. But incubi and succubi are more closely related to mortals—we can still kill them." I glanced at Flynn's unmoving form. "Obviously."

I shuddered in disgust. "They feed on emotion; that's why she was always so eager to make us squirm. I should have known."

Shay uncoiled the end of the whip from her arm. "And what do wraiths feed on?"

"Pain," I replied, glancing at the whip in his hand. "Indiana Jones, huh?"

He smiled, nodding as he coiled up its length.

"Good role model. Bring that with you; I'm afraid we might need it."

I touched his face, relieved that he hadn't been hurt. "Why didn't you change form?"

"I thought I wasn't supposed to," he said.

"I didn't realize I needed to point out that if we are attacked by a fire-breathing bitch, you can change forms." I punched him on the arm.

"Check, fire-breathing bitches make Shay a wolf boy." He shook the whip at me. "I have more practice using these than my teeth anyway."

"Right." The Guardians' cries still floated toward the moon. How long would they call before they came looking for me? "We have to get out of here. Before they realize what's happened."

"But we can't outrun them, can we? Even as wolves?" He followed my glance toward the flickering torches.

"We have to try," I said, starting to walk away.

"Wait." Shay clasped my arm, turning me toward him. "Calla, you know, right?"

"Know what?" I asked, caught in the mystery of his eyes.

"That I love you too."

With tears stinging the corners of my eyes, I shifted into wolf form, licking Shay's fingers once before I darted into the woods.

THIRTY-THREE

WE WOVE THROUGH THE MAZE OF PINE TREES.

The woods thinned; spears of moonlight created columns of ghostly light that split the darkness.

Shay ran so close his fur brushed against mine. *Where are we going?*

Where is Haldis? And the book? My ears flicked back and forth. The chorus of howls had stopped, allowing a terrifying quiet to settle upon the forest.

My house. I heard the fear in his reply. *We have to get them, don't we?*

They're the only clues we have left. I wished the forest would come back to life, reassuring me with its usual sounds. But there was nothing, just emptiness. *Plus the Keepers want them, which means we need to take them as far away as we can.*

Far away where? he asked. *Where will we go?*

I don't know. The world had turned upside down; I had no answers. *Anywhere but here.*

I can live with that. Here isn't working out so well for me.

I nipped his flank playfully, grateful for his attempt at humor. Even after facing tonight's horror, he was still trying to lighten my heart.

Did we lose them? Shay leapt over a fallen log. *I don't hear the howling anymore.*

My inner smile faded at his reminder that the night forest remained silent, sending a chill scurrying beneath my fur.

Just keep running.

Out of the corner of my eye I caught a brief, shadowy movement. Uncertain of what I'd seen, I put on a fresh burst of speed. Snow churned up around me as I raced toward the opening in the trees ahead.

Calla! Shay's cry of alarm sounded in my mind as a massive shape loomed from the forest, crashing into me.

All breath was forced from my lungs as I tumbled through the deep powder. My attacker and I rolled over and over until I found myself on my back, pinned down. In the next moment Ren's human face hovered over me.

Startled and utterly bewildered by the sight of the alpha, still dressed in his tuxedo, tie hanging loose and shirt rumpled, I shifted into human form and stared back at him.

His fingers dug into my shoulders as he continued to hold me down. His words tumbled out, broken and fearful.

"I've been sent to kill you, Calla. To kill you and bring Shay back. *Why am I here to kill you?*"

"Ren." My own voice quaked. "Let me explain. I can explain."

Before I could speak again, a low growl sounded nearby. In his wolf form, Shay stalked toward us, his pale green eyes locked on Ren, baring razor-sharp fangs. Ren's brow furrowed as he stared at the wolf. His eyes widened and his face paled. I tensed, expecting him to shift instantly and fall on Shay. But he didn't. Instead he jumped to his feet, backing away from me. His eyes moved from my face to the new wolf.

"You turned him." Ren's voice cracked.

He stumbled backward as if he'd been blinded and fell against the thick trunk of a pine tree, his fingers tearing at the bark.

Shay hunched low, ready to strike. I rolled onto my feet and darted in front of him, blocking his path to Ren.

"No, Shay! Don't!" I said. "I need to talk to Ren alone. Please."

Then a boy stood before me again. "No way." Shay was still looking past me, eyes locked on Ren, fangs catching the pale moonlight as he glared at the alpha.

"It will be all right. Just a few minutes, I promise." I pointed in the direction I wanted him to run. "Now go."

"Are you insane?" he snarled. "He's one of them, Calla."

"No. He's not," I said. "He won't hurt me."

And I knew it was true.

"Run. I'll catch you." He started to protest, but I cut him off. "*Now,* Shay. The others can't be far behind him."

He hesitated before slinking into the thick woods.

I stumbled through the deep snow toward Ren. His eyes were closed; his hands bled where the sharp bark of the tree had ripped away the skin of his fingers.

"Ren, look at me, please." But his eyes remained shut.

"I knew it. This is what you want. You want him." His eyes slowly opened; the pain reflected in his dark irises made my heart falter. "That scent—he was with you in the cave. He's the lone wolf."

"Ren, they're going to make us kill him!" I blurted. "The Keepers were going to sacrifice Shay tonight. He's our kill."

He was silent for a moment, and I knew at least a part of Ren wanted to kill Shay. All his instincts as an alpha would push him toward that conclusion, to possess me and destroy the usurper, especially now that Shay was one of us. But another part of him, and I hoped it was the stronger part, had to know that killing Shay was wrong.

"That's impossible," Ren said at last, shaking his head. "There's no way, after all they've asked of us. We've taken care of him; it's sick."

"It's true," I said, waves of relief coursing through me. "Shay went with me to the cave and he did kill the spider. But it bit me and I had to turn him. I would have died without pack blood. We had no choice."

I didn't want to think about how much it would hurt Ren now that he knew how long I'd kept secrets from him. How much I loved having Shay in his wolf form, running at my side. All these secrets and lies, rising from the dark unknown, circling like vultures.

"Calla, what the hell are you talking about? Why did you go to the cave with him in the first place?" Ren snapped. "None of this makes sense. Why would the Keepers ask us to kill him?"

"Shay isn't just a human boy. He's special." Ren winced at the word, but I pressed on. "He's the Scion, someone the Keepers see as a threat. He fulfills a prophecy they're afraid of."

"What prophecy? Calla, if our masters say he's a threat, then why are you helping him?" he roared. "We follow the Keepers' orders. We protect the sites."

"No, we don't. At least we shouldn't. We've been lied to." I tightened my hold on his arms. "I've read the *War of All Against All*, Ren. Shay found it in his uncle's library and I read it."

Ren's eyes went wide with fear and fascination. "You read the Keeper's text?"

"They lied to us, to all of us," I said. "They're not who they claim to be, and we're not their loyal soldiers. We're their slaves. Guardians have fought back in the past, resisted. Our ancestors tried to take another path, and the Keepers killed them for revolting. It's all there, all in the history we've been forbidden to learn.

"I can't live like this anymore." My angry tears came faster. "I hate what they can do to us. What Efron does to Sabine. What could happen to Mason, to Ansel, to Bryn . . . to any of us or all of us. I don't want to submit, Ren. I'm an alpha."

And then I was clinging to Ren, sobbing, even as I drove my fists into his chest.

"Calla," Ren whispered hoarsely. "If this is about what happened on the mountain, I'm sorry. I didn't mean to hurt you. I don't want to rule you. You're my mate and I respect your strength. I always have."

He paused, taking a deep breath. "I'm not my father."

Not yet. I couldn't hide from my own fears about Emile and my mother's words about the Bane alpha. *Could Ren be so different?*

"That doesn't matter now," I said. "None of it does. I'm leaving. I have to help Shay get out of here. I won't let him die."

"Why?" Ren hissed. "What about him is worth risking your own life?"

"He's the Scion," I whispered. "He might be the only one who can save us. All of us. What if our lives only belonged to us? What if we didn't serve the Keepers?"

Ren's arms wrapped around me, pulling my body tight against him. "I don't know how to believe you. Any of this. What else is there? This is who we are."

"That doesn't make it right. You know I wouldn't abandon my pack unless I had to," I said quietly. "Unless it was the only way to help them."

His eyes met mine, strained and uncertain.

"We don't have much time," I said. "How did you get ahead of the others?"

He glanced in the direction from which we'd come. "There was an uproar when they found Flynn's body, but I caught your scent and took off. The rest of them were still regrouping. My father's pack. The elder Banes."

He tensed and cold flooded my limbs.

"What about the Nightshades?" I asked.

"They're being held for questioning."

He caught me just as my muscles went limp and I collapsed. Images too hideous to face began to flash through my mind. My pack. My brother. Wraiths. My stomach turned over and I thought I would vomit.

Ren's strong arms supported me while I sought the strength that had fled my body.

"What do they know, Calla?" he whispered.

"Nothing," I said. "None of them know who Shay is or what I've learned. I didn't want to endanger them . . ."

I shook away the horrible thoughts. "If anything happens to them now, it's my fault. You have to help them. You're the only one who can."

"No. If you're in trouble, I'll help. I'll go with you." He gritted his teeth. "Even if that means protecting Shay."

"You can't go with me," I argued. "I need you to go back. Create a diversion to buy us some time. Please, Ren."

He sucked in a sharp breath and stared at me. I held his gaze, forcing strength into my voice.

"I need you to do this. Tell them we fought and you injured me badly enough that I ran, but Shay wasn't with me, that I was leading you on a false trail. He's who they want; they'll follow you if you take them in another direction."

The words were as difficult for me to say as I could see they were for Ren to hear.

His eyes were sad but resigned. "And where will you go?"

I couldn't keep the fear out of my reply. "I don't know."

"Please don't do this," he whispered. "Come back with me. We'll talk to Logan; there has to be an explanation. The Keepers need us; we're the alphas. We'll figure this out. They won't hurt you. I won't let them."

"It won't matter that I'm an alpha." I drew a sharp breath. "Ren, listen to me. This isn't just about Shay; there's more. You have to know the truth. It wasn't the Searchers who killed your mother; it was the Keepers."

He stared at me.

"We found records at Rowan Estate, the history of the Vail packs," I continued. "Your mother allied with the Searchers and led a Guardian revolt when you were an infant. She was executed because of it."

"That's impossible," he whispered.

"It's the truth," I said. "I read it myself. The Keepers killed your mother. I'm so sorry."

"No. It's not true." He closed his eyes, shaking his head. "It can't be."

"Help me. Please."

Far in the distance a howl sounded, then another. I shuddered.

"I'm out of time," I said. "What are you going to do?"

His eyes opened slowly. He lifted his hand and touched my cheek. "I'll do what you want."

"I owe you my life." I turned my face, kissing his palm. "Tell them we fought but that Shay wasn't here. He doesn't have a human scent now. They wouldn't know to track him when he smells like a wolf."

"Tell me you'll come back for the pack. For me." His eyes were bright with tears. "I don't want to lose you."

I couldn't speak. Tears welled in my eyes and I stepped away from him. But Ren caught me in his arms.

"Do you love him?" His eyes searched mine.

"Don't ask me that," I said, lips still burning from my confession to Shay, now stinging with this deceit. "This isn't about love. It's about survival."

"No, Calla." His voice became hushed. "This is only about love."

And then he was kissing me. His lips moved over mine in a slow caress, hands running over my body, every touch begging me to stay. I could tell he believed he would never kiss me again. Part of me wanted to linger, clinging to him, knowing all the ways we were meant for each other, how well we fit. But another part tugged me away, already running through the forest, chasing after a fate unknown. I choked back a sob when Ren released me and turned away.

The charcoal gray wolf paused and looked back once more before disappearing into the trees. I picked up Shay's trail and plunged through the snow. From behind me, I heard the lone cry of a wolf. The howl echoed as it rose toward the full moon, a sound full of agony and irreparable loss.

THIRTY-FOUR

SHAY WAS RUNNING THROUGH THE GARDENS

of Rowan Estate by the time I caught him.

I nipped at his heel. *You're fast. I'm impressed.*

An arc of shimmering snow crested around him when he skidded to a halt and whirled to face me. *Are you all right?*

I'm fine. I darted past him. *Don't stop running, we need to hurry.*

What happened with Ren? He kept pace beside me.

He's going to buy us a little more time.

We flew through the sculpted hedges and past the stillness of the marble fountains in the estate gardens.

Are you sure you can trust him? I could hear the angry edge in his question.

Yes. Don't worry about Ren, worry about getting us out of here. We haven't made it yet.

We both shifted into human form when we reached the manor's steps. Shay unlocked the door and grabbed my hand, and we ran to the stairs. Our footsteps rang in the empty corridors as we dashed through the east wing toward his room. Moonlight poured through the tall windows; long, spindly shadows ebbed and flowed over the walls and pooled like ink on the pale marble floors. All my nerves were screaming, but I managed not to jump when we passed the sculpture of the incubus.

Shay flung open the door to his room. "Okay, let's grab what we need and get out of here."

He grabbed a hiking pack from his closet while I paced by the door. Hands still full of clothes, he stopped and looked at me.

"Do you want to borrow some jeans and a sweater? They'd be too big but probably better than your dress." He looked me up and down. "You're stuck with whatever shoes you're wearing, though. Sorry."

My cheeks burned as I glanced down at my dress, its hem soaked by melting snow and almost black from the dirt of the forest floor. "It's okay. They're ballet flats, so it's not torture to walk in them. But changing into your clothes sounds good."

He watched me for a long moment, and the heat spread from my cheeks, tiny flames stroking my skin.

Finally he cleared his throat and tossed me a pair of jeans and a black lamb's wool sweater. "Here, these are on the smaller side. I'll . . . uh . . . keep my back turned while you change."

"Okay," I murmured, trying to stretch my hands around to un-button my dress. After three failed attempts I swore, wondering how Bryn had expected me to ever get out of the gown. Then I thought of Ren and blushed, full of guilt and conflicting desires.

"You okay back there?" Shay asked, but kept his back to me.

My heart began to pound. "I need you to unbutton my dress."

"What?" Though I couldn't see it, I could easily envision the thunderstruck expression on his face.

"My mom designed the dress, and Bryn helped me put it on. It has a bazillion tiny buttons and I can't reach them. Please just do it so we can get out of here."

"Uh. Okay." He came to my side, but I immediately turned my back on him.

He had about half of them undone when he paused and I heard him suck in a sharp, startled breath.

"What?" I asked, turning slightly, but I couldn't twist my neck far enough to see his face.

"You're not wearing a bra." His words came out with a rush of breath.

"It's a specially tailored bodice. The bra is built in," I said. "Come on, Shay, just get the gown off me!"

He was silent for a moment and I felt him continue to unbutton the dress. He began to laugh.

"What is it now?" I snapped.

"That's not exactly the way I imagined you asking me to take your clothes off," he said softly.

"The way you imagined what?" I gasped, trying to step away from him, but he held the now-open back of my dress firmly in his grasp.

One of his hands released my dress and slipped around my waist while the other touched the bare skin between my shoulder blades and slowly moved along my spine toward my lower back. I shivered, closing my eyes. His lips pressed against the curve between my neck and shoulder. Soothing warmth pooled at the site of his gentle kiss, poured over my shoulders, and cascaded through my limbs. The world fell away, as it always did when he touched me.

His hand slid beneath the loosened bodice from my back to my bare stomach, pulling me against him. I could feel every inch of his body touching the length of mine, the strength of his wanting matching my own, breath for breath. His fingers slid down and I gasped. My eyes wandered to his bed. It was so close. He could easily carry me there.

We can't. Not like this, not with everything that's happening.

"Don't," I murmured, head and body battling each other. "Please don't."

I twisted away from his lips, fighting the flood of emotions his soft touch provoked, needing to quell the ache his hands had left lingering deep within me. The faces of my packmates passed before my tightly closed eyes. Faces I feared I might never see again. Ren's face. I swallowed the thickness in my throat, pulling the bodice tight across my chest.

"Right. I remember. No kissing without loss of limbs. My limbs, that is," he said. "Sorry, I was caught up in the moment."

Shay resumed his task of unbuttoning in a more-chaste manner.

I cleared my throat, wanting to sound more confident than I felt. "It's okay. We just need to hurry. No distractions."

His hands dropped from the fabric. "You should be able to wiggle out of that now. I'll wait in the hall."

"That's probably a good idea."

I shimmied out of the dress. With considerable relief I pulled on Shay's jeans and sweater and then braided my hair, ripping a ribbon from my dress to tie it.

A faint cracking sound reached my ears, sharp and brittle like too much weight on thin ice. My breath came more quickly.

"Calla," Shay called from the hall. "Without your nakedness to distract me, I'm remembering that we're in serious trouble. Hurry, please."

"All set." I grabbed the Keeper's text from Shay's nightstand and left the room, throwing it on top of his hastily packed clothes. "Haldis?"

"Already in here." He patted the bag. "It was hidden in the back of my closet."

"Let's get out of here." I grabbed his hand and we ran back down the hallway. When we turned into the main corridor, I froze. He paused beside me.

"What's wrong?"

I pivoted, staring at the thin flakes of marble that littered the floor.

"Where is the statue?" I murmured. "The incubus?"

"What?" His voice was hoarse.

A soft rustle like the wind lifting a pile of dead leaves came from above us. I glanced up.

The incubus grinned at me, spreading its wings and unhooking its talon-like nails from the ceiling.

"Run!" I shoved Shay forward and shifted into wolf form. In the next moment a golden brown wolf ran beside me.

Our toenails scraped the marble floor as we tore down the hallway. Something whistled past my shoulder and the incubus's spear clattered on the stones a few feet in front of me. The sound of beating wings filled my ears. Shay glanced over his shoulder.

There's more than one chasing us.

How many?

Another spear sailed past us.

I'm not sure.

We reached the top of the staircase and I yelped. The chimera crouched halfway down the steps, its serpent tail hissing and weaving hypnotically while a forked tongue darted from its mouth and its lion head roared, its mane of snakes striking at the air, hundreds of needle-sharp teeth flashing. Two succubi hovered in the air above the chimera. They shrieked at the sight of us. One drew its bow taut and loosed an arrow at me. I threw my body to the side as the arrow buzzed past, scrambled to my feet, and ran along the balcony with Shay at my heels.

I bolted toward the corridor that led to the west wing. A rush of sighs like the collective release of breath wafted through the hall, making me skid to an abrupt halt. A long moan echoed around us; it became louder and louder, rising to the ceiling in a dense fog of wretched sound.

What was that? The terror in Shay's question was as shrill as nails on a chalkboard.

Oh God. I scuttled backward as two grasping arms and then a flailing body dropped out of one of the tall portraits that hung on the walls.

The figure jerked to its feet and ambled toward us, its moans constant, growing more and more desperate. All along the halls bodies lurched and rolled from the paintings until the corridor was filled by the scrape of slow-moving feet on the stone floor. Dozens of the moaning creatures came forward at an awkward, jerking gait.

The first of them emerged from the dark corridor and was suddenly bathed in moonlight. I whined, swaying on my feet. Despite the sunken features and vacant expression, I would have recognized him anywhere. It was the Searcher whom I'd turned over to Efron and Lumine for questioning. My muscles quaked and I thought my legs might give out.

Calla! Shay's alarm brought me back to my senses. *What the hell is happening? What are those things?*

I don't know, but there are too many. I couldn't hide my own panic. *We can't fight them.*

Shay darted past me, shifting forms. "Come on!" He hurled himself against the library door, flinging it open, and I rushed after him into the dark room. The moment I was through the door, he slammed it shut and locked it. He banged his forehead on the wood, drawing a ragged breath. I could hear the screams of the succubi on the other side of the door.

"Damn," Shay whispered.

I shifted forms. "I know. We have to find a way out of here."

"That's not it." He was shaking his head.

"What are you talking about, Shay?"

"The door, Calla," he murmured. "The library door. It wasn't locked."

My throat closed.

"They weren't chasing us," he continued. "They were driving us."

I jumped as a ruddy orange glow poured through the library. Flames burst to life, dancing and weaving in the fireplace. A lone figure stood in front of the roaring fire, his frame outlined by the flickering light. Fear wormed beneath my skin. The shadow cast by the Keeper wasn't the shape of a man. I didn't know what it was.

"Very perceptive of you, Shay." Bosque Mar smiled, his eyes rolled up at the portrait above the mantel. "Your parents would be proud."

"Uncle Bosque." Shay's voice quaked. "You're here."

Bosque continue to smile, the play of light and shadow from the undulating fire etching his face into a grotesque mask. The cruelty of his expression made my knees weak.

What is he? I grabbed Shay's arm, tugging him back.

"I was called back from business," he said. "It seems things in Vail have gotten a bit out of hand."

His eyes moved to me, narrowing into slits. "Tell me, Calla. When precisely did you turn my nephew into one of your own kind?"

I forced steel into my voice. "He is not your nephew."

Bosque's laugh was like shattering glass. "How very little you understand. You're a warrior, a leader of warriors." He took a step forward. "I never expected such foolishness from an alpha Guardian."

"She isn't foolish," Shay said, twining his fingers in mine.

"She belongs to another and she betrayed her own kind. She is the embodiment of rash decisions." Bosque glanced at our clasped hands and shook his head. "I'm afraid this will not do."

"Who are you?" Shay managed to keep his voice level, though I could feel his pulse pounding.

"The only family you have left," Bosque murmured. He glanced at the painting again. Tristan and Sarah's faces appeared even more sorrowful than when I'd first gazed at the portrait. "I'm the one who knows what's best for you."

"You want to kill me," Shay whispered.

Bosque cocked his head, smiling. "Why would I want to kill my own nephew?"

I gripped Shay's hand. "Stop it. No more lies. They tied him up! Brought him to be sacrificed at the union. We know about the prophecy, the sacrifice. We read *The War of All Against All*."

"I know," Bosque replied smoothly. "But why do you think we forbid the study of that volume?"

"To protect yourself and the Keepers," I said. "To keep us from knowing the truth about our past. You've enslaved us."

"No, dear girl. We saved you." Bosque assumed a pained expression. "Keepers have always been the caretakers of our Guardian soldiers. That book is poison, full of lies produced by the Searchers. It has been circulated by our enemies for centuries in an attempt to seduce others to their wicked cause. We work hard to suppress it because of the harm it can do. And look at what has happened because of it. That text has brought bloodshed to our very doorstep."

"It wasn't the book that attacked us!" I shouted. "I don't even have a name for what came out of those paintings." I pointed at his bizarre shadow. "Or for you! What are you?"

Bosque's face darkened, but a second later a placid smile rested on his lips. "I'm sorry if you were frightened, but this exceptional circumstance made it necessary that I gain a captive audience with the two of you. You must listen to reason."

"Reason?" Shay spat. "I want to know the truth!"

"Of course you do, Shay." Bosque nodded quickly. "If I'd realized what an independent spirit you'd developed, I would never have put this library off-limits. What else would a bright young man like yourself do but find a way in? Your thirst for knowledge is admirable."

His smile had the keen edge of a blade. "I blame myself. I still think of you as a little boy. I wanted to protect you from your enemies, but I failed to see how much you've grown up. I've neglected you, and for that I have much regret."

Shay's fingers clutched my hand so tightly it hurt. "Tell me who you really are."

"I'm your uncle," Bosque said calmly, walking toward us. "Your own flesh and blood."

"Who are the Keepers?" Shay asked.

"Others like me, who want only to protect you. To help you," Bosque replied. "Shay, you are not like other children. You have untapped abilities that you cannot begin to imagine. I can show you who you truly are. Teach you to use the power you have."

"If you're so invested in helping Shay, why was he the sacrifice at my union?" I pushed Shay behind me, shielding him from Bosque.

Bosque shook his head. "Another tragic misunderstanding. A test, Calla, of your loyalty to our noble cause. I thought we offered you the best of educations, but perhaps you aren't familiar with Abraham's trial with his son Isaac? Isn't the sacrifice of one you love the ultimate gauge of your faith? Do you really believe we wanted Shay to die at your hands? We've asked you to be his protector."

I began to shake. "You're lying."

"Am I?" Bosque smiled, and it almost looked kind. "After all you've been through, have you no trust in your masters? You would never have been made to harm Shay—another kill would have been provided in his place at the last moment. I understand such a test may seem too terrible to be fair, too much to ask of you and Renier. Perhaps you are too young to have faced such a trial."

I couldn't answer him, suddenly questioning everything I'd done up to this moment, wondering if my own desires had carried me far off course, skewing my ability to see the truth. I didn't know what to believe.

"I've cared for Shay since he was a tiny child. Provided for his every want and need. Surely that proves my concern for his welfare." Bosque paused a few feet short of us, stretching his arms out to his nephew. "Please, give me your trust."

The stained glass windows behind Bosque exploded into a shower of multicolored shards. I pushed Shay to the ground and curled my body around his, shielding him from the jagged rain. I threw an arm up to cover my face while the falling glass sheared the fabric of my sweater and sliced my skin.

Shouts sounded in the room, the pounding of footfalls on the library floor. I raised my face to see at least twenty Searchers leaping through the shattered windows, surging in a wave of glinting steel and buzzing arrows toward the Keeper. The air around Bosque shimmered and the flurry of projectiles sailing at him bounced back like they'd slammed into a shield. Bosque raised his arms. The leaping flames of the fire extinguished and the red haze illuminating the room gave way to the blindness of heavy shadow.

A few of the Searchers stumbled and fell; others jerked awkwardly to a stop, struggling to regain their bearings. Shay pushed me off him and rolled to his feet.

"What happened?"

"Searchers," I hissed. "More than I've ever seen."

Bosque threw his head back and cried out. I covered my ears against the sound, which made the library's books vibrate on the shelves. The darkness covering the room collected into distinct pools that rose into the air and slowly took shape. I gasped and grabbed Shay's arm.

"Are those . . ." His voice was tight.

"Wraiths," I murmured. "But it's impossible."

"Why?" His eyes were wide as the shadow guards descended upon the invading force.

I could barely draw breath to get the words out. "No one can summon more than a single wraith at a time. They're too hard to control."

"Wraiths incoming!" one of the Searchers shouted. "Ethan,

Connor! Get the boy and get out now! The rest of you clear a path for them!"

Another Searcher, a woman, screamed when black tendrils snaked around her waist. Yet another hacked futilely with his sword at the looming wraith that engulfed him; he made strangling sounds as his body disappeared into the black veil.

"Go! Go! Go!" the first Searcher yelled.

Bosque's face twisted, full of outrage. With fingers extended like talons, he pointed to the library door, twisted his hand, and jerked his arm back. The door flew open and the horde that waited on the balcony sprang to life, rushing into the fray. Succubi and incubi hissed and screeched as they flew through the library, spouting flames while the Searchers' arrows buzzed through the air. Several of the winged creatures screamed and dropped to the ground, feathered shafts protruding from their chests.

The chimera bounded into the room and pounced on a Searcher who screamed as the lion's jaws clamped on his shoulder, its serpent tail striking at his legs over and over. Shuffling feet and moans announced the arrival of the painted undead, who lurched into the battle, jaws agape, eyes hollow and hungry. A few of the Searchers dropped their weapons, screaming at the sight of these slow-moving, desiccated creatures.

Bosque began to laugh and waved his arms as though conducting a symphony. The chorus of moans grew louder.

"Don't look at the Fallen!" the first Searcher shouted. "Our target is all that matters!"

"Monroe! The boy is over here!" A man bolted from the other side of the room toward us. I recognized him instantly, even without blood gushing from his nose.

I bared my teeth as he raised his crossbow.

"No talking this time," Ethan said.

I shifted forms, launching myself at him, but my breath came whistling back out as a pair of crossbow bolts buried in my chest. The force of my leap sent Ethan and me tumbling over each other across the floor. I smashed into the far wall. Pain rocketed up my spine. I could feel blood running over my stomach as I fought to remain conscious.

"Calla!" Shay hurled himself at us, shifting in midair. Ethan swore, twisting away from Shay's snapping jaws.

"Monroe, Connor! Get over here now! They've turned the Scion," Ethan yelled, and another string of curses erupted from his throat.

A blurred figure sped across the room, weaving through the chaos of wings, claws, and weapons. I saw Connor fling his body across the floor, rolling just out of reach of the slithering shape of a wraith. He leapt to his feet and bolted toward Shay, who snarled when Connor drew his swords. He held the blades low, wolf and Searcher stalking in a slow circle facing each other.

"I don't want to hurt you, kid, but we don't have time for this."

I watched them struggle through a haze of pain. My breath sounded wet each time I sucked in air. Despite the spike of pain I tried to drag myself toward them.

While Shay's eyes tracked Connor, Ethan struggled to his feet. His hand dipped inside his leather duster and he threw himself onto the wolf's back. Shay yelped when the Searcher plunged a syringe into his neck. Shay bucked, snarling, and Ethan flew back onto the stone floor. The wolf pivoted, muscles bunched to leap at Ethan, but abruptly shook his head. His limbs shuddered and he whimpered, swaying on his feet and collapsing onto the floor. He didn't move again.

I howled, struggling across the floor to his side. Each step was agony. The crossbow bolts still protruded from my chest. The blood in my lungs was slowly drowning me.

When I reached him, I shifted forms, buried my hands in his fur, and shook his shoulders.

"Shay! Shay!" Even as I clung to him, I could feel strength ebbing from my limbs.

"Enchanted bolts; hope you're enjoying the ride." Ethan's gravel-rough voice drew my eyes to the side. He had the crossbow trained on me once more. "Are you the one who turned him?"

My chest was on fire, my vision blurred. I nodded and slumped to the floor, rolling alongside Shay. *So this is how I die?* I reached for his hand.

Ethan's finger tightened on the trigger. A long moan from behind me pulled his eyes away. He gasped, stumbling back. "Kyle?"

I twisted my neck. Through a haze of pain I saw the corpse-like Searcher who'd emerged from one of the paintings ambling toward us, his arms grasping mindlessly at the air in front of him.

"No!" Ethan started toward the lurching body.

The Searcher who had been shouting orders loomed over me, blocking Ethan's view of the moaning creature.

"Get out of the way, Monroe," Ethan said. "I have to help him."

"He's not your brother, Ethan." Monroe gripped the other man's arms. "That isn't Kyle. Not anymore. Forget him."

I heard a choked sob as Ethan's shoulders crumpled.

"We need to get out of here," Monroe said. "Stay at Connor's back in the retreat."

Ethan's face was tight with grief, but he nodded. "On it."

"Now, Connor," Monroe said. "Hurry."

Connor crouched beside Shay, gathering the wolf in his arms.

I cried out when Shay's fingers were wrenched from mine.

"Got him," Connor said. "Let's go."

"After you." Ethan lifted his crossbow.

Connor raced across the room with Ethan at his side, firing bolts as they ran. Monroe turned to follow.

"Wait," I whispered hoarsely.

He looked down at me and frowned. "Who are you?"

"I'm trying to help Shay."

"You made him like you? A Guardian?"

"I had to." The room began to fade in and out.

"Did the Keepers make you turn him?"

"No." I winced, closing my eyes against the pain. "They didn't know."

One of his eyebrows shot up. "You defied the Keepers?"

I nodded. My body convulsed and I coughed up blood.

There was a long moan and the slow scrape of feet along the stone floor grew louder. I wondered how close the creature that had been Kyle was . . . and how strong it might be.

Monroe's gaze flitted behind me. His brow knit and his eyes fell on me again, watching me struggle to sit up.

"I'm sorry about this," he said, raising his sword, and brought the hilt down on my skull.

A lightning strike of pain seared through me before I sank into darkness.

THIRTY-FIVE

I LIVED IN THE SPACE BETWEEN THE CONSCIOUS

and the unconscious. Brief flashes of light and sound occasionally pierced the veil that smothered my senses. I felt movement, but not any I made on my own. My limbs were numb. Arms, legs, torso all felt heavy; painless, but waterlogged and beyond my control.

Was I dragged or carried? I couldn't be sure. I was only vaguely aware of my body being lifted, jerked, passed from one pair of arms to another. Was this actually happening? I felt warm, drowsy. My eyelids were like lead curtains.

"*I hear we've bagged an alpha.*"

Voices. Rough speech that belonged to strangers, enemies. Words that made no sense.

"*Corinne's son? Monroe must be relieved.*"

"*No. It's a female.*"

"*That's a shame. We're not keeping her around, are we?*"

"*Not sure. I think Monroe's weighing our options.*"

Someone gripped my hand and I heard the voice of a friend.

"*It's going to be okay, Calla. I swear I won't let them hurt you.*"

"*Shay, get over here,*" a gruff but strangely familiar voice ordered. "*I've asked you not to speak with her.*"

"*You're being unreasonable.*"

"I think you'll find I'm very reasonable, but you haven't earned my trust yet."

"Is that what I'm supposed to be doing?"

"You'd be the wiser for it."

The world came rushing back, strange sights and scents swirling around me. I was lying on my back, and there was a dull ache in my chest. My eyes struggled to adjust to the dim light. Something cold with sharp edges clamped around my left wrist. A sudden heavy weight brought my arm down hard against my body and my eyes squeezed shut again. I winced at the tenderness in my rib cage.

"Ethan, stay close to Connor in case she wakes up," Monroe said.

"Why are you doing this?" Shay said. "You don't need to. She isn't your enemy. Not anymore."

"Sure, kid." Ethan laughed coldly. "Whatever you say."

"Hand me the other one, Ethan," Connor said.

The same cold grip seized my right wrist and pressure pinned my arm against my torso.

"That should do it," Connor said.

"You said she'd be okay," Shay growled. "You promised."

"And I'll keep that promise," Monroe said. "She hasn't been harmed."

"She looks okay to me," Ethan added. "What do you think, Connor?"

"I think she's kind of cute," Connor replied.

A snarl and a scuffling sound reached my ears.

"Whoa! Hang on there, kid. Lucky you ducked, Connor, I think that's the same left hook that broke my nose last round," Ethan said. "You got him, Monroe?"

"He's not going anywhere," Monroe said with a grunt. "Stop struggling. Connor didn't mean anything by it, Shay. You don't need to fight him."

"Let me go!"

"Scrappy one, isn't he?" Connor said. "You're sweet on this girl, huh? Interesting."

"If you touch her, I swear—"

"Calm down," Connor muttered. "I was just joking around."

I forced my eyes open, but everything remained blurry. My throat was parched and I struggled to swallow, to find my voice.

"We had a deal, Shay," Monroe said firmly. "You can't stay here any longer."

"But—"

"You'll see her again. You have my word."

"When?"

"That depends on you."

"I don't know what you mean."

"You will. Now it's time to go. Today is the day your real life begins."

The light winked out and shadows engulfed the room. The long screech of a rusty metal hinge was followed by a dull clang. The voices began to fade.

I parted my lips, my voice emerging in a quiet rasp.

"Shay?"

Silence. I was alone in the darkness.

Maybe it was a dream.

Anger seized me and I screamed at the shadows that filled the room, but there was no enemy to fight, save my gnawing fear of the unknown. I began to tremble.

You're an alpha, Calla. Get it together.

The unyielding darkness pooled in the pit of my stomach.

What does it mean to be an alpha if you've abandoned your pack?

I was glad to be alone when the tears finally came. At least no one would witness the shame that rolled swift and hot down my cheeks. Streaks of moisture reached my lips and tasted sharp and bitter, reminding me of the choices I'd made. Of how I'd taken so many turns that brought me here—to a place so unfamiliar that it felt like the end of everything.

Where did running away lead me? Straight into the arms of the only enemy I've ever known? To my own death?

For the first time I could remember, I was truly alone. I stared into the empty room, grasping for a sliver of hope.

I'd risked everything to save Shay. Letting stillness ease my trembling limbs, I closed my eyes and saw his face, remembering the freedom I'd felt in his arms, the possibility of a life unlike any I'd imagined. I wondered if my capture had snuffed out that dream ... if it had ever stood the chance of becoming real.

Despair threatened to drag me down, but I fought back, clinging to a single, flickering thought. *Shay loves me.* He would risk everything to find his way back to my side and set me free. *Because that's what love is, isn't it? It has to be.*

ACKNOWLEDGMENTS

Acknowledgment doesn't phonetically evoke the grace and fortitude provided by colleagues, friends, and family, whose presence made this novel possible. Richard Pine and Charlie Olsen of Inkwell are my knights in shining armor. Charlie—thank you for loving this book, guiding me, and indulging phone conversations conducted fully in Star Wars metaphors. Richard—I'm still dazzled whenever you call! I couldn't have better writing mentors than Michael Green and Jill Santopolo at Philomel. Michael, thank you for your wonderful words and questions as I started this journey. I'd especially like to thank Jill for bringing incredible skill and kindness to our work together. The entire team at Penguin Young Readers has been wonderful. Thank you Don Weisberg, Jennifer Haller, Emily Romero, Erin Dempsey, Shanta Newlin, Jackie Engel, Linda McCarthy, Katrina Damkoehler, Felicia Frazier, Scottie Bowditch, and Julia Johnson for your incredible support and enthusiasm. I'm thrilled to be part of the Penguin family!

I'm indebted to Stephanie Howard and Lisa Desrochers for being great critique partners. Lindsey Adams and Gina Monroe made my Internet digs fabulous by sharing their artistic gifts. John and Natalie Occhipinti taught me that strangers on a plane can become your first fans. Corby Kelly, thanks for lending your mad language skills. Kristin Naca, you are a goddess, keep it up. Casey Jarrin, your brilliance makes everything around you sparkle, this book being no exception. This writer's mind flourished in a little-known corner of the globe: Ashland, Wisconsin, I love you like no other place in the world. FISH CAMP! Ed and Maribeth, thank you for reading from the first hope. Katie, thank you for knowing.

None of this would have happened without the love and support of my family. Aunt Helen, thanks for all the books. Mom, Dad, Garth, you are the threads that weave through everything, always. And for Will, who dances with me whenever I am sad—I may not like *The Young Ones,* but I love you more every day.

The story continues in

Turn the page for an exciting preview . . .

I.

I couldn't shut out the screams. Darkness surrounded me. A terrible weight pressed into my chest, making me struggle for each breath as I lay drowning in my own blood. I sat up with a gasp, blinking into the shadows.

The screaming had stopped. The room became still, flooded with silence. I took a couple of painful swallows, trying to moisten my parched mouth. It took me a moment to realize that the screams had been my own, each cry clawing my throat until it was raw. I brought my hands up to my chest. My fingers moved along the surface of my shirt. The fabric was smooth, with no sign of rips or tears from the crossbow bolts. I couldn't see well in the dim light, but I could tell this shirt wasn't mine, or rather, wasn't Shay's borrowed sweater—the one I'd been wearing the night everything changed.

A blur of images rushed through my head. A blanket of snow. A dark forest. The pounding of drums. Howls calling me to the union.

The union. My blood grew cold. I'd run from my own destiny.

I'd run from Ren. The thought of the Bane alpha made my chest tighten, but when I dropped my face into my hands, another figure replaced him. A boy on his knees, blindfolded and bound, alone in the forest.

Shay.

I could hear his voice, feel the brush of his hands on my cheek as I'd slipped in and out of consciousness. What had happened? He'd left me alone in the dark for so long. . . . I was still alone. But where?

My eyes adjusted to the low light of the room. The cloudy skies filtered sunlight through tall leaded windows stretching the length of the opposite wall, tingeing pale shadows with a rose-hued gleam as I scanned the room for an exit, finding atall oak door to the right of the bed. Ten, maybe fifteen feet from where I sat.

I managed to slow my breathing, but my heart was still pounding. Swinging my legs over the edge of the bed, I tentatively put weight on my feet. I had no trouble standing and felt each muscle spring back to life, coiled and taut, ready for anything.

I'd be able to fight, and kill, if I had to.

The sound of booted footsteps reached my ears. The knob turned and the door swung inward to reveal a man I'd only seen once before. He had thick hair, deep brown like the color of black coffee. The contours of his face were cut at strong, chiseled angles, slightly worn with lines and covered with the shadow of several days unshaven, salt-and-pepper stubble—neglected but still appealing.

I'd last seen his face seconds before he coldcocked me with the pommel of his sword. My canines sharpened as a growl rumbled deep in my chest.

He opened his mouth to speak, but I shifted into a wolf, crouching low, snarling at him. I kept my fangs in plain view, a steady growl rolling out of my throat. I had two options: tear him to pieces or bolt past him. I was guessing I only had a few seconds to pick one.

His hand went to his waist, pushing back his long leath
to rest on the hilt of a long, curving saber.

A fight it is.

My muscles quivered as I hunched down, angling for his th

"Wait." He moved his hand off the hilt, lifting his palms in an attempt to pacify me.

I froze, stunned by the gesture and a little irked at his presumption. I wouldn't be calmed that easily. After a quick snap of my fangs, I risked a glance toward the hall at his back.

"You don't want to do that," he said, stepping into my line of sight.

I answered with a growl.

And you don't want to find out what I'm capable of when I'm cornered.

"I understand the impulse," he continued, folding his arms over his chest, the sword in its scabbard. "You might get past me Then you'll run into a security detail at the end of the hall. And if you get past them—which I think you probably could, given that you're an alpha—you'll hit a larger group of guards at any of the exits."

"Given that you're an alpha." How does he know who I am?

Still growling, I backed off, throwing a glance over my shoulder at the tall windows. I could easily smash through them. It would hurt, but as long as it wasn't too high a drop, I'd survive.

"Not an option," he said, glancing at the windows.

What is this guy? A mind reader?

"That's at least a fifty-foot drop onto solid marble." He took a step forward. I backed up again. "And no one here wants to see you get hurt."

The growl died in my throat.

His voice dropped low and he spoke slowly. "If you'd shift back into human form, we could talk."

I gnashed my teeth, frustrated, sidling along the floor. But we both knew I was feeling less sure of myself by the minute.

"If you try to run," he continued, "we'll be forced to kill you."

He'd said it so calmly that it took a moment for me to process the words.

I let out a sharp bark of protest that turned to dark laughter as I shifted into human form.

"I thought no one here wanted to hurt me."

One corner of his mouth crinkled. "We don't. Calla, I'm Monroe."

He took a step forward.

"Stay where you are," I said, flashing my canines.

He didn't come any closer.

"You haven't tried to kill me yet," I replied, still scanning the room for anything that would give me a tactical advantage. "But that doesn't mean I can trust you. If I see that steel hanging from your belt move an inch, you lose an arm."

He nodded.

Questions pounded in my skull, making my head ache. The sensation of breathlessness threatened to overwhelm me again. I couldn't afford to panic. I also couldn't afford to show any weakness.

Memories stirred deep within me, swirling beneath my skin and raising gooseflesh along my arms. Cries of pain echoed in my head. I shivered, seeing wraiths ooze around me like nebulous shadows while succubi screamed overhead. My blood went icy.

"Monroe! The boy is over here!"

"Where is Shay?"

I choked on his name, terror welling up my throat as I waited for Monroe's response.

Snatches from the past flitted through my mind, a blur of images that wouldn't stay in focus. I struggled with the memories, trying to catch them and hold them in place so that I could make sense of what had happened, how I'd gotten here. I remembered racing through narrow halls, realizing we'd been cornered, and finding our way into the library at Rowan Estate. Shay's uncle, Bosque Mar, eroding my outrage with doubts about what was happening to us.

Shay's fingers clutched my hand so tightly it hurt. "Tell me who you really are."

"I'm your uncle," Bosque said calmly, walking toward us. "Your own flesh and blood."

"Who are the Keepers?" Shay asked.

"Others like me, who want only to protect you. To help you," Bosque replied. "Shay, you are not like other children. You have untapped abilities that you cannot begin to imagine. I can show you who you truly are. Teach you to use the power you have."

"If you're so invested in helping Shay, why was he the sacrifice at my union?" I pushed Shay behind me, shielding him from Bosque.

Bosque shook his head. "Another tragic misunderstanding. A test, Calla, of your loyalty to our noble cause. I thought we offered you the best of educations, but perhaps you aren't familiar with Abraham's trial with his son Isaac? Isn't the sacrifice of one you love the ultimate gauge of your faith? Do you really believe we wanted Shay to die at your hands? We've asked you to be his protector."

I began to shake. "You're lying."

"Am I?" Bosque smiled, and it almost looked kind. "After all you've been through, have you no trust in your masters? You would never have been made to harm Shay—another kill would have been provided in his place at the last moment. I understand such a test may seem too terrible to be fair, too much to ask of you and Renier. Perhaps you are too young to have faced such a trial."

I balled my hands into fists so Monroe wouldn't see them shaking. I could hear the screams of succubi and incubi, hear the hissing chimeras and the shuffling gait of those horrible, desiccated creatures that had crawled out of the portraits lining Rowan Estate's walls.

"Where is he?" I asked again, grinding my teeth. "I swear if you don't tell me—"

"He's in our care," Monroe said calmly.

There was that half smirk again. I couldn't puzzle out this man's reserved but confident demeanor.

I wasn't sure what "care" meant in this case. Keeping my fangs bared, I edged across the room, waiting for Monroe to make a move. Even as I watched him, blurry images of the past wavered before my eyes like watercolors.

Cold metal encircling my arms. The click of locks and the sudden absence of weight from my wrists. The warmth of a gentle touch rubbing away the icy chill on my skin.

"Why isn't she awake yet?" Shay asked. "You promised she wouldn't be hurt."

"She'll be fine," Monroe said. "The enchantment from the bolts acts like a heavy sedative; it will take some time to wear off."

I tried to speak, to move, but my eyelids were so heavy, the darkness of slumber pulling me beneath its surface again.

"If we can reach an agreement, I'll take you to him," Monroe continued.

"An agreement?" I was right about not wanting to show weakness. If I was making any sort of deal with a Searcher, it had to be on my terms.

"Yes," he said, risking a step toward me. When I didn't protest, he began to smile. He wasn't being deceptive—I didn't catch the scent of fear—but his smile was chased away by something else. Pain?

"We need you, Calla."

My confusion buzzed more loudly, forcing me to shake it off like a pesky swarm of flies. I had to appear confident, not distracted by his strange behavior.

"Who exactly is 'we'? And what do you need me for?"

My anger had dissolved, but I concentrated on keeping my canines razor sharp. I didn't want Monroe to forget for one minute who he was dealing with. I was still an alpha—I needed to remember that as much as he needed to see it. That strength was the only thing I had going for me right now.

"My people," he said, vaguely gesturing behind him toward whatever lay beyond the door. "The Searchers."

"You're their leader?" I frowned.

He looked strong but grizzled—like someone who never got as much sleep as he really needed.

"I'm *a* leader," he said. "I head up the Haldis team; we run operations out of the Denver outpost."

"Let's talk about your friends in Denver".

Somewhere in the recesses of my mind Lumine, my Mistress, smiled and a Searcher screamed.

I crossed my arms over my chest so I wouldn't shudder. "Okay."

"But it's not just my team that needs your help," he continued, turning suddenly to pace in front of the door. "We all do. Everything has changed; we don't have any time to waste."

He ran his hands through his dark hair as he spoke. I considered bolting—he was clearly distracted—but something about his manner mesmerized me, enough so that I didn't know if escape was what I really wanted anymore.

"You might be our only chance. I don't think the Scion can do this alone. You might be the final part of the equation. The tipping point."

"The tipping point of what?"

"This war. You can end it."

War. The word set my blood boiling. I was glad for it; the heat coursing through my veins made me feel stronger. This war was the one I'd been raised to fight.

"We need you to join us, Calla."

I could barely hear him. I was trapped in a red fog—thoughts of the violence that consumed so much of my life filled my being.

The Witches' War.

I'd served the Keepers in their battles against the Searchers since I could cut flesh with my teeth. I'd hunted for them. I'd killed for them.

My eyes focused on Monroe. I'd killed *his* people. How could he possibly want me to join them?

As if sensing my wariness, he froze in place. He didn't speak but clasped his hands behind his back, watching me, waiting for me to speak.

I swallowed, forcing steadiness into my voice. "You want me to fight for you."

"Not just you," he said. I could tell he was fighting to control his words as well. He seemed desperate to flood the air between us with his thoughts. "But you're the key. You're an alpha, a leader. That's what we need. It's what we've always needed."

"I don't understand." His eyes were so bright as he spoke I didn't know whether to be afraid or fascinated.

"The Guardians, Calla. Your pack. We need you to bring them over to us. To fight with us."

It felt like the floor had dropped out beneath me and I was falling. I wanted to believe what he was saying, because wasn't this the very thing I'd hoped for?

A way to free my pack.

Yes. Yes, it was. Even now my heart was racing with the thought of returning to the Vail, of finding my packmates. Of getting back to Ren. I could take them all away from the Keepers. To something else. Something better.

But the Searchers were my enemies . . . I could only tread carefully if I made a pact with them. I decided to play up my reluctance.

"I don't know if that's possible. . . ."

"But it is!" Monroe lurched forward as if to grab my hands, a mad glint in his eyes.

I leapt back, shifting into wolf form, and snapped at his fingers.

"I'm sorry." He shook his head. "There's so much you don't know."

I shifted back. His face was etched with deep lines. Haunted, full of secrets.

"No sudden moves, Monroe." I took slow steps toward him, extending my hand, warding off another approach. "I'm interested, but I'm not convinced that you know what you're asking of me."

"I do." He looked away, almost flinching at his own words. "I'm asking you to risk everything."

"And why would I do that?" I asked.

I already knew the answer. I'd risked everything to save Shay. And I'd do it again in a heartbeat if it meant I could get back to my packmates. If I could save them.

He stepped back and extended his arm, clearing my path to the open door.

"Freedom."